OFFICERS DOWN

ELIOT SEFRIN

A Novel

ISBN: 978-1-66782-237-2 (softcover)
ISBN: 978-1-66782-238-9 (eBook)

To Rosalyn, who lived this story in nearly every possible way.

Part 1

There it was. The dirty, stinking block. The ugly gray and red tenements … were crowded close together and rose straight up … to shut off all but a narrow expanse of sky. It was as if nothing bright would ever shine on Amboy Street.

—Irving Shulman, *The Amboy Dukes*, 1947

Chapter 1

EVEN IN THE GLOW OF MORNING there was darkness. It was all that Matt Holland could see. Dank and dreary, like the cellar in which it dwelled, it had clung to the embattled New York City police officer all through his hellish ordeal, swallowing him up like a savage beast before burrowing deep inside him, as if to find a permanent roost.

Even now, with daybreak burnishing a cloudless, azure sky, Holland couldn't stop thinking about how pitch-dark it had been in the cellar, black as a cave in the dead of night. He was blind, for all intents and purposes, when that shadow rushed him from out of nowhere. Never knew who or what it was. Never saw it coming until it careened headlong into him. Never fully grasped what had taken place until he was back at the 73rd Precinct station house with the Internal Affairs Division investigators lobbing questions, and NYPD brass flocking to the precinct in droves, and the darkness of the cellar engulfing him, part of him forever now.

"Detective Sergeant Holland," an IAD investigator chirped, poking his head into the precinct commander's office, where Holland awaited questioning.

Holland squinted, as if awakening from a long, deep slumber. It was seemingly all he had the strength to do, the past nine hours having drained him like a spent battery. His close-cropped, dusky hair was matted and flecked with droplets of blood, his complexion sallow, his eyes sunken and lifeless. Seated behind Captain Borelli's outsized desk, the veteran officer seemed gnarled and shrunken from his normal six-foot frame, like a punch-drunk fighter slumped on his stool.

"Two minutes," the investigator said. "We're about ready to tee things up again."

But the IAD shoofly may well have been invisible; Holland saw nothing of him. Instead, all he saw were the same vivid, jolting images that had haunted him all night. He saw the muzzle flash of his service revolver light up the apartment-building cellar on Amboy Street. He saw spidery silhouettes skitter across the musty, ashen vault, looming ominously on the ceiling and walls. He saw his partner, Rachel Cook, gasping for breath before dropping to her knees. He saw the boy's face, ghostlike in the beam of Cook's flashlight, appearing joyful at first, then frightened and bewildered.

> ... Then the angry throng of onlookers, cursing and shouting, as a phalanx of fellow officers hustled him and Cook into a waiting patrol car.
>
> ... Then the sterile, emerald corridors of Brookdale University Hospital, lined with gurneys and wheelchairs and empty, pained faces.
>
> ... Then his wife Katie, tremulous and tearful, reaching out to hold him close.
>
> ... Then the darkness again, desolate and suffocating and forbidding.

Everything would have been so different if it hadn't been so dark down in that cellar—that's what Matt Holland kept thinking now. None of this would have happened. He and Cook would have handled the 911 call routinely, nothing unwonted for a normal four-to-midnight tour, and everyone would have gone their merry way. The boy who'd run into him would be all right, tucked in bed at his family's apartment, or waking to a gorgeous, summer day. The other kids in the cellar would be all right, too. So would Cook, off by now on that July 4th Fire Island junket she'd gushed about for weeks.

And Holland? He'd be all right, too.

By now, he would have arrived at Katie's parents' beach house, down the Jersey shore, waking from a good night's sleep as daylight brightened the horizon and a balmy breeze blew in off the ocean. By midday, he'd be grilling steaks on the backyard deck, watching his eight-year-old twin girls romp along the shoreline and the seawater glint off Thomas's skin as his twelve-year-old son barreled through the surf on a boogie board. There would have been fireworks at the boardwalk by nightfall and a festive Independence Day parade, with costumes and marching bands and floats. Then custard and saltwater taffy, and back to the house with Katie and the kids. Everything normal. Everything intact. The arc of his life pregnant with glowing possibilities, joyous memories, and an abundance of priceless riches.

Instead ... there was *this*.

Instead of a much-anticipated holiday weekend off, Matt Holland sat in the fusty bowels of the 73rd Precinct station house in the Brownsville section of Brooklyn—exhausted, bewildered, pondering how everything in his life had gone so swiftly and frighteningly awry.

The IAD investigators were coming off a short break now, their interrogation having already stretched since shortly before midnight. There were hours to go yet before the dour-faced men with the tape recorders and legal pads would wrap things up and move their investigation to NYPD headquarters, where the probe would continue interminably.

"I'm sorry as hell that all of this happened, Matty," Capt. Borelli said at the outset of Holland's questioning. "My heart's breaking for you. I just pray that you and Katie can stay strong through it all."

Holland, though, could manage no more than a tepid smile.

By then, the officer had signed his formal statement and convened with Patrolmen's Benevolent Association President Red McLaren, PBA shop steward Angelo De Luca, and union attorney Eddie Shearson. Capt. Borelli had handed his *Unusual Incident Report* to the I-24 man for typing. Holland and Cook, per NYPD protocol, had surrendered their uniforms and firearms and been discharged from the hospital, where they'd been examined for injuries and trauma.

"If there's anything I can do for you, Matty," Capt. Borelli had said, looking ashen and shaken himself. "Anything in the world ... anything."

But there was nothing Capt. Borelli could do ... nothing *anyone* could. And so, the precinct commander had grudgingly left Holland alone, pledging that he'd keep an eye out for Katie when the investigators marched the officer downstairs.

First in line for the questioning was the deputy inspector in charge of the ten-precinct Brooklyn North. Next up were detectives from Firearms and Homicide, followed by investigators from the district attorney's office and, finally, the shooflies from Internal Affairs. By then, the station house was flooded with NYPD brass, and the investigators were forced to move their interrogation from Capt. Borelli's cramped, second-floor office to the precinct muster room downstairs.

Along about 2:00 AM, they delivered sandwiches and sodas, and broke for a while so that everyone could use the restroom. Portable fans were brought in, but they hadn't helped. Heat poured in through open windows as if from a blast furnace. Flies and mosquitoes buzzed about. The entire muster room—crammed with unshaven, growly investigators—reeked of cigarette smoke, stale cologne, and human sweat.

The 73rd Precinct station house felt much the same. Drab and dimly lit, its white-tiled ceilings were stained with moldy watermarks … its paint-peeled walls plastered with official notices and *WANTED* posters. Adjacent to the muster room, a sergeant sat behind a massive wooden desk, cradling a telephone between his shoulder and ear. At a smaller desk, the I-24 man cranked out reports, the clacking of his typewriter keys echoing through a row of empty jail cells.

Outside the station house, it was obvious that something unusual was going on. Dozens of plainclothes officers—I.D.s dangling from breast pockets and neck chains—milled about on the sidewalk, mingling with late-platoon cops and others arriving for the eight-to-four tour. Patrol cars and unmarked sedans sat parked at odd angles to the curb. Even the station house itself looked especially weathered. A dingy, turn-of-the century Gothic structure, its begrimed windows were nearly opaque, its stone façade speckled with pigeon droppings. Amber metal lanterns flanked a pair of twelve-foot-high wooden doors, over which the precinct's number was etched in glass. A sun-bleached American flag hung limply over the entranceway. Beyond the fortress-like structure, Brownsville stretched for blocks, blighted and morose in the early morning haze.

"What the fuck is goin' on here?" a slack-jawed officer from the eight-to-four tour inquired. He was dressed in faded jeans and a blue-white *New York Yankees* tee shirt. A freshly laundered uniform was slung on a hanger over his shoulder.

"Ain't ya heard?" a mutton-chopped cop named Terry replied. "It's all over the radio an' TV. Front page of the mornin' papers, too."

The other officers broke the news.

"Holy shit!" the newly arrived cop exclaimed. "Who was it?"

"Matt Holland," Terry said.

"*Holland*? You're shittin' me!"

"Last guy you'd ever imagine, huh?" Terry said.

"Fuck, yeah!" the cop in the *Yankees* shirt said. "Who was he partnered with?"

"Rachel Cook."

"*Who*?"

"Cook. A rookie. Female. On the job all of eight months."

"Jesus Christ!" the cop in the *Yankees* shirt said. "Where'd it go down?"

"Amboy Street." Terry dragged on a half-smoked Marlboro. "Cellar of some shithole apartment building."

"When?"

"About nine last night."

"What the fuck happened?"

"No one's sure yet," Terry said. "They're still sorting things out."

"Where's Holland now?" the newly arrived cop asked.

"Capt. Borelli's office," Terry said and nodded toward a second-floor window. "They're still questionin' him. Been at it since about midnight. No letup."

"Puttin' the poor bastard through the ringer," a plainclothes cop said, shaking his head. "I hear they already took his bullets. Probably will cut his nuts off next."

"Ain't that the truth," Terry said and flicked his cigarette butt to the curb. "And he's already in bad shape. I know, 'cause we were one of the backup units called to the scene. Poor guy was all broken up, cryin' like a baby. Tough as hell to see."

"What about his partner ... Cook?"

"She's upstairs, too," Terry said. "Scared shitless, from what I hear."

"Wouldn't *you* be?'

"Guess so."

"Who's up there with them?" the cop in the *Yankees* shirt asked.

"Who *ain't* there ... that's a better question." Terry sneered. "Coupla three-stars. Patrol commander. Division commander. Borough commander. Half of Brooklyn North. You name it, they're there."

"Lotta shooflies, too," the plainclothes guy said. "Homicide. Internal Affairs. D.A. investigators. Suits from City Hall."

The cops paused in their chatter as a trio of police brass emerged from a shiny, black Mercury and ambled up the station house steps, uniformed cops snapping to attention and saluting as the high-ranking officers passed.

"See what I mean?" Terry grumbled. "They're pullin' people in from all over the goddamned city for this."

"Anyone from *our* side in there?" the cop in the *Yankees* shirt asked.

"Red McLaren's upstairs," the plainclothes cop replied. "So's Angelo De Luca, an' that lawyer the PBA brings in for the heavy-duty shit."

"You mean Eddie Shearson? The guy who looks like *Columbo*?"

The cops chuckled at the reference to the popular TV detective.

"Holland's wife is there, too," the plainclothes cop said. "Drove in 'round midnight with her old man. Poor kid. They won't even let her in to see him."

"Barely gave him time to take a piss," Terry growled. "Been grillin' him nonstop for hours."

"An' the boy?"

"Under the knife, last I heard. Don't look good."

"Don't look good for Holland either," the plainclothes cop said. "Right or wrong, the poor bastard's in for a long, hard ride."

All of that seemed evident by the tortured look on Matt Holland's face. Closeted away in Capt. Borelli's office, the veteran cop, head hanging, was unhearing, unseeing, as troubled and forlorn as a man could possibly be.

"Ready now, detective?" the IAD investigator asked. "Time to get goin' again."

Nodding grimly, Holland rose slowly from his chair, wondering all the while if he'd be able to explain how what happened in the Amboy Street cellar had been a tragic accident—*a reflex, nothing more*—the single, gut-wrenching, life-changing instant that every police officer feared. Wondering if anyone would believe his account of the incident. Wondering, too, if the darkness that shrouded him now would ever fade to light, and if that light would ever shine again on the man he once was, and all the brave and noble acts that once defined his life.

Chapter 2

ONCE HE WAS A HERO, honored and celebrated by the City of New York. There were all those commendations to show for it, of course. All the headlines. All the notoriety. All the accolades across sixteen years on the job.

There was the time he came across that woman and her baby girl during the Blizzard of '69, when a fierce Nor'easter roared in and crippled half the East Coast. No one expected a storm like that ... caught everyone by surprise. Twenty-six inches of snow in a single day, drifts four feet high. Schools and businesses closed. Power lines down. People trapped in homes and stranded at airports, train stations, and bus terminals. Nothing much moved in New York for the better part of three days—not a bus or a subway car, not a fire engine or a snowplow, not a police car or an ambulance.

But Matt Holland woke at 3:00 AM that day and figured that the 73rd Precinct would probably be shorthanded. Dennis and Kevin Molloy, a pair of firefighters who lived nearby in Staten Island, were going to try to make it to work, too. Nothing could keep guys like that from the job back then—certainly not a snowstorm.

The three of them threw some tire chains on Kevin's big four-wheeler, jumped in, and headed to Brooklyn in heavy, blinding snow. The four-wheeler, chains and all, fishtailed and strained as it plowed through wind-whipped drifts. The icy roads were barely visible.

Exiting a parkway ramp, Holland caught a fleeting glimpse of something peculiar. Turned out, it was the antenna, roof, and rear window of a station wagon, half-buried in a massive snowdrift. Then he noticed a telltale fog on the wagon's rear window, and tiny rivulets running down the glass.

When Holland and the Molloy brothers dug barehanded through the snow and pried open a door, they discovered a panicked young mother lying face down across the rear seat. Nestled beneath her, blue-lipped and bawling, was a six-month-old baby girl.

Years later, Matt Holland would tell people that when he and the Molloy brothers trudged through waist-deep snowdrifts, carrying that woman and her infant daughter to the hospital—knowing that his simply coming to work had saved two lives—it was the single finest moment he'd ever have as a cop. The NYPD gave him an Exceptional Merit Award in recognition. Holland, as was his wont, shrugged the honor off. Said it was no big deal. Said guys in Emergency Services and the FDNY did things like that every day and people hardly noticed.

Then there was the other rescue, the one in 1971. That one *was* a big deal. Especially for the NYPD.

The '70s, in many ways, were the worst of all times for modern-day New York. Nearly bankrupt then, the city was crumbling under the weight of an unprecedented fiscal crisis. Crime and unemployment were soaring, racial tensions spiking, the city's social fabric frayed. Hospitals, libraries, and firehouses were closing, municipal services being cut, layoffs and hiring freezes imposed, the subways and streets rife with vandalism and drugs. An exodus of middle-class white residents was draining the city of tax revenue, threatening its very existence. Just as troubling, the relationship between police and the public had reached a dark, disturbing nadir.

Traditionally revered by most New Yorkers, city police had been stained in recent years by a recurrent pattern of corruption, labor disputes, and charges of misconduct. On the front lines during civil rights and antiwar demonstrations, police had been taunted, cursed at, and scorned. Seen by many as symbols of a corrupt, broken, racist establishment, they bore the brunt of frustration over housing shortages, service cuts, and other policy failures—their actions challenged by the public, the courts, political interests, and the media.

Accompanying the backlash were demands for reform. Protests, fueled by a powerful wave of activism, rocked minority neighborhoods as pressure mounted to upgrade law enforcement and place it in the framework of a modern-day society. Civilian review boards sprang up. Longstanding units were disbanded. New policies were implemented on everything from patrol practices and nomenclature to hiring procedures and the use of firearms.

All of this had a corrosive, crippling effect. With recruitment at a trickle, and veteran cops opting for early retirement, the NYPD was losing more than a hundred officers a month through attrition. Productivity was down, morale at an all-time low. Worse yet, a heightened sense of insularity gripped most precincts, as the schism between police and civilians heightened, and cops became, in effect, a closed society. Under attack from seemingly all sides, their feelings alternated from frustration and mistrust to self-pity and confusion. Viewing their plight as hopeless, their hands as tied, cops saw themselves as pariahs, martyrs, scapegoats, victims. Embattled. Maligned. Misunderstood. Oppressed. Traumatized. Alienated. Bitter.

Then things got even worse.

By the summer of '71, radical black militants had mounted an organized terror campaign against law enforcement. Suddenly, it was open season on New York City police. One after another, cops were assaulted, ambushed, and assassinated in deliberate, unprovoked attacks—each incident drawing extensive press coverage, each building upon the other, each seemingly more random and maniacal. Letters filled with chilling revolutionary-style rhetoric—issuing threats and claiming credit for the slayings—were delivered to newspapers. Attackers exulted as officers lay dying on the streets. Minor incidents flared into armed confrontations. Police headquarters was dynamited. Inspectors' funerals—with their recurrent imagery of grieving widows, distraught children, police pallbearers, motorcycle processions, and coffins draped in white-and-green NYPD flags—became a familiar ritual.

Angered and stunned, cops battled back. Teams of officers combed the streets in NYPD-sanctioned manhunts for suspected terrorists. Extra tours of duty were authorized. Heavy weapons, armored cars, and other militarized vehicles were stockpiled for the first time. Apartments were raided with increased regularity, hand grenades, shotguns, assault rifles, and other weapons seized.

The all-out warfare only exacerbated the impact on cops. Petty crimes and traffic-stops frequently went ignored for fear they'd escalate into deadly confrontations. Volunteers in plainclothes and unmarked cars began riding backup for uniformed officers on routine calls. Rifles were no longer locked in the trunk of patrol cars, as mandated by regulations. The PBA issued advisories for its members to purchase shotguns and wear bulletproof vests. The regulation .38-caliber Smith and Wesson service revolver, and the smaller off-duty gun, were no longer seen as enough. Many cops started carrying seconds: nine-millimeter Browning automatics or twenty-five-caliber automatics concealed in belly and ankle holsters. Others carried throwaways—guns that couldn't be traced—along with deadly, hollow-point bullets. Wary and on edge, symbolic of their feelings of isolation and besiegement, cops began nicknaming precincts after noted forts. Bedford-Stuyvesant had the "Alamo," the South Bronx, "Fort Apache." The 73rd Precinct was known as "Fort Zinderneuf," a French foreign legion outpost in the movie *Beau Geste.* Cops in Brownsville called it "Fort Z," for short.

In the middle of all this, Matt Holland made his second rescue.

He was walking foot patrol late one day on a busy thoroughfare that ran under an elevated subway line when a building caught his eye. It was a nineteenth-century dwelling, typical of many Old Law tenements in the city's poorest neighborhoods: three stories high, flat-roofed, wood-frame construction, with a brick-and-mortar veneer front, the final building in a row of three. Fire had destroyed the two adjoining dwellings, eroding the support on the building's side. To the naked eye, nothing was amiss. There were no telltale signs of trouble, no warnings. The building wasn't tilting or leaning; no walls were splitting, or windows cracking. Still, Holland knew something wasn't quite right. This time, it wasn't something he saw, rather an odd sound he heard.

At first it sounded like the rumble from an elevated train, only it came from *inside* the building and was more like a labored groan, the sound of something weary and about to surrender. Thankfully, Holland knew all about building construction. All those weekends on job sites with Katie's father, building and remodeling homes; all those warnings from firefighters about abandoned buildings collapsing in ravaged, inner-city neighborhoods like Brownsville. Holland knew what was happening the instant he heard the building groan. What he *didn't* expect to hear, though, were screams. The building, condemned months earlier, was presumed empty. No one knew that a family of squatters was living there.

Instantly, Holland realized that he had mere seconds to act. Instinctively, he raced up the front stoop and was barely in the downstairs vestibule when a pair of children raced down a flight of stairs. They were eight, maybe ten years old—a boy and a girl—immigrants from Nigeria. Instantly, Holland snapped the girl up in his arms. The boy leapt, piggyback style, onto the officer's back. Then Holland spun about, and the building surrendered with an earsplitting sound as its walls collapsed inward, its upper floor pancaked downward—and the entire structure, drawn by the weight of its metal fire escapes, came crashing down in a heap. Holland barely made it out with the children when a mighty gust of debris hurled the three of them twenty yards into the street. Two other children and their parents perished in the rubble. Holland suffered a broken collarbone and multiple contusions. The children he'd rescued survived without a scratch.

For his actions that day, Holland received the Medal for Valor, the third-highest honor the NYPD could bestow. It was a stunning medallion, its imagery symbolizing sacrifice, service, gallantry, and honor. Engraved evergreen laurel leaves rung the medal's centerpiece. The words *For Valor, Police Department City of New York* were etched in gold on its face. On the reverse side, the name *Matthew William Holland* was engraved under an image of the Police Memorial Statue, the monument that had stood for decades at the entrance to NYPD headquarters. Depicted was the image of an officer standing alongside a young boy—symbol of the protector, guardian of those in need. It was an image that Holland would forever cherish.

Just like he'd cherish the day the medal was awarded.

It was regal in many ways—that Medal Day ceremony, steeped in the finest traditions of the NYPD. The Blue Room of City Hall had just been refurbished—with decorative woodwork and flooring, cornice-and-rope moldings, blue velvet ropes, new wainscotting, and door surrounds. The flags of New York, the United States, and the NYPD stood on either side of an historic marble mantelpiece. Portraits of Thomas Jefferson, DeWitt Clinton, and other New York notables adorned the walls. A stunning ornamental medallion hung directly overhead. At the rear of the room, above massive entry doors, an acanthus leaf molding and wooden plaque marked the date of the city's charter, *1811*.

Matt Holland, in crisply pressed dress uniform, stood that day behind a podium fronted by the city's official seal, at the very spot where New York mayors, for the better part of two centuries, had greeted presidents, ambassadors, and heads of state. NYPD brass stood at attention. Fellow cops flooded the gallery. Cameramen snapped photos. Katie, Thomas, and the Hollands' twin girls, Angie and Jenny, sat alongside other family members, beaming as New York's mayor pinned the medal on Holland's chest.

"What we have in Matt Holland," the mayor said, "is an example of why New York City police officers are called 'The Finest,' and why we should never forget, when we think of our police, that there are heroes out on our streets. It's through the actions of these heroes that we find inspiration to continue our tradition of service to the public, no matter the risk or peril."

Embarrassed by the accolades, Holland tried to deflect it onto his fellow cops.

"I didn't do anything that thousands of other police officers, rescue personnel, or firefighters wouldn't have done," he told the press. "I shouldn't be singled out. I'm only happy I was in a position to do my job."

The story, of course, went national.

Still under attack, desperate to repair its tattered image, and seeking to rally support around its beleaguered cops, the NYPD was hungry for the kind of hero the public once revered. Someone who could put a human face on the NYPD. Someone who could change the image of the cop from that of the callous, corrupt thug. Someone who could win the people back.

The department's PR minions pushed the story hard; the press corps ate it up. The *Daily News* and *New York Post* each ran front-page photos of Holland holding the children he'd rescued while standing at the entrance to One Police Plaza, the words **HERO COP** surprinted over the photos in block-cap headlines. Coverage was picked up by radio, TV, and syndicated wire services for publication in newspapers across America. And virtually overnight, Matt Holland became the NYPD's favorite son, a poster boy for the modern-day, big-city police department, the hero the department so desperately craved.

Touted as a throwback to the beloved beat cop of the past, he was hailed as the living embodiment of *the cop who cared*—the officer who walked a beat, day in and day out, with no fanfare and little regard for race, class, or his own safety, spilling his guts out under the most harrowing conditions simply for the good of the public. A newspaper in Staten Island featured him as their *Hero of the Year*. A special "Matt Holland Day" was celebrated at the schools his children attended. His family was handed V.I.P. tickets to the Macy's Thanksgiving Day Parade, and they sat in the reviewing stand near Central Park, alongside all the other dignitaries, close enough that they could almost touch the mammoth floats as they moved along Broadway.

The toast of the town, Holland was awarded a gold shield, designating him as a detective, promoted to sergeant, and offered a transfer to any command in the city. He decided, however, to remain in uniform, on street patrol, as a field training officer at the 73rd Precinct, a high-crime command in Brownsville. He believed he could have the greatest impact at a command like that, honor the role he'd been celebrated for, in a neighborhood where New York needed good cops the most.

That was the height of Matt Holland's exemplary police career. By no means, however, was it the sum. Aside from the Medal for Valor, there'd be four Exceptional Merit Awards, nine Excellent Police Duty Citations, two Meritorious Duty Awards, and six honorable mentions over the course of sixteen years on the job.

Katie had her father build a glass case for all the awards, and they surprised Matt with it as a Christmas present in 1971. And what a Christmas that was: Matt's brother Dan and his family in from Long Island; Katie's and his parents singing Christmas carols and cooking in the kitchen and unwrapping presents by the tree; the house all lit up and crawling with kids; everyone laughing and toasting and wondering what the rest of the '70s would be like.

Then there was Katie, so warm and close that night—stroking his face; telling him how proud of him she was, and how special he made her and the children feel; telling him how all the medals were nice, but what was more important was how he'd never let police work *claim* him, how he'd never become sullied or jaded or burnt-out or bigoted, like so many others; telling him, too, how all that truly mattered—all that *ever* mattered—was that he'd just keep coming home each day to her and the kids.

Even now, five years later, Matt Holland remembered how Katie had loved him that night—her skin so silky and sweet-smelling, her hair spilling across his chest, the taste of her on his lips and tongue. He remembered, too, how everything seemed so right and ascendant just then: his wife at his side; their kids asleep in their bedrooms; the house quiet except for a gentle snowfall tapping on the roof; everything he loved most in the world young and full of life, and there for him to have and to hold.

But that was before today—before the darkness barged in and the world went black, before Holland's life, and his city, were changed in the blink of an eye.

It was before he and Rachel Cook answered the call that took them into the cellar on Amboy Street, before Brownsville would be reduced to rubble and flames, and the off-duty cops would come with shotguns and rifles to guard Holland's house, and the anti-police demonstrators would start calling for his head, and the NYPD would hang him out to dry. It was before the investigations, the racial politics, and the telephone threats, the sleepless nights, and the tortured freefall into anguish and guilt and doubt. It was before Katie would cry herself to sleep and struggle to hold their marriage together, and the twins would be shipped off to live with their grandparents, and his brave little Thomas would begin stammering and wetting his bed.

It was before Cook would get banished by the NYPD, too—transferred to a meaningless, shit-fixer post in Coney Island, reduced to doing strip searches and chasing derelicts off the boardwalk, her bright, budding police career in ruins.

Poor Cook.

Such a pioneer. Such a rising star. Finest rookie, male or female, Holland had ever trained. So smart and compassionate, gutsy and tough. So wide-eyed and frightened at times, but so willing to learn and put her trust in him; defying the hubbub, the stereotypes, and the resistance to women on street patrol; working so hard to gain acceptance from the naysayers and skeptics; so determined to prove that women could be cops, could be *anything* they wanted to be.

And now? *Who knew*?

Who knew if his rookie partner would be able to cling to her perspective, her steely resolve, her sense of hope? Who knew if she could keep from growing lonely and lost, jaded and bitter? Who knew if she'd even be able to survive?

And what about the boy?

That was the worst part of it all.

There'd never be a day in his life, from that day on, when Matt Holland wouldn't think about what happened to the boy. There'd never be a day when he'd stop wishing he could make all of it go away. There'd never be a day when he wouldn't bleed a bit for the boy he shot, and pray for his family's forgiveness, and whisper to himself that he was sorry for everything that took place down in the cellar on Amboy Street.

Chapter 3

DESPERATELY AS SHE TRIED, Rachel Cook couldn't fully catch her breath or halt her body from trembling like a tuning fork. Nearly nine hours had passed since her nightmarish ordeal began, but even now Cook couldn't keep from quaking. It had been that way from the moment the powerful surge of adrenaline had knocked the rookie officer off her feet—the echo of Matt Holland's gunshot exploding like a thunderclap—then all through the ride to the hospital and back to the 73rd Precinct station house, where the partners' four-to-midnight tour had kicked off.

Already, Cook had been briefed by PBA officials regarding her rights as a police officer, along with what to expect in the muster room, where NYPD investigators were hours into their probe. Capt. Borelli had stopped by for a fleeting pep talk, too—extolling Cook's virtues, encouraging her to remain strong, and assuring her that things would work out in the end, as long as she told the truth.

But neither the PBA's guidance, nor Capt. Borelli's assurances, or all the hours that had passed since 9:00 PM the previous night had assuaged Rachel Cook's all-consuming angst. Nothing had halted her mind from racing or helped her grasp the gravity of what had occurred or quelled the terrifying sensation of plunging headlong into a dark and bottomless pit. Even on the cusp of a glorious summer day, the clock pushing 5:00 AM, Cook couldn't keep her extremities from quivering, or her heart from racing, or frosty shivers from rolling up and down her spine.

Down in the cellar, before being whisked from the scene by fellow cops, paramedics had examined Cook for injuries and trauma, covered her with blankets, and cleansed the bilious gobs of vomit that had splattered her pant-legs and blouse. Her fetid, urine-stained uniform—like Holland's—had been confiscated, replaced with civvies, and hauled off in a plastic bag to be examined as evidence. Blood samples from the two officers had been rushed to a lab, to be tested for alcohol or drugs. Droves of senior officers and investigators had also arrived at the scene, floodlights erected, the building's entrance cordoned off, the partners separated and advised, under Miranda, to invoke their right to counsel. And before she knew it, Cook was seated on an examining table in a flimsy hospital gown, shivering like she'd just emerged from a neck-deep tub of ice.

"Your name, officer?" the emergency room doctor asked at the start of her exam.

"Cook," she replied, arms wrapped around herself, eyes bloodshot, streaks of mascara running down her cheeks. "Rachel Cook."

The young male doctor, stethoscope around his neck, peered into Cook's eyes with a penknife flashlight.

"In a million years," he said, jokingly, "I'd never take you for a cop."

"I've heard that before," Cook said, dryly. "Many times."

And indeed, she had. Petite in stature, with delicate features and shoulder-length auburn hair, Cook possessed neither the size nor physical bearing typically associated with police officers. To the contrary, clad in a baggy sweatshirt and bell-bottom jeans, she more closely resembled a college co-ed than a cop. Besides, people weren't used to seeing female police officers. Not on the streets of New York. Not *anywhere*.

"Do you remember what today's date is?" the doctor asked.

Cook blinked. For an instant, she wasn't certain.

"July 4th, 1976," she stammered, correctly.

"Do you know where you are?"

"Brookdale University Hospital. Brooklyn, New York."

"Do you understand what's taken place?"

"I think so," Cook said hesitantly, although the full scope of what had occurred was impossible at this point to comprehend.

Cook inhaled deeply, trying to slow her wildly beating heart, but the simple act of breathing was like sucking air in through a straw. The doctor used a rubber reflex hammer to tap Cook's knees, fingers, and ankles, then ran his fingertips along her extremities, her temples and scalp.

"Were you wounded in any way?" he asked.

"I don't think so," Cook replied, tentatively.

"Struck by a ricochet, perhaps? A flying object?"

"Not that I can tell."

"Bleeding?"

"Uh-uh."

"Any trouble breathing?" The doctor placed his stethoscope to Cook's chest. Inhaling, the officer emitted a croupy cough.

"I guess so, maybe," Cook said.

"Is there anything else out of the ordinary you want to tell me about?" the doctor asked.

Cook pointed to where she'd struck her elbow when she'd dropped to the cellar floor, and told the doctor about her body aches, her dizziness, and the sharp, incessant ringing in her ears.

"When did the ringing start?" the doctor asked.

"The instant," Cook said, "that I heard the gunshot."

Then the doctor asked if Cook was injured in any other discernable way, and she remembered wanting to reply that yes, she was—but not in a way that she could possibly explain or that he could treat. It was then that they rolled in an I.V. hookup with antibiotics to lower Cook's blood pressure, handed her a couple of aspirins, treated her tinnitus with eardrops, and walked her to X-ray for a look at her elbow.

"Anything else I should be aware of?" the doctor asked, prior to discharge.

"Just this." Cook raised a quivering hand. "For the life of me, I can't stop shaking."

"That's understandable," the doctor said. "You're in a deep state of shock."

Seven interminable hours later, the same thing could be said.

Matt Holland, by then, was downstairs in the 73rd Precinct's muster room, surrounded by a bevy of investigators. In fifteen minutes, it'd be Cook's turn. But now, she waited in a vacant office near the Precinct Investigation Unit, rocking nervously in a swivel chair. Her body aches had coalesced to a sharp, stabbing pain at the base of her skull. Her hair, unpinned from how she wore it under her police cap, dangled loose and stringy to her shoulders, as if she'd been caught in a sudden downpour. An hour earlier, to her immense shame, she'd squatted over the toilet bowl in the bathroom near Capt. Borelli's office and emptied her bowels in loose, watery stools. Streaks of excrement stained her undergarments now. Rings of perspiration soiled the underarms of her sweatshirt.

Outside the office where Cook waited, the detective's squad room was eerily quiet. Desks, telephones, and rows of metal file cabinets sat unattended, as if the detectives and Street Crimes Unit had abandoned the station house for a fire drill. A trio of IAD investigators huddled near a water cooler, conversing in hushed tones. A solitary prisoner stared forlornly from a holding pen. And Cook sat deep in thought, imprisoned in a jail cell of her own.

Frightened and alone, the officer sipped from a cup of lukewarm tea, reliving all that had occurred that night, and thinking that it wasn't supposed to happen this way—not according to the plan she'd so carefully conceived; not eight months into a job she'd worked so long and hard for; not after such a promising start as a probationary New York City police officer.

Police work was going to be so different, Rachel Cook thought. Never in her wildest dreams was it going to be like this. Never was it going to take such a woeful, terrifying turn.

Chapter 4

IT STARTED AS AN AUDACIOUS ADVENTURE. Rachel Cook craved one at the time—*needed* one, too, or so she thought. Twenty-two years old and footloose, Cook needed to do something bold and brassy with her life, something different from other women her age, something that would allow her to step outside the life she'd been living, the role she was expected to play.

But while she craved adventure and distinction, all Cook had ever been handed was a blueprint. Fashioned from gender expectations and age-old stereotypes, it was a blueprint that detailed precisely what women like Cook—born and raised in the postwar, middle-class enclaves of Brooklyn—were *supposed* to do with their lives.

In the blueprint, work was merely transitory, little more than a stopgap between high school and marriage, never to be viewed as a substantive, fulfilling endeavor. Long-term, meaningful careers were exclusive to women of different pedigrees, or restricted at the time solely to men. In Cook's world, young women pursued "suitable" professions, primarily as secretaries, nurses, social workers, or teachers. Genuine fulfillment couldn't be attained until a woman married, raised a family, and managed a household.

By the time she'd emerged from adolescence, however, Rachel Cook had adopted a radically different mindset. On the cusp of graduating from Queens College, part of New York's tuition-free university system, Cook was vying for anything but a traditional path. Marriage wasn't in the cards, at least not yet. Notions about female stereotypes and traditional gender roles seemed archaic, almost absurd. The world beckoned with other possibilities. Cook wanted to free herself from the shackles of the blueprint she'd been handed all her life. She was setting her sights on bolder, more exciting paths.

But there was more to Cook's internal stirrings than simply a sense of restlessness and ennui. In a strange kind of way, Cook felt frightened, too. And what frightened her, as much as anything, was the idea that her life might somehow remain tiny and invisible, a mere whisper in a city of salient voices and audacious dreams. Marriage and children were fine—they just weren't for *now*. Cook wanted something else, something more. She wanted to step away from what she was supposed to do, spread her wings. More than anything, she wanted to soar.

Her timing, as it turned out, could not have been better.

For decades, the New York City Police Department had drawn its officers from the ranks of young, working-class white men—generally of Irish or Italian descent, and often linked to law enforcement through lengthy bloodlines. The '70s were witnessing a sea change, however. Anxious to upgrade its image and attract better educated and more ethnically diverse officers, the NYPD had begun recruiting for the first time on college campuses, as well as among the city's ethnic and racial minorities. The department was also promoting a wealth of burgeoning new opportunities for women. That's when Rachel Cook came across an NYPD recruiter at a special "Career Day" several weeks prior to college graduation. And that's when she first became intrigued.

Women had been employed for years by the NYPD, although never as bona fide police officers. Tied closely to traditional gender stereotypes, their responsibilities had been confined to roles that women were *expected* to play. They performed administrative and other non-patrol functions; guarded and searched female detainees; and were employed in social-advocacy roles, usually involving domestic disputes, missing persons, juveniles, rape, and spousal abuse.

But that, too, was changing.

Just as the civil rights movement was opening doors for racial and ethnic minorities, the women's movement was doing the same for women. Barriers were tumbling, opportunities emerging, gender roles changing, stereotypes being discarded. Feminists were questioning the authority being wielded over decisions regarding their bodies, their morality, and their status as second-class citizens. Women were speaking out, opening the public discourse to issues like gender equality, voting rights, reproductive rights, and female-health issues. Activists were challenging the ways patriarchy and sexism objectified women, limited their independence, and capped their talent and potential.

By the time Cook reached her teens—wrestling with questions of self-identity, attempting to define her values, her goals, her beliefs—the women's movement was in full flower. The blueprint Cook had been handed was no longer valid, women no longer destined solely to roles as housewives, mothers, and second-class citizens. Women had the freedom now to make their own choices, the right to embark on bold new paths of fulfillment and self-discovery. Indeed, months before Cook's college graduation, Congress had passed a sweeping amendment to the Civil Rights Act, banning job discrimination based on gender. No longer could a woman be denied employment simply because an employer preferred a man, or because a job had traditionally been handled by men. No longer could a woman's opportunities be denied simply because she was a woman. The government, backed by the courts, had opened a door. And women were walking through it.

Equally sweeping changes were also taking place within the NYPD itself. The traditional, gender-based segregation of police duties was clearly discriminatory now; so were separate promotional policies, pay scales, and job titles. Positions that once belonged exclusively to men were fair game now for women, too. The terms "policeman" and "policewoman" had been abolished from the department's lexicon and replaced by the gender-neutral designation, "police officer." The Policewoman's Bureau, to which females had traditionally been assigned, was disbanded. Quotas on the number of women who could join the NYPD were eliminated. Height and other entrance requirements were modified.

In truth, all these changes were more than simply a matter of law; in many ways, they'd also become a matter of choice. Responding to public pressure, police departments across America were rethinking their approach, experimenting, innovating, re-examining the very definition of police work. No longer was it enough to simply catch criminals and toss them in jail. Police departments were being required to become less a *force* and more a *service*. Programs were launched to improve police-community relations. Public-relations efforts were attempting to transform the image of the cop from that of a brutish, graft-prone flatfoot to that of an officer as likely to use his brains as his muscle.

In line with this broadened notion of police work, most police departments were trying to present a softer, more "human" image of the cop. Women, it had been decided, could be a part of that new approach. The qualifications for being a cop had clearly changed. Who said a cop had to be a certain height and weight to be effective? Who said they had to be big and tough? Who said being a police officer was something only a man could do? Clearly, the vast bulk of police work had nothing to do with chasing and locking up criminals; it required neither great strength nor extraordinary agility. Other qualities were equally, if not more, important: common sense, communication skills, intelligence, maturity, compassion, empathy. Men certainly couldn't boast exclusivity to those qualities. To the contrary, each characterized *women* far more than it did men.

For decades, the notion that women were "too soft" for street patrol had rendered female officers all but invisible. But with police departments looking for a new kind of police officer, precisely the opposite was true: women were actually being sought to fill jobs as cops and serve in groundbreaking new roles.

And they were putting a whole new face on the NYPD.

Indeed, women were now doing virtually everything male officers did. They trained alongside men and were required to meet the same physical and academic standards. Assigned on a gender-blind basis wherever they were needed, they worked all kinds of tours and on special details. In the most revolutionary move of all, they were being deployed in small but growing numbers on uniformed patrol in each of New York's seventy-five precincts. They walked beats, stood fixed posts, rode in patrol cars and even on horseback. Pioneers and groundbreakers, they were symbolic of the NYPD's bright new vanguard and its bold new reality. On the verge of Rachel Cook's college graduation, two hundred women were employed as part of New York's thirty-thousand-member police force. By then, Cook had decided to become one of them.

In many ways, it was a perfect fit. Cook was precisely the kind of recruit the NYPD was seeking. A straight-A student throughout high school and college, with a bachelor's degree in political science, she'd been toying with the idea of a graduate program in city administration, perhaps even law school. A law enforcement background, she reasoned, would be a natural steppingstone for either. Police work would also certainly be interesting and challenging. Obviously, it was vital. Cook felt she could make a difference, touch people's lives in a positive way, and be an integral part of the city she loved—one that needed young, energetic, dedicated women like her.

The NYPD?

Wow.

It was brassy, different, just the kind of adventure Cook was seeking. So what if people might think it was "unsuitable" for a woman—too edgy, too dangerous, not right? As far as Cook was concerned, that was all the better. With this job, she'd not simply be breaking the mold, she'd be *shattering* it—defying the blueprint, busting free from all the old, repressive stereotypes.

Besides, who cared anymore what other people thought? Cook was a child of the 1960s: liberated, rebellious, willing to take risks. Breaking new ground held enormous appeal. Being a pioneer was more than alluring. *Why not become a cop?* Cook had nothing to lose. If she fell on her face, she'd just pick herself up and start over with something different. There were plenty of other things she could do. The whole world was out there, waiting, beckoning. Cook was still young, after all. Anything was still possible.

NYPD job recruiters enticed her with an offer of a twelve-thousand-dollar starting salary and a two-hundred-dollar uniform allowance, wage hikes based on seniority and rank, the opportunity for overtime, and any number of benefits—including health care, time off, and a lifetime pension after twenty years.

The department even sweetened the pot. Based on her academic record, her recruiter explained, Cook would qualify for a special master's degree program at the John Jay College of Criminal Justice, where twice a week—as part of her job—she'd take courses in police administration, policy analysis, forensic science, and similar subjects. If the NYPD liked what it saw, the recruiter told her, Cook would be groomed for an executive role in criminal justice, with a path to a potential career in federal law enforcement, perhaps even the FBI.

Rachel Cook was swept off her feet.

To her, working for the NYPD would be the job of a lifetime, one that she'd embrace, and one that would embrace her in return. It would be a modern-day, urban fairy tale, charged with glamor, excitement, and unbridled promise. There'd be fast-paced action, romance, suspense. Cases to be solved. Lives to be saved. Headlines to be generated. High drama, too—tense stakeouts, heart-stopping struggles, dramatic courtroom confrontations. And everything would *work*. Issues would be clearly defined. Stakes would be eminently clear. Complex, twisting plots would lead like puzzles to logical, bloodless conclusions. Crimes would be solved, cases won, justice triumph. And Cook would be smack in the middle of it: one of the good guys, a guarantor of order, a flagbearer for the women movement, an inspiration to others. She'd make arrests and receive commendations, all while breaking new ground. She'd work alongside skilled, highly trained, caring professionals, part of a team that depended upon her, needed her, drew strength from her. She'd be part of a great tradition, too, one of *New York's Finest*. Doing what she believed in. Doing what was right. Young, daring, and hip. Satisfied, committed, and fulfilled. Working hard to attain something of value. Putting herself on the line. Making a difference. A dedicated public servant helping to save her city.

All of that was present in Rachel Cook's grandiose, private vision.

Deep down, she knew police work could never truly become all of that. *No job*, after all, could reach such lofty heights. Even in her abject naiveté, Cook recognized that. Still, she imagined that police work might mirror, in some small way, the fantasy that she harbored, the vision that she'd pieced together from TV shows and feature films, magazine articles and pulp fiction, fanciful illusions and blind faith. To Cook, all of it was possible, all of it within her grasp.

Right from the start, all Rachel Cook had ever wanted was for her artless fantasy to remain intact, her bubble never to burst. All through her Police Academy training, and each day as a rookie cop—a trailblazer, a role model, a pioneer—she'd prayed that the job would be everything she'd imagined it could be.

And now, terrified and forsaken, trying to quell her nausea, she sat in a tiny office inside the 73rd Precinct stationhouse, waiting to be interrogated by NYPD brass and thinking about how her bright, budding police career was suddenly in tatters, all of it wrested from her grasp. She thought about Matt Holland—the field training officer she'd come to idolize, the decorated cop she'd put her faith in for the past eight months—and how he suddenly seemed distant and out of reach, his career demolished, his life turned upside down. She thought about the boy she and Holland had unwittingly crossed paths with in the cellar on Amboy Street, and the angry throng of people outside—shouting, cursing, and threatening the officers as they were led, faces shielded, from the scene.

Rachel Cook wondered what would happen to her brazen ambitions, the dauntless adventure she'd embarked upon. She wondered what it would be like downstairs in the muster room, where NYPD investigators waited with their barrage of questions. She wondered what her family would think, her fellow cops, her friends, her city. She wondered if there was any way she could marshal her flagging spirit, or muster her waning strength, or quell her wildly beating heart—and if there'd ever be a moment in her life when she could stop her mind from rambling, her arms and legs from trembling, her dreams from running for the hills.

Chapter 5

THE CALL WAS RECEIVED AS A 10-31, NYPD radio-signal code for a burglary-in-progress.

Phoned in to the city's command-and-control system, and relayed through the 73rd Precinct dispatcher, it was radioed to the patrol car of Matt Holland and Rachel Cook, assigned that night to a twelve-square-block sector of Brownsville. The caller who'd phoned 911 reported that she'd heard loud, suspicious noises—shrieks, bodily movement, possibly a gunshot—in the cellar of her apartment building at 118 Amboy Street. Holland and Cook were advised to proceed with extreme caution to the location. Suspects, perhaps armed and dangerous, were presumed to be either at the scene or in the immediate vicinity.

Matt Holland swung the officers' blue-and-white cruiser onto Amboy Street, a one-way stretch of squalid tenements, brownstones, and red-brick apartment buildings that cut a swath through the impoverished, predominantly black, Central-Brooklyn neighborhood.

Like many thoroughfares in Brownsville, there wasn't much to the desolate street, most of whose dwellings had either been fire-damaged, abandoned, or leveled as part of an aborted slum-clearance project. Amboy Street was also a well-known "hot spot" for 73rd Precinct cops, designated by police commanders as posing a distinct threat. Muggings, robberies, and drug-related crimes were commonplace on the street. Indeed, several nearby buildings had been the target of recent break-ins tied to the theft of plumbing fixtures and other valuables.

The side of the street to which Holland and Cook were summoned contained a pair of six-story, art deco apartment buildings abutted on either side by rubble-strewn lots. Number 118 was a fifty-year-old building fronted by a waist-high, wrought-iron fence and concrete stoop. A pair of granite gargoyles glared at the street from above the building's entrance.

Confirming their location, Holland pulled up in front of the building and parked in a vacant spot near a fire hydrant. It was 8:46 PM on a Friday, the Fourth of July, and a blistering blanket of heat was scorching New York. Even at night, the air was sweltry and stifling, dozens of residents having poured onto sidewalks, fire escapes, rooftops, and stoops to escape searing billows of indoor heat. Long rows of people sat on milk crates and folding chairs, playing cards and dice in the amber glow of streetlamps. Gaggles of children romped across the gummy, chalk-scribbled blacktop or played atop rusted, abandoned cars. Music blared from boom boxes set along the curb.

Holland and Cook, both white, were eyed warily as they exited their patrol car and made their way toward the building. The officers were dressed in summer uniforms—short-sleeved powder-blue shirts, navy trousers, and peaked service caps—their duty belts laden with handcuffs, portable radios, batons, service revolvers, and ammunition.

Flashlights on, the officers proceeded cautiously down a concrete stairwell to an alleyway that ran the length of the building and reeked with the scent of urine, musty cardboard, and rotting trash. Shards of broken glass crunched underfoot. Rats combed through piles of refuse. New York, like much of America, had embarked on a weekend-long celebration marking the nation's Bicentennial. Fireworks cascaded in colorful circles across the sky. Firecrackers and cherry bombs exploded every few seconds.

Proceeding with extreme caution, Holland and Cook cut the volume on their radios and inched their way past a coal-chute door and a trio of trashcans, the beams from their flashlights reflecting off broken glass and other debris that scrunched underfoot. Several yards ahead, a doorway leading to the building's cellar had been left slightly ajar, a shard of light visible. As the officers approached, a shadowy figure spotted them and bolted down the alleyway, disappearing into a courtyard behind the building. Holland and Cook, taking the person for a lookout, let him escape. Their attention was focused on the cellar door—and whatever was behind it.

At Holland's whispered command, Cook twisted her service revolver from her holster and slipped the safety off, her firearm pointed downward, her forefinger parallel to the barrel of the gun. Holland did the same. As a sixteen-year veteran, he was far more practiced than his rookie partner at brandishing his firearm. In eight months on the job, Cook had never removed her gun from its holster, except on the police firing range.

Holland placed a finger over his lips, signaling silence. As her field training officer, the veteran cop was charged with the indoctrination and evaluation of probationary cops like Cook.

"Are you alright?" he whispered.

Cook nodded silently, her breath coming in shallow spurts, her senses heightened, her movements timorous. A rush of adrenaline had set her heart racing. Rivers of sweat darkened the sides of her blouse.

"We're going in," Holland whispered.

Gripping her .38 Special tightly, Cook slid her finger into the trigger guard of the service revolver. Like Holland, she used her thumb to gently pull the hammer away from the chamber. Both weapons were cocked and ready.

The officers, listening intently, hesitated for several seconds. There was noise emanating from behind the cellar door. Indistinguishable to the officers, it sounded like muffled voices, labored grunts, the movement of a heavy object. There was the sound of a hammer rapping on wood, then a popping noise, like the bursting of a balloon.

Holland motioned to Cook that he'd shove the door open and she should follow him in. Cook, drawing deep breaths, tried to slow her racing heart. Droplets of sweat dribbled off her forehead, burning her eyes. Blaring rap music echoed across the alleyway. Fireworks exploded from a block party down the street.

"You ready?" Holland whispered.

Swallowing hard, Cook nodded that she was.

"Okay … in we go!"

Lowering his shoulder, Holland shoved the cellar door open forcibly and—flashlights on, firearms drawn—the pair of officers barged in.

Chapter 6

Pulling on a stubby Lucky Strike, the attorney for the Patrolmen's Benevolent Association eyeballed Matt Holland, his expression conveying the utmost gravity.

"Are you all right, detective?" the PBA attorney inquired, in a near-whisper.

Holland blinked, as if trying to awaken from a dream.

"It's been a rough few hours, I'm sure," the attorney said, "but I want to assure you that we're here to assist in every way possible."

Holland nodded wordlessly. He was seated behind Capt. Borelli's desk, before a wall plastered with NYPD memorabilia, including a photo of the 73rd Precinct commander standing alongside the hero cop on the steps of City Hall, pointing proudly to the Medal for Valor around Holland's neck.

"You with me, Matty?" The PBA attorney snapped his finger.

Glassy-eyed, Holland nodded.

"Good," the attorney said, "Because it's critical that I have your attention."

Clad in a ratty beige suit, the union lawyer was seated in a guest chair before Capt. Borelli's desk, directly facing Holland. Seated alongside the attorney was PBA shop steward Angelo De Luca. Both men fingered copies of Holland's formal statement, along with Capt. Borelli's *Unusual Incident Report*, required for occurrences outside the realm of routine operations. Relieved of his uniform, Holland had changed into a short-sleeved shirt, blue jeans, and running shoes. A clock on the wall read 11:45 PM.

"You're in the best possible hands here, Matty," Angelo De Luca said as he gestured at the attorney. "This is Eddie Shearson. I'm sure you know who he is."

Holland knew all too well. Indeed, most New York City cops knew who Eddie Shearson was, although they just as surely prayed that they'd never require his services. Indeed, Shearson had developed a unique specialty in legal circles. He was on an annual retainer from the PBA, his sole function defending officers charged with wrongdoing.

Like most of the cops he represented, Shearson was the product of a working-class upbringing, and had put himself through St. John's University's law school at night while juggling a series of menial jobs. Thirty years earlier, he'd begun his legal career as an investigator for the Queens County District Attorney, before opening his own practice and developing a reputation for providing representation and amicus-brief preparation in high-profile police cases.

What endeared Shearson to cops, however, wasn't so much his curriculum vitae as his skillfully crafted persona. Colorful and pugnacious, Shearson was a legal bulldog who never gave an inch in court and steadfastly defended the clients he served, cleverly seizing on obscure details and legal technicalities to consistently win over prosecutors, judges, and juries. Cops got a charge from the theatrical nature of his *schtick*: unkempt, baggy suits; a raspy voice, and a mushy, unkempt persona that, appearances aside, was hard as nails. The city's tabloids ate it up, too, portraying the attorney as a legal celebrity akin to a Broadway star. Shearson, for his part, was equally enamored of playing the role of the scrappy, streetwise underdog who somehow managed to outthink, outtalk, and out-finagle the highbred government officials who generally opposed him.

"Let's talk about what's going to happen tonight," the lawyer told Holland. "I'm here to walk you through the process for standard investigative protocols … to familiarize you not only with departmental policies and procedures, but also with your rights as a police officer."

Shearson pulled again on his cigarette.

"First," he said, "I want to assure you that the family members you've designated in the event of an on-duty emergency have all been contacted."

"My wife?" Holland raised an eyebrow.

"Katie's downstairs with the desk sergeant," Angelo De Luca replied.

"How is she?"

"Pretty shaken up … like everyone."

"Is someone looking after her?"

De Luca nodded. "She's here with your father-in-law, Matty."

"And my kids?"

"They've been brought to your in-laws' house. All three are fine."

Holland tilted his head. "Can I get to see Katie?"

"Not now," Shearson said.

"When?"

"After your initial round of questioning. Prior to them taking the investigation downtown."

Holland lowered his head, his eyes bloodshot, his pallor ghostlike. De Luca offered the officer a glass of water. Holland's hand shook as he slowly took a sip.

"Matt, you're about to be questioned about an act that may involve a criminal charge, and because of that you have the right to an attorney," Eddie Shearson said. "Under Miranda, that right 'attached' the instant you invoked your right to counsel. "That's why you were advised to do so before you even left the scene of tonight's incident."

"*Capiche*?" Angelo De Luca asked.

Holland nodded, drifting in and out of muddled thoughts.

"What you're about to go through represents the first of a multi-phased departmental investigation," Shearson resumed. "It's standard procedure, purely administrative. As an NYPD employee, you're obligated to provide a detailed account of what took place tonight, to answer the questions of superiors or face disciplinary penalties."

Holland blinked as though to clear his eyes.

"You also need to understand that you're a citizen as well as a police officer, and as such you have every citizen's right against self-incrimination," Shearson continued. "In other words, from a legal standpoint, you don't have to submit to questioning at all. You can invoke your right to remain silent."

"To tell you the truth, Matty, you're caught between a rock and a hard place," Angelo De Luca said gravely. "Any officer who invokes the right to remain silent under Miranda must immediately be suspended. It's department policy. You don't answer their questions, you're out of a job. On the flip side, no attorney would ever advise you to answer questions that may eventually result in criminal charges. In other words, you can waive your legal rights and agree to cooperate in the internal investigation, or you can be instantly suspended. You've got to choose."

"It's what's called a 'Hobson's choice,'" Shearson said. "In other words, you don't have much of a choice at all."

Holland stared blankly at the lawyer. "So, what should I do?"

"Answer their questions," Shearson advised, "and I'll hold your hand."

Just then, the door swung open and in walked someone even more well-known to New York cops than Eddie Shearson.

Tommy "Red" McLaren was president of the PBA, a thirty-thousand-member army of officers that comprised the largest municipal police union in the world. A veteran cop, McLaren had drawn his nickname not so much from his ruddy complexion as from his roots in Red Hook, an earthy, Irish enclave in South Brooklyn.

"Hey, partner ... how you holdin' up?" McLaren asked, extending a hand the size of a catcher's mitt.

McLaren's handshake was firm enough to make most men flinch. Even in his mid-fifties, he clearly was someone not to be trifled with. Broad-shouldered and hulking, he looked every bit like a lumberjack spoiling for a fight—and he'd been in more than his share of scraps.

Indeed, Red McLaren had gotten his initial taste of power as the leader of a cohort of cops who, shunned by the entrenched PBA leadership, had launched a battle to stamp an activist imprint on the police union. Appealing to a wide swath of cops, McLaren had risen to prominence by charging that the city and the NYPD's top brass were tearing the heart out of the cop on the street, compromising officers' wellbeing with policies that were outdated, counterproductive, and politically motivated. His fiery rhetoric hammered incumbent PBA leaders for being weak-kneed diplomats and dealmakers, far too controlled by City Hall bureaucrats. He advocated work slowdowns, and even strikes, as legitimate forms of protest—even though such actions violated state law. Vocalizing the frustration and bitterness that most cops felt at the time, McLaren pledged that he'd no longer tolerate further erosion of either their image or their morale. New York City cops, he swore, would no longer be the city's whipping boys.

McLaren's rebellious stance had resonated with the PBA's rank and file. In a stunning landslide, he'd been elected union president three years earlier, and was now at the height of his popularity. Nothing less than the voice of the cop on the street, he was respected for his willingness to ferociously protect cops' interests. He was equally admired for his ability to rankle city officials with actions and language that were cleverly contrived to keep adversaries off balance. In tandem with Eddie Shearson, he was as formidable an ally as any police officer could possibly have.

"We're here to help pull you through the legal minefield you're in," said McLaren, turning to Shearson for an update on what had already been discussed.

"Complicated, huh?" The PBA president sighed, rolling his eyes. "I know. There's a lot of legal shit surrounding incidents like tonight's and things are changing all the time. New precedents. New rulings. New suits at City Hall and One Police Plaza."

He bummed a cigarette from Shearson and fired it up.

"Listen, partner," said McLaren, exhaling a twisting plume of smoke. "We'll try to keep this as simple as possible. I'm sure your mind is running wild. But just know that we, and a lot of other people, are fully on your side. And we'll fight like hell for your interests."

Holland nodded. McLaren motioned for Shearson to resume his prep.

"Okay, so here's what's going to happen," the attorney began. "You've already submitted a formal statement about what took place tonight. Now, you'll be questioned regarding specifics, the precise nature of the incident, and the circumstances surrounding it. The purpose is to determine whether your actions were compliant with department procedures, as well as the law."

"Are you with us, Matty?" Red McLaren snapped his finger.

Holland stared trance-like at the PBA president and nodded.

"There are multiple layers to this kind of investigation, to ensure that a thorough, impartial, and transparent probe is conducted," Shearson continued. "The aim is to examine not just the particulars of the incident, but your state of mind: what you saw and felt to make you act the way you did; what you knew; what you didn't know; what you suspected. The department's goal is to determine whether you erred in judgment, exercised poor decision-making, violated policy, or acted with malice or intent based on other factors, like race."

"I didn't—" Holland began.

"*We* know that," Red McLaren said. "You need to let *them* know it, too."

Holland, seeming distracted, stared at the wall behind Capt. Borelli's desk.

"Who'll be handling the questioning?" Angelo De Luca asked.

"A lot of people will be involved," Shearson replied. "Patrol commanders, Internal Affairs, Homicide, Special Investigations Units, the Kings County D.A., and other entities you've probably never heard of. All of it will be recorded and videotaped. While any number of investigators will be present, you can only be questioned by one at a time, and only for reasonable periods."

"What does 'reasonable' mean?" Red McLaren asked.

"It means," said Shearson, "that they'll allow you to have bathroom breaks if you request them. Otherwise, the questioning can last for hours—and very likely will."

Holland sighed.

"A lot of the questions they ask may seem redundant, even hostile," Shearson resumed. "It may seem like they're asking you the same things repeatedly, only with a different slant. They'll be trying to trip you up, catch you in a contradiction or a lie."

"Any advice on how he should answer, Eddie?" Angelo De Luca asked.

"Just tell them the truth," Shearson said. "Tell them what happened and why."

"Our collective-bargaining agreement with the city also allows you to bring legal counsel into an administrative interview," De Luca explained.

"That will be my role," Shearson said.

"A PBA representative can also be present," De Luca said.

"That," said Red McLaren, "will be me."

Shearson nodded. "I'll be there to protect you against the interrogation turning adversarial, rather than as an objective effort to elicit facts. If the questioning gets confrontational, I'll jump right in."

"Eddie and I will be there to keep everyone in line, Matt," McLaren said. "Your partner, Officer Cook, will receive the same level of support."

Holland's eyebrows arched. "How is she?" he asked.

"Pretty shaken up, as you might expect," Shearson said. "The two of you have been placed on sick report, effective immediately. The trauma you sustained from tonight's incident is considered grounds for that."

Holland let loose a deflated sigh.

"As I've said, at this stage, the investigation is purely administrative, aimed at determining if NYPD policies, procedures, and training were followed," Shearson explained. "There'll be a series of interviews, here at the station house and afterwards at police headquarters. The findings of the internal investigation will inform any criminal charges or administrative discipline that might result, as well as liability that may attach to you or the department."

"What if this turns criminal?" De Luca asked.

"We'll cross that bridge if and when we come to it," Shearson said and doused his cigarette. "But at some point, prosecutors from the D.A.'s office will surely get involved, too."

"What determines that?" De Luca asked.

"It depends on whether they think there's enough evidence for a criminal case, which is impossible to tell at the moment—or whether there's political pressure," Shearson said. "In either case, the D.A.'s prosecutors will probably lie back for the time being and see how things go."

"And the Justice Department?" Red McLaren asked. "What if they jump in and this becomes a civil rights case?"

"Let's not go down that rabbit hole just yet," Shearson said.

Holland sipped absentmindedly from his water glass.

"How else can you advise Matt?" Red McLaren asked.

"What I can tell you," Shearson said, "is that officers under investigation cannot be threatened with disciplinary action during their interrogation. If you're threatened, whatever you say following the threat cannot be used against you in any criminal proceeding that may arise. Any statements you make can be used only to determine possible disciplinary action by the NYPD. Understand?"

Holland nodded, weakly.

"You'll continue to receive full pay and benefits unless you're suspended," Shearson said. "A violation of that right can result in a dismissal of any potential charges against you."

"How about the NYPD?" De Luca asked. "What can we expect from them?"

"The NYPD doesn't take incidents like tonight's lightly, especially in the current racially charged climate," Shearson said. "There's a lot at stake: civil-liability issues, potential community unrest, political careers, the perception of the NYPD, future department policies. In the final analysis, though, police departments are bureaucracies, fickle as hell. They're under intense scrutiny, enormous pressure."

"In other words," McLaren said, "the NYPD is going to cover its ass."

"And the media?" De Luca asked.

Holland looked up, seeming alarmed.

"I'm afraid so." Shearson nodded. "The NYPD has no choice but to get the media involved. The public has a right to know, and the department has an obligation to assure that there's a thorough, timely, and impartial investigation. These kinds of incidents can get emotionally charged. I'm sure you know that."

"History is weighing heavily against you, Matt," Red McLaren said gravely. "Let's face it: Cops have a piss-poor reputation in minority neighborhoods like Brownsville. There's a lot of anger and bitterness. What I'm saying is that a lot of people will be out to get you, justified or not, to make you pay for sins of the past. A lot of people are going want to make what happened tonight into a racial incident. A lot of them will be out for blood."

Holland placed a hand over his forehead, as if to shield himself from a blinding light.

"One final thing," Shearson said. "There's no way to minimize the gravity of what happened tonight. This incident is going to garner widespread attention. It'll likely trigger protests, even violence, in the community, and a shit-storm of controversy. It's going to be an emotional and legal nightmare for you, Matt. Your life will likely be turned inside out, your sanity tested."

"That's the truth," Red McLaren nodded. "You're walking in a minefield now, Matty. Your entire career is at stake … maybe even your life."

"It's also going to be a long, drawn-out struggle," Shearson said. "These investigations can take months, even years, to get resolved. The bottom line is you're in for a long, tough haul. But you've got to pull yourself together and get through it somehow. You've got to stay strong."

With that, Matt Holland lowered his head, rested it in his hands, and began, openly, to weep. Red McLaren and Eddie Shearson moved consolingly to the officer's side. Angelo De Luca bit his lip and looked away.

"Hey, partner," Red McLaren told Holland. "What do you say we forget about how tough this might be, and just try to get through it one day at a time?"

That's when they walked Matt Holland in to waive his right to silence, affirm his formal statement, and answer the barrage of questions that seemed as if they, like the night itself, would never end.

Chapter 7

Matt Holland sipped gingerly from a smudgy water glass, its contents having long since gone murky and tepid. Dawn was breaking over a sleepy city and Holland was already into his sixth full hour of questioning, seated at a lengthy conference table under harsh fluorescent lights in the 73rd Precinct's muster room.

Seated at the officer's right arm, PBA attorney Eddie Shearson sat chain-smoking and scratching notes on a legal pad. At Holland's other arm, union president Red McLaren drummed his fingertips absently on the tabletop, staring balefully at the Internal Affairs investigator spearheading Holland's interrogation. More than a dozen uniformed and plainclothes officials from the NYPD and the Kings County District Attorney's office were jammed into the roll-call area, its conference table cluttered with tape recorders, coffee containers, and ashtrays littered with cigarette butts. The heat was stifling, the air as stale as a gymnasium locker.

"Detective Sergeant Holland—" the IAD investigator began, coughing into a fist. Holland squinted, pulling away from somewhere deep inside himself.

"Referring to your recollection of last night's incident, the call to which you and your partner responded," the investigator said. "It was what, exactly?"

The investigator, eyebrows arched, shuffled through a ream of paperwork. He was slightly built, with a pockmarked face that resembled a golf ball, his hair coiffed and sprayed to look fuller. Alongside him sat a detective from Firearms, his pallid, bloated face looking as if he'd spent several days underwater. Behind them, Chief of Department Patrick Delaney—the NYPD's highest-ranking uniformed officer—stood ramrod straight, his crisply pressed reefer strung with multicolored medals, his service cap wrapped with a gold-colored braid. Other uniformed and plainclothes officers of various ranks looked on.

"The call we responded to," Holland recounted, "was a 10-31."

"A burglary-in-progress?"

"That's correct."

"And the location to which you responded?"

"An apartment building, at 118 Amboy Street."

"Number of officers responding?"

"There were two of us. Me and my partner, Rachel Cook."

The investigator glanced at his tape recorder, to assure it was spooling properly. His scrawny fingers, clubbed and yellowed from nicotine, poked at the collar of a Ban-Lon shirt.

"And the 10-31," he inquired, "it was received at what time?"

"8:46 PM," Holland replied, referring to his written statement.

"And the time of your arrival?"

"8:57 PM."

The IAD guy wrote the information down.

"Time of arrival of backup officers?" he asked, without looking up.

"I believe it was 9:15 PM," Holland replied.

The firearms investigator nodded to confirm the accuracy of the response.

"And you're Officer Cook's field training officer, are you not?" the IAD guy asked.

"I *have* been ... yes," Holland said.

"And for how long have you been her FTO?"

"About eight months, ever since she was assigned to our precinct."

"And the two of you were in uniform when you responded to the call ... clearly identifiable as police officers?"

"We were."

The investigator glanced at his notes, then back at Holland.

"The *NYPD Patrol Guide*," he intoned, "provides detailed guidelines for display of shield, voice commands, and other measures to avoid use-of-force incidents. You're aware of those guidelines, are you not?"

"I am," Holland said.

"And among them," the investigator continued, "is the stipulation that any application of force must be 'reasonable' under the circumstances … and if the force used is 'unreasonable,' it'll be deemed excessive and in violation of department policy. You're aware of that, as well?"

"I am."

"Detective Sergeant Holland," the investigator inquired, "why did you feel, at the time you entered the cellar, that it was necessary for you and Officer Cook to unholster your service revolvers?"

Holland drew a deep breath, sipping again from his water glass.

"Decisions like that," he said, "are left to an officer's discretion, based on whether they're encountering what they consider to be extreme and particularized danger."

"And you felt as if the two of you were?"

"Officer Cook and I were responding to a 10-31 at a location that had been the scene of past criminal activity, and we were entering a part of the building that we believed represented a potential threat," Holland said. "Based on the call we received, we had to assume there was a crime-in-progress, with possible shots fired, and that suspects were either at, or close to, the scene."

Holland sipped again from his glass as the investigators took notes and NYPD brass sat silently and watched, faces ashen and rigid.

"Rooftops, stairwells, alleyways, and cellars like the kind Officer Cook and I entered are considered danger zones, especially if they're dimly lit," Holland elaborated. "We had no idea what we'd find down there."

"But usually, these types of calls amount to nothing, isn't that correct?" the investigator asked, skeptically. "They turn out to be a short-circuited alarm, or a phony 911 call, or someone doing something perfectly innocent. Isn't that correct?"

"Yes," Holland nodded. "But you never know what to expect on any call. As a police officer, you're always on guard. I felt that preparing ourselves as we did was completely appropriate under the circumstances."

"So, you drew your firearm?"

"Yes."

"And Officer Cook did the same?"

"At my command ... yes."

"And then you pushed in the door and entered the cellar?"

Holland stared blankly into space.

"I tried to push the door in gently at first," he recalled, after a brief pause, "but it seemed as if it were jammed, or something was blocking it from the other side. So, I shoved it forcibly with my shoulder, and the door flew open."

"And you and Officer Cook entered the cellar?"

"Yes."

"Tell us what happened then."

* * *

When Holland and Cook burst into the apartment-building cellar, they realized instantly that there *had* been something blocking their entry—a person trying to hold the door shut.

Whoever that person was was knocked to the floor by the force of Holland's shove, as the officers—crouched combat-style, handguns married to their six-cell flashlights—rushed in. There was an instant commotion, frantic shouts, a high-pitched shriek. Suddenly, the cellar was full of movement and clamor. In the dim light, people who were barely discernable seemed to be careening about, their shadows swooping like angry raptors across the cellar's concrete walls.

Holland shouted forcefully.

"Halt ... Police!"

He shouted the command two, three times. Cook shouted it, as well.

"Halt ... Police! Halt ... Police!"

But the officers' commands were ignored. The commotion in the cellar only intensified, shadows swirling, high-pitched squeals echoing off the walls. Wide-eyed and breathless, the officers braced for an attack. Then, almost instantly, the light was extinguished, and the entire cellar went black, rendering Holland and Cook utterly blind.

"Hmm," the IAD investigator mumbled, scribbling notes. Others sat stone-faced, squirming in their seats.

"One more time," the investigator resumed, "can you describe the lighting in the cellar after you and Officer Cook burst in?"

Holland looked up, pulling himself free from his harrowing flashback.

"It was dim but lit well enough to see when we initially entered," he recounted. "Officer Cook and I used our flashlights to try and get our bearings. The cellar was illuminated by a single lightbulb hanging from the ceiling over a large, butcher-block-type table. Everything went completely dark, though, seconds after we entered."

"And what caused that?"

"At first," Holland said, "someone shouted, 'Police ... Run!'"

"And then?"

Lowering his head again, Matt Holland drew a deep breath.

"Almost immediately," he replied, "whoever was there started to run toward a small flight of steps leading to the outside courtyard. I saw someone reach up and pull the cord on the light."

"By that point I take it you and Officer Cook had identified yourselves by issuing assertive voice commands?" the investigator inquired.

"We had."

"How soon?"

"Immediately upon entering the cellar."

"How many times did you shout, 'Halt ... Police!'?"

"Once, when we entered. Two or three times after that."

"Was there a response to your commands?"

"Not that I could tell." Holland shook his head. "Whoever was in the cellar just kept racing about."

"Do you feel your commands were forceful and clear?"

"Yes. Both Officer Cook and I shouted the same command, loudly and forcefully, several times."

"How many people did you assume were in the cellar?"

"It seemed like maybe five or six."

"What assumption did you make from the fact that they seemed to be running away?"

"I assumed that they were startled and were trying to exit the cellar."

"Anything beyond that?"

"Only that they were trying to leave for a specific reason."

"And what did you believe that reason to be?"

"That whoever it was," Holland said, "didn't want to make contact with the police."

The investigator scribbled a note to himself. Red McLaren leaned over and whispered into Eddie Shearson's ear. Nodding, the attorney placed a hand consolingly on Matt Holland's forearm.

"Take your time, Matty," Shearson said. "You're doing fine."

Holland took a deep breath before continuing.

When the cellar went black, he recounted, he and Rachel Cook—service revolvers and flashlights in hand—were frozen in place for a split-second, unable to see beyond their flashlight beams piercing the darkness. There was chaos, Holland remembered, frantic shouts, people scurrying about. Holland saw nothing but darkness. What happened next, he said, happened in the blink of an eye.

"And exactly what was that?" the investigator asked.

"I thought I saw something coming at me," the officer replied.

"You saw it—or *thought* you saw it?"

"It was more like I *sensed* it," Holland said. "It's difficult to describe. Whatever it was … I never fully saw it."

"Approaching from your right side or left?" the IAD guy probed.

"Slightly toward my right side," Holland replied. "It was like a shadow, nothing more than a dark shape coming quickly at me. I couldn't tell what it was. It was pitch-black and it happened so fast. This shadow … it just kept rushing at me. I wasn't sure why. It was as if whatever it was completely ignored my and my partner's commands."

"What were your thoughts at that instant, detective?" the IAD guy probed.

"I couldn't tell if I was being attacked, or if someone was about to run into me inadvertently, because the cellar was so dark."

"How much time elapsed from the time the lights went out until you saw this so-called shadow," the investigator asked.

"A second … maybe two," Holland said.

"Could you determine if the 'shadow' was a person or an object, male or female, young or old, black or white?"

"No … I couldn't tell a thing."

"Did you have any suspicion of drug or alcohol use by the subject?"

"There was no way of knowing."

"Any knowledge of the subject's mental status?"

"None."

"Criminal intent?"

"No."

"Weapons he or she might have possessed?"

"Again … no way of knowing."

The investigator pensively scratched his chin.

"Your training, along with established NYPD procedures, offered you many response options—among them command presence, verbal direction, and persuasion," he said. "You're aware of those de-escalation techniques, are you not?"

"I'm well aware," Holland said.

"Were all of them employed?"

"They were."

And even as he replied, Holland's thoughts drifted back to that harrowing moment in the cellar. It was then, he remembered, that *whoever* it was that rushed him let loose a high-pitched squeal, and then lurched chest-high into the officer's right side. The surprise impact was jarring. So was the muzzle flash from Holland's service revolver, filling the cellar with a thunderous sound and a blinding light, as if a violent storm had suddenly struck. Holland felt the jolt from the gun's recoil run like an electric shock up his arm, and then ducked reflexively as something struck him atop his head.

"What happened then?" the investigator inquired.

And Holland recounted how Rachel Cook instinctively dropped to the floor, along with the shadowy figure that had rushed the officers, and how there was only stillness and darkness and the smell of cordite now, and powdery grains of concrete dust falling like snowflakes from the ceiling.

Chapter 8

When their paths first crossed, eight months earlier, neither one knew what to expect. Neither could imagine what it would be like working alongside the other. Neither could fathom what their future as partners might be. How could they possibly know? How could anyone?

It was Rachel Cook's first day on the job, and she was fresh out of the NYPD Police Academy, raw and green as a rookie could possibly be—and the only female among the thirty-six officers assembled for the 8:00 AM roll call at Brownsville's 73rd Precinct.

All through that initial muster, Cook found herself equally anxious and self-conscious, uncertain about how to look or sound, only half-listening to the precinct's hardboiled sergeant barking out a litany of instructions. Instead, Cook's mind wandered almost in free flight. She wondered—at five-foot-three, the first female ever assigned to the seven-three—if she looked enough like a cop to command the credibility and respect of the other officers. She wondered how she'd be welcomed into the ranks—*accepted, ridiculed, scorned?* She wondered which of her fellow officers was Matt Holland, the veteran cop assigned as her field training officer.

She didn't have to wait long to find out.

"You Cook?" a uniformed officer asked, approaching her after roll call.

She nodded, nervously.

"I'm Detective Sergeant Matt Holland," he said, extending a hand. "I'm gonna be your FTO."

Cook was taken aback. For some reason, she'd envisioned her FTO as looking more like the stereotypical cop—hardboiled, imposing, and gruff. In contrast, Matt Holland looked nothing at all like that. Slender in build, with fair-skinned features sunburned from months on patrol, Holland appeared far younger than his forty-two years, his double-breasted reefer fitting snugly, his cap tilted over his eyes. A trio of chevrons on his upper right sleeve signaled his rank as sergeant; a quartet of hash marks denoted his years of service. A string of medals, along with a detective's gold shield and nameplate, adorned his chest. Gold pins with the precinct number, 73, were pinned to each collar.

"How are you doing?" he smiled in a sparkly kind of way.

It was, Cook thought, a smile that hinted at an innate humanity, a kindness unscathed by the rigorous demands of big-city police work. Cook instantly felt at ease. All through her final weeks at the Police Academy, she'd wondered about her FTO—his expertise, his integrity, his demeanor—wondered if he'd be lenient or a hard-ass, supportive or a ball-buster. Now, she'd finally met him, and he seemed pleasant enough, even potentially funny. Cook saw him instantly as someone she could work alongside, even someone she could come to like.

Holland, for his part, seemed unsure precisely what to think. Slack-jawed, he simply stared at the female probationary cop, equally curious, amused, and perhaps a bit apprehensive.

All of which was understandable.

For one thing, Holland, like nearly all of the 73rd Precinct's officers, had never even *seen* a uniformed female cop, let alone worked alongside one. The sight of Cook alone seemed to take Holland a moment to absorb. And if Holland didn't resemble the stereotypical cop, Cook looked even less the part. Shoulder-high to her FTO, with dimpled, flushed cheeks, Cook's long, dark hair was barely visible beneath the brim and sides of her police cap. To Holland, she seemed almost shy, greenish eyes sparkling with equal measures of steely determination and unbridled anxiety. Holland saw grit and substance in Cook's eyes—an innate toughness and intelligence—but got the distinct impression that his rookie partner wasn't sure, at that moment, exactly what to feel.

He was right.

But while Rachel Cook was hardly the kind of physical deterrent that the NYPD traditionally sought in its officers, it was obvious that she took very good care of herself. Four months of running, weight-training, calisthenics, and self-defense courses at the Police Academy had rendered the rookie cop hard as nails, as physically fit as she was resolute and smart. She had studied diligently, too, absorbed everything her instructors had thrown at her. Despite her diffidence, she was as prepared to go to work as any probationary cop could possibly be.

"I've heard a lot about you from Capt. Borelli," Holland grinned. "Good things."

Cook felt instantly relieved. Joseph Borelli, commanding officer of the 73rd Precinct, was a well-respected captain whose opinion carried weight. Apparently, he'd been impressed about what he'd heard regarding Cook, who days earlier had graduated from the NYPD Police Academy number one in a class of four hundred recruits.

"Exactly what have you heard?" Cook inquired, smiling.

"That you're extremely intelligent and highly motivated ... handpicked for a master's degree program at John Jay," Holland said. "Pretty impressive stuff."

"Well, I've heard a lot about you, too," Cook said.

"Really? What?"

"Well, I've heard you're an exemplary officer—experienced, decorated, and highly respected by the NYPD and the people here in Brownsville."

"Anything else?"

"I heard about how you saved those children from that building collapse, and some of the other things you've done in the neighborhood."

"I see," Holland said. "Allow me to let you in on a secret, though."

"What's that?"

"Don't be overly impressed by everything that you hear."

"What do you mean?"

"I mean, all that 'hero' stuff is well and good," Holland said, "but I don't take it too seriously and neither should you. It's *history*, understand? Being a 'hero' a few years ago doesn't count for much today. On this job, you're judged by other criteria—not just something big—and certainly not by something you may've done years ago."

Holland studied Cook. “Think you can remember that?”

Cook nodded. “Sure.”

“Good.” Holland smiled. “Now we can begin.”

* * *

It was hardly an accident that the two of them were a team. Unlike most sets of patrol partners, thrown together at random, the NYPD had paired Matt Holland and Rachel Cook with a specific purpose in mind. It was part of a well-conceived plan.

For years, New York’s police brass had cut down on neighborhood foot patrols in favor of more mobile, efficient, two-officer patrol cars. That policy was being re-evaluated, however. Community policing had become the backbone of an experiment that proponents saw as vital to the relationship between police and the public. Concurrent with other changes in law enforcement, foot patrols were being resurrected, not simply as a deterrent to crime but as a way of reconnecting police with the communities they served. Special units, deployed in select neighborhoods, were expressly aimed at increasing the number of positive contacts between police and citizens, humanizing cops, and making them allies rather than adversaries. At the same time, precinct commanders were being mandated to conduct regular meetings with community leaders. A variety of outreach programs were aimed at neighborhood youths.

Matt Holland—an exemplary, decorated officer—was an integral part of the community policing approach at Brownsville’s 73rd Precinct. Rachel Cook had been handpicked to join him.

In several ways, the Holland-Cook pairing was also part of a bold, new experiment in police chemistry. Holland—streetwise, professional, and mature—was considered among the top FTOs in Brooklyn. It was believed that he also possessed the ideal blend of experience, personality, and perspective required to nurture a rookie, in Cook, whom NYPD brass viewed as a potential superstar.

Just as importantly, Holland—unlike most male cops—was at least willing to give the strategy of deploying females on patrol a chance. It was similarly believed that Cook would bring her own special attributes to the team. Exceptionally bright and eager to excel, she'd contribute a level of sensitivity and communications skills rare in most cops. She'd also, in theory, soften the image of the patrol team, have a calming effect in high-stress situations, and help establish greater levels of police-community trust.

While Cook was serving in Brownsville, her partnership with Holland would be closely monitored to determine if it could serve as a potential model for similar pairings. Holland would also evaluate Cook's performance regularly, mentoring her on the ins and outs of policing in a poverty-stricken, high-crime, minority neighborhood. The officers would partner for Cook's entire twelve-month probationary period. At that point, assuming Cook passed muster, she'd be ready for an assignment to NYPD headquarters or in one of the department's elite anti-crime or investigatory units. A couple of years in that role, coupled with her continued education, and who knew? With Cook's potential, it was thought, the sky was the limit.

Holland and Cook, it was believed, would help usher in a whole new era of rapport between police and Brownsville residents. They'd talk to people on the streets, help reduce fear, solve problems instead of simply responding to calls, and reconnect the police to the community in a new and constructive way. In time, it was believed, the partners might give a whole new meaning to the term "New York's Finest," comprising nothing less than the ideal New Age police team.

That, at least, was the plan.

"You need to know right up front that it's not going to be easy for you," Holland told Cook that first day.

"Why is that?" she asked.

"Lots of reasons," Holland said. "You're a female. You're a rookie. You're new to the neighborhood. The seven-three, as I'm sure you know, is an 'A' house. A lot of poverty, crime, things that are extremely difficult for most people to see. What I'm saying is that it's hardly an easy assignment. You're going to be pushed to the brink, tested in ways you can't even imagine. And lots of people will be watching, evaluating, maybe even criticizing."

The pair took seats in the muster room, empty now with the precinct's other cops having left on patrol.

"It's very different on the streets than it is at the Police Academy," Holland said. "What you did in training doesn't carry a whole lot of weight in a neighborhood like Brownsville."

"Look," said Cook, "I know I've got a lot to learn and it's not going to be easy. I have no idea how I'll do, but I want you know that I've trained very hard, and this job is extremely important to me. I'm ready to learn, and I'll work my ass off to prove myself to you and everyone else at the seven-three."

"Well, that's refreshing!" Holland chuckled. "Most rookies come to work thinking they're so smart they should be training their FTO!"

"That's not me," Cook said. "I'm here to learn and to do a good job. All I want is a chance to show what I can do."

"Fair enough." Holland grinned. "I understand that you did exceptionally well at the Police Academy."

"I did all right," Cook said, nonchalantly.

"Yeah?" Holland asked. "Exactly *how well* did you do?"

* * *

In reality, the term "all right" was a gross understatement. Rachel Cook had literally sailed, like few recruits ever, through her four months of training. Indeed, to Cook, the NYPD Police Academy had been everything a training ground could possibly be—and more. Aside from that, she was making history.

The NYPD Police Academy was housed in downtown Manhattan, in a newly opened, ultra-modern building that stood in stark contrast to the antiquated training facility used for decades. When Cook entered, in 1975, it was among the busiest times in the Academy's history. Emerging from its fiscal crisis and responding to a sharp rise in crime, the city had ordered a speed-up in training. Recruitment was ratcheted to new heights. Stretched to the limits of its capacity, the traditional training period cut from six to four months, the Academy was graduating four hundred officers a month. And for the first time ever, men and women were training alongside each other.

But it wasn't merely the history being made, or even the fact that she was training for a dream job, that made Cook feel so bullish. It was the Academy, itself. There, for the first time in her life, Cook felt that school truly had a purpose, and there was a rationale for everything that was being taught. Every course seemed to have a distinct objective. Every program built upon one another. Everything Cook learned helped her feel more confident, better prepared for what she'd face.

There were courses in Constitutional law, criminal law, and traffic law; courses on the city charter and on New York's administrative and health codes; courses in police science and NYPD procedure; in the rituals of patrol; and in investigative procedures like interviewing, fingerprinting, and evidence preservation. There were other courses, too—in psychology, sociology, and first aid—and workshops on the urban environment, family crisis intervention, on-the-street problems, and police ethics. Then there was the physical stuff: calisthenics, search-and-frisk techniques, self-defense, crowd control, and drills on the use of the nightstick. Lastly, there was firearms training: round after round of practice at police shooting ranges; dry firings; practicing in daylight, dim light and total darkness; firing combat-style; kneeling to the left, kneeling to the right, flat on her back, flat on her stomach, standing behind an object; firing at paper bullseyes and life-size silhouettes of faceless forms pointing guns; practicing until Cook got comfortable with the feel of the gun, the sound of the shot and the power of the recoil; practicing until her scores were nearly perfect.

Rachel Cook loved every minute of it.

At the Police Academy, she'd poured herself into her studies as never before, willingly embracing everything she was taught—and mastering it, too. Indeed, Cook's four months of training had ended on equal notes of triumph and promise, and an ending she'd always remember:

> … graduation ceremonies at the landmark Seventh Regiment Armory on Manhattan's Park Avenue.

... row upon row of rookies, all clad in crisp NYPD reefers, white gloves, and spit-polished shoes.

... crowds of onlookers in the gallery, smiling and waving and taking photos.

... the mayor and top police brass standing at attention, alongside the NYPD's color guard.

Cook would remember it all.

She'd remember taking an oath that bound her, body and soul, to a police department that the mayor called the finest in the world. She'd remember being stirred by the speeches: about the need to bring the highest level of service to the public; the need to never forget the dignity of each person with whom she'd come in contact; all the ways that her city needed and respected its officers.

She'd also remember the memo she received from the police commissioner himself, congratulating her on her stellar academic achievement. Then, she'd remember being called up on stage and hearing the armory explode in cheers as she accepted congratulations for achieving the highest academic rank in her training company, highest in the Police Academy's hundred-and-twenty-year history.

Four hundred recruits graduated the Police Academy that day. Rachel Cook was first in her class.

She'd remember leaving the stage, clinging to the award certificate and the $2,500 check that she'd wind up using as a security deposit and month's rent for her first real apartment. She'd remember the party that night, the kind of raucous celebration a person could carry with them forever—music pounding, strobe lights flashing, hundreds of rookie officers dancing and toasting one another in a loft overlooking the city's downtown skyline. She'd remember wondering, too, if the other rookies felt like she did—so worthwhile, so charged, so full of the moment. She'd remember wondering if they, like her, believed in the speeches, if they, too, wondered how it all might work out. Would their glittering new careers stay aloft, or would they crash and burn on the city's streets? Would they become good, productive cops, or would they wind up bruised and burned out and just putting in their time? Would they win awards for their achievements, or would they end up in an alley somewhere with their eyes shot out—bleeding and frightened and alone?

Cook remembered all of that now.

She remembered wondering, as she left the Academy, about how her bold new journey might unfold. Would it live up to the radiant possibilities she imagined? Would she emerge from the other end with her body and senses intact, boundless in her resolve, clinging to her hopes, still trying to greet new challenges with everything she could muster?

And she remembered, as she spoke to Matt Holland on their first day together, how she knew she didn't have any answers, only that she'd put her faith in everything that she'd learned—and put her faith in Holland, too—and that she'd pour her heart and soul into her job as a cop, and give it every ounce of energy and courage she possessed.

* * *

Matt Holland shrugged nonchalantly after listening to Cook's recitation of her Police Academy accolades.

"Wow!" he said, smiling. "Sounds like you broke new ground."

"I guess so," Cook grinned, haughtily.

"Then," said Holland, "why don't we start your 'real' training now."

He pulled a radio from his belt and handed it to Cook.

"What about this?" he asked.

"What *about* it?"

"Well … did you learn how to use it?"

"Excuse me?"

"At the Police Academy … did they teach you how to operate a radio?"

Cook hesitated, nonplussed. "Uh, actually, I can't recall that they did."

"You mean, you didn't have a course on how police officers communicate with each other on the street?" Holland asked, mockingly.

"To be honest with you," Cook replied, sheepishly, "I never even *saw* a radio at the Academy."

"Well, that's interesting," Holland said, wryly. "How about a summons? Do you know how to fill one out?"

"Uh ... we spent a day on it. They didn't go into much detail."

"How about a 61 ... a complaint report?"

"No."

"A logbook?"

"Not really. They told us that when we got on the job, we'd be reporting our activities ... but they didn't actually tell us how."

Holland then inquired, in staccato fashion, about Cook's familiarity with other routine procedures and forms. She wasn't aware of one. She *was* aware by now, however, that Holland's questions were aimed more at making a point than at eliciting information—and she was equal parts speechless and deflated.

"Look," Holland said. "I don't want you to feel that you're going to be a liability on patrol, but we've got to close the loop on a lot of things very quickly. Understand? Like I said, reality is very different from training school."

Cook simply nodded.

Holland broke into a broad grin.

"Okay," he quipped, "so let's start your training the *right* way."

He led her out of the station house and down the street to a coffee shop. "The doughnuts," he said, "are on me."

At least she'd been right about her FTO having a sense of humor, Cook thought. Hopefully, she mused, he had more to offer than simply that.

* * *

He did.

Starting with the simplest of basics, and assuming nothing, Matt Holland began Rachel Cook's field training, working like a paint-by-numbers artist and coloring in everything left blank by the Police Academy.

He began that first day by showing Cook around the station house, introducing her to the roll-call man, desk officers, and the I-24 man, who handled the precinct's clerical work. They visited the property clerk to procure the supplies Cook needed. The two of them then walked through the *NYPD Patrol Guide*, a detailed manual on police policies and procedures, and reviewed the forms that Cook needed on patrol: summonses, complaint reports, patrol reports, domestic incident reports, aided cards, and booking sheets.

After that, they turned to the radio. Holland instructed Cook on the proper way to speak into it: articulate and forceful. He then reviewed the NYPD's myriad incident code signals: possible crimes, crimes in the past, crimes-in-progress, non-crime incidents, rapid mobilization and all the others. He drilled Cook on the differences between a 10-10—a call to investigate a suspicious person or a burglar alarm—and a 10-34, an assault-in-progress. They reviewed the definitions of a 10-53, a street accident; a 10-52, a noise or dispute; and a 10-67, a traffic or parking condition. He reminded her that a 10-06 meant "stand by" and, laughingly, that a 10-63, meant you were out of service for a meal.

"Then there's this," said Holland, grim-faced, pointing to the signal code 10-13. Next to the code, were the bold-faced words: **Assist Police Officer.**

"This one is big-time trouble, understand?" he said. "If you hear the code 10-13, you drop whatever you're doing and rush to the scene as fast as possible. A 10-13 means that an officer needs immediate assistance. You don't wait for an explanation. You just get to his or her side quickly as possible."

Holland paused, as if to be sure Cook fully understood.

"We never leave a police officer out on the street when they're in trouble—*never*!" he said. "But you knew that already, didn't you?"

"Yes," Cook said, "that much I know."

It would be another three days before they'd even leave the station house.

"I think it's time for you to get a taste of Brownsville," Holland said.

"I'm ready," Cook said.

"Oh yeah?" Matt Holland grinned. "We'll see about that."

Chapter 9

THERE WAS NO WAY she could have been ready—not really—no way that Rachel Cook could have ever prepared for what she saw when she ventured for the first time into the heart of the central Brooklyn neighborhood known as Brownsville.

Ready or not, though, there Cook was. And there, before her eyes, was Brownsville.

Developed initially as a middle-class suburb of New York, Brownsville had been one of the city's most vibrant neighborhoods in the decades prior to World War II, drawing its primarily Jewish population from Manhattan's Lower East Side. Often called the "Jerusalem of America," the neighborhood was dominated then by Old World customs and had the look and feel of an Eastern European shtetl. Yiddish newspapers, totems, and signs marked the landscape. Pushcart peddlers lined the major thoroughfares. Synagogues and cheders, where Jewish children received instruction in Orthodox customs and traditions, could be found on nearly every street.

Like other Jewish settlements in New York, Brownsville also seethed with political rhetoric and social protest. Socialists and Communists, anarchists and labor leaders, Zionists and atheists clashed on street corners and in cafes. Traditional European values and customs warred with modern Western lifestyles. Pockmarked with overcrowded Old Law tenements, dreary railroad flats, and decaying sections, Brownsville was also a breeding ground for crime. Murder, Inc. found a home there. So did any number of notorious youth gangs.

But despite its roots in poverty and crime, the neighborhood for years flourished as a folksy, bustling community—in many ways both a mass experiment in Americanization and a lush garden for ideas and talent. It served as home to many of the city's most prominent businessmen and best-known writers, entertainers, educators, scientists, and politicians. It also became one of Brooklyn's most important retail centers.

After World War II, however, Brownsville began to change.

Once the postwar celebrations died down, the very people who'd settled the neighborhood began to flee, joining waves of other upwardly mobile, middle-class, white residents as they flocked to other neighborhoods, or to New York's burgeoning suburbs. No longer drawing refugees of the Jewish diaspora, Brownsville began to attract another cohort of America's poor: the descendants of the slave ships and cotton fields of the Deep South, the sugar cane factories and tobacco farms of the Caribbean, the sweat shops and rice paddies of the Far East.

As the new minorities arrived, the exodus of whites only quickened—prompted, in part, by the disruption that defined the city's attempts at urban renewal. Under those failed programs, vacant apartments in Brownsville became a dumping ground for poor, dislocated welfare clients from other parts of New York. As new welfare clients arrived, old-time residents panicked, and more apartments emptied. A growing number of real estate agents began "blockbusting," illegally inducing white homeowners to sell by spreading fear of a minority incursion. Banks started to "redline" the neighborhood, refusing mortgage loans, driving property values down, and forcing people to sell. Soon, rather than pay taxes and provide maintenance for property they were making no money on, landlords simply abandoned their buildings, leaving tenants without heat, hot water, and other services. Squatters moved in, driving out still more tenants. Vandals went after abandoned buildings, stripping them of appliances, plumbing fixtures, and other valuables. Other buildings were leveled by the city. Merchants, businessmen and professionals also fled the disintegrating community, leaving the remaining residents void of shops, restaurants, entertainment, and services.

As time passed, the complex social forces reshaping the neighborhood continued to eat away at Brownsville's infrastructure. Many longtime residents, subsisting on fixed incomes, had neither the resources to abandon the neighborhood nor any place to go. Others, tied to welfare requirements that mandated lengthy leases, found their movement restricted. Fear set in. Desperation and panic followed. And after a while, Brownsville began to burn.

Fire had become an act of social protest by the 1960s, and arson fires soon swept through Brownsville like an unchecked epidemic. Residents seeking relocation money or attempting to move up the waiting list for public housing literally began setting fire to their homes. Greedy landlords and local businessmen, seeking an insurance payoff, hired professional arsonists to destroy their buildings. Neighborhood youths began torching apartments as a routine pastime. All the while, attempts at community resurrection were failing. Federal, state and city funds dried up. Efforts at commercial and industrial development failed to deliver new jobs. Attempts at providing school aid, job assistance, and community development programs proved more cosmetic than substantive. Pleas for urban aid, anti-poverty programs, and social services went ignored. Programs aimed at providing new housing were riddled with corruption and suffocated by disputes between community groups and developers. Battles raged over literally everything, especially control of the schools, lighting the fuse of racial hostility.

By the time Rachel Cook arrived in Brownsville as a cop, the neighborhood's metamorphosis was complete. An ugly, barren ruin, Brownsville had been transformed into a tragic showplace for America's urban maladies, a synonym for the decay of the nation's inner cities. Its population had plummeted to half of what it once was. Once almost entirely white, most of its residents were now black or Hispanic. Many were dependent on the government for shelter, medical assistance, clothing, day care, and food. Many lived with no heat, hot water, or electricity. Unemployment was twice the citywide rate, the high school dropout rate greater than that. Alcoholism and drug addiction—along with infant mortality, juvenile delinquency, and venereal disease—ran rampant. And Brownsville's crime rate was a staggering eight times the city's average.

The twelve-square-mile neighborhood had also taken on the look of a charred and crumbling war zone, consisting of aging, decaying, abandoned, and burned-out buildings, and choked by a prevailing mood of despair.

Referred to in the city's tabloid newspapers as *Bombsville*, residents saw it as a neglected stepchild of New York. Others saw it as nothing less than a tangible sign of the collapse of American civilization.

"Welcome," Matt Holland said, and grinned when he showed Cook around the neighborhood for the first time. "Welcome to your home away from home."

* * *

Home.

It was an interesting choice of words. Ironic, too.

Matt Holland didn't realize it when he described Brownsville that way, but sixteen years earlier, Brownsville really *had* been Rachel Cook's home, the neighborhood in which she'd spent the first six years of her life. Brownsville, like New York, was very different then. And so, of course, was Cook.

An only child at the time, Cook lived with her parents and grandmother in a two-bedroom, railroad apartment above a flower shop on one of Brownsville's busiest streets. Like most walk-ups, the apartment was tiny and cramped, Cook sharing a bedroom with her grandmother. But the apartment was clean and bright and spacious enough for the four of them, with sunlight streaming in through big French doors, and the scent of fresh-cut flowers pervasive from the shop below.

As a child, Rachel would peer through the shop window, see row upon row of beautiful bouquets, and imagine that all there was to the world were flowers and colors and fragrant smells. In many ways, for her, it was true.

Through Cook's childhood eyes, postwar Brownsville was dazzling and exciting, a wondrous extension of the flower shop itself. Stretching outward from the family's apartment, for block upon city block, Rachel Cook's Brownsville was alive with sights and sounds. Everything her family needed could easily be found. Grocery stores, pharmacies, laundromats, barber shops, bakeries, butcher shops, delicatessens, and produce stands—all within walking distance—were built into the fronts of the brownstones and two-story buildings that lined the streets. On Brownsville's main thoroughfare,

Pitkin Avenue, retail outlets sold furniture, appliances, linens, clothing, chinaware, shoes, radios, and television sets. At fine department stores, uniformed chauffeurs would wait near idling, double-parked limousines, while wealthy patrons hunted for bargain prices. Out along an open-air market on nearby Belmont Avenue, pushcarts overflowed with roasted peanuts, knishes, and jellied apples, while vendors hawked Italian ices, hot dogs, pretzels, and fruit pies. At Dubrow's, a legendary New York automat, people bought food from behind glass cubicles and sat at lacquered tables, eating and laughing and sharing tales about the Old Country. At the Loew's Premiere, an Art Deco movie palace, audiences sat under a simulated night-sky ceiling, gazing up at faux clouds that moved and stars that twinkled, and marveling at huge chandeliers, plastered ornaments, lavish statuary and marble fountains in the lobby. In the meantime, out on the streets, hordes of people, rubbing shoulders as they walked, strolled along narrow sidewalks, a great flowing mass of humanity, window-shopping, stopping to eat, and taking it all in.

And Rachel Cook was there, right in the middle of it all.

A part of Brooklyn's vast working class, Cook's parents couldn't afford a car then. But that didn't matter. Their greatest joy was simply walking the streets of their bustling Brooklyn neighborhood. And walk, they did.

Every Sunday in the summer, Cook and her parents would walk Brownsville's streets.

> … past jewelry stores, where tea sets and sterling silver vases glittered in mahogany-framed glass cases that rolled out from the walls;
>
> … past clothing stores with sleek, well-dressed mannequins in the windows;
>
> … past ice cream parlors with black-marble counters and high, spinning stools and ice chests full of frosted, floating soda bottles;
>
> … past toy stores where groups of children stood in front of window displays, watching electric trains go round and round;

> … past candy stores with chewing gum machines and soda fountains and shelves of newspapers and comic books and candy bars.

Then they'd walk some more.

They'd walk past knots of Brooklyn's Hasidim: past bewigged women in patent-leather shoes and high-necked, ankle-length dresses; past men with unruly beards and long side locks, in white shirts, fur-brimmed hats and belted black robes; past frenzied radicals arguing politics on street corners; past elderly people playing mah-jongg and pinochle on folding bridge tables; past young mothers rocking baby carriages, crocheting blankets and knitting sweaters, embroidering tablecloths, and making basket bags out of straw. Sometimes, they'd walk all the way to Eastern Parkway, a broad tree-lined thoroughfare stretching for miles through the heart of Brooklyn. That was Rachel's favorite—one of the most magnificent streets you'd ever see in an American city. Just like a glorious promenade in Paris.

All along Eastern Parkway towering, graceful oaks and pink-blossomed magnolia trees overhung a roadway lined with wooden benches and paths for walking and riding bicycles. On the opposite side of the boulevard was a bridle path for horseback riders. On both sides of the six-lane thoroughfare stood long rows of luxury apartment buildings, their baroque lobbies full of antique furniture, varnished wood floors, marble staircases, and ornate plasterwork. Alongside them were supper clubs, skating rinks, places of worship, and attached, two-story brick homes with gardens enclosed by hedges and trellises bursting with flowers.

To Rachel Cook, Brownsville was the center of the universe, and Eastern Parkway was the gateway to the world. On it, she imagined, people could truly *go places*. Traffic swirled and moved away off into the distance, for as far as you could see—all the way to the huge, white-stoned Brooklyn Museum and the massive public library at Grand Army Plaza, where a colossal triumphal arch commemorated the Civil War; all the way to Prospect Park, with its gentle lakes and undulating lawns and tree-lined walking paths and zoo; all the way to the jagged skyline of Manhattan and to places that were even more exotic than New York—as if that was even possible.

Rachel and her parents would walk. Sometimes for hours.

Sometimes, her parents would hold her hand and swing her by the arms. Sometimes, her father would carry her, or let her straddle his shoulders, his face smelling of cologne, scratchy against Cook's little girl's skin. They'd stop and buy egg creams, lime rickeys, patent leather shoes and ribbons for Rachel's hair. They'd peer into shop windows. They'd chat with people they'd meet. They'd sit on the benches of Eastern Parkway, as the traffic rushed by.

Then they'd walk some more, just Rachel and her parents: her father, with his bright, laughing eyes and his dark hair piled in a pompadour; her mother, with her brown curly hair flowing down to her shoulders and her cheeks flushed with rouge, wearing pearl earrings and a necklace and a summer dress of soft pastels.

They'd walk together like that all day long, talking and laughing and singing and loving each other. They'd walk together, as if it would always be that way—sunny and simple and easy. They'd walk together, as if they'd always be just like that—young and innocent, together and happy.

* * *

"So, what do you think?" Matt Holland asked, as he drove Cook around Brownsville for her first time as a cop.

Cook was speechless, numb. She hadn't been back to Brownsville in the sixteen years since her family had moved—part of the upwardly mobile white exodus abandoning the neighborhood after World War II—and she was hardly prepared for what she saw now.

Brownsville's streets, buildings, stores, even its gardens and trees, seemed devoid of all color. Charred, splintered timbers jutted awkwardly from rubble-strewn lots, where rows of houses once stood. Abandoned buildings—their roofs gone, insides ravaged, doors sagging off hinges, windows covered by cinder blocks—stood decaying like rotting vegetables, their darkened windows looking like the haunted eyes of skeletons. Other ruined buildings spilled out into the streets, as if they had been crushed by a mighty blow.

Block after block, Brownsville's unspeakable tragedy unfolded. Trash, picked at by stray dogs, was strewn along the curbs. Lots were overgrown with weeds and filled with old refrigerators, tires, auto parts, furniture, shopping carts, discarded mattresses, and other rubble. Grass grew through cracks in the pavement. Stripped and abandoned cars, their hoods and trunks open, rested on wooden blocks. Derelicts warmed themselves around trashcan fires. Homeless drifters, covered with blankets and newspapers, slept on fire escapes or in the doorways of tenements. Others pushed shopping carts down streets in search of empty bottles, cans, and scrap metal.

Holland drove some more, as Cook, in stunned silence, struggled to reconcile her childhood memories of Brownsville with everything she was seeing now. It was nearly impossible. To Cook, seeing Brownsville again was like visiting a sickly relative for the first time in years; it was jarring to see how tired and feeble it had become. Familiar landmarks were either entirely gone or virtually unrecognizable. Storefronts were boarded up. Factories were abandoned. Many streets were deserted, reduced to piles of rubble. It was hard to believe that many of the buildings lying in ruin had once been homes at all, places where people had laughed and loved, raised families, and celebrated birthdays, anniversaries, and other special occasions. It was hard to believe anything joyous could have taken place in Brownsville—ever.

Holland and Cook drove past movie theaters that were converted to churches of obscure denominations. They drove past libraries whose Doric columns were chipped and worn; past schools whose bricks were weathered and covered with graffiti; past the site of what once had been the flower shop over which Cook had lived.

But that was gone now, too.

The walk-up apartment that was always full of sunshine and sweet smells was nowhere to be found, the building that had housed it crumbled and burned. Little remained—just the pastel-colored paint from what had once been a bedroom wall, peeling in the sunlight; a stairway leading to nowhere; and a brick chimney jutting upward, like a finger pointing toward the sky.

"Oh, my God," Rachel Cook gasped.

And it was all she could do simply to keep from crying.

Chapter 10

But Rachel Cook's personal history meant little to the NYPD. Nor did the jarring dissonance between her childhood memories and the broken and wounded neighborhood she witnessed now. Like other rookie cops, Cook hit the streets shortly after arriving in Brownsville. She couldn't have been handed a tougher patrol assignment in all of New York.

The 73rd Precinct had been designated as a high-crime command—an "A" house in NYPD parlance—for good reason. The shriek of police sirens and whirl of turret lights were part of the natural order in Brownsville, no more out of place in the fractured, inner-city neighborhood than a hungry infant crying in the night.

Cook may have been inexperienced, and unaccustomed to the pace, but that didn't matter. She and Matt Holland caught the same barrage of calls as other precinct sector cars. They were summoned to break up fistfights and domestic disputes on mangled streets and in apartments reeking of urine, feces, and rotting trash. They raced to crimes-in-progress and assisted at fires, auto accidents, and medical emergencies. They issued summonses, gathered evidence, wrote reports, delivered warrants, testified in court, searched for missing persons, escorted arrestees to jail, and transported the homeless and mentally ill to public shelters and psychiatric facilities.

On some tortuous, eight-hour tours, there was barely time to breathe. Brownsville, Cook discovered, was a neighborhood of victims—victims of illness and crime; victims of misfortune and chance; victims of the penury and despair that rained relentlessly on the wounded, crime-wracked neighborhood.

Brownsville's victims, Cook discovered, were everywhere to be found—damaged hearts; battered souls; people empty and hopeless and unhinged;

people whose dreams were trampled, and aspirations devoured, by the harsh realities engulfing their lives.

Naïve and sheltered her entire twenty-two years, Cook had never seen anything like this before, or even imagined it. But she saw it now, in full. She saw the crushing weight of poverty on people's shoulders, desperation and defeat in their eyes. She saw the neighborhood devour the destitute and the sickly; claim its children through acts of cruelty, abandonment and neglect; claim its elderly, too: shrunken old women pushing grocery carts along broken sidewalks; people trapped inside their homes by real or imagined fear; longtime merchants with nowhere to go, standing sorrowfully in front of their shops; aging Jews walking to synagogues where stacks of tattered talliths lay draped on clothing racks, fading in dusty beams of sunlight.

Each tour brought Holland and Cook into the lives of Brownsville's residents. Sometimes, the officers entered as intruders, through doors that were bulldozed or windows that were jimmied, to kicks and punches, curses and screams. Other times, their presence was hailed, and they arrived as heroes and saviors, a lifeline to people in need of comfort and support. Sometimes, Cook discovered, it took something dramatic to reach people and make a difference. Other times, she found that all it took was a simple gesture—talking to them; helping them solve a problem; assuaging their confusion and fear, helping them find reassurance and hope.

Police officers like her, Cook also discovered, never stayed for long. Usually, they stepped into the middle of things, did their job, and then moved on. Bit players in the daily drama unfolding before them, they arrived somewhere in the middle of the action, but rarely stayed for the denouement. There were few lasting relationships, little engagement beyond a moment of crisis. They touched people's lives, sometimes profoundly, but it was a fleeting brush rather than a lasting embrace.

"It's not our job to be important to people for more than a few minutes," Holland told Cook. "There's always another call, another crisis."

Most of those calls, Cook realized, were nothing extraordinary—the kind of incidents that were never noted anywhere other than a cop's logbook, little more than notations on a blotter, the daily rumblings in the chest of a neighborhood that was rheumy with an illness that neither Cook nor Holland could ever pretend to cure. But that was the job. That was police work.

Cook realized soon enough that being a cop wasn't about jumping off rooftops to thwart crimes-in-progress. It wasn't about the shootouts and stakeouts and investigations she'd fantasized about—the things that she saw on TV or read about in newspapers and novels. Nor was it solely about courage under fire or performing acts of heroism.

No.

Police work was simply about *being there*. It was about letting people know you were a telephone call away if they needed you—and that you'd arrive quickly, day or night, come hell or high water, for whatever reason you were summoned. It was about letting people know there was someone who would stand on their side, establishing a quiet, steady, day-to-day rhythm in which you subtly made a difference. It was about helping to hold the line, preserving what was lawful and right, providing people with confidence enough to simply carry on.

You were *there* for people—that's what mattered. Sometimes, you were there to throw the bad guys in jail. Sometimes, you were there to serve as a mediator or a doctor, an advisor or a minister, a judge or a shrink. Sometimes, you were there to bring people peace of mind, guide them through a difficult moment, and help them shoulder the weight.

It didn't matter *why* you were there—just that you were.

"I think you're seeing how much people in neighborhoods like Brownsville rely on the police," Holland said one day. "I think you're beginning to understand why we're so important to people here."

Holland, of course, was right. Cook saw that soon enough. And, strange as it seemed, she was also discovering that she needed people as much as they needed her. Contacts with Brownsville's victims made Cook feel good, brought her the sense of purpose she sought from the job. It was important for Cook to feel that she was somehow helping, preserving a degree of sanity and order, bringing a measure of relief and hope into the lives she brushed against. It didn't matter how routine the call was. It was only important for Cook to come away knowing that her presence had helped, that people could rely on her. She felt good knowing that she was needed, that she was making a difference. For Cook, the rewards were simple: a thank you, a smile, a handshake, a hug. That's what it was all about.

Sometimes, Holland pointed out, a police officer could take the greatest of satisfaction from the simplest of acts. And he was right. Rachel Cook was discovering, with her FTO's help, just how often she could unearth those nuggets of buried treasure. The real trick, she'd discover with time, would simply be to remember how to muster those feelings at the moments she needed them the most.

* * *

But if Brownsville was a challenging assignment, Cook realized soon enough that she couldn't have been assigned a better FTO to help her through the job's ineluctable learning curve. Matt Holland, to Cook's abiding relief, was as good as they came. Not only did he know police work inside and out, but he possessed precisely the right personality and temperament to mesh with Cook's. He was thorough, organized, concise, professional, and prepared. He was also exceptionally patient.

He had to be.

Cook may have been raw and unsure of herself at times, but she was extremely energetic, highly intelligent, and far more inquisitive than any of the dozen male cops Holland had previously trained. Unlike most rookies, she rarely shied away from action, even if she occasionally blundered. She also asked dozens of questions, many of them far more sophisticated than those of the typical rookie. And she was like a sponge.

Holland was blown away by how quickly Cook absorbed things and challenged him with questions. Nonetheless, he fielded each query patiently, explaining things in detail, correcting Cook's mistakes, and rarely making assumptions. Occasionally, he delayed answering a question until a critical prerequisite could be hammered home. Often, he wrote things down so that Cook could study them off-duty. He also made a concerted effort to bring Cook along at a comfortable pace, never force-feeding her more than she could handle, guiding the action while his rookie partner hung back and observed.

Cook marveled at the way Holland worked, how easy he made such a challenging job look. It was as if he had a sixth sense, a blend of instinct and experience that allowed him to instantly size up a situation, react in precisely the right way, and never let circumstances get out of control. Like all great cops, Holland was never reckless, highly observant, and a master of psychology. If he had to come on strong, he could manage that; if he had to be gentle and funny, he could handle that, too. Sometimes, he'd simply stand back and let a problem resolve itself, stepping in only if necessary. No one had to tell him what to do. He just looked and listened and *knew*—knew what he could get away with and what he couldn't; knew how to apply just the right touch; knew what each incident, each encounter, needed in order to be satisfactorily resolved.

Watching him, Cook thought, was like watching a master billiards player. Holland saw the entire table, alternating delicate bank shots with a touch of English and a hard, powerful stroke. There was little wasted motion. Holland could always pull something, if needed, out of his bag of tricks. And he never failed to set himself up for the shot that followed.

"Most people think police work is about brawn, but it's really all about what's going on between your ears," he told Cook. "You've got to be able to think on your feet. A lot of it is what I call 'jawboning'—just knowing how to talk to people. A good cop can handle almost anything by talking. Don't get me wrong, you've got to give the impression that you can back up what you're telling people. In reality, though, it usually never gets to that point."

Just *looking* the part, Holland told Cook, was half the battle.

"A lot of it is commanding respect by the way you carry yourself—your attitude, your body language," he explained. "You can't afford to come off as being uncomfortable or apologetic. You don't have to be nasty or overly tough, either. You can be quiet and still make forceful statements."

Holland also explained that cops often operated largely on instinct.

"Over time, you just develop a feel for how to handle things," he said. "It's a combination of training, experience, observation, and what you feel in your gut. You learn as you go along. You've got procedures to follow, and the law. That's the structure you operate in, and then you ease your way into it. There's no set of instructions, no textbook. A lot of times, it almost feels like you're making things up as you go along. You experiment, see what works, and develop a style."

Holland's focus in training Cook wasn't as much on theory as it was on the kind of common-sense, practical matters that cops in Brownsville needed to know. He pointed out known drug locations, explained how street pushers operated, taught Cook to keep her eyes open for visual cues, and always ask herself questions. Holland also enlightened Cook about what he called "inside dope." Absent of cynicism or bitterness, he talked about how the NYPD often malfunctioned; the tendency for policy to be shaped more by politics than by reason; the gaps between how the law was supposed to work and the way it actually did.

"You won't see much of this until you're on the job a while, but I don't want you to be surprised," he told Cook. "Part of my job is to open your eyes. But I also want to give you a sense of perspective, so you don't stumble when you see things for yourself ... so it doesn't hurt you or shock you quite as much."

Holland was careful not to let those things happen. His training seemed to follow a logical sequence, allowing Cook to learn while retaining her balance. At times, it was as if he were building a house from the ground up. Each lesson built on the one before. Each served to shore Cook up and make her a better cop.

Holland walked Cook through the various scenarios they were likely to encounter, so that she could anticipate how to react. He reviewed the kinds of questions that should be asked in different situations, so that she could quickly obtain relevant information. He rehearsed mock confrontations, drilling Cook on how to respond, teaching her how to use different degrees of escalating force to get a point across. He also demonstrated how she could disarm people simply by employing humor.

"No matter how much verbal abuse you encounter, you need to remain courteous and in control," he explained. "You give someone a ticket and they curse your mother? Your response is, 'Sir, it's regrettable that you're making a negative reference to a beloved family member. However, you did make an illegal left turn, and I am required by law to cite you for that.'"

Cook loved that one.

She also loved learning the cop's colorful lexicon.

Holland taught her, often laughingly, that an arrest was a "collar," and a bad guy was a "skell." He taught her that "writing paper" meant issuing a summons; that a "rip" was a complaint against an officer; that "cooping" meant sleeping on the job, and that sergeants came around to give you a "scratch," or sign your memo book to verify you were on patrol. Cook also learned how the unique police nomenclature could pertain to politics and careers—discovering that a "rabbi" was someone who could pull strings for you; that "gold tin" meant a detective's shield; that "back in the bag" meant being busted to foot patrol; and that a "shine" was a bureaucrat who wore out the seat of his pants from sitting and doing nothing.

Intertwined through each of Holland's lessons, though, was Brownsville.

Holland, it was obvious, knew the neighborhood inside out. He drove Cook around, explaining how each of Brownsville's police sectors was defined: "A" through "M," Adam through Mike. He briefed her on nicknames for different parts of the community; showed her how addresses ran; which thoroughfares ran parallel to one another, which ones intersected, and which were dead ends. He noted boundaries, accident-prone locations, landmarks, and the best places to eat. He even jokingly pointed out good "coffee blocks"—deserted streets where cops could take an unofficial break.

"Not that I ever expect *you* to do that!" he told Cook, laughing.

But Holland knew more about Brownsville than simply its landmarks, boundaries, and streets. To Holland, Brownsville was a neighborhood that had many dimensions. Despite its harrowing reputation and downtrodden presence, it was a neighborhood that had a heart, a soul, and a network of people who refused to surrender to the squalor and hopelessness, who continued to inject the neighborhood with energy, laughter, and hope.

"People call Brownsville a 'ghetto,' but how do you pin a label like that on a neighborhood like this?" Holland asked. "Some of the nicest people I've ever met live here ... good, friendly, honest, hardworking people who are just trying to exist from day to day, raise their families, make a better life for themselves. Black or white, it doesn't make a difference. You may not hear about them much, and they may not always be visible, but they're here, believe me. There's plenty of people who give a damn, and they want to save this neighborhood more than anyone because they're the ones who live here. The good people in neighborhoods like Brownsville need the police more than people in so-called better neighborhoods because if they didn't have us, they'd have nothing standing between them and chaos."

"Look carefully," Holland would tell Cook, as the two of them drove around. "See beyond what's on the surface."

And then he'd point out things he wanted his rookie partner to take notice of: parents holding their children's hand as they walked them to school; homes with well-tended lawns; boys and girls strolling out of libraries cradling books. To Holland, they were totems, reminders of glowing possibilities, symbols that rose above the neighborhood's pervasive squalor like monuments to the notions of resiliency and faith.

"Just remember," he'd say, "Brownsville has all kinds of people living here. You've got winos passed out on the sidewalk and parents who stay up all night to keep rats off their children. You've got kids shooting dope, and others painting a mural on the side of a church. You've got people who pee in their hallways and others who keep their homes so immaculate you could eat off the floor. The point is Brownsville is not one-dimensional; it's far more complex. You've got to be here day in and day out to understand it. And whatever you do as a cop, you've got to stay in touch with people's aspirations, their challenges, their pain."

But Holland did more than simply talk about those kinds of things. Often, he'd nudge Cook out of their patrol car so that the two of them could walk the streets, see things up close, and interact with people.

"This is what community policing is all about," he'd say. "This is how we build bridges. Police work isn't simply about controlling crime. It's about dealing with people, getting to know them, eliminating their fears, breaking down stereotypes. If you start making those kinds of connections, you're not just a 'cop' anymore—you're a person, too. But you've got to get out of your patrol car to do it. Somewhere along the line, police officers got into cars and lost contact with the people they serve."

Holland said he never wanted to police Brownsville without a level of positive contact. And that approach had seemingly paid off.

It was clear to Cook that her FTO had an easy rapport with many people in Brownsville, people who'd known him for years, people who respected him. He shook hands and joked, often in broken Spanish, with residents and merchants. Others, he waved to as he passed on foot or in their patrol car. Still others, he introduced Cook to, or put in a good word for her.

The network of people Holland knew in Brownsville was far-ranging, cutting across ethnic and racial lines. He introduced Cook to an aging Italian immigrant, whom he called the last of the great Brooklyn shoemakers. He brought her to meet a pastor who'd personally laid the concrete for the construction of his church. They met a former pro basketball player who was running a program for troubled youths. There were others, too—regular, run-of-the-mill people: a local haberdasher whose family had owned a store in Brownsville for forty-eight years; a butcher who'd survived the Holocaust and put two sons through medical school; a bodega owner who'd played sandlot ball with Roberto Clemente in Puerto Rico; a teacher whose classroom was alive with maps and drawings and posters, even though the walls were peeling and the ceiling was leaking and the windows were broken each day.

Cook loved the way Holland talked about being a cop—so full of passion, so able to put his finger on everything the job meant to him and all the ways that police work moved him. To Cook, Matt Holland was exactly the kind of cop New York was lucky to have: a blend of toughness and compassion, experience and energy; sensitive but not too soft; realistic but not impenetrable; neither naïve nor jaded, wide-eyed nor hardened beyond redemption; insightful, yet fully aware that there were always new things to learn.

Just the kind of cop that Cook wanted to be.

Considering all the time he'd spent on the job, Holland's perspective on Brownsville was as miraculous as it was unfettered by the ruinous battle scars Cook saw on other cops. Remarkably, his view of the neighborhood was in utter balance. Despite all he'd seen across sixteen years as a cop, Matt Holland still managed to retain his faith in the essential goodness of the neighborhood's people. Sixteen years on the job and he'd never become cynical or racist, burnt out or callous. Sixteen years on the job and he still believed there was room for hope.

* * *

For all she was learning, however, Cook's transition from the Police Academy to the streets was far from easy. Despite Holland's efforts, she was uptight and stiff, especially in the beginning, struggling like a newborn fawn to find her legs.

"I want to project the right image," she said, two months in. "I want my voice to sound just right. I want to appear competent and in command."

"You don't feel that way now?"

"Uh-uh," she said as she shook her head. "To be honest with you, Matt, sometimes I'm afraid I'm going to walk up to someone to assume command of a situation, and the person will simply break out laughing and say, 'Who the hell are you kidding, sister? Get me a *real* cop.' I guess I'm afraid of losing face and not knowing how to handle it."

"Don't worry," Holland assured her, "that won't happen. First off, don't underestimate the power of your uniform, especially your gun. That makes a very strong statement. When people see that, they'll take you seriously ... believe me."

Holland did that often, especially at the start. Aside from being an exemplary officer, and excellent teacher, he was able to consistently bolster Cook's confidence, help dispel her doubts. Even when he was critical, which wasn't often, he was always encouraging and unfailingly supportive.

"A lot of patrol cops feel what you're feeling," he'd say. "It's not easy on the streets of an unfamiliar neighborhood with a bad reputation. It's doubly hard being a white cop—let alone a female—in a minority community, battling with innate hostility, cutting through barriers to trust. But all of that's normal. Just hang in there. You'll feel more confident, and more in control, with time."

"You're not just saying that?"

"Hell, no; I mean it. If I didn't think you could do the job, I wouldn't be giving you this much of my time. I've got better things to do than train rookie cops who can't make the grade. Don't worry about coming up short at times. I've worked alongside some very good cops, but I've never met one who didn't have a downside."

"So, you don't mind having me as a partner?" Cook asked.

"No," Holland said. "Besides, the hazardous-duty pay I get for partnering with you pays a lot of bills."

"*What*?"

"I'm just kidding!" He laughed. "No, I don't mind having you as a partner, Rachel. You're doing just fine. All you need is experience. Learning this job takes time, but you're picking things up fast. Hell, you're already better than most of the men I've worked with. Some guys I know have been on the job for years and still can't write out a simple report. Others don't give a damn or are lazy and simply go through the motions. You're a lot smarter than all of them combined—and you truly care. That counts for a lot. Being a good cop has a lot to do with caring, especially after the job knocks you on your ass a couple of times."

"Well, I do care," Cook said. "I hope you know that."

"There's no doubt in my mind," he said. "I knew it right from the start."

Cook felt good about that. It was important to her that Holland knew she really cared—about the job, the city, Brownsville, and him. It was equally important to her that her FTO could feel confident when he partnered with her, regardless of her gender, inexperience, and occasional lack of confidence. She wanted him to be certain, if nothing else, that she'd always be there for him, that he could always depend on her. Even if he was sure of nothing else, Cook wanted Holland to know he could always lean on her in a pinch—that he'd never have to question her integrity, her intentions, or her heart.

"Matt, there's something that's very important for me to say," she told him earnestly, four months into the job.

"What's that?"

"I want you to know that I'll be there for you if the shit ever hits the fan," she said. "I'll be at your side come hell or high water if you ever need me. You know that ... don't you?"

"I have no doubt," Holland said.

"No matter what happens," Cook pledged, "just know I've got your back. I'll fight if I have to. I'll call for backup. But I'll never leave you alone."

And she wouldn't.

Of that much, Cook was certain. At the very least, she'd hold her ground, no matter how difficult things got. She might flinch or duck or be frightened in ways she couldn't even imagine. But when push came to shove, she knew she'd never run. It wasn't so much a matter of loyalty or adoration, duty or respect—although all those things played a part. It was because Cook knew she could never live with herself if her partner got injured or killed because she failed him. She knew she could never live with that guilt or pain. She'd almost rather be dead herself than feel those things, she thought.

"You're signing out with me every time we work together," she told Holland. "Hear that? No matter what, I'm signing out with you, Matt."

"That's important for me to know," Holland said, smiling. "Thanks."

Chapter 11

THE INTERNAL AFFAIRS INVESTIGATOR thumbed through a copy of Capt. Borelli's *Unusual Incident Report*, before training his beady eyes Matt Holland. The clock in the 73rd Precinct muster room was pushing 8:00 AM already. The day had dawned sunny and hot.

For the past eleven hours, Holland and Cook had been separated to prevent the officers from potentially collaborating on a bogus account of what had occurred the night before. Both had been subjected to mandatory blood tests for alcohol, drugs, or other substances that could have impaired their judgment; examined at the hospital, discharged, and driven back to the station house. They'd also been instructed not to discuss what had happened with anyone other than their union rep, attorney, or authorized investigative personnel. A noon press conference to address the incident had been scheduled by NYPD officials.

"So, let me summarize what you told us took place," the IAD investigator said, as the muster room came to order.

Holland, seeming disoriented, struggled to focus his gaze.

"Are you telling us that your service revolver 'discharged' when you made unexpected physical contact with this so-called shadow in the cellar?"

Tugging at his shirt collar, the investigator glanced around the room, as if seeking support regarding his apparent skepticism. All eyes were on Holland, however.

"Yes," said Holland, his voice quaggy and hoarse. He was struggling to focus, lapsing in and out of flashbacks. PBA president Red McLaren slung an arm around the officer's shoulder as Holland coughed weakly into a fist. Attorney Eddie Shearson offered him a fresh glass of water.

"Which is your shooting hand, detective?" the investigator asked.

"I'm right-handed," Holland replied.

"Your firearm was in your right hand the entire time?"

"Yes."

"And what was the direction of the muzzle at discharge?"

"Upward … to the ceiling."

"That's where you're losing me," said the investigator, seeming puzzled. "Why were you shooting *upward* if the perceived threat was coming from your right?"

"At the last instant," Holland recounted, "I pulled my arm up."

"Pulled it up?"

"Yes," the officer nodded. "Instead of pointing my gun at the suspect, I was pointing it at the ceiling."

"What made you do that?" the investigator asked.

"At the last split-second," Holland recounted, "I thought that maybe I didn't *have* to shoot … that maybe whatever was coming toward me wasn't really a threat."

"What made you feel that way?"

"I don't know," Holland said and shook his head. "I just sensed it. I'm not sure why. My instincts just told me: *Don't shoot … don't shoot!*"

The investigator squinted. "Weren't you fearful that you were being attacked and that you should shoot to save your life, and perhaps that of your partner?"

Holland looked away, as if eyeing something in the distance.

"It was very strange," he said. "At first, yes, I was fearful for my life—and that of Officer Cook—and I felt compelled to shoot. Then, at the last instant, I wasn't sure. I still had a doubt. I wasn't certain I was being attacked, but it was impossible to know for sure. There simply wasn't time."

Holland looked at the roomful of NYPD officials, many of them former street cops. *Maybe they understand what I'm talking about,* he thought. *Maybe they've experienced similar moments themselves.*

"I didn't want to take the chance that I might be wrong, that I might injure or kill an innocent person," Holland said. "I've always believed that an officer should wait to shoot until he has absolutely no doubt."

"Even if it meant *not* shooting at a perceived threat?"

"Yes."

"Even if it meant potentially losing your own life or that of your partner?"

"I suppose so."

"And yet," the investigator said, "you shot in this instance?"

Holland, his hand shaking, took a sip of water.

"Actually, I tried at the last second to pull back," he said. "I'd actually made my mind up *not* to shoot."

The investigator scrunched his eyes.

"Are you saying, then, that your gun just 'went off'?"

"The gun," said Holland, "discharged when I was run into by the suspect."

"This so-called shadow that you saw coming at you?"

"Yes."

The IAD examiner glanced at his notepad. Everyone was deathly silent, their attention riveted on Holland. Portable fans hummed. Papers shuffled. Tape recorders whirred.

"How many times," the IAD guy asked, "did your gun discharge?"

"Once," Holland replied.

"And what happened then?"

"I remember being struck atop my head by a falling chunk of concrete from the ceiling, and I felt something lying across my feet," Holland recalled. "I still couldn't see a thing. My eyes hadn't adjusted to the darkness yet."

"Then what?"

"I dropped to my knees and felt a body. I shined my flashlight on it and … could see it was a boy."

"And then?"

"I yelled to Officer Cook to try and find the light cord."

"Had your partner fired her service revolver, too?"

"I don't believe so. I never heard a second shot. Everything in the cellar stopped moving and went quiet once my firearm went off."

Matt Holland drew silent, sipping again from his water glass.

"What happened next?" the investigator asked.

Holland drew a deep breath. The silence in the cellar, he recalled, didn't last for long. There were times, he'd wish later, that the moment could have lasted longer than just those few fleeting seconds, times he'd wish it could have lasted forever. There were still other possibilities during those several seconds when everything went quiet and still. There was still a chance that everything wouldn't turn out like it did.

But the silence faded almost instantly, Holland recalled. And through the darkness of the cellar, Holland remembered calling out to his partner.

"Cook, are you there? Rachel! Rachel!"

"I'm here!" Cook's voice was hoarse, crackling like a distant radio signal.

"Were you hit? Are you okay?"

"I'm okay. You?"

"Get the light cord!" Holland shouted. "The light cord, Rachel! It's up there somewhere!"

Rachel Cook stumbled to her feet, using her flashlight to scan for the light cord dangling from the ceiling. It was all she could do to simply move. Her legs felt leaden. She could barely lift her arms. Her breathing was shallow, her vision obscured, as if she were lost in a tunnel.

When Cook found the light cord and tugged at it, the enormity of what had happened became all too apparent: a young black boy, slight of build, lay on the floor, face up. His eyes, half-open, stared blankly at the ceiling. A pair of eyeglasses, shattered at the bridge, lay at his feet, alongside a tiny hammer and a *New York Mets* baseball cap.

Cook was stunned by the sight of her partner hunched over the boy. For an instant, she simply stared in horror. Then, as if awakening from a trance, she shouted into her radio.

"10-85! 10-85! Shot fired! Need immediate backup and EMS! Suspect down!"

Holland recalled how frantic and tinny his partner's voice sounded then, even as he stared in disbelief at the boy who'd been felled by his single errant gunshot. And he felt the life go out of him, the same way it was spilling at that very moment from the boy he'd just shot.

"Was the victim moving at all?" the IAD investigator asked.

"No," said Holland, shaking more discernably.

"What did you think?"

Holland paused, seemingly drawing on every ounce of his waning strength.

"I couldn't believe it," he finally said. "I knew my shot had gone up, not out. As I said, I had decided *not* to shoot. If anything, I thought my shot might have hit the ceiling. I couldn't believe it might have struck the boy. I thought that maybe he'd tripped and fallen, that maybe his head had hit the ground and he was stunned, or maybe my shot just grazed him. I didn't see blood. I couldn't believe he really might be hurt."

"What did you do next?" the investigator asked.

With that, Matt Holland took another sip of water.

"I tried," he said, voice cracking, "to save the boy's life."

Chapter 12

THE BOY'S NAME WAS CLIFFORD JOHNSON, but everyone who knew him called him, simply, C. J. He was familiar to most of his neighbors on Amboy Street, a friendly eighth-grader, well cared for by his parents—Charles and Eunice Johnson—popular among a tiny circle of friends.

Frail and bespectacled, C. J. was far shorter and more lethargic than most fourteen-year-olds, and often mistaken for a younger child. His size, however, was simply a reflection of a far greater problem.

As both an infant and toddler, C. J.'s growth had been normal. Indeed, he'd reached all his key developmental milestones by the age of six. It was then, however, when signs emerged that something wasn't right. By the time he entered kindergarten, C. J.'s growth had noticeably slowed, and he was in only the tenth percentile for his height and weight. His attention span had also become truncated, rendering him restless, irritable, and moody.

Then the symptoms grew even more acute.

C. J.'s kindergarten teacher informed Charles and Eunice Johnson that their son was growing increasingly impulsive, was having difficulty following even simple instructions, and required frequent naps. The diagnosis was hyperactivity. Ritalin was prescribed.

Doctors didn't diagnose what was truly wrong until a year later. By then, C. J. was experiencing headaches, abdominal cramps, and periodic bouts of vomiting. He was noticeably behind his peers in fine motor skills, language ability, and hand-eye coordination. He couldn't count past the number five or correctly name the primary colors. His walking was labored, his eyesight and hearing strained. There was also occasional blood in his stool and a strange purplish line on his gums.

At the advice of friends, the Johnsons took their only child to a neurologist. When the specialist joined Charles and Eunice in his office, neurological and blood-test results in hand, his questions were puzzling.

"Is anyone in your household a plumber?" the doctor asked.

"No," Charles said and shook his head.

"An auto repairer?"

"No."

"A construction worker or gas station attendant?"

"No."

He asked the Johnsons if they lived near any industrial facilities or hazardous waste sites, or if their apartment had recently been remodeled, or if they had household pets. He asked about hobbies, the family's medical history, even how their food was served. The Johnsons answered each question, growing more puzzled by the minute. The doctor then asked if C. J. had any siblings or playmates who'd ever been diagnosed with lead poisoning.

That's when they knew.

According to the doctor, C. J. Johnson's illness—high-dose lead poisoning—had likely originated from the paint on the walls, windowsills, and woodwork of the apartment in which the Johnsons had resided the past eleven years.

"Are you saying that our apartment is ... *poisoned*?" Eunice Johnson asked.

"I'm afraid, in a way, it is," the doctor said. "There are many older residences in neighborhoods like Brownsville that contain lead-based paint and lead-contaminated dust. Adults who work with batteries, do home renovations, or work in auto repair shops also might be exposed to lead. In many cases, the paint in homes is peeling, flaking, and chipping. It's extremely hazardous when it comes in contact with young children. Lead poisoning, unfortunately, is very common among children in neighborhoods like yours."

"I never heard of such a thing," said Eunice, clutching her husband's hand.

"It has only recently come to light," the doctor explained. "And it's only recently being regulated."

"But how did C. J. get it?" Charles asked.

"He contracted the disease, I'm afraid, simply by being a child," the doctor said. "Many children chew on their nails or mouth their toys and hair. Those habits are normal, and most children eventually outgrow them. Other children, however, ingest loose chips and flakes of paint due to a disorder called 'pica,' the compulsive eating of non-food items. Flaking paint is among the most common items eaten."

"Are you saying," Eunice asked, "that our son ate paint?"

"Actually, I don't think that's what happened in C. J.'s case," the doctor replied. "Although even tiny amounts of lead can cause problems, lead poisoning generally occurs when lead accumulates in the body over months or years. Children who are C. J.'s age have a high risk for it because they have a significant amount of hand-to-mouth activity. As they learn to walk, or play on the floor, they hold onto walls and windowsills, and then put their hands in their mouth. They can be exposed through skin contact or simply by inhaling lead dust in the air or on the surface of floors, toys, furniture, and other objects."

"You mean C. J. got sick simply from breathing?" Eunice slumped in her chair.

"In all probability ... yes."

"How serious is this?" her husband asked.

The doctor shook his head. "To be perfectly candid, Mr. Johnson, I can't be sure yet. Because children C. J.'s age are still developing, toxic substances like lead can affect many areas of the body. Even in tiny concentrations, the effects could be ... profound."

"What do you mean?"

"What I mean is that even a single paint chip the size of a thumbnail ingested by a child like C. J. can cause permanent brain damage."

"Will our son die?" asked Eunice, weeping now.

"No," the doctor said, informing the Johnsons that, fortunately, C. J. would survive. In many respects, he said, their son was *lucky*. X rays revealed that the lead toxin had yet to enter his bones.

"There's no question, however," the doctor added, "that your son will face serious difficulties and challenges."

He then informed the Johnsons how exposure to lead could attack virtually every part of the body and could have a wide range of effects on a child's development and behavior—damaging kidneys and other organs, causing a reduction in speech and muscle strength, stunting growth, and robbing children of such skills as reading, writing, concentration, and abstract thinking.

He then prescribed a treatment.

C. J. would be admitted to a hospital, where his stomach would be pumped. He'd then begin a treatment called chelation, a series of injections that would force the lead to be excreted through the boy's urine. A special diet, low in fat and high in calcium and iron, would be prescribed as well. Beyond that, there wasn't much else they could do, the Johnsons were told. Medical treatments could only reduce blood toxicity levels and minimize further damage.

"But whatever neurological damage C. J. has already sustained," the doctor said, "I'm afraid that's irreversible."

The symptoms of that damage, aside from C. J.'s stunted growth, would be varied. Learning disabilities would tax his ability to become truly self-sufficient. Certain motor skills would remain crude and poorly coordinated. There'd be a significant reduction in his ability to respond normally to most environmental stimuli, rendering him easily befuddled. And C. J. would also suffer a pronounced loss of hearing.

Unless he was facing someone in full light and able to read their lips, or unless he was wearing a specially made hearing device, it was highly unlikely that C. J. Johnson would be able to respond appropriately in an uncertain or threatening environment to events unfolding rapidly around him. It was equally unlikely that he'd hear very much—not even the vehement commands of a pair of frantic police officers repeatedly ordering him to halt.

Chapter 13

KNEELING ON THE CELLAR FLOOR seconds after his gunshot, Matt Holland holstered his service revolver, frantically feeling for a pulse on C. J. Johnson's neck.

The boy's face looked rigid and ashen, as if cast in cement. Holland searched desperately for a wound, finding no marks, no torn clothing, nothing. Only after seconds did he notice a splotch of blood in C. J. Johnson's hair, at the crown of the boy's head. And the officer traced its path as it flowed in a twisting rivulet along the boy's temple, seeping from C. J. like liquid through a crack, before collecting in a pool under the boy's body.

That's when Matt Holland knew that the boy who he never really saw had been gravely wounded by the gunshot he'd never intended to fire—a shot that had headed upward after Holland's contact with the victim, and then ricocheted downward off the concrete ceiling of the cellar. And that's when the entire world seemed to close in on the officer, who suddenly felt as if the cellar was wobbly and blurry, and caving in all around him.

"I take it you called for paramedics then?" the IAD investigator asked.

"Officer Cook radioed for an ambulance," Holland said, haltingly.

"She also summoned backup units to the scene?"

"That's correct."

The investigator, seeming pained, wrote the information down. Several of the others in the muster room squirmed silently in their seats

"How long after the shooting did Officer Cook radio it in?" the investigator resumed.

"From what I could tell, almost immediately," Holland replied.

"And while Officer Cook was summoning the ambulance and backup—?"

"I was administering medical assistance to the boy."

Matt Holland paused again, choking on his words. PBA attorney Eddie Shearson leaned over and rubbed the officer's back. Hardened NYPD officials were fighting to retain their composure. Several blinked away tears.

"Where was the boy at this time?" the investigator asked.

"Flat on his back," Holland replied, "bleeding from the top of his head."

"Did you try to staunch the bleeding?"

"I did."

"How?"

"I applied my fingers directly to the wound and pressed downward."

Holland, eyes welling, faltered for several fleeting seconds.

"I picked up his baseball hat," he stammered, "and used that, too."

From the back of the muster room, you could hear someone sniffle, as if stifling a sneeze. Other than that, you could hear a pin drop.

"Could you tell if the boy was breathing?" the investigator asked.

"I'd say yes, but abnormally so," Holland recounted. "His breathing was shallow and labored. He was struggling to draw breath … gasping."

"Any pulse?"

"Irregular. Very weak."

"You made an effort to revive him?"

"Yes."

"How would you describe it?"

"I tried everything I was ever trained to do," Holland said.

"Cardiopulmonary resuscitation?"

"Yes."

"What kind?"

"Hand-over-hand chest compressions, fingers interlocked, hard and fast to the center of his chest. I also pried the boy's lips open with my fingertips and attempted artificial ventilation."

"Mouth-to-mouth resuscitation?"

"Yes."

"Was he responsive?"

"Once," Holland said, "I saw him open his eyes."

"And then?"

"His eyes rolled back in his head, and he closed them again."

The investigator checked his recorder, its spool of tape running low.

"For how long did you apply CPR?" he asked.

"I'm not sure," Holland replied. "I lost all track of time. Maybe ten, fifteen minutes in all. I didn't stop until the paramedics arrived and took over with a defibrillator and oxygen."

The officer hesitated, staring off, deep in thought.

"I tried as hard as I could to bring him back," he finally said. "I knew it was likely going to be futile, but I didn't want to stop."

Holland sipped from his water glass, before resting it on the table.

"I desperately wanted the boy to live," he said.

The officer then lowered his eyes and began, without embarrassment or shame, to openly weep. The IAD investigator halted his interrogation. The other men diverted their eyes. Red McLaren handed Holland a tissue, and the officer blew his nose.

"What, specifically, can you recall from that time on?" the investigator resumed after a lengthy pause.

"Not much," Holland said. "To be honest with you, the life just went out of me. I knew I had either badly wounded or killed a young boy. I remember lights, noise, an ambulance, and backup officers arriving at the scene. I know they got the boy to the hospital, and my partner and I were transported there as well. But I don't remember much more than that … until I was taken to the station house."

There was more that Matt Holland remembered, although he couldn't put it into words. Not then. Maybe not ever.

What he remembered was how empty and helpless and frightened and sorry he felt—all at once—and how it was as if his own life was flowing out of him as C. J. Johnson lay bleeding on the floor. He remembered how C. J. had clung briefly to his leg as the boy tumbled to the floor, and how he'd gotten on his hands and knees and cradled C. J.'s head and wiped the chalky concrete off his face, breathing into the boy's mouth and begging him not to die. He remembered how his police cap fell to the floor and how the photo of Katie and his children tumbled out from where he kept it in the lining. He remembered how the lights came on in the courtyard outside the cellar, and how they reflected off C. J. Johnson's shattered eyeglasses, and how he picked the eyeglasses up, wanting to fix them and hand them back.

And there was more.

Matt Holland remembered C. J. Johnson's face, staring at him with a peculiar expression, seemingly of wonderment—as if he were seeking answers to a million unformed questions—before his eyes rolled back in his head and he drifted off to someplace far away.

"Is that all you can recall?" the investigator asked.

"I remember that I wanted him to live," Matt Holland said. "I wanted him to live as much as I would have wanted my own children to live, but—"

Hesitating again, Holland lowered his head, as Eddie Shearson put an arm around him, and Red McLaren looked away.

"Yes, detective?" the investigator persisted. "You were saying that you wanted the boy to live … but what?"

Holland hesitated, as if trying to steel himself.

"I was trying to say that if the boy was going to die, I wanted him to die quickly," Holland said. "I didn't want him to suffer. And I wanted him to know that I didn't mean to shoot him, that I was sorry. And that—"

Holland halted again.

"Yes?" the investigator prodded.

"And that I wanted the boy, somewhere in the depths of his heart," Holland said, "to find a way to forgive me."

Chapter 14

RACHEL COOK RAISED THE WATER GLASS tremulously, but even the simple effort of taking a sip was taxing beyond anything imaginable. Cook's hands quivered as she sat in the 73rd Precinct's muster room, surrounded by NYPD investigators and police officials. Her throat, parched and scratchy, felt as if she'd slept open-mouthed for hours. The stabbing pain that had begun as a dull ache at the base of her skull had spread to her shoulders, back, and neck.

"It's gonna be all right, Rachel," Red McLaren whispered consolingly at the outset of Cook's preliminary interrogation.

Cook wasn't sure she believed him, wasn't sure of *anything* anymore—except that something unspeakably tragic had taken place, and her auspicious, eight-month-old police career was imploding before her very eyes.

"I'm sure you're frightened and confused—it's perfectly understandable," McLaren said. "But rest assured that the most powerful police union in the world, and a whole lot of other people, have your back."

Cook mouthed a thank-you as she sat anxiously at the head of a conference table cluttered with tape recorders, legal pads, and copies of the statements she and Matt Holland had filed with 73rd Precinct commander Capt. Robert Borelli.

McLaren slid in alongside the officer.

"Every man and woman who wears a badge in America understands what you and your partner faced in that cellar," the PBA president said. "Just know that we'll be at your side, every step of the way, to defend you and protect your rights."

Cook nodded self-consciously. The muster room, crowded with grizzled investigative personnel, was stifling, the station house seemingly swaying like a dinghy on a roiling sea. Cook was the only woman in the room—and the youngest by far. She felt as if a spotlight was shining on her from the ceiling, and there was no way to turn it off, nowhere to hide.

"Remember, no one is saying that you did anything wrong," union lawyer Eddie Shearson said, reminding Cook that interrogations of the type she was about to undergo were mandatory for officers who'd witnessed a shooting—even if they themselves hadn't fired their gun.

"No one here is charging you with misconduct, departmental violations, or criminal activity," Shearson said. "You're simply here to offer testimony as a material witness to what occurred … understand? All you need to do is answer their questions, to the best of your ability. Think you can do that?"

"Uh-huh," Cook replied absently, reaching shakily for her water glass.

But answering investigators' questions wasn't going to be so easy. Cook was anxious, more so than at any time in her life. Her cheeks were deeply flushed. Beads of sweat dotted her forehead. She wondered if she'd even be able to utter a coherent word.

"Let's begin," the Internal Affairs investigator said, turning on his tape recorder.

The muster room grew silent, all eyes riveted on Cook, who wished she could crawl into a hole and disappear.

"Officer Cook," the investigator began, "do you fully understand what transpired last night?"

"I believe so … yes," Cook replied, voice cracking.

"And have you spoken to anyone regarding the incident?"

"I've spoken to Mr. Shearson," Cook replied, glancing at the PBA attorney.

"And I assume you've also spoken to your union president, Mr. McLaren."

"I have."

"And to Mr. De Luca, your shop steward?"

"Yes, I've spoken to him, as well."

"Anyone without privileged communication? For example, family or friends … perhaps a roommate?"

"No."

"What about officers or medical personnel at the scene, at the hospital, or in the station house?"

"Only a doctor at the hospital … but strictly about my physical condition."

"Not about the incident itself?"

"No."

"And what about your partner?" the investigator scrunched his eyes. "Have you spoken to Detective Sergeant Holland—either at the scene of last night's incident or any time afterward?"

"No," Cook replied. "We've been separated and instructed not to speak."

The investigator paused, his coiffed hair fluttering with the breeze from a portable fan. Red McLaren freshened Cook's glass from a pitcher of water and Cook took a sip, feeling shriveled and unkempt. She had the unsettling feeling of being eyeballed by higher-ups from head to toe. Evaluated. Judged.

"The call to which you and Detective Sergeant Holland responded to," the investigator resumed, "it was received as a 10-31, correct?"

"That's correct," said Cook, swallowing hard.

"And the location to which you responded, the cellar on Amboy Street … it had been the scene of criminal activity in the past, had it not?"

"Apparently so," said Cook. "We'd been warned about it previously. It was considered one of many 'hot spots' in Brownsville."

"For what kind of criminal activity?"

"Mostly drugs and petty theft," Cook said. "A while ago, I believe, there was a rape reported there. Prior to that, there was a shooting."

"But last night's call," the investigator probed, "that was supposedly a burglary-in-progress?"

"Yes," Cook said, voice quavering. "But—"

"But *what*?"

"But as any police officer knows, with a call like that it could have been anything—shots fired, weapons possession, a prowler," Cook said. "There was no way for either my partner or me to know what we were *really* walking into down there."

"Understood," said the investigator, fingering a sheath of papers. "Nevertheless, your statement describes how you and Detective Sergeant Holland entered the partially-lit cellar—forcefully and with your service revolvers drawn—encountering an unspecified number of suspects before identifying yourselves several times as police officers and commanding the people you encountered to halt. Is that correct?"

"Yes," Cook nodded, making a concerted effort to speak more assertively.

"Where were you, exactly, when you and Detective Sergeant Holland entered the cellar?" the investigator probed.

"I was directly behind him," Cook replied.

"How far?"

"About two feet."

"Were you able to see him?"

"Yes. I could see his back—that is, until the light went out."

"Then what?"

"Then for several seconds, I couldn't see anything, only pitch black."

"What did you see prior to the instant the light went out?"

"Only my partner's back and a small portion of the cellar."

The investigator dragged on a cigarette, exhaling a column of smoke. "Could you make out what was there?"

"A wooden table and several chairs," Cook said. "Things happened too quickly to see much more. And the cellar was dimly lit."

"Did you hear anything?"

"I heard someone holler that everyone who was present should run."

"What happened then?"

"People were racing about, trying to escape through a rear door to the courtyard outside."

"Did you see anyone approach your partner?"

"No, I only saw his back. Then everything went completely dark. A split-second later, I saw the cellar light up again, as if someone used a flash camera. There was a loud bang. Then the cellar went dark again."

"What were your thoughts then?"

"At first, I thought someone had set off a firecracker. Then, instantly, I realized it was a gunshot."

"Did you know whether it was your partner, or someone else, who shot."

"At that point, no."

"What did you do then?"

"I immediately dropped to the floor."

"Were you knocked over, or was your reaction instinctual?"

"It was instinct. I was diving for cover."

"You weren't shot, yourself?"

"No."

"Did anyone in the cellar make contact with you?"

"No."

"Was your firearm unholstered?"

"Yes."

"Why did you not discharge it?"

"Personally, I never saw a direct threat."

"Did you not see what Detective Sergeant Holland saw?"

"I don't know exactly what my partner saw ... only that it was something that obviously caused his gun to discharge."

The investigator looked skeptically at Cook and then, peripherally, at the others in the room. No one moved or uttered a sound.

"Were any efforts undertaken by you to reduce or eliminate the necessity for your partner to discharge his firearm?" the IAD guy resumed.

Cook straightened in her chair. "Excuse me?"

"Did you attempt, in any way, to de-escalate the situation?"

"I didn't have a chance to do anything," Cook said. "Everything happened in the blink of an eye."

The investigator paused to scratch out some notes. Cook, hand shaking, reached for her water glass but lowered it without drinking, feeling clumsy and foolish all the while.

"How long would you say you were on the floor?" the IAD guy resumed.

"A couple of seconds, maybe," Cook replied. "I was trying to adjust to the darkness. I didn't know if I or my partner was going to be attacked, or who was there, or what was going on."

"Did you call out, at that point, to Detective Sergeant Holland?"

"Yes. I called to him several times … trying to determine if he'd been hit."

"Did he respond?"

"I heard him mutter something, but I wouldn't really call it a 'response.'"

"What was it?"

"It was more like a gasp."

"Excuse me?"

"I heard my partner make a sound," Cook said, "as if he were trying to catch his breath."

"What happened then?"

"I called to him again."

"Did he respond this time?"

"Yes, he just responded that he wasn't hit. Then he asked if I was all right. I told him that I was. Then he instructed me to use my flashlight and try to find the cord to the lightbulb over the table."

"Did you?"

"Yes. I reached up to pull the cord and when I did, the light came back on."

"You were able then to see?"

"I was."

"And that's when you realized it was your partner—not someone else—who'd discharged his gun?"

"That's correct."

"Did you radio for an ambulance and backup at that time?"

"It took a few seconds for that. I was still trying to assess what happened."

"So, what did you do?"

"I did a quick visual sweep," Cook replied. "I checked under the table in the middle of the cellar, behind some bicycles and baby carriages lined against a wall, and under the stairs leading to the courtyard."

"Was there anyone in the cellar besides you, your partner, and the victim?"

"There were several other people."

"How many?"

"I'm not sure. My guess is about five. Two or three escaped the cellar as soon as my partner and I entered. Then there were two others. I saw them when the light came on, hiding under the stairway to the courtyard."

"What did you do then?"

"I ordered them to emerge and lie face-down on the floor."

"Did they comply?"

"Yes."

"Without resistance?"

"Yes."

"And then?"

"I searched them."

"Were they armed?"

"No."

"Did you cuff them and place them under arrest?"

"No," Cook said. "I just ordered them to stay on the floor and not move."

"Did you perceive them to be a threat?"

"No … they seemed like nothing more than frightened teens."

"Male or female?"

"Female."

"What made you feel as if they were frightened?"

"Both of them," Cook said, "were crying."

Cook was trembling noticeably now. She tried, vainly, to compose herself, and the investigators in the room shifted uneasily in their seats.

"The suspects who exited the cellar," the investigator continued, "they were never pursued or apprehended?"

"No."

"Why not?"

"Foot pursuits, I've been taught, can be extremely taxing and dangerous," Cook replied. "I reasoned that it would be more fruitful if I remained at the scene, at my partner's side, to summon backup, await emergency medical personnel, identify potential witnesses, and assist in any way I could. Besides, I didn't think there was any way I could catch whoever it was that escaped."

Several of the onlookers snickered, although Cook hadn't meant her observation to be humorous. She felt further diminished by the investigators' response.

"Were there firearms or other weapons at the scene?" the IAD guy resumed.

"Nothing more than a handsaw, a stapler, and a hammer," Cook replied. "I didn't perceive them to be weapons."

"Anything else?"

"Just the table at the center of the cellar."

"Anything on it?"

"Bags of popcorn, potato chips, bottles of soda, party goods."

"Is that when you summoned backup and an ambulance?"

"Yes."

"And what did you see then?"

"I saw my partner, hunched over a body lying on the floor."

"Talking? Moving? Face up? Face down?"

"Face up. Not talking or moving. I could tell it was the body of a boy."

"Black or white?"

"Black."

"And your partner ... what was he doing then?"

"He was on his hands and knees, hunched over the boy."

"What was he doing?"

"He was administering CPR. Chest compressions, and then mouth-to-mouth. And he seemed to be talking to the victim."

"Could you make out what he was saying?"

"Not really. It was difficult to hear. He'd breathe into the boy's mouth, and every time he drew a breath, he'd repeat something. I can only tell you what it sounded like."

"And what is that?"

Cook's voice quavered.

"It sounded to me like he was saying: 'Please don't die … please don't die.'"

"Are you sure?"

"I'm pretty sure that's what my partner was saying."

"And why do you suppose he would say that?" the investigator asked.

"I think he realized he'd unwittingly shot a young boy, and I imagine that he was deeply disturbed," Cook replied.

"You could tell that from his demeanor?"

"I know my partner well," Cook said, "and I could tell he was deeply disturbed."

"And you?"

Cook reached for her water glass, quickly put her trembling hand under the table, and rested it, out of sight, on her lap.

"I was deeply disturbed, too," she said, "as disturbed as if I'd shot the boy myself."

Chapter 15

IT HAD BEEN SUCH A JOYOUS DAY until then, too—such a proud and glorious celebration filled with laughter, music, and song.

All along Seventh Avenue, in the heart of Manhattan, massive crowds had lined the sidewalks, waving American flags, singing patriotic tunes, and cheering as marchers paraded under a blizzard of confetti loosed from windows of midtown office towers. Bands from local high schools, scout troops, the New York City Fire Department, and the NYPD's Emerald Society—bagpipes, drums, and horns reverberating—led the parade into Times Square, where the marchers paused at the statue of Father Francis P. Duffy, the famed military chaplain, to observe a moment of silence. Then the veterans' groups, the labor unions, the uniformed services workers, and thousands of others wound their way uptown to Columbus Circle, past a reviewing stand of dignitaries. An open limousine carried a Medal of Honor winner who smiled broadly and waved. Behind him, a sleek, white convertible, its sides pasted with banners, reminded people not to forget the MIAs from Vietnam. Then came row after row of soldiers, sailors, airmen, and marines—smiling, waving, and catching hardhats lobbed to them by saluting construction workers.

But there'd been more to the day's festivities than simply a celebration of America's Bicentennial. Independence Day this year had been especially exciting for C. J. Johnson. There was the spectacle of the parade, for one thing—the fireworks and the historical displays, the twirlers and drum majors, the revelers in Revolutionary War costumes. For the Brownsville teen, however, there was more than that to this glorious Fourth of July: C. J.'s brother, Marcus, was being discharged from the U.S. Army after a yearlong tour of duty in Vietnam, and C. J. could hardly wait to see him.

Technically, Army Specialist Marcus Williams was C. J.'s *cousin*—not his brother—although the pair had been raised like siblings. The son of Eunice Johnson's sister Clara, Marcus had come to live with the Johnson family in Brownsville when he was nine and C. J., three. It had been a blessing for everyone concerned. A single mother, and indigent, Clara Johnson could hardly afford to raise Marcus and her four other children in rural South Carolina. The Johnsons more than welcomed a companion for C. J.

Despite the cousins' age disparity, Marcus connected with C. J. right from the start, helping the Johnsons raise their lead-poisoned son, and teaching him the ins and outs of their hardscrabble neighborhood. Marcus played hide-and-seek with C. J. in the hallways of their building, and in the alleyways and streets near their home. He took C. J. to the Brownsville Boys Club, a local recreation center, where he taught his cousin how to swim; took C. J. to the movies and to the basketball courts on Stone Avenue, where the boys cheered as the city's premier schoolyard players put on a show. At night, Marcus played imaginary basketball games with C. J., using a rolled-up sock as a ball and a lampshade as a basket, clowning and imitating the moves of their favorite players. He introduced C. J. to video games, teaching his cousin hand-eye coordination, as the two of them battled gunslingers and space aliens on the family's console TV. He also spent hours with C. J. compiling a loose-leaf scrapbook containing photos and newspaper clippings about their favorite sports heroes: football legend Jim Brown; basketball star Willis Reed; baseball great Willie Mays; boxing champ Muhammad Ali.

C. J. had always cherished that scrapbook. He'd cherished Marcus even more, idolizing his cousin with an adoration and devotion generally reserved for the sports heroes he worshipped.

Raising Marcus, however, hadn't been easy for Charles and Eunice Johnson. As a teenager, Marcus ran for a while with the wrong crowd, getting bounced from high school and prompting his surrogate parents to consent to him enlisting, at age seventeen, in the U.S. Army. His tour in Vietnam had awakened Marcus to both life's fragilities and its possibilities. Training in electronics had proffered him a palpable skill set and potential career path. Aged twenty now, his army hitch nearly at an end, Marcus Williams was returning to New York. In several weeks, he'd be formally discharged, returning to Brownsville to start an electrical-union apprenticeship. Today, along with the rest of his army company, he was marching through the streets of Manhattan in the city's Bicentennial parade.

C. J. Johnson had risen especially early that day, barely able to contain his excitement. He and his parents had gotten dressed in their finest clothing for the subway ride to Manhattan, where they'd snapped photos and waved excitedly as Marcus marched past. Then, after lunch, they'd joined the tens of thousands who'd filled the parks and shorelines along the Hudson River to see the flotilla of naval vessels and tall-masted sailing ships anchored in New York Harbor as part of Operation Sail.

C. J. was even more excited, though, about what would happen next. Marcus would be spending several hours in Manhattan with his army buddies. Then, that night, he'd be coming to Brownsville for a visit. A surprise homecoming party was being planned. The party, it had been decided, would be held in the cellar of the Johnsons' apartment building. A group of friends had volunteered to help C. J. set the cellar up with decorations, junk food, and party favors.

C. J. Johnson couldn't wait to surprise Marcus with the party. All day, he'd barely been able to contain himself. All his closest friends, girls and boys, would be joining in the celebration.

C. J. had decided what to wear and how to comport himself that night. He'd wear his eyeglasses because he could barely see without them, but had decided, self-consciously, to leave his hearing aid in a bedroom drawer. It didn't matter that he'd barely be able to hear much of anything without the clunky device in his ear. He couldn't wait to rush into Marcus's arms and welcome his beloved cousin home.

Chapter 16

WITHIN MINUTES of Rachel Cook's radio call, police backup units screeched to a halt in front of 118 Amboy Street, lighting up the thoroughfare with their pulsating turret lights, and filling the air with staticky radio chatter. More than a dozen officers leapt from their patrol cars, hustled through a gathering throng, and flooded into the cellar.

When the backup officers accessed the shooting scene, they found Matt Holland—his uniform bloodstained, his police cap on the floor—hunched over the body of C. J. Johnson, frantically attempting lifesaving resuscitation. Rachel Cook had her firearm trained on the two girls she'd ordered to lie on the floor. Quaking and in tears, the girls were quickly cuffed, informed of their rights, and led away.

With the girls in custody, Cook moved tentatively toward her crestfallen partner, who was surrounded by officers attempting to pry him from the body of the fallen youth. A team of paramedics had also arrived and began positioning a defibrillator on C. J. Johnson's chest, and an oxygen mask over his nose and mouth.

Cook saw her partner raise himself to his feet, and then teeter like a drunk before slumping into the arms of fellow cops, his anguished sobs echoing off the walls and ceiling of the cellar. Choking back tears, Cook reached in to touch his shoulder.

"Matty," she said softly, as if trying to rouse him from sleep. But Holland never saw nor heard her, weeping unabashedly as the backup officers encircled him, trying vainly to console the grieving cop.

"Matt—" Cook said, choking on the word. But Holland seemed in a world apart, someplace where he could neither see nor hear.

"Where's that fuckin' bus?" a cop shouted into his radio. "We need that goddamned ambulance *now*!"

But the backup officers knew that the ambulance might not arrive so promptly and there wasn't time to waste if C. J. Johnson had any chance to survive. Better to rush the wounded boy to the hospital themselves rather than wait, the officers reasoned. So, one of them gingerly lifted the boy and carried him, arms and legs dangling, from the cellar. Another officer, his hand pressed against C. J.'s wound, walked alongside as the fallen teen was brought outdoors, through a hushed crowd, and placed onto the rear seat of a waiting patrol car.

Then suddenly empty and freezing, Cook slumped to the cellar floor, head between her knees, and threw up over her pant-legs as her partner, surrounded by other cops, collapsed in their arms and uncontrollably wept.

* * *

"One final question, officer," the IAD investigator asked near the end of Cook's testimony, eleven hours after the incident.

"Yes?" Cook said, trying desperately to focus, the others in the 73rd Precinct muster room seeming blurry and distorted, like characters in a film melting under heat.

"Did it ever occur to you—either at the time of the shooting, or in the hours since—that the victim may not have heard either your or Detective Holland's commands to halt, and that he may never have heard you identify yourselves as police officers?" the investigator asked.

Cook stared at him, emptily. "No."

"And why is that?"

"Our commands were very forceful," Cook said. "The command to 'halt' was given loudly, and several times, by both Detective Sergeant Holland and myself. We identified ourselves as police officers, repeatedly."

"And yet those commands were ignored?"

"Yes."

"Why do you suppose that was?"

"I think whoever was in the cellar was trying to escape."

"And yet the shooting victim neither halted nor tried to escape, did he?" the investigator said. "In fact, he actually ran *toward* Detective Holland and made physical contact with him. Now, why do you suppose he did that?"

"I've thought about that all night." Cook sighed. "And I just don't know."

Hand shaking, Cook sipped warily from her water glass.

"I can't imagine that our commands weren't heard," she said. "I could only assume that, for some reason, they were being ignored."

Then she looked away, to someplace only she could see.

"But I don't know," she said. "It's the strangest thing. It was almost as if the boy was expecting to greet someone he knew. It was almost as if he couldn't hear a word we said."

Chapter 17

IT HAD ALL BEEN GOING SO WELL FOR HER until then, too. Everything was going according to plan.

Eight months into her job as a New York City cop, police work had become everything Rachel Cook had ever envisioned it could be, and more. At times, it seemed to Cook as if she'd achieved nothing short of an impossible dream—the job, though daunting at times, rewarding beyond her wildest imagination, nothing like the puerile fantasy she'd once harbored but in many ways far more gratifying.

Though prone, like most rookies, to occasional lapses in judgment, Cook for the most part was standing on her own two feet halfway through her yearlong probationary period, having mastered the rudiments, the vernacular, and the ins and outs of police work. Despite his role as Cook's FTO, Matt Holland was purposefully letting her take the lead on traffic stops, ambulance cases, auto accidents, and other routine calls—and she was handling them with professionalism and proficiency.

As envisaged by NYPD brass, Cook was proving a natural in employing the attributes modern-day law enforcement was trying to emphasize—utilizing intellect, sensitivity, communications skills, and problem-solving acumen in her contacts with the public, rather than defaulting to authoritativeness and force. Instinctively, she leveraged the fact that she wasn't as physically intimidating as the typical cop, instantly creating the perception that she was more empathetic, more pliable, and easier to deal with. Her presence alone produced an instant calming effect on emotionally charged situations, and was highly impactful in defusing aggressive, dangerous behavior. Time and again, she successfully juggled the challenging, often conflicting, roles of psychologist, social worker, diplomat, referee, minister, and legal expert.

Mirroring this performance, Holland's monthly evaluations were overwhelmingly positive. Having partnered with burnouts, bigots, incompetents, and malcontents, Holland found himself inspired by Cook's intellect and tenacity, her sensitivity to the community, and her fierce determination to prove herself as a woman in a domain populated almost exclusively by men. Cook was consistently graded as trustworthy, respected, and motivated to serve the public. Her interpersonal and report-writing skills were off the charts. She was also judged as highly unlikely to violate a citizen's civil rights, revert to the use of force, engage in corruption, or be subject to a civil or criminal lawsuit. By nearly every quantifiable measure, she was as good a cop as any rookie on the streets of New York.

"There's only one category I can't rate you as 'exceptional' in," Holland joked. "I can't stretch the truth when it comes to 'physical bearing.' Let's face it, Rachel, at five-foot-three, a hundred-and-ten pounds, you don't exactly look like the stereotypical cop."

"That's fine with me," Cook said. "Truth is I don't want to be a 'stereotype.' I want to be *me*. Besides, 'physical bearing' is overrated when it comes to being a successful cop. Other qualities are far more important."

In Cook's case, those qualities were being increasingly acknowledged. By midyear, NYPD officials, as promised, had not only enrolled Cook in a postgraduate program at the John Jay College of Criminal Justice, but had her conducting weekly visits to public schools throughout the city, where Cook was building bridges between police and the public, while delivering a message about the limitless possibilities that students' lives could hold.

The students Cook addressed nearly always were spellbound, enthralled. Most had never seen a uniformed female police officer before. They sat in rapt silence, mouths agape, as Cook addressed them in classrooms and assemblies, telling them about police work, demonstrating her radio, and showing them her flashlight, logbook, nightstick, and handcuffs.

"Are you a *real* police officer?" the students would ask.

"Yes," Cook would reply. "There are women, like me, who are police officers and do everything that male officers do."

"Do you like being a police officer?" they'd ask

"Yes, I like it very much," she'd say. "It's interesting and important work."

"Is your job hard?"

"Sometimes," she'd say. "There are times we have to go to places that are dangerous or unpleasant, and we have to work hard to make things safe for everyone."

"Do you put people in jail?"

"Only when they break the law. Mostly, we help people who need us."

"Is that a real gun?"

"Yes."

"Can you take it out and show us?"

"No. A gun is not a toy, or something you show off or play with. It's part of my job, and it's used to help people. But it's dangerous if not handled properly."

"Did you ever shoot anyone?"

"Thank goodness, no. Police officers try to never shoot anyone, but, in rare cases, we must ... if someone breaks the law or tries to harm other people."

At the end of her presentations, the students would applaud.

"Remember," Cook would say. "Never stop dreaming. Always follow your heart. Some people think I can't be a police officer because I'm a woman, but I've become one anyway because that's the job I've chosen. You can do that, too. You can do, or become, anything you want to be. Your life can be as big and bold as any dream you have, if you just give yourself a chance."

And all of that was true, wasn't it? After all, wasn't Cook living a big and bold dream, too?

Indeed, by midsummer, Rachel Cook was literally *soaring*, the police job opening doors, inside and outside herself, to worlds she never knew existed. Cook felt alive as never before, energized by burgeoning opportunities to discover a whole new her: someone who felt competent and worthwhile, someone breaking new ground, someone achieving a sense of mission that was both heady and fulfilling. Cook was helping people through their darkest moments. She was contributing something worthwhile to her city. She was helping make a difference.

Equally gratifying for Cook was the opportunity to see the NYPD moving in the direction it was, attempting to redefine the age-old image of the patrol cop and change pernicious public perceptions. Cook also loved being on the cusp of the women's movement, rejoicing in how women were playing a greater role in the workplace, how inequities were being eradicated, female stereotypes crumbling, opportunities emerging. She felt gratified to be helping write a bold new chapter in the history of the NYPD, being part of something so cutting-edge, so new. Female officers had been working street patrol for mere months; there was but a handful of them in all of New York. No one knew quite what to make of them, what to expect, how to react to their presence. Cook quietly reveled in that, basking in the attention that women officers garnered, being the centerpiece at parties, loving how people were instantly drawn to her, asking questions, showing interest, wanting to hear her story.

Yes—eight months into her job as a cop, Rachel Cook had truly arrived. She wasn't simply a faceless person lost in a crowd, the nobody she'd once been terrified of becoming. Her life was nothing like the inconsequential whisper she'd always feared it would become. Her life had gotten big. It had gotten bold. It had gotten special.

Eight months into police work, Rachel Cook felt certain that she could fully embrace police work and ride it as far as her talent and ambition would allow. There were no barriers anymore, nothing standing in her way. Everything had fallen into place, just as she'd hoped. All of it was tangible now, endlessly exciting. Eight months into police work, the sky, for Rachel Cook, was truly the limit.

* * *

Not that Cook, by any stretch of the imagination, was achieving success all on her own. Detective Sergeant Matt Holland—as steady a presence as Cook could have ever wished for—was working alongside his rookie charge, training her, supporting her, and helping her win the acceptance of the 73rd Precinct's male cops.

Indeed, while women may have been equal to men in the eyes of the courts, they were far from equal in the eyes of most male cops, and were often denigrated, rejected, and subjected to far more scrutiny and criticism than their male counterparts.

As Cook soon discovered, most male cops staunchly resisted the idea of women on street patrol, arguing that females didn't possess the requisite strength, endurance, self-confidence, and assertiveness required in handling police work. Critics further argued that women were too emotionally unstable to withstand the job's pressures, were more likely to panic in life-or-death situations than tackle those crises head-on, and thus were more likely than male cops to get their partners injured or killed.

Much of this, of course, was tied to archaic female stereotypes and longstanding police culture. The traditional image of the cop, after all, had always been "manly." Police officers, by definition, were aggressive, strong, unemotional, courageous, decisive, dependable, and patriarchal. Women, in contrast, were seen as the antithesis of that: passive, weak, emotional, fearful, indecisive, erratic, and motherly—in short, everything that a "good" cop wasn't. Most men believed that for a woman to perform effectively as a police officer she'd have to achieve what amounted in essence to a reversal of cultural roles. And that, they reasoned, was all but impossible.

Typical of his mindset about most things, Matt Holland had risen above the anti-female hysteria pervading the ranks of the NYPD. While he wasn't entirely thrilled with the notion of women on street patrol, he was at least willing to give the idea a chance. Throughout her eight months on the job, he'd purposefully helped Cook win acceptance among many male cops in the 73rd Precinct, endorsing her virtues, and getting the men to acknowledge that there were attributes beyond raw physicality for evaluating cops. He'd also helped Cook weather a series of demoralizing, citywide demonstrations by police officers' wives, denouncing so-called Cop Couples. He'd even helped reinforce Cook's belief that the resistance to women on patrol was based largely on threats to male cops' masculinity, along with wives' fears of potential infidelity.

"Police officers have been exposed to a lot of change recently, and most of the men are fed up with the constant change," Holland explained. "They've also had it up to here with the women's movement—at home and in the workplace. To most men, the station house has always been 'sacred turf,' the last bastion of all-male territory that still exists. But now women have invaded that, too. It's the final straw for many guys, the demise of policing as they've known it. They resent the hell out of women like you."

"But just because we're women, it doesn't mean we're automatically unfit to be police officers," Cook argued. "I just wish the men would give us a chance to prove ourselves."

"That's exactly the point," Holland said. "It's not so much that men are afraid that women *can't* do the job—they're afraid that women *can*. Think about it: What if women can do a job most men thought that only men could do? How does that diminish the men? The point is, Rachel, women are perceived as a threat. That's why you're running into such staunch opposition."

Holland's insights helped. So did his calming, reassuring presence and the way he indoctrinated Cook and slowly brought her along. As the months wore on, Holland's lessons about police work evolved from the most rudimentary basics to the more sophisticated and nuanced. He taught Cook about the need to control her emotions, and suspend her imagination, on frightening calls, so that she wouldn't freeze up and become ineffectual. He taught her ways to keep from feeling demoralized and defeated; how to escape the job's pressures and cope with its emotional ferocity; how to close the door on Brownsville at the end of each tour and find a release, an escape, a relationship—*anything* to get her mind off work.

Still, what helped the most was simply that Holland told Cook he believed in her, and that the job would get easier with time. Cook was never entirely sure whether Holland's supportive words were earnest, or simply a ruse to make her feel better. But it didn't really matter. Holland was *there* for her, giving her exactly the kind of support she needed. He didn't smother her with advice, didn't bury her with criticism. Mostly, he just gave her a chance.

Each day, Cook was learning new things—learning, mostly, to stand on her own two feet. But it was comforting to know that someone as experienced and proficient as Matt Holland was there to help her through the rough spots—even protect her, if that's what was needed. Cook took shelter in Holland's words, found reassurance in his encouragement, his actions, and his very presence.

As long as Matt Holland was her partner, Cook was convinced, very little could ever go wrong.

Chapter 18

THE SCREAM could be heard for an entire city block, a piercing, high-pitched shriek that echoed through the concrete-and-asphalt canyons of Brownsville, rattling the neighborhood like a mighty clap of thunder.

"Dear Lord … No! No!" Eunice Johnson wailed as she made her way from her apartment toward the patrol car where her fourteen-year-old son lay motionless across the rear seat, wounded by the bullet from Matt Holland's gun.

"Don't tell me that's my little boy in that police car!" Eunice bellowed as she tottered along the sidewalk, parting the crowd of onlookers that had gathered on either side of Amboy Street.

"Please, dear Lord!" C. J. Johnson's mother yowled. "Don't tell me you're gonna take my baby from me!"

The crowd was silent and stunned. Dozens of police officers stood transfixed, frozen in their tracks.

"Don't … let … that … be … my … baby!" Eunice Johnson gazed to the heavens. "Please, dear Lord … don't take my baby from me!"

But the sobbing, grief-stricken mother never reached her fallen son. Eunice made it only as far as the rear of the patrol car, before hurling her body across the vehicle's trunk and reaching vainly for its rear window. Her anguish pouring from her in heaving, gut-wrenching sobs, she then slid down the length of the trunk and plopped face-first onto the asphalt.

"Please … tell me no, Lord!" she wailed, slapping at the ground with a bruised and bloodied palm. "No! … No!"

Just then, a Black man emerged from the Johnsons' apartment building, clambering down the stoop and running frantically toward the patrol car in which C. J. Johnson lay. Portly in stature, his hair thinning at the crown of his head, he was clad in the navy-blue blazer and slacks of a New York City Transit Authority worker.

"Please," he wheezed breathlessly to a cop, "that's my son in that car!"

"We've got to get your son to the hospital ... *now*!" the cop said. "An ambulance is on the way, but we can't afford to wait!"

"Then let me go with him," C. J. Johnson's father implored.

And the officer let him slip into the rear seat of the patrol car alongside his fallen son, whose head he cradled gently as the RMP, siren wailing, sped through the streets of Brownsville on its mile-long journey to the hospital.

"I'm here for you, Son," C. J. Johnson's father whispered, as he stroked his fallen son's blood-stained hair. "Hang on, C. J. Please don't leave us now. There's still so many things the two of us have left to do."

* * *

One hour later, alone in a waiting room near the first-floor nurses' station at Brookdale University Hospital, Charles Johnson maintained a prayerful vigil as a team of doctors and nurses worked feverishly in an operating room down the hall to save the life of his son.

His Transit Authority blazer and slacks spattered with C. J.'s blood, his mind in a flutter, Charles paced anxiously, then made his way to a corner of the room and lowered his head to pray.

A devout Baptist his entire life, Charles believed, fervently, that the God he worshipped was benevolent and merciful to pious disciples like Charles, a devoted church congregant who'd given himself wholly to his faith. Charles also believed that God, in His infinite wisdom, acted in ways that mere mortals couldn't possibly comprehend, and that there was a purpose to those actions, an objective that might seem obscure at first but would be revealed with unmistakable clarity over time.

Now, head bowed, fingers interlocked, Charles fell to his knees and began to pray. "Almighty Lord," he said, in a guttural, heartfelt whisper. "You've been at my side from the instant of my first breath, and you'll be with me 'til my dying breath ... and I'm grateful for the blessings you've bestowed upon me."

Charles closed his eyes, oblivious to the staticky voices on the hospital loudspeaker, the hospital personnel and visitors shuffling by in the hallway outside.

"I've never asked you for much of anything, Lord," Charles said, "but I beg you now—"

Choking on his words, Charles begged God to forgive whatever sins he may have unwittingly committed, sacrifices he'd failed to make, or character flaws he might have exhibited, but to please spare the life of his beloved son, whom he imagined tethered to a fragile string about to fray, allowing C. J. to drift away, forever out of Charles's reach.

"I beg you, Lord, to provide healing for Clifford's body and spirit, and to make me strong for the difficult days that lie ahead," Charles prayed. "Help me to not allow my struggles to yield bitterness, disillusionment, or exhaustion. Know that my greatest desire in life is to reflect your everlasting light on our broken world. I beseech you, Lord—for you and you alone are able to help me. I love you and need you on this day, as always. Amen."

Rising unsteadily to his feet, Charles slumped into a chair, his thoughts on C. J., connected by now to life-support equipment in an operating room down the hall.

How in God's name could this be happening? Charles thought. *How could something so terrible be happening to C. J. again?*

* * *

For the longest time after C. J. contracted his lead poisoning, Charles Johnson had been unable to forgive himself for the challenges surrounding his only child. Where was he, after all, when C. J. was breathing in the dreaded lead toxin? How could he not have been aware? Why couldn't he make enough of a living to move his family from the kind of poverty-stricken neighborhood that could breed such a wretched disease?

"Don't blame or punish yourselves," the doctor told Charles and Eunice Johnson. "Lead poisoning can be insidious and extremely difficult to diagnose. It's even called the 'stealth disease' because children can be exposed to lead for months without exhibiting any symptoms at all."

The doctor had been sympathetic, as had family and friends, the support group Charles and Eunice had joined, and the priest and parishioners at their church. But how could he not blame himself? Charles thought. How could any father not bear responsibility for what had happened—or escape the guilt?

For weeks after C. J.'s diagnosis, Charles had gone to sleep each night, sobbing and praying and holding Eunice, trying desperately to ease the couple's anxiety and amplify C. J.'s recovery. Rooted in evangelical traditions common among Blacks in Central Brooklyn, the couple had turned to religion, immersing themselves in Brownsville's Good Shepherd Baptist Church, where they'd met and married eighteen years earlier. They helped found clubs, assisted with fundraisers, sang in the choir, and cared for the needy, serving as champions for human rights and racial justice.

At forty-eight and forty-six years old, respectively, Charles and Eunice Johnson had become respected church elders who tried in every way to be there for their son. Any form of help that C. J. needed, they provided—regardless of expense. Intensive speech therapy had enabled the boy to learn simple words by the age of six. A hearing aid had helped, as well. So had school. Assigned at first to a class for disabled children in the basement of his elementary school, Charles and Eunice lobbied to have C. J. mainstreamed, a novel approach that enabled special-needs children to attend regular classes and avoid the stigma tied to their disability.

But with everything they'd tried, all the assistance they'd procured, what helped C. J. the most was simply his parents' steadfast attention. Charles, especially, made it a point to spend every possible waking minute with his son. He calmed his son down when C. J. grew restless and agitated. He played with the boy and talked to him, took him to church and taught him things. Each night after work, he spent an hour at bedtime, reading to C. J.—classic comic books, fables, sports stories, and, finally, poems.

And through those poems, father and son forged a special bond.

Nonsense poems in particular, Charles found, contained a rhythm, a rhyme, an iambic pentameter that captured C. J.'s attention, sparked his curiosity, and invariably made him laugh. Poems weren't as intimidating or as frustrating as long-form stories. They didn't distract C. J. as much or make him irritable. They contained words he could break apart, sound out, memorize.

So, Charles read his son poems that were simple, emotional, introspective, funny. He focused C. J.'s listening skills by asking that the boy signal when he heard rhyming words. He taught him to recognize sounds by asking him to point out words that ended in the same letter, and then patiently explained the meaning of each word. He allowed C. J. to invent his own words and to draw pictures to illustrate the poems. He used the poems to teach C. J. the notion of time, how to distinguish the seasons, how to read a calendar. Other poems helped C. J. with color recognition and the rudiments of reading.

There were plenty of times when Charles was unsure whether his words were truly reaching his son. But that didn't stop him from trying. Even people in comas, Charles knew, could be reached through sounds; so, in his mind, could C. J. Besides, so what if C. J. didn't grasp all the meanings? So what if all the reading wasn't helping the boy? At least C. J. had to know that his father was there for him—talking to him, engaging him, loving him, and trying to rescue him from whatever feelings of loneliness, hopelessness, or despair he may have had.

Charles knew he couldn't undo the damage wrought by the lead poisoning—couldn't *will* C. J. to be normal. But he could always be there for his son. He'd do whatever it took. He'd work one, two—ten jobs, if necessary—to get C. J. the care that he needed. He'd spend every waking moment he could with his son, for as long as C. J. wanted him around. That much, he vowed.

Charles Johnson would be someone who'd help dispel the odious, age-old stereotypes about Black fathers and how they treated their families. He'd be the Black father who'd work hard and never drink, never grow violent, or squander his money. He'd be the Black father who'd never cheat on his wife, never be a deadbeat dad, never abandon the people who needed him the most. He'd be the Black father who'd always provide for his dependents, always display his love, always be there.

And now, as he prayed for God to spare the life of his son, Charles prayed, too, that C. J. would somehow hear his words and sense that Charles, as always, was at his side—supporting the boy, pulling for him, loving him with every ounce of his being.

And as the agonizing minutes passed, Charles couldn't help but think not simply about his fallen son, but about the entirety of his life, the long and arduous journey that had led him to this fateful day.

* * *

His was a familiar Deep South story. A familiar New York story, too.

Born to the teenaged descendants of former slaves, Charles Johnson was raised on the outskirts of Claymont, South Carolina, in a countryside dotted with cotton and tobacco fields, sun-parched roads, and the ghostly ruins of antebellum plantations.

Nestled in the Appalachian foothills, in a region known as the Piedmont, Claymont was squarely at the center of the cotton-mill world—a village of little more than a general store, gas station, post office, bank, and rows of company-owned shotgun houses. Life there, as in other Piedmont towns, was dominated by the local cotton mill, which drew its workforce mainly from destitute yeoman farmers who'd succumbed to the lure of factory wages in lieu of bankruptcy.

Known as "lintheads," Claymont's mill workers labored round the clock, producing carpet yarn, grain sacks, and canvas for military tents. Production schedules were grueling, the work tedious, noisy, and dangerous. Entire families of mill workers—breathing in the lint-filled air, trying to steer clear of roaring spindles and looms—labored in twelve-hour shifts. Children were worked as hard as their parents. Injuries cost workers their wages, and often their employment.

And those were the *best* jobs to be had.

South Carolina in the 1920s was White Man's Country, and the Southern textile industry was exclusively a white domain. With blacks barred from work at the cotton mill, Charles's father, Wilbur, was forced to eke out a living as a day laborer, while his mother, Gladys, was employed by a mill family to cook, clean, and babysit five children—all while raising six children of her own. The Johnsons lived in a three-room, dirt-floor shack devoid of running water, electricity, or indoor plumbing. Charles and his siblings helped the family make ends meet, earning pennies an hour picking cotton and baling hay.

But like other Black South Carolinians, the Johnsons lived as much in terror as in abject poverty. Life in the Deep South then was totally segregated, with citizenship a racial privilege and civil rights meaningless to a white establishment that clung to Old Southern ways. Jim Crow laws governed where Blacks could walk, talk, rest, play, and eat. Voting rights were nonexistent, with Blacks excluded from politics, and government services divided into separate "White" and "Colored" domains. Charles and his friends walked three miles one way to a dilapidated, one-room schoolhouse, while White children rode on buses to a separate, modern school, spitting out the windows and calling the Black kids niggers, burrheads, and coons.

But that was hardly the extent of the torment that Charles and other Blacks were subjected to. Eighty years after the Civil War, the legacy of slavery reverberated in backwater southern towns, where racial tensions often bubbled over into bloodshed. Blacks were barred after nightfall in "sundown" towns like Claymont, whose surrounding countryside was ruled by White supremacists, paramilitary groups, vigilantes, and Ku Klux Klansmen. Black men were routinely beaten, bludgeoned, and knifed for even imagined violations of southern racial etiquette. Black women were routinely assaulted and raped. Criminal charges were systematically covered up by local authorities. Lynching was a way of life.

Ineligible for military service due to poor eyesight during World War II, Charles was in his twenties, working as a dollar-a-day gas station attendant, when he discovered that while the War for Democracy had ended triumphantly overseas, a different kind of war was raging at home, as civil rights activists fought to eradicate deeply rooted Old South traditions.

The civil rights movement brought court challenges, lobbying efforts, fundraising, and similar efforts at ending racial discrimination to towns like Claymont. Marches, sit-ins, and boycotts were staged at white-only public facilities. Churches, grassroots groups, and fraternal societies mobilized volunteers to participate in acts of civil disobedience. Civil rights organizations sponsored freedom rides and other anti-segregation efforts.

To most Southern Whites, however, the civil rights movement was little more than another unwelcomed Northern incursion into the Southern way of life. South Carolina quickly became a flashpoint for challenges to White supremacy, with civil rights advances met by a powerful backlash. State officials balked at enforcing federal mandates. Voter registration drives were thwarted. Poll taxes, residency requirements, and literacy tests stripped blacks from voter rolls. Efforts at school desegregation were blocked, protests squelched, anti-lynching legislation defeated. Worse yet, blacks were subjected to a virulent new form of white rage.

Klansman, vigilantes, and insurgent white supremacists terrorized Black neighborhoods in and around Claymont. Homes were ransacked, schools dynamited, churches burned, civil rights activists assaulted. With National Guardsmen summoned to protect rights, and Blacks employing guerilla warfare as a means of defense, the climate grew even more hateful, and race relations more tortured than ever.

In his twenties by then, Charles had left Claymont for a month-long visit to relatives in New York and, upon his return, discovered that a newly formed "White Citizens Council" had circulated a list of Black voters—permitting banks, stores, restaurants, and gas stations to deny Blacks essential services. Charles's parents had also been evicted from their home and forced, along with other Blacks, to live in a makeshift tent city. All the while, efforts aimed at halting the oppression were met with opposition from the White Citizens Council, local and state police, and the Klan. Protestors were greeted with tear gas, billy clubs, mass arrests, and firehoses. Charles's father was blacklisted at White-owned farms, and his mother fired from her housekeeping job. The family's church was firebombed. For Charles, there was no way to protest what was happening—except with his feet.

Lured by jobs in wartime defense factories, legions of southern Blacks had been abandoning the agricultural South for several years, part of a massive migration to northern industrial cities. New York was, in many ways, the Promised Land, light years ahead of South Carolina on the issue that mattered most: democracy was more elastic there, nor reserved solely for Whites.

New York was far more progressive than most U.S. cities when it came to integration, housing, education, and other racial divides. It was headquarters to nearly all the leading civil rights organizations, home to the major radio networks and most of America's liberal newspapers. Teachers in its schools openly discussed controversial Black leaders like Paul Robeson and Malcolm X. Students were permitted to read writers like Langston Hughes, Richard Wright, and Booker T. Washington.

Charles knew of several South Carolinians who'd settled in Brooklyn. Civil rights, he'd heard, had a different meaning in Brooklyn than in Claymont. Indeed, parts of the borough had become hotbeds of social consciousness. Community and religious leaders were openly preaching integration of housing, factories, and schools. A progressive trade union movement was underway. Jackie Robinson, the first Black player to break Major League Baseball's color barrier, had been summoned from the Dodgers' farm team to play for the parent club in Brooklyn.

To Charles, when Jackie Robinson took the field for the Dodgers, in 1947, it was an act that in one transcendent moment epitomized promise, hope, and a new order that stood in vivid contrast to the age-old ways of the South. If Jackie Robinson could play big-league baseball on America's greatest stage, then anything, to Charles, was possible. And if Jackie Robinson could live and play ball in Brooklyn, then Brooklyn was a place where Charles, too, could build a life of his own.

Brooklyn was by no means perfect, people said, just a whole lot better than Claymont. Brooklyn had its own ugly forms of racism, people warned, but at least there were no cross-burnings, no fire-bombings, no Jim Crow traditions to endure. In New York, there'd be none of the masks that Blacks in Claymont were forced to wear simply to survive: no more mumbled *yassirs*; no more tipped hats; no more moving to the back of the bus; no more stepping to the curb to let white folk pass.

Stirred by the notion of living in an America like that, Charles fled the South. Stuffing all he could carry into a battered cardboard suitcase, he and a cousin hitched a ride to Memphis, where they slept in haylofts and roadside ditches, and picked up low-wage jobs to finance their travels. They arrived on the final leg of their six-month journey on a train to New York. It was 1951. Charles was twenty-six years old, penniless, and overwhelmed by what he saw.

Overjoyed, too.

When he arrived at a bustling Penn Station, two things caught Charles's eye. The first was a huge American flag, void of an accompanying Confederate standard. The second was a billboard. It depicted two White boys holding baseball gloves, a Black boy standing off to the side. A White woman was frowning in displeasure.

"But what does race got to do with it?" one of the White kids was saying. "He can pitch!"

Charles Johnson was moved to tears when he saw that.

Then he and his cousin left the railway station and walked through midtown Manhattan—East Side to West, one street at a time, bucking the traffic and the crowds. Into the blazing neon canyons of Times Square and up to the lush, sprawling pastures of Central Park. Past Rockefeller Center and Saint Patrick's Cathedral and the Empire State Building and the United Nations. Past the glittering Broadway theaters and the famous hotels and the massive office towers and the fine restaurants and the world-renowned museums. For seven hours, they walked through the electric city, agape at its magnitude, mesmerized by its movement, caught up in its energy, its strength, all its radiant possibilities.

And strangely, Charles felt at home.

One week later, the cousins went to see Jackie Robinson play. It was another sight that Charles would never forget: crowds pouring out of subways and lining up at the gilded ticket windows of Brooklyn's Ebbets Field; vendors hawking peanuts, hot dogs, scorecards, and souvenirs; children armed with baseball gloves being led into the cozy, misshapen big league ballpark.

Charles remembered that day, twenty-five years later, as if it were yesterday: entering the ballpark's circular rotunda, enclosed in marble and tiled like the stitches on a baseball; taking in the ads plastered on the outfield walls; marveling at the playing field, more verdant than any farmland he'd ever seen.

Charles then saw Jackie Robinson emerge from the Dodgers' dugout, his black face in stark contrast to his brilliant home whites. Charles saw the crowd in the grandstand and bleachers begin to stir. Then he saw Robinson standing in the batter's box, bat held high, lining a curveball to the concave wall in right-center field, and then sweeping around the bases, before sliding into third in a cloud of dust as the crowd stood and roared. All of it in the melting pot of a big-league stadium. All in a place where blacks and whites were seated together, rooting aloud for the same team.

And Charles knew, then and there, that New York and Brooklyn would be a new beginning, everything that Claymont wasn't. It didn't matter that Charles was part of the very influx of poor minorities that was causing whites to flee. It didn't matter that he had to live with his cousin in a roach-infested, cold-water flat with gaping holes in the ceiling; or there was no hot water and no heat except from a gas stove; or that the two men had to use candles to light the apartment at night. Nor did it matter that the best job Charles could find for his first two years in Brooklyn was a lonely, low-level job working nights in one of the city's rail yards, cleaning subway cars for the New York City Transit Authority.

None of that mattered.

It didn't matter because, to Charles, Brooklyn was alive in a way that no home of his had ever been, vibrant and welcoming and flush with possibilities. And so was the larger city in which the borough was nestled: the City of New York.

The childhood wounds that Charles incurred in Claymont would never completely heal or be forgotten. In his adopted city, however, Charles could at least assuage his bitter Deep South memories. New York would be a city that Charles would come to call home; a city in which he'd live and work, marry and raise a son; a city in which he'd never feel as humiliated or as inconspicuous, as frightened or as hopeless as he once had in the South.

Charles thought about all of this, as he kept his vigil at Brookdale University Hospital, praying and waiting for word on C. J.'s fate. He wondered if God would be good to him on this otherwise-celebratory night: Independence Day 1976, symbolic of all that was great and good about a nation in which he'd found redemption, buoyancy, camaraderie, and hope. And he wondered if, God forbid, the worst were to happen, how he'd ever be able to deliver that sorrowful news to Eunice, deep in prayer herself at the couple's Brownsville apartment.

Chapter 19

BACK AT THE SHOOTING SCENE, the mammoth weight of what had occurred bore down on Matt Holland and Rachel Cook, as if the entire building was caving in and crushing the officers under a landslide of rubble, heartache, and disbelief.

Both officers were beyond merely distraught, seemingly shattered in some permanent, intractable way. Holland's face, ashen as a corpse, was twisted like a pretzel as he wandered aimlessly about, C. J. Johnson's blood sticking like maple syrup to the soles of his shoes. Cook, eyes glazed, seemed sallow and emaciated as she sat shivering beneath a pile of blankets against a graffiti-scrawled wall.

By now, senior command staff and NYPD investigative personnel had flooded the Amboy Street cellar. Holland and Cook's patrol car had been removed from the street, the perimeter around the apartment building cordoned off, officers posted at the entrance to the cellar and in the ovular courtyard at the rear. Throngs of onlookers stood behind police barricades. TV- and radio-broadcast crews, along with newspaper reporters and photographers, were also arriving in droves. At the same time, plainclothes detectives mingled with onlookers, canvassing for potential witnesses to the shooting, while other investigators knocked on doors, seeking anyone who might have had a view of what transpired.

Down in the floodlit cellar, forensics specialists, homicide detectives, and other investigative personnel were already busy mapping and photographing the scene—studying everything from the distance and trajectory of Holland's gunshot to the officers' proximity to C. J. Johnson, and the entry and exit points of the bullet. Latex-gloved forensics personnel scoured the cellar floor with flashlights, searching for shell casings. High atop a ladder, an investigator studied the concrete ceiling where Holland's gunshot had left a dint before ricocheting downward and striking C. J. Johnson atop his head. A chalk outline marked the bloodstained spot where the teenaged shooting victim had fallen, a plastic cup covering the spent slug from Holland's service revolver.

There wasn't much to the shooting scene itself. Forty-by-sixty feet in size, and illuminated by a sixty-watt incandescent bulb dangling from its ceiling, the cellar had once been used as a perambulator room, a storage space for baby carriages and bicycles. Dank and mildewed, it wasn't used for much of anything anymore. Discarded appliances, plumbing fixtures, and similar debris lined its walls. Ashes sat piled at the base of a coal-burning furnace. Backflow from an open sewer collected in a torpid pool near a former trash chute. At the cellar's midpoint, a six-foot-long wooden table surrounded by metal folding chairs was laden with soda bottles and bags of pretzels and potato chips. Party streamers hung from the table's sides. Balloons, taped to a wall, surrounded a crudely printed cardboard sign that read simply: *WELCOME HOME.*

By now, news about the shooting was spreading like wildfire throughout Brownsville and adjacent neighborhoods. Spreading, as well, was a virulent form of hysteria, born of a longstanding antipathy toward the police. Threats were being issued, anger building, charges voiced that Holland and Cook had killed C. J. Johnson in cold blood. Several onlookers charged that the two White officers had been seen drinking in their patrol car prior to the shooting. Others said they saw the patrol partners joking about the incident after the fact, while attempting to concoct a cover-up for what had happened. Instances of arson, along with looting incidents in protest of the shooting, were being falsely reported. Cops in riot gear were said to be massing on the outskirts of Brownsville.

By now, Holland, as per NYPD protocol, had been relieved of his firearm, and the 73rd Precinct's patrol supervisor summoned to verify both his and Cook's identities and the specifics of their assignment. Evidence was being carted off in boxes and plastic bags, radio voice transmissions being reviewed. Both officers' service revolvers were confirmed as being authorized, checked for state of load and powder residue, and certified to be functioning properly. A detective confirmed a single spent round from Holland's gun, emptied the remaining cartridges, and bagged the weapon. That, along with blood tests and the personnel records of Holland and Cook, was already on its way to Borough Command.

The collective bargaining agreement between the PBA and the city required that Holland and Cook remain at the shooting scene until the arrival of the union's shop steward. It would be forty-five minutes before Angelo De Luca would arrive to inform the officers to formally invoke their right to counsel, and to neither make statements nor answer questions unless a PBA attorney was present. Only after they'd agreed to that were Holland and Cook escorted from the cellar by a protective phalanx of fellow officers.

"Racist murderers!" a voice rang out.

"Sons of bitches!"

The crowd surged forward, held at bay by a line of police. People began cursing, jeering, pointing fingers. Photographers' flashbulbs lit up the street.

"Fuckin' pigs ... you're gonna pay for this!" someone shouted as Holland and Cook, their faces shielded by other cops, were hustled into the rear of a waiting patrol car and quickly whisked away.

Chapter 20

INSIDE BROOKDALE UNIVERSITY HOSPITAL ninety minutes after his son's shooting, Charles Johnson was joined in his private vigil by the Reverend Josiah Watson, who strode unnoticed past the first-floor nurse's station and entered the waiting room in which Charles remained deep in prayer.

As pastor of Brownsville's Good Shepherd Baptist Church, Josiah Watson had presided for thirty-plus years over the largest Baptist congregation in Central Brooklyn, many of whose worshippers had been drawn to New York to escape their southern roots—and drawn to the church by its spiritual overseer himself.

A descendant of a long line of Black Pentecostal preachers, Josiah Watson, at fifty-two, had made a name for himself on the front lines of the civil rights movement, while serving as a social justice advisor to three U.S. presidents and assisting in nationwide campaigns to integrate housing, workplaces, and schools.

Rev. Watson viewed his pastoral role as offering more than simply spiritual guidance, and his ministry not merely as the religious heart of Brownsville and surrounding communities but, in many ways, as their cultural womb and soul. His efforts had given birth to a wide range of businesses, along with initiatives in day care, adult education, and vocational guidance. His ties to the upper echelons of Black society had lured Mahalia Jackson, Aretha Franklin, and other renowned artists to perform with his church's acclaimed gospel choir.

But Charles Johnson and Josiah Watson also shared a personal bond that transcended their spiritual link. For the past eighteen months, Rev. Watson had been mentoring Charles through a five-year course to become a deacon at the Good Shepherd Baptist Church. He'd also been instrumental in helping his congregant pass his New York State Civil Service exam, paving the way for Charles to land his current job as a subway token clerk.

"My dear friend," the pastor whispered, placing a hand on Charles's shoulder as he approached from behind, officious in his velveteen pulpit robe and clerical collar.

Charles, teary-eyed, rose from his knees and the two men embraced.

"Our entire congregation is standing at your side—praying for you, Eunice, and C. J.—and lending our strength as you face this mighty struggle," Rev. Watson said. "As always, the Good Lord is with you. And with C. J., as well."

Charles thanked Rev. Watson for his sympathetic words and inquired about Eunice, who, the pastor informed him, was under sedation at the couple's apartment, accompanied by several church congregants, along with C. J.'s cousin Marcus, who'd arrived in Brownsville minutes after the shooting.

"Eunice and I wouldn't know what to do without our church," Charles said.

"Of that, you'll never have to worry … nor fear that you'll have to shoulder your burden alone," Rev. Watson said. "Our circle, as you know, is very supportive and close."

Charles thanked him again as the men, facing one another, joined hands.

"Difficult times like these call for prayer," Rev. Watson said.

"I've been doing that," Charles said, "and trying to find a reason why God would—"

"Why *would* he, you ask?" the pastor said.

Nodding, Charles stared at his feet and began to openly weep.

"Perhaps not immediately, but in time you'll come to see that what happened tonight, like everything, is the will of God … part of a much larger plan," Rev. Watson said.

"A *plan*?" asked Charles.

"Yes." Rev. Watson nodded. "God has a plan in mind for all of us. It's not our place to question that plan … but merely to embrace it."

Rev. Watson tightened his hand in Charles's.

"Perhaps it's the Good Lord's will to have C. J. at His side," the pastor said. "And perhaps His plan is for you to be tested so that even through your heartbreak and uncertainty you might become something greater than who you are now."

Charles wanted desperately to believe that, and tried to, even though it was impossible for him to believe that God, as part of any plan, would want to take an innocent boy like C. J. and test Charles in this way.

Rev. Watson bowed his head.

"Dear Lord," he prayed, "Thank you for being at our side. We confess that we don't understand why tragedies like this happen, but we're comforted in knowing that you're here with us, you love us, and that you'll never forsake us."

"Amen," Charles said.

Absorbed in prayer, the men didn't notice when a doctor entered the room. Clad in blood-stained surgical scrubs, cap, and booties, the doctor looked sorrowful and drawn, like someone who'd been laboring long and hard. Slipping off his latex gloves, he extended a hand.

"I'm Dr. Robert Fredericks," he said. "Chief neurosurgeon at the hospital."

"I'm the boy's father," said Charles, shaking the doctor's hand, "and this is Rev. Josiah Watson, pastor of our church."

The doctor nodded grimly and then ushered Charles and Rev. Watson to a row of chairs where the three of them took seats, Dr. Fredericks positioned between Charles and the pastor.

"I'm very sorry for what's happened to your son," the doctor said.

"How is he?" Charles asked.

Dr. Fredericks sighed. "Well, your son, as I'm sure you're aware, was gravely injured ... struck at the top of his skull by a bullet that penetrated his brain."

Charles recoiled, as if he'd been struck by the bullet himself.

"As you might suspect," Dr. Fredericks explained, "injuries like this are most severe in 'friable' organs like the brain."

"*Friable*?" Rev. Watson asked.

"I'm sorry for sounding clinical," Dr. Fredericks said. "Being 'friable' describes the tendency of a solid substance to become dislodged, or break into smaller pieces, under contact or pressure."

Charles cringed.

"In your son's case," Dr. Fredericks resumed, "the bullet that struck him was traveling in such a way that bone fragments from the entry wound were propelled deeply into the brain, causing significant damage."

"What type of damage?" Charles asked.

"I'm afraid," said the doctor, "that every meaningful bodily function—breathing, motor skills, cognitive ability, major organs—was seriously compromised. It's also impossible for us to control the bleeding."

"Is my son still in surgery?" Charles inquired.

"At the moment, he's out of surgery but remains in our O.R., on equipment that enables him, technically, to cling to life."

The doctor then informed Charles and Rev. Watson that while his surgical team had tried everything possible to save C. J.'s life, there was unfortunately little more that they could do.

"Even with the life-support system that he's on," the doctor said, "your son won't be with us for very much longer. I'm terribly sorry."

Doctor Fredericks then told the men that they were welcome to join him in the operating room, where Rev. Watson, with Charles's blessing, could administer to C. J. the last rites of the church, and Charles could have an opportunity to bid his beloved son goodbye.

Chapter 21

IT WAS IMPOSSIBLE to recall anymore—perhaps it *always* would be—but Matt Holland and Rachel Cook somehow always found time to laugh. Laughter was a release, an escape, a way to assuage the air of melancholy and dread that that could sully cops in ravaged neighborhoods like Brownsville. Sometimes, it seemed like the only way to stay sane.

Paired for tedious, often perilous, eight-hour tours, Cook and Holland cracked sardonic jokes, exchanged wisecracks, engaged in dark, gallows humor, and found laughter in incidents that bordered on the frivolous and ludicrous:

> … An eccentric woman standing atop a kitchen chair, fending off an outsized rodent with a broomstick handle.
>
> … A stopped-up toilet that flooded an apartment with rancid waste.
>
> … A larceny suspect who caught his penis in the zipper of his pants.

Once, responding to a 911 call about lusty, unseemly sounds, Cook and Holland discovered that the disturbance was emanating from a trio of lovers engaged in kinky sex. Another time, the officers intervened in a domestic dispute only to find a forest of marijuana plants sprouting from a bathtub.

At times, Cook evoked riotous laughter simply through her ungainly attempts at performing a task or mastering a skill. Holland doubled over hysterically when his rookie partner inadvertently depressed the emergency brake of their patrol car while trying to access the headlights' high beams with her foot. He laughed equally hard when Cook accidentally sideswiped a car in which a pair of teens was making out.

Holland also loved to chide Cook about the first time he ever laid eyes on her, when the rookie officer, toting a pair of shopping bags laden with personal belongings, reported to the 73rd Precinct for her first day as a cop.

"That was a classic," he'd chortle. "You looked like you were delivering bags of groceries to the station house. Guys were doing a double-take, asking: 'Who the hell is that? *That's* what the NYPD sends us to police a neighborhood like Brownsville?'"

"I wish you'd forget about that," Cook would invariably respond.

"I wish I could," Holland would say. "But no one who was there will ever forget the day our precinct's first female officer made her grand entrance!"

Cook never took the ribbing the wrong way; it was simply good-natured fun. Besides, by then, the officers had become regular partners whose mutual respect and admiration transcended idle jibes.

Cook, for her part, was blown away by Holland's proficiency, his record of heroism, and the approbation he was afforded throughout Brownsville. Having been on the job sixteen years, Holland had pretty much seen it all, demonstrating dedication, compassion, resilience, and courage under fire. Widely respected throughout the community, he was known by seemingly everyone, from merchants and school principals to building superintendents and religious leaders. The annual Labor Day Weekend camp he'd helped organize had also won plaudits for affording Brownsville's special-needs children an opportunity to escape the city and experience the upstate New York countryside.

But Holland and Cook, by midyear, had become more than simply regular patrol partners. They'd also become confidantes, allies, friends.

Their bond, in large measure, was forged through the daily drama they witnessed, their interdependence, and an abundance of shared emotions: triumph and setback, heartache and joy, fulfillment and frustration. They rejoiced when justice was done and criminals were taken off the street, and lamented when their efforts were thwarted by judges, juries, politicians, and a criminal justice system that all-too-often seemed dysfunctional. They shielded one another from the perils posed by Brownsville and took delight in providing comfort and support to the people the neighborhood preyed upon.

Yet there was more to the officers' relationship than the sum of all those parts. Just as they were able to mesh as partners, Holland and Cook were also able to mesh as *people.* Each found the other likeable, honest, compassionate, funny, and human. Each admitted to frailties, aspirations, disappointments, and fears. Each spoke openly to the other in conversations that were far-ranging, illuminating, and seemingly endless.

The job, of course, was a prime topic of conversation—not simply the ins and outs of daily patrol, but also about what police work had been like in the past and how it had changed along with both the city and society.

The two of them lamented about how public trust in law enforcement had withered; how what was formerly admiration and respect had morphed into resentment and fear; how police were often seen by inner-city neighborhoods like Brownsville as little more than an invading army, punitive figures whose role was to enforce an unjust system, symbols of everything oppressive, insulting, demoralizing, and intrusive about people's lives.

"Some of that, frankly, is our fault," Holland observed. "There've been too many years of confrontation between police and the community. The stereotypes, attitudes, and patterns of interaction are set in stone. A huge gulf exists."

Holland, clearly, was right about that. The 73rd Precinct, like others in minority communities, had earned a reputation for subpar policing in the past. Brownsville's cops, almost exclusively white, had been cited on numerous occasions for abuse of power, excessive use of force, and other civil rights violations. Departmental investigations had invariably cleared officers charged with malfeasance and misconduct. Others who'd committed policy violations and criminal acts had gone unpunished.

In truth, much of the bad blood between Brownsville residents and police had been fostered under the watch of 73rd Precinct Commander Joseph Borelli's longtime predecessor, a zero-tolerance hardliner who believed that even minor crimes like loitering created a climate that fostered more serious offenses. Among his commonly used tactics had been a controversial practice known as "stop-and-frisk," in which police randomly stopped minorities without cause, searching them for weapons, drugs, and other contraband. Borelli had since halted the practice, focusing instead on fostering a positive relationship between police and Brownsville residents.

"Things don't have to be the way they are between police and the community," Holland said. "I want people to know that I'm not their enemy—that I'm here to make their lives better, to enforce the law but to do it civilly, justly."

"That's why I'm here, too," Cook said.

"Good." Holland smiled. "Then maybe the two of us can make a difference."

But beyond their convivial banter and heartfelt conversations, Cook and Holland's bond was anchored by something far stronger: an abiding sense of confidence. Like many regular police partners, Cook and Holland had grown to trust one another with their lives. It was only natural that they could trust one another in other ways, too.

Before long, Cook found that she was able to confide in Holland about far more than simply the nuances of police work. The two of them talked about families and childhoods, movies and books, music and fashion, politics and religion, and the major issues shaping 1970s America: civil rights, feminism, urban decay, welfare reform, the energy crisis, and a public that had grown weary, divided, and cynical.

Cook talked to Holland about her parents and siblings, her upbringing, past and current boyfriends, and what she was seeking in a lifelong partner. She talked about how much she loved taking long, meandering drives through the upstate fall foliage, losing herself in cool and tranquil mountains, the lush, deep forests, the colors of the trees. She told him how much she cherished summer afternoons at the beach, when the crowds were gone and all that remained were the ocean breeze and the crashing of waves and the scent of sunshine on her skin. She told him how much she wanted one day to have children, an admission she'd made, until that moment, to no one else.

Cook couldn't help but think at times that she hardly knew Holland well enough to usher him into her life in such an intimate way. He was, after all, still a stranger in many ways. But he was a cop, just like her, and he was her partner. And that meant she could trust him as much as anyone—in some ways even more.

Holland, for his part, had come to feel much the same. He never admitted it openly, but inwardly he was pleased to be partnering with a woman because he found himself able to confide to Cook in ways that he never could with a man. Like Cook, Holland knew he was on safe ground with his partner—that she was someone he could trust, someone who'd never ridicule or betray him. And so, he opened himself up to her, candidly and with few holds barred. He talked about his parents and older brother Dan; his wife Katie, and son Thomas, and twin daughters, Angie and Jenny. He talked about what had drawn him to police work, what the job meant to him, and how it still motivated and moved him after all these years.

As they conversed, Cook and Holland discovered, too, that for all their differences in gender, age, religion, experiences, and marital status, they had far more in common. Both were products of New York's working class, born in similar, blue-collar enclaves to parents who'd struggled to make ends meet but somehow managed to never allow their children to feel unhappy or deprived. Both had attended New York City public schools. Both had been raised on tales about the ruinous nightmare of the Great Depression, the arduous ordeal of World War II, and the unbridled optimism that pervaded New York in the postwar years.

Their politics and religious practices weren't all that dissimilar, either. Left-leaning while in college—during the height of the Vietnam War protests, the women's movement, and civil rights demonstrations—Cook found it comforting to learn that Holland's politics weren't as far right as those of most cops, and that he kept an open mind about things like race relations and women's rights. She also found that her FTO wasn't as strictly tied to religion as most cops, even though he'd been raised in a traditional Catholic household. Sure, Holland went to church. But he also skipped services regularly, opting to spend time on home remodeling projects, or in coaching Thomas in Little League, or spending weekends at the Jersey shore, where his in-laws owned a house.

What Cook and Holland had in common beyond even that, though, was the City of New York and the Borough of Brooklyn, where each had been raised and each had been indelibly shaped by the experience.

Holland and Cook spent hours engaged in Brooklyn nostalgia, sharing memories of the borough when it seemed more innocent and unfettered, an almost-mythic realm alive with history, people, and stories. They talked about the borough's patchwork of neighborhoods and how each was an entity unto itself, defined less by geography than by the nationality or ethnic group residing within its boundaries. They talked about what it was like walking as children to six-story, red-brick schools, and laughed about what it was like playing in asphalt-covered schoolyards and on narrow, congested streets while dodging passing cars.

Holland reminisced about steel trolley cars and flocks of pigeons swooping overhead; about children playing curbside in rivers of gushing water from open fire hydrants; about men coming around to sharpen knives and fix umbrellas and deliver block ice and milk; about backyards and side yards transformed into flower and vegetable gardens. Cook talked about hiding under her desk during Cold War Era air-raid drills, and dressing in red, white, and blue for weekly assemblies; talked about acting in school plays and attending pajama parties at which she and her girlfriends spent hours fixing their hair and listening to forty-five-RPM records, practicing dances, and wondering what it would be like to kiss a boy.

"Brooklyn will always be part of us, I suppose," Cook said, "the emotions, the experiences, the memories."

"I'm grateful for that," Holland said. "Brooklyn was a magical place to grow up in. You could walk anywhere, all hours of the day. Windows were open. Doors were never locked. People may have been frightened of many things, but no one was frightened of Brooklyn."

That wasn't necessarily the case anymore, however. Holland and Cook talked about that, too—about how Brooklyn was different now, how it had been wounded and transformed by crushing loss.

Bled by the middle-class flight to the suburbs, Brooklyn's population had plummeted in recent years. Jobs had dried up. Factories and docks had closed. Businesses, restaurants, and breweries had been shuttered. Worst of all, the beloved Dodgers had fled to California, transforming Ebbets Field into a low-income housing project.

All this, of course, had robbed Brooklyn of its uniqueness, its vitality. Once a commercial and cultural powerhouse, the borough had been reduced to something ordinary. Streets had grown meaner. People had grown afraid. Doors and windows were bolted shut, protective gates erected, car alarms being installed. Worse yet, what was unfolding in Brooklyn was happening elsewhere in New York. Crime was up. The school system was crumbling. Subways were decaying. Streets were strewn with litter. Drugs were ravaging entire neighborhoods. Dwindling finances were forcing services to be cut.

And it wasn't just a local issue.

People were talking not only about New York's demise, but also about the death of the American City itself. Cities, it was said, were becoming little more than congested, crime-riddled magnets for the poor, and no one seemed capable of reversing the tide. The commitment to neighborhoods like Brownsville had seemingly vanished. Pleas for federal and state aid were falling on deaf ears. Symbolic trash burnings and school boycotts had little effect. Other forms of social protest had proven fruitless. The prevailing trend now was simply to turn the other cheek.

About all of this, Cook and Holland were well aware. And so, even as they spoke with fondness about Brooklyn's past, they spoke with sorrow over its current state, its seeming demise.

Other than the times he talked about his wife and children, Cook would never hear Holland speak so lovingly as he did when he talked about the Brooklyn of his youth. Nor would she ever see his smile fade so quickly as when he spoke about how that Brooklyn seemed so lost and distant and broken now.

"The Brooklyn you and I came from is history," he told Cook one day. "It's *gone*. I wish we could bring it back, but I guess we can't, can we?"

"I'm afraid this is what we're left with," said Cook, nodding in the direction of Brownsville's broken, tired streets. "This and the question: where's it all headed?"

"Actually, there's one other question," Holland said.

"What's that?"

"It's 'What can the two of us do to help save what's left?'"

* * *

But there was far more about her FTO that Rachel Cook came to learn.

For one thing, Matt Holland was unlike most New York City cops, at least in terms of lineage. He had no uncles or cousins or brother on the job, no bloodline ties of any kind. Nor was he even native to the boroughs outside of Manhattan from which the NYPD generally drew its cops.

Holland's parents, of Norwegian descent, had their roots in Canonsburg, Pennsylvania, where Matt's father, Carl, worked for years at the nearby Bethlehem Steel plant. By 1940, however, Carl Holland had his sights on New York—moving with Matt's mother, Irma, to Greenpoint, a working-class enclave on the Brooklyn-Queens border. Matt was six years old at the time. His brother Dan was eight.

With America on the brink of World War II, jobs in New York were plentiful for ironworkers like Carl, who quickly joined the workforce of what was then the city's largest employer: the Brooklyn Navy Yard.

In existence already for more than a century, the Navy Yard had a proud and weighty history, as the birthplace for hundreds of legendary warships and historic vessels. In 1940, the Yard was busy round the clock, building much of America's two-ocean fleet. Working sixty hours a week in twelve-hour shifts, workers like Carl labored on blistering-hot decks under beach umbrellas during the summer, makeshift shelters during snowfalls, and the glare of massive floodlights at night.

When Matt and Dan were still young, Carl took them to his celebrated, bustling workplace. The boys were flabbergasted. All around them was motion and clamor: metal being bolted and drilled; freight cars being loaded with raw steel and prefabricated components; heavy-duty cranes hoisting bulkheads, engines, propellers, smokestacks, fuel tanks, cannons, decks, and superstructures. Showers of sparks rained from the decks of giant warships.

Forges blazed. Torches popped, as men welded cast-iron plates in air thick with clouds of spent acetylene and diesel exhaust.

Carl Holland and his sons, wearing hardhats and work gloves, meandered about as electricians installed signal systems, machinists worked on gun turrets, ship joiners crated equipment, draftsmen designed ventilating systems, and plumbers molded fittings from sheet lead. All the while, Carl explained the complex choreography unfolding around them: the planning and coordination; how everyone played a critical role; how all of them worked as part of a team.

Matt Holland's life was indelibly shaped by imagery tied to America's industrial home front. Some nights, as World War II raged overseas, air raid sirens would sound, and the family would lower their blackout curtains and huddle in their dinette, quiet and still, waiting for the all-clear. Sometimes, Matt and Dan would sit with Carl in the living room, listening to war reports on the family's Philco console, then poring over *The New York Times* war map as their father detailed the Allied and Axis strategy and explained how so many brave people were fighting hard so that all of them back home could remain strong and free.

Brooklyn, like much of the home front, was fully immersed in the war. Gun emplacements sprouted up on rooftops. Searchlights crisscrossed the nighttime sky. Patrols scoured beaches in search of enemy submarines. The Hollands did their part, as well. Matt's mother, Irma, served as a School Defense Aid volunteer. Matt and Dan participated in scrap metal drives. And four nights a week, Carl Holland donned a helmet, whistle, and armband, serving as a volunteer air raid warden.

Some nights, Matt and Dan—donning armbands, toy whistles, and flashlights—would accompany their father to their sixth-floor rooftop, manning the searchlight to help keep people safe. And that's when it first occurred to Matt that he, like his father, might one day do his part to help protect the city he loved. That's when it occurred to him for the first time that he might one day become a New York City police officer.

All he ever wanted from the job, Holland told Cook, was a chance to make a difference. It wasn't about the NYPD's steady, middle-class paycheck, or the union-protected benefits, or the lifetime pension he was entitled to after twenty years. Nor was it about anything heady or heroic. Holland, instead, was drawn to the notion of resurrection—and even a renaissance—for the city he loved. He hated it, he told Cook, when people saw New York as a sad and passé joke, its decline inevitable, its greatness a distant memory. Instead, Holland saw New York as a living, breathing entity—forever evolving, forever rebounding, forever worth saving. And he saw himself as someone, like his father, who could help preserve it and somehow make it better.

Holland carried that ambition through high school and beyond. By then, he'd met the woman he'd marry.

Katie Maglio was a fellow student at Grover Cleveland High School. The only child of Irish-Italian parents, she excelled at academics and was active in the drama club. Her first love, however, was photography. Indeed, Katie Maglio could take the most exquisite photos, with an eye for capturing human emotions. Her photos, stories, and poetry appeared regularly in the school newspaper and literary journal. And that's how she and Matt first crossed paths.

Matt was setting long-distance running records as a senior and was training for the biggest track meet of his life, the New York City Championships. Katie was assigned to write an article about him for the school paper.

Years later, Katie would tell family and friends how surprised she was to discover that Matt was nothing like the shallow, haughty, self-centered jock she'd envisioned. Instead, she found him humble, polite, and funny, with the sweetest of smiles. Matt, for his part, thought Katie was smart and sensitive and easy to talk to—and had the most beautiful eyes he'd ever seen.

Katie posed him on the track, gazing into the distance as if in search of a prize. He laughed and grew excited when he read her article, which included flattering references to his looks. She sent him several of the photos she'd taken, along with a gracious note. They fell in love on their first date and were inseparable throughout high school and two years of community college. A year later, they were married. And soon after that, they were moving from Brooklyn.

Staten Island had always been the most isolated of New York's boroughs—quiet, remote, and sparsely populated. For decades, it had been accessible only by ferry. Linked to the rest of the city by the Verrazano-Narrows Bridge, however. The once-forgotten borough was experiencing an unprecedented land rush. New residents flooded in. Homes, shopping centers, and schools sprouted up on what formerly was unsettled farmland. Nearly overnight, the island was transformed from a semi-rural area of tiny villages into a densely populated bedroom community. And Katie Holland's father, Ray, was smack in the middle of it.

With Staten Island's housing boom fully underway, Ray Maglio's four-man roofing-and-siding business quickly grew into a thriving company whose former focus—the renovation of aging farm-like dwellings—quickly took a back seat to a flurry of business on another front. The company was soon building single-family tract homes throughout Staten Island.

Despite its growth, Staten Island remained far quieter and more pastoral than most of the city, soon becoming a bastion for police officers, firefighters, and other civil servants. Matt and Katie moved to the Castleton section, a modest neighborhood of split-level and Cape Cod-style homes. Their modest Cape Cod, on a quiet cul-de-sac mere minutes from Katie's parents, had a fenced-in backyard, steeply pitched gable roof, and window flower boxes along its front and sides. Katie furnished the house mainly with hand-me-downs, and filling the flower boxes with roses, geraniums, and begonias. Ray Maglio helped Matt finish the basement, remodel the bathrooms and kitchen, and build a backyard deck.

And Katie and Matt Holland began raising a family.

When Rachel Cook visited the Hollands' home for the only time, four months after she'd joined the NYPD, Matt Holland was working on an addition to the dwelling. His twin daughters, eight years old, had always shared a single bedroom. It was time for each to have a room of her own, just like the Hollands' twelve-year-old son, Thomas.

"I guess you probably know this already, but Matt's a handy guy to have around the house," Katie said, while serving dinner. "Don't get me wrong;

he's got his faults, believe me. There isn't a man alive who doesn't. But he can build anything he sets his mind to and fix anything that's broken."

Leaning over, she kissed her husband gently atop his head.

"All except Brownsville," she laughed. "Even *you're* having trouble fixing that, aren't you, Matty?"

"Maybe so," Matt winked. "But we're working on it—aren't we, Cook?"

"We sure are," Cook said.

"Oh yeah, and I forgot to mention that he's also the world's greatest optimist," Katie joked. "You know, he still believes the Dodgers are returning to Brooklyn!"

"When we finish cleaning things up, they will!" Holland laughed. "You'll see. Brooklyn's coming back. One day, people are going to pay big bucks to live there. Mark my words!"

Later that day, he proffered Cook a gift. It was photo Katie had taken, several years earlier, when Matt was going through a troubling, job-related feeling of despair.

"Police work and Brownsville were making me feel like the entire world had been drained of color," Holland explained. "It was like being trapped in a black-and-white movie. Everything seemed bleak and somber. Anyway, one day I mentioned this to Katie. Next thing you know, these photos start showing up."

"Photos?"

"Yeah, photos that Katie took. They just start showing up, all over the house. Then they start showing up in the mailbox, in the pocket of my uniform, on the seat of my car."

"What were they?"

"They were photos of butterflies."

"Butterflies?"

"Uh-huh," Holland said, "go figure. Butterflies—on the branches of trees, on flowers and shrubs, flying around."

"And they had lots of color?" asked Cook, catching on.

"Every color you could possibly imagine," Holland said.

Butterflies, Katie told her husband, were the most colorful things she could capture in the lens of her camera, her special way of helping her husband retain his sense of balance. The photos she took were more than just skillfully composed images on film, more than simply gifts. In their own way, they were nothing less than love letters—gentle, everyday reminders of the presence, even in her husband's troubled world, of the brightest and most beautiful colors.

Holland handed Cook a photo of a yellow-and-indigo butterfly taking flight.

"Hold onto this as a reminder that everything isn't as colorless and bleak as the things you might see in Brownsville," he said.

Cook was speechless.

Holland then showed his partner where he kept an identical photo tucked inside the lining of his police cap, along with a holy card of Saint Michael, the patron saint of cops, and a photo of Katie and the kids.

"Hang onto it," he told Cook. "Remember what it's about. You never want to feel hopeless or alone when you're out there on the street."

* * *

It would never become anything sexual. Oh, occasionally there may have been the kind of playful flirting that sometimes transpires between men and women who work in close quarters. Other times, there'd be a closeness and warmth spawned by shared exposure to danger, trauma, and stress. And every so often, Rachel Cook couldn't resist a fleeting, half-baked fantasy about what it would be like to become intimate with a man she had truly come to love.

But that's as far as it ever went.

For one thing, Matt Holland was unfailingly devoted to Katie and his children; to Cook, he'd always be forbidden fruit. A dalliance would be not only insanely inappropriate, but also diminish the stature Cook desperately wanted to hold her partner in. Cook saw Holland as a big brother, and that's how she loved him. Besides, what attracted her to her partner as much as anything was his very inaccessibility—the bond he had with Katie, his fidelity, the couple's connection to each other. It was comforting for Cook to believe that such a firm and lasting bond was possible between man and woman. It was something to aspire to. Cook would admire the Hollands' marriage from afar and do nothing whatsoever to damage it. To hurt Matt Holland in any way, to stain him or damage what he had, Cook felt, would be like destroying a dream of her own. Instead, she admired Holland from her unique vantage point, as his partner.

And there was much to admire.

Holland, after a stint in the Navy, had become a police officer at age twenty-six, his sixteen-year record impeccable, his status nearly exalted. To the cops of the 73rd Precinct, Matt Holland had done something far more important than winning medals and honors—he'd paid his dues, and gained their respect, by virtue of his work ethic and character. His performance was worthy of the highest form of compliment any police officer could proffer: Matt Holland was a standup guy. Day in and day out, he did his job, absent of griping or histrionics—an honest, solid professional who could always be counted on and always did things the right way.

Along with his Medal for Valor had come a gold shield, a promotion to first-grade detective, his assignment as FTO, and a bump in salary. The NYPD had offered him a transfer to the Detective Division, too; to a special unit, or even to a precinct on Staten Island, a cushy, quiet "C" House close to home.

But he turned the transfers down.

Instead, Matt Holland informed NYPD brass that he preferred to stay in uniform, at the precinct level. Believe it or not, he told them, he'd grown to like it in Brownsville, loved the spontaneity and pace of street patrol, the variety of calls, and the people he came across. He'd become involved in the community, too, especially with the Labor Day Weekend camping trips for special-needs children that he and other cops conducted, sojourns that were so popular there was a two-year waiting list to attend.

Other perks, Holland admitted, had also been too good to pass on. They came with seniority and were quietly proffered by the precinct's desk sergeants: A steady seat in a patrol car; a regular partner; first crack at vacation time; and, most importantly, no more rotating tours. For Matt Holland, there were no longer grueling midnight-to-eights—no more four-to-midnights either, unless he volunteered for them, or a fill-in was needed for someone on vacation. Holland had earned the right to work straight eight-to-fours, weekdays only. Normal hours, so he could spend time working around the house and on construction sites with Ray Maglio. Normal hours, so he could spend time with Thomas and the twins. Normal hours, so he could come home every night and be with Katie.

"Has the job worked out for you, Matt?" Cook asked one day.

"Well, I can't say it's been a disappointment." Holland shrugged. "It's got its ups and downs, like anything else. You take the good days with the bad."

Pausing, he smiled. "But I love it. I really do. It gets in your blood, you know, becomes part of who you are. I've always loved being a police officer. I think being a New York City cop is the greatest job in the world."

The greatest reward, Holland said, wasn't the medals or the acclaim or all the perks. It was simply knowing he was doing the job right, that he was making a difference. The record bore him out, too. Aside from all of Holland's medals and citations, there'd been two hundred-and-twenty felony and misdemeanor arrests, countless acts of patience and compassion, and not a single civilian complaint.

No shootings, either.

Despite all the action across all the years, in the most crime-ridden neighborhood in all of New York, never once had Matt Holland brutalized a prisoner, or abused a citizen, or taken a bribe. Never once had he drawn a reprimand, or failed a partner, or saw Brownsville and its people through a lens of hatred or callousness, apathy or race. Never once in sixteen years on the job had he ever so much as fired his gun.

Chapter 22

IT WAS SHORTLY BEFORE 11:00 PM, roughly two hours after the shooting, when Matt Holland and Rachel Cook were transported under heavy police guard from Brookdale University Hospital to the 73rd Precinct. And it was only after hours of grueling interrogation that the officers—Holland initially, and then Cook—were made aware of the full scope of that evening's tragedy.

"Officer Cook," an Internal Affairs investigator said near the end of Cook's interrogation, "we've become aware, even in the initial stages of our investigation, that the 911 call the station house received—and the subsequent 10-31 radio code that was relayed to you and Detective Sergeant Holland—created a grossly false impression."

"A *false impression*?" Cook was nonplussed.

"In other words," the investigator said, "the call that you and your partner were responding to made what was happening in the cellar seem like something that it wasn't. Are you aware of that?"

"No, I'm not." Cook glanced at Eddie Shearson. The PBA attorney seemed equally confused.

"Did you ever consider what I just informed you about to be even a possibility?" the investigator pressed.

"I'm not sure I understand the question," Cook stammered.

"Did you ever think, Officer Cook," the investigator elaborated, "that the 911 call you and Detective Sergeant Holland responded to last night might not have been a burglary-in-progress at all ... that it might have been something else?"

"No." Cook shook her head. "We both assumed—"

"We know what the two of you *assumed*, officer," the investigator said curtly. "But did it ever occur to either you or your partner that perhaps the person who'd called the police might've been mistaken about what was taking place—and the 'burglary-in-progress' she reported might not have been a crime at all, but something entirely different?"

"No." Cook felt a sinking feeling in the pit of her stomach. "That never occurred to me … or, I believe, to Detective Sergeant Holland."

"And what about *now*?" the investigator asked. "Do you still believe that you and your partner responded to a burglary-in-progress in that cellar?"

"I'm not sure anymore what we walked into down there," Cook replied. "I only know what wound up happening."

"Well, let me tell you what our preliminary investigation suggests," the IAD guy said, stonily.

He then proceeded to tell Cook the same thing he'd told Matt Holland at the conclusion of Holland's questioning. He told her that the fourteen-year-old boy that Holland had shot apparently suffered from some sort of unspecified physical disability, and that very likely the boy was hearing-impaired—and because of that, as far as anyone could tell, he was virtually incapable of responding appropriately to the officers' commands. He also told Cook that the 10-31 the officers had responded to was not a burglary-in-progress at all but had emanated instead from a group of six teenagers preparing the cellar for a surprise homecoming party, and that the supposed gunshot the 911 caller reported was likely an exploding firecracker from the July 4th celebration on the street. He further informed Cook that the shooting victim had apparently mistaken Matt Holland for his cousin—a soon-to-be-discharged army soldier—and had assumed that one of his friends, attempting to enhance the element of surprise, had switched off the light when the officers burst into the cellar. And instead of running to attack her partner, Cook was told, the boy who'd been shot—the so-called shadow that rushed the officer—was actually attempting to greet his cousin with a welcoming embrace.

It was also then that police officials informed Cook that, roughly an hour earlier, the teenaged boy that Matt Holland accidentally shot had succumbed to his wounds on the operating table at Brookdale University Hospital.

"There was ... no way for either of us to know any of that," Rachel Cook sputtered, feeling the muster room sway.

She then whispered something inaudible and asked to be excused, feeling that, once again, she was once again going to be violently ill.

* * *

By the time they wrapped up the initial questioning, it was shortly after 9:00 AM, nearly twelve hours since the shooting. One by one, the investigators and police brass who'd crowded into the 73rd Precinct muster room dispersed, pausing to chat with officers gathered outside. Off in the distance, the skyline of Manhattan could be seen jutting through a gauzy summer haze. That's where the investigation would be headed now.

Matt Holland was escorted to the precinct locker room by plainclothes detectives. There, he gathered his belongings and stuffed them into a gym bag, before being marched to a holding area, where his wife and father-in-law had been waiting for the past nine hours.

"I love you, Matt," Katie Holland said as she ran up to embrace her husband.

"I didn't mean it," said Holland, his eyes empty and glazed. "I never meant to hurt that boy."

"I know," Katie said, tearfully. "We *all* know."

"I'm sorry, Matty," said Ray Maglio, embracing his son-in-law.

"Me too, Pop," Holland said.

"Just know that we believe in you and we're here for you, every step of the way," Ray Maglio said.

Holland nodded, burying his head on Katie's shoulder.

"It's all right," Katie said, stroking his face. "I'm here with you now."

And there the three of them stood, holding one another as the precinct's other cops, unable to watch, stood to the side, barely noticing as Rachel

Cook, glassy-eyed, walked past them, arm-in-arm with her sister Susan, before quietly exiting the station house.

A sergeant was dispatched to escort Katie Holland and Ray Maglio to the Hollands' home, so that the NYPD could take possession of the officer's off-duty firearm. Holland was then led out the door and down the station house steps, past the knots of cops gathered outside, and off to police headquarters.

"Hang in there, Matty!" a cop shouted, as they placed Holland in the rear seat of an unmarked car, a pair of detectives flanking the officer.

"Stay strong!" another cop shouted, as the squad car pulled from the curb, disappearing like a ghost into the steam-like haze.

"You can kiss his ass goodbye," a cop on the station house steps said. "His entire life just turned into a living, fuckin' hell."

"I wouldn't want to be in his shoes," a plainclothes guy said. "Worst nightmare you can imagine for any cop. He'd be better off dead himself now."

"Better circle the wagons, boys," the first cop warned. "The shit's gonna fly around here like none of us have ever seen."

He nodded toward a group of people huddled in a doorway across the street, pointing at the officers and whispering among themselves.

"Mark my words," the cop said. "White cop shoots Black kid—you know how that story goes. *Phewee*! The fuckin' lid's gonna blow off Brownsville now ... just you wait and see."

Part 2

Show me a hero and I will write you a tragedy.

—F. Scott Fitzgerald, *The Crack-Up*, 1945

Chapter 23

THE PROTESTS BEGAN almost immediately. Indeed, no sooner had news of C. J. Johnson's shooting reverberated throughout Brownsville than hordes of angry demonstrators began gathering outside the 73rd Precinct station house to voice their outrage over the incident.

"Another Black child has been taken from us by a police officer's bullet!" a protest leader shouted into a bullhorn, his tightly coiffed Afro-style hair a burgeoning symbol of Black pride.

"Once again," the burly protestor shouted, "an innocent Black life has been snuffed out callously and without justification by the brutal, racist officers sworn to serve our neighborhood. And once again, we're left to mourn and beg for answers!"

The speaker pointed to a bedsheet mounted across a pair of metal poles. On it, a single word was scrawled in red paint:

ENOUGH!

"We're gathered here today to say 'enough'!" the speaker proclaimed. "The shooting of this young boy is the breaking point! We will no longer tolerate racially motivated acts of police brutality, excessive use of force, or lack of accountability. This time, we demand action! This time, we demand justice!"

Their ranks rapidly swelling, the protestors shouted their concurrence.

"Brownsville lost an innocent young boy last night and we're not only grieving, but we're also outraged!" said the speaker, sweating profusely in the fierce summer heat.

"The police shield in America has become a license to kill," he told the crowd. "But we're tired of being terrorized by police, tired of burying black children! It's time we sent a message that these shootings are unacceptable ... that it's time for police officers who wantonly kill to face the music!"

Other speakers, leaping atop the roofs of parked cars, took turns with the bullhorn, their sentiments fueled by years of community-police antipathy. Curses were voiced. Fists were raised, bottles and rocks hurled at the station house, whose doors and windows were shuttered and bolted shut.

Within the hour, another crowd had assembled, this time in front of the Amboy Street apartment building where the shooting had occurred, directly outside the Johnson family's second-floor window. Passersby swelled the irate throng. Protests were audible for blocks.

Sensing the potential for civil unrest, the NYPD issued a hastily written press release, urging calm and pledging a comprehensive, impartial, and timely probe into the shooting. Specially trained crisis counselors were also dispatched to Brownsville. Neither of those actions, however, did anything to calm emotions. Bogus accounts of the shooting were being voiced now, as supposed eyewitnesses emerged to provide chilling details of alleged police misdeeds. A teenager claiming to have been in the cellar at the time of the shooting swore that Matt Holland had tried to suffocate C. J. Johnson, pinning the youth to the floor before shooting him at close range in the head. Holland and Rachel Cook, it was charged, had kicked in the door to the cellar and wantonly sprayed it with gunfire. Others charged that the two White cops had ignored the defenseless teen's pleas to spare his life, hurling racial slurs as each officer fired a fatal shot.

Within minutes, a virulent form of hysteria was spreading through the agitated horde, as allegations of police misconduct grew increasingly outlandish, and protestors lashed out blindly at the two White officers. A building tenant swore that C. J. Johnson was shot *not* in the cellar, as police claimed, but in the courtyard behind the building—his body then dragged to the cellar so that police could concoct an excuse for the teen's cold-blooded murder. Another tenant said she'd heard that the fourteen-year-old was purposely allowed to bleed to death rather than being transported immediately to the hospital. Yet another supposed eyewitness condemned police for allegedly handcuffing the mortally wounded boy and callously dumping him into a patrol car, all while fending off agitated bystanders at gunpoint.

"An innocent Black boy was shot dead by two White police officers who did not exercise restraint, did not exercise sound judgment, and were aggressive and reckless!" a speaker declared. "This shooting is not simply another 'isolated incident' or another 'terrible mistake' or another 'unfortunate tragedy,' as the police like to call them. No! It's part of a pattern of callous, unjustified brutality, systemic racism, and officers who abuse their authority … a pattern of 'business as usual' for the NYPD."

Pausing for effect, the speaker scanned the crowd.

"When do we finally say enough?" he implored. "Enough of police acting without fear of consequence! Enough of police exercising the power of judge, jury, and executioner! Enough of police getting away with murder!"

He then pointed in the direction of the 73rd Precinct.

"We've let 'business as usual' continue for far too long in Brownsville!" he shouted. "We will no longer stand for what has been considered 'normal.' This incident is our rallying cry! We must not allow this moment of protest to simply fade away! We're here to tell our city and our police: No more! Never Again! Enough is enough!"

"Enough is enough!" the protestors shouted in unison.

"Enough is enough … enough is enough!"

The raucous, angry throng cheered. Wildly enough so that its cheers and its chants could be heard in all ends of the community. Wildly enough so that it was apparent that a compelling drama was unfolding in Brownsville, gaining momentum by the minute, and threatening to fracture the neighborhood's fragile, uneasy peace.

Chapter 24

By the time Matt Holland arrived home, drained from his eighteen-hour ordeal, his house was flooded with well-wishers. It was 3:00 PM by then, but smatterings of supporters had begun gathering at the Hollands' modest dwelling since early that morning when news about the shooting first broke.

By then, coverage of the incident—including photos of Holland and Rachel Cook being led from the Amboy Street cellar—was front and center in the city's newspapers, the focus of nonstop TV and radio coverage. And although neither Holland's nor Cook's identities had been divulged, word of mouth about the pair's involvement in the shooting had quickly spread within police circles. By midday, the Hollands' house was filled to the brim with supporters, including a sizeable contingent of off-duty cops.

In the kitchen, family and friends congregated around a tearful Katie Holland, who sat, downcast and crying, at the kitchen table. Nearby, Matt's brother, Dan, huddled with Father Michael Caruso, chaplain of the NYPD's Holy Name Society, while Carl and Irma Holland, Matt's parents, chatted in hushed tones with Katie's parents, Ray and Ruth Maglio. The entire scene resembled a wake.

Fresh off his second round of questioning, at NYPD headquarters, Matt Holland was driven home by PBA President Red McLaren. Awake for more than thirty hours by then, Holland was disoriented and queasy. Katie greeted him at the front door with a tearful embrace. Holland's eight-year-old twin daughters ran to embrace him, as well. Thomas, chest-high to his father, hugged him as if he'd never let go.

"You alright?" Katie whispered.

Holland nodded, clinging to her tightly.

"Remember, Matty," Katie said, "I'm here for you. I'll *always* be here."

"I know," the officer said, softly.

Holland hugged Thomas, kissing his son atop his head. He then swept the twins up, one in each arm, and kissed them, as well. Carl and Irma Holland embraced their son, and then Ray and Ruth Maglio did the same, and Matt's brother Dan—and, one by one, all the others in the house.

"I just want you to know, Matty, that every cop in the city is behind you a thousand percent," said Bobby Foster, a fellow cop from the seven-three. "All of us understand what happened down in that cellar. We know it was a 'clean shoot.' You've got our total support, brother."

Matt Holland mouthed his gratitude, and then caught the eye of Father Michael Caruso. "Pray for me, Father," he said.

"I'll pray for *everyone*," the priest said. "God knows, all of us will need it."

And then, all the well-wishers backed away, so that Matt Holland could enter his home, and his children could be driven to stay with Katie's parents, and Holland could grab something to eat and get some sleep before he'd have to report downtown, first thing in the morning, to answer another round of questions.

"Tell me about it," Katie said, when the two of them were alone.

"I don't know if I can," Matt murmured.

"You're safe with me, Matty," Katie said. "You know that, don't you?"

Holland nodded. "That much I've always known."

"And you've always known we can talk about anything in the world, right?" Katie said. "No holds barred."

"Yes," Matt Holland said, beginning to cry. "I've always known that, too."

* * *

When the phone call came, she was at her parents' beach house, down the Jersey shore, waiting for Matt to join the family for their July 4th weekend celebration. He was expected sometime in the wee hours, after the four-to-midnight he'd been working only because he'd traded the tour out with another cop.

Only, he'd never made it to the house.

Instead, it was shortly after 10:00 PM when the telephone rang. The kids were asleep by then, drained from a sun-splashed day at the beach. Katie's parents were asleep, too. Katie, however, was wide awake. Matt, after all, was still on the job.

"There's ... been an incident, Katie," the 73rd Precinct desk sergeant said, his voice scratchy, almost dreamlike.

This time, however, it wasn't one of Katie Holland's dreams.

For the past sixteen years, in those dreams, there'd be phone calls like this one in the middle of the night—calls that would jolt Katie awake and summon her to some dreary city-run hospital where off-duty cops would be rushing in to donate blood, and the mayor and police commissioner would be talking to reporters, and Matty would be lying in the ICU, tied to intravenous drips and ventilators. There were other people in Katie Holland's dreams, too: nurses and doctors; paramedics and priests; friends and family members crying and praying and offering consolation; neighbors and police wives delivering platters of food and telling Katie how she had to stay strong, for Matty and the kids.

It wasn't quite like that when the actual call came. Sure, Katie Holland found herself racing in the middle of the night to a hospital in Brooklyn, but at least Matt hadn't been injured or killed. Something unimaginably tragic had happened, to be sure, but at least her Matty was alive. At least he'd be coming home to her and the kids.

Matt Holland was alive, all right—even though by the time Katie got to see him, it seemed as if no small part of him had died.

Katie had waited with her father for more than eight hours at the 73rd Precinct station house, all through Matt's examination at the hospital and his preliminary interrogation. That was difficult enough in itself, knowing that Matt had to weather his melancholy ordeal alone, that she couldn't console him or talk to him, that all she could do was stand by helplessly and wait.

Just like she'd done, for all the years Matt had been a cop.

Like most police wives, Katie Holland had long ago learned to live with her nightmares about phone calls in the middle of the night, and patrol cars pulling up in front of the house with news even more dire than tonight's. She'd adapted to the stark realities of police work: the dangers, the unpredictability, the incessant crises, the loneliness, the fear. What she'd never been able to completely shake, however, was a different kind of fear. It wasn't the thought of Matt getting injured or killed. It was the thought that police work might somehow cripple or destroy their marriage.

Katie Holland was onto police work in that way, fully aware of the job's occupational hazards—the absence of a spouse at critical times; the need for one parent to assume dual roles; the changing work schedules; the pressures of living in the public eye; the loneliness and the fear—and how each of those things could be the kiss of death for a marriage. She knew about how the job could change people, slowly, insidiously, from the inside out; saw cops who policed their families the same way they policed the streets—domineering, critical, unyielding, overprotective; knew all about the cops who experienced so much stress that they wound up cynical and alienated and moody, paranoid and bigoted and angry, apathetic and bitter and burnt out; heard all about the cops who drowned their sorrows in alcohol and self-destructive acts, and distanced themselves to a point where they couldn't bring themselves to love their wives or hug their children. She'd heard about others, too. Ruined by the job in some permanent way. Incapable of spontaneity. Devoid of intimacy. Unable to communicate or trust.

More than anything, *that's* what Katie Holland feared. She feared silence and evasiveness in her marriage. She feared a husband who was callous and withdrawn, who couldn't risk being vulnerable, who couldn't touch her or share things with her, a husband who was mangled up and dead inside.

All of that, to Katie Holland, was a fear far more powerful than that of Matt being injured or killed on the job. And while she understood she might not be able to fend off the job's physical dangers, Katie knew she could try to prevent the other repercussions she feared, the psychic wounds. It didn't matter if the stories about police marriages were realities or myths; Katie Holland wouldn't chance it. She wouldn't close her eyes to the things she feared the most, nor pretend they didn't exist. She wouldn't allow Matt's job to kill the precious gift the two of them had, or become a scapegoat for a failed marriage.

And so, she'd worked at it. Worked long and hard.

Katie Holland knew that her love, enduring as it was, wasn't nearly enough—that it would take more than the usual amount of commitment, understanding, and patience to make her marriage work. So, she'd done more than simply *love* Matt. She became the best wife a police officer could possibly have.

When she heard about how cops on four-to-midnight tours would come home to a darkened, quiet house, and unwind with a drink and late-night TV, she left the lights on for Matt, and assigned him household chores to help him shift gears and unwind. When she heard about how cops could become disconnected from their families, she left him notes about the children's activities. When she heard about how the accumulated stress of the job could crush even the strongest of spirits, she devised ways to engage Matt in lighthearted distractions and made it a ritual for them to be together. Out to a movie. Out to dinner. Out shopping. Out for an overnight. Anywhere as long as the two of them were together.

Over the years, Katie had also learned to control her anxiety. She'd learned when to talk to Matt about the job, and when *not* to; learned not to get too emotional or be too judgmental; learned not to berate the criminals or curse the bureaucracy or condemn the politics or try the cases. Mostly, she learned to listen. It was perfectly okay, she made it clear, for Matt to talk about police work; he didn't have to shield her. He could be sickened, saddened, humiliated, outraged, frustrated, elated, defeated—it didn't matter. Anything he felt was acceptable. He could lose control, let his guard down, do whatever he needed to, and Katie was there. If he wanted a sounding board, she was there. If he needed a sympathetic witness, she was there. If he needed a shoulder to cry on, she was there. There was never a need to hold back. It would always be okay, always be safe.

Katie would always be there.

Because of this, their marriage had flourished, grown to a point where they were able to reconcile the dreadful things Matt experienced as a cop with a view of the world that was nevertheless optimistic and hopeful; grown to a point where Matt had learned how not to bring the job home with him but also knew, in the instances when he *did*, that it wouldn't be a problem; grown to a point where they were both secure in their roles and knew that they shared something special that each of them could draw on whenever it was needed.

And they'd done just that—through eighteen years of marriage, three children, and sixteen years of Matt as a cop. They were doing it still, even in the face of Katie's persistent nightmares.

But Katie Holland had quietly nurtured yet another dream across the entirety of her married life, a dream she'd clung to since her teens, a dream that she'd willingly deferred: Katie wanted to open a photography studio and exercise the talents stymied by her role as housewife and mother. Indeed, several years earlier, when their daughters were old enough for pre-school, Katie had taken on part-time work for a local photographer specializing in family portraiture. Quickly, she'd developed a specialty all her own: a creative, new photographic style that defied convention, broke new ground—and sold like hotcakes.

Unlike traditional portrait photographers whose work was often clinical and static, Katie posed her subjects outside the studio, in natural settings, and in ways that enabled her to capture her subjects' persona and spirit in compositions that were at once stylish and unique. Katie photographed children at play, families kissing and hugging, couples dancing and laughing, people immersed in pastimes they loved. She experimented with advances in photographic technology: darkroom procedures, lighting techniques and depth of field, using different shutter speeds, filters, lenses, and backdrops to create stunning contrasts and compositions of shadows and light, capturing certain features in sharp focus while allowing others to be rendered gauzy and almost dreamlike.

Even working only part-time, Katie had made a name for herself. Several of her photos found their way into ads and brochures. A neighborhood weekly ran a feature story. A local library showcased her work. And her services were soon in such high demand that prospective clients had to wait weeks for an appointment.

Still, Katie purposefully held back from going any further in her budding career. Held back to be the devoted mother and the supportive wife. Held back because there were other, more important, things to do, and it wasn't yet *her time*. Like so many women of talent and ambition, Katie would have to wait to act upon her special gift. All she'd allowed herself for now was a fleeting taste of the endeavor she was born to pursue. Serious, full-time photography would have to wait. Matt and the children came first.

"I believe you," she said when Matt recounted, in excruciating detail, what had transpired in the cellar on Amboy Street. And she held him close as he told her how sorrowful he was, how empty and broken inside, and how frightened over the ramifications of what it might mean to them as a family.

"I know that you'd never do anything to harm an innocent boy," Katie said.

She then let her husband talk some more, his emotions spilling from him in gut-wrenching sobs as she held him close, until the two of them fell asleep in each other's arms, tangled up and aching in the stillness of their dark and deserted home.

Chapter 25

RACHEL COOK WENT HOME THAT DAY, TOO.

Departing the 73rd Precinct after her initial round of questioning, the rookie officer was driven by her sister, Susan—first to gather some belongings at the apartment Cook shared with a roommate, and then to her family's residence in Brooklyn. There, Cook felt, she could melt into familiar and comforting surroundings, and find shelter from the maelstrom engulfing her partner and her.

She was wrong.

For while Cook's family surroundings were certainly familiar, they were anything but a comfort or a shelter to her now.

"How in God's name could this have happened?" Frieda Cook fretted, as she puttered about the family's apartment, in a public-housing project in Brooklyn's Canarsie section.

"A young boy is dead, you and your partner are under investigation, there are demonstrations in Brownsville," Frieda Cook said. "Dear God, Rachel ... what's going to happen next?"

"Please, Mom ... *not now*!" Cook beseeched. "I didn't come home for this. A tragic accident has taken place—and yes, all those other things are going on. But please don't make things worse for me than they already are."

"But I'm frightened to death," Cook's mother said.

"So," said Cook, "am I."

At forty-one years old, Frieda Cook was a shrunken, frail woman who'd been a housewife and mother since the age of nineteen. And through all those years, like many women of her ilk, she'd harbored the belief that a woman's place was at home. It was a belief that was as ingrained in Cook's mother as it was conventional—and one that had been applied for twenty-two years to the eldest of her three children.

Indeed, Frieda Cook had never wanted Rachel to become a police officer and had vehemently opposed the idea, right from the start. To Frieda, police work was far too demanding, far too dangerous, far too *inappropriate* for a woman. In Frieda's world, young Jewish women became secretaries or teachers, nurses or bookkeepers, nutritionists, or social workers—or, more likely, housewives and mothers.

But a *cop*?

It was unfathomable, a rarity even for Jewish men. Why couldn't her daughter find a job that was more suitable? Frieda Cook wondered. Why put herself in harm's way? And what was all this talk about a *career*, being a pioneer and a spear-carrier for the women's movement? A feminist? What in the world was that? Why couldn't Rachel be like all the other daughters who were going steady and getting married, starting households, and having babies?

"I think you'd be far better off with another job," Frieda had said all through Rachel's training at the Police Academy and her assignment to Brownsville.

"But the job is right for me," Rachel would say.

"What can be 'right' about a young, White woman carrying a gun and walking patrol in a high-crime, Black neighborhood?" Frieda would ask.

"Because it's something I want to do," Rachel would counter. "It makes me feel worthwhile and special, as if I'm contributing something positive to the city."

"Contribute in another way! Women don't belong on a job like that, plain and simple!"

"That kind of thinking is archaic," Cook would say. "Women today are not the same as in your generation, Mom. They're breaking barriers, proving just as qualified as men. They can hold any job they wish."

"But is being a police officer worth risking your life for?"

"The risks are exaggerated."

"Are they?"

"Yes. Very few officers actually get injured or killed on the job."

"But how can you be happy being a cop?"

"Because I am."

"And why do you have to be so different from other young women."

"Because I am."

It was always the same: do what was conventional; do what was safe; do what other young women did; live your life according to the blueprint Cook had been prescribed; be everything she didn't want to be, at least for now.

"I feel like I'm failing miserably as a mother by allowing you to continue working as a cop," Frieda would lament.

"I'm sorry to break the news to you, Mom, but this isn't something you can control," Cook would say. "I'm all grown up now. You don't have to take responsibility for my decisions. I will."

"I only wish you could be like other daughters," Frieda would say. "They bring home babies ... you bring home a gun."

And that's where their conversations about police work abruptly ended—if they even took place at all anymore. The exchanges, over time, had become far too acerbic—always the same questions, the same answers, the same outcome. After a while, it seemed pointless to talk. Each person—mother and daughter—stood firm, their viewpoints resolute, the wall between them hardening, the distance growing. Indeed, over the past eight months, it felt to Rachel at times as if the job she'd grown to love was like a powerful current, pulling her downstream from a family she loved just as much. Her bond with her mother, once tender and strong, had grown testy and frayed. Contacts with family, once a weekly ritual, had dwindled to a random phone call or occasional visit. Conversations about the job were strictly off-limits. When she wasn't doing so vocally, Frieda Cook protested Rachel's job tacitly, by refusing to allow her daughter to enter the family apartment unless she first removed her off-duty revolver—as much a *symbol* now as a hazard—and tucked it in a closet. Though invited repeatedly, Frieda wouldn't even attend Rachel's Police Academy graduation, refusing to acknowledge the occasion when her daughter had so proudly graduated number one in her class.

"I don't know what I'm going to do about everything that's happening," Frieda lamented, striking a match to light the Sabbath candles, and then placing a kerchief atop her head and reciting her ritual prayer.

* * *

Rachel Cook sat deep in thought as Frieda Cook mouthed her Sabbath blessing, seeing her mother, for the very first time, as a woman who'd aged far beyond her years—becoming, at the same time, intractably withdrawn, fretful, and alone.

"Baruch atoh Adonoy, eloheinu melech ha'olom ..."

Frieda whispered her prayer in Hebrew, her hands moving in circles over the candles.

"... Asher kid'ashanu b'mitzvotav v'zivanu 1'hadlike ner shel Shabbat."

Rachel watched as her mother covered her eyes with both hands and asked that God be with her and her children, and grant them all wellbeing, fulfillment, and peace. Then Rachel's eyes wandered to a photo on the kitchen wall. It was a long, rectangular, black-and-white photo of a company of U.S. Army soldiers, taken during World War II, during boot camp somewhere in Alabama. In the middle of five rows of khaki-clad G.I.s, gazing out from under the brim of his service cap, stood Rachel Cook's father.

David Kaminsky was twenty-two years old in 1943, strikingly handsome in his army uniform, looking proud and fit and ready to go to war. Rachel tried to imagine what he was thinking at the instant the photo was snapped. She wondered if he was frightened or excited, lonely or homesick, troubled or steadfast; wondered if he ever dreamed of coming home from the war and having a daughter like her.

She was happy that he had.

Cook had always had a special kinship, a closeness, with her father. He was very much like her, after all. David Kaminsky, like his eldest daughter, had been an adventurer. He, too, had never been afraid take chances, follow his heart, walk an uncommon path.

Cook's paternal grandparents, Ashkenazi refugees, had immigrated to Cuba on the eve of World War I, chased from Hungary by persecution, poverty, and pogrom. At the time, Cuba had adopted an open-door policy, and Jews were flooding onto the island, seeking refuge from the misery they faced in Eastern Europe. Most saw Cuba as a temporary layover on a journey to America. Others, like David Kaminsky's parents, settled permanently in Cuba—and for good reason. Acts of religious hatred were banned on the tiny island nation, anti-Semitism virtually non-existent. The year-round tropical climate was equally welcoming and there was plenty of work to be had. The Cuban sugar industry was growing by leaps and bounds, as was the island's garment trade and tobacco business. Any number of Jews were prospering in those industries, others finding work as merchants and peddlers in the cities and pueblos dotting the countryside.

David Kaminsky's parents settled in La Habana Vieja, the old quarter of the Cuban capitol, where David was born in 1921. By the time the family immigrated to America, during a pre-World War II Cuban democracy, their surname, like those of many Jews, had been anglicized—the new name decidedly non-denominational. And shortly after he'd returned from the war, David Cook was immersed in a livelihood common to New York's Jewish working-class army: each day, he commuted to Manhattan's bustling Garment Center, where he labored as a needle-trade worker, making women's blouses and skirts.

Studying her father's photo now, Rachel thought about her childhood in Brownsville—the apartment she'd shared with her parents and grandmother above the sweet-scented flower shop; the walks they'd taken through the bright, eternal sunshine; the way all of it had seemed so loving, enduring, and secure. She then thought about the family's move to the modest, three-bedroom apartment she'd lived in through elementary school, high school, and college—fifteen years in all. Rachel was six when the family fled Brownsville and moved to Canarsie. She had a younger sister by then. A brother would soon follow.

For decades, Canarsie, an isolated section of Brooklyn, had possessed huge expanses of open space, sandy flats, and brackish marshes crisscrossed by channels and canals. By the 1950s, however, developers were filling in the swamplands and building neighborhoods of modest, attached one- and two-family brick homes. A home of their own was out of the question for the Cooks. Instead, they moved to a sprawling public-housing complex of umber, eight-story buildings called Bay View, named for its panorama view of nearby Jamaica Bay.

Their apartment had five rooms in all, including a bedroom that the three children shared. It didn't matter that the family's rent doubled. David and Frieda Cook were frightened by the changes taking place in Brownsville; wanted to cleanse themselves of an encroaching feel of poverty, a growing fear of the minorities flooding into Brooklyn. Canarsie was a mere four miles away but, in many respects, seemed a world apart—a place to start anew, a neighborhood populated mainly by white, upwardly mobile, second-generation Italians and Jews, and thousands of Baby Boom children.

It was 1955—an era of innocence, exuberance, and seemingly endless possibilities—when the Cook family moved to Canarsie. A flood tide of postwar optimism was washing over much of New York, pundits talking about a Golden Age of sorts for America, a life that was better, richer, fuller. Even the Dodgers at long last had won their first World Series. Victory banners were slung across Brooklyn's streets. The prevailing mood was buoyant, hopeful, and celebratory.

Best of all, David Cook was still alive.

Studying his Army photo, Rachel remembered playing for hours in the vest-pocket park nestled in the tree-lined walkways of their housing project, then walking to the bus stop to wait for her father to return from work. She remembered how she'd watch for him through the windows of his bus as it wheezed to a stop, waiting for the other workers to disembark until her father would be standing at the curb, sports jacket slung over his shoulder, necktie undone, eyes bright and sparkling in the waning light.

"So," he'd say, smiling, "how's daddy's little girl?"

Cook remembered now how he always called her that. Even as a young girl, she knew it was a cliché. Many fathers said it, but Cook didn't care. She knew it wasn't a cliché to her father. Something in his eyes told her that, something in the way he smiled. David Cook couldn't help but smile when his eldest daughter was by his side. Rachel smiled a lot then, too.

She remembered how some springs, during the Garment Center's slack season, her father would walk her to elementary school—just the two of them, talking and giggling and greeting people they met. She remembered how her father had been the centerpiece of their family, a lover of life who masked whatever sorrows he may have had behind laughter and songs and stories about his former life in Cuba:

> ... about tropical nights, when Havana was lit up and alive with people.
>
> ... about the clean, salty scent of the Caribbean, and how the lights of the Cuban capitol glistened on the waters of the harbor.
>
> ... about cobblestone streets and walks along *El Malecon*, out along the coastline, past palm trees and stately mansions and old colonial fortresses.

David Cook lit up their lives with stories like those, did the same when he danced to the music he'd carried to America from Cuba—Tito Puente, Johnny Pacheco, Celia Cruz, Papo Lucca, Jose Albert, Polito Vega. David Cook loved their energetic, soulful sounds: the conga drums, maracas, claves, trumpets, and bells. He'd raised his family to the flamboyant, foot-tapping sounds of mambo, rumba, cha-cha, reggae, salsa—all of it mixed with the Four Seasons and the Beach Boys and Motown and the music of his young American family.

Rachel remembered the songs her father loved, and how he danced, and the happy, carefree way he smiled. Then, she remembered the phone call that pulled her out of a sophomore political science class at Queens College.

Go home, she was told.

Right away, they said.

Heart attack, they told her.

And she remembered how, blinded by grief, she had to be driven home by a college administrator, feeling as though her entire world had crumbled around her.

David Cook died on the morning of his forty-second birthday; the family was set to mark the occasion that very night. Rachel could never get over that cruel and ironic act of fate, or that she never had the chance to say goodbye. She couldn't get over how, by the time she arrived home, the family's apartment was flooded with neighbors and Frieda Cook was lying on the living room floor next to her husband, a bed sheet over his body. Nor could Cook get over what happened across the days that followed: the rabbi's mournful eulogy; the funeral procession through the sullen, rain-slicked Brooklyn streets; the seven days of *shiva*, when the apartment's mirrors were covered with pillowcases and Rachel and her siblings sat on wooden boxes, mourning ribbons pinned over their hearts.

For weeks, Rachel couldn't get over the thought that a life that had inspired such powerful and joyful emotions in her could have been so anonymous and trifling to the rest of the world. Her father's life, like his passing, had gone so unnoticed, hadn't made a difference, hadn't changed a thing. And now, with his death, Rachel was suddenly fearful that her own life would play out in a similar way. Only years later, did she realize how that singular thought, more than any other, had driven her to try to lead a life that was extraordinary and different, a life as a New York City cop.

* * *

The Sabbath candle that Frieda Cook once lit for her husband hadn't burned for four years now. In its place was a yahrzeit jar, a Jewish symbol of mourning.

The past four years hadn't been easy for Frieda Cook. Of that, Rachel was painfully aware. Frieda and David Cook had been joined at the hip since the day they'd met; they'd been married for twenty-six years, with David's death delivering a crushing blow to his widow.

For nearly four years now, Frieda hadn't been able to as much as look at a photo of her late husband without breaking into tears. Nor had she found the courage to become independent and strong. Like many women of her time, Frieda had drawn nearly all her strength from her husband. David had brought home the paychecks, made the major decisions, set the ground rules for their family. Frieda, in contrast, had been the Good Wife: loyal, dutiful, dependent, passive. When David died, it was as if someone had cut loose a dinghy moored to its dock; Frieda Cook drifted, as if lost at sea. For the first time in her adult life, she didn't have a husband to lean on. Jobless, living off a meager union pension, with three children to support, she didn't even know how to write out a check.

For nearly four years, Rachel had let her mother lean heavily on her, playing the role of both daughter and husband as she finished high school and entered college. She'd helped Frieda make decisions, taught her how to manage money, contributed income from part-time jobs, and tried to fill the gaping void in the lives of her sister and brother. She'd stayed home with her mother nearly every night for the first two of those years, tutoring her siblings, eschewing dates and social occasions, trying to help her mother shoulder the burden of her emptiness and grief.

"It's all right, Rachel," Frieda would assure her. "Go out. You have your own life to live. Don't let me be an anchor."

But Rachel didn't. She couldn't. Her mother's emptiness made her too heartsick to even try. Her guilt was overwhelming. Her desire to live her own life felt like a cruel form of betrayal.

Until one day, just like that, it changed.

It was shortly after Rachel got the police job when she decided it was time to stop drowning in grief and guilt. Encouraged by friends, and using her Police Academy graduation award, she rented a tiny apartment with a former college classmate in a section of Queens known as Bayside.

And, slowly, she began to live again.

Adjacent to the Long Island Sound, Bayside was a pleasant departure from the concrete and clutter of Canarsie. Cook's bedroom window, in a two-story garden apartment, overlooked streets lined with quaint boutiques and eateries. Sailboats and other watercraft sailed in and out of the Sound. People picnicked and flew kites along the shoreline. Each morning, Cook woke to the caw of seagulls, the scent of saltwater mixed with honeysuckle.

Finally, she was *free*.

"If he were alive, he would have stopped you," Frieda Cook said, nodding toward the photo of David Cook. "Believe me, he would've fought you tooth and nail over your godforsaken police job!"

More than ever, Rachel knew, her mother wished her late husband was alive. He'd help Frieda resist the path that Rachel was taking. He'd help his wife shoulder the weighty burden she carried now.

"It wouldn't have mattered a bit, Mom," Rachel said. "If Daddy were alive, I'd be telling him the same things I've been telling you."

"Even now ... with all that's happened, with this horrific shooting?"

"Even now."

The Sabbath candles danced in the lamplight of the kitchen. It was dark outside now. Cook stared out a window, but all she could see was the reflection of her mother standing behind her, as if Frieda was outside the window, somewhere beyond Rachel's reach. It certainly felt that way. Cook knew that her mother was struggling mightily. Worrying, more than ever, was her nature.

"I'll tell you, Rachel, I'm frightened to death over what's going on in Brownsville," Frieda said. "I don't want to light a yahrzeit candle for you, too. I don't want to lose my daughter the same way I lost my husband."

Rachel felt something inside her melt. It was the way her mother looked: so vulnerable, so pained, so old. Even with the challenges she was facing now, Cook didn't have the heart to give Frieda a hard time.

"You won't have to light a candle for me, Mom," she said, softly. "I promise."

"Are you sure?"

"Yes, Mom, I'm sure."

Frieda approached Cook, gently cupping her daughter's face with both hands.

"Don't be angry with me, Rachel," she said. "All I care about is that you're safe. I just want you to come home every night. Nothing else matters."

"I'll come home, Mom." Cook caressed her mother's cheek. "Don't worry. Everything will be all right. I promise. I'll always come home."

Then Cook walked to her childhood bedroom to hide away and wait for whatever was about to unfold for Matt Holland and her and the City of New York. And as she left the kitchen, she paused briefly to touch the photo of her father.

"Help me, Daddy, please," Cook whispered. "Help me find a way to weather the terrible storm that I'm surely about to face."

Chapter 26

AFTER NIGHTFALL, the protests turned ugly.

Like other minority communities across America, Brownsville had witnessed violent racial unrest in the past. Mere months earlier, bitter clashes between Black and White construction workers had flared during an attempt by civil rights activists to integrate a local building site. Days later, a wave of looting had erupted after a pair of white cops roughed up a black man accused of a petty crime. And now, twenty-four hours after the C. J. Johnson shooting, the incident was threatening to wreak yet more havoc on the troubled, inner-city neighborhood.

Although anti-police protests were peaceful through much of the day, the mood of demonstrators had grown far more militant as nightfall approached. Attempting to short-circuit potential violence, NYPD officials had once again issued a statement in which they expressed sympathy for the Johnson family and reiterated their pledge for a swift, unbiased investigation into the shooting. While few details regarding the incident were disclosed—nor were Holland's or Cook's identities divulged—the NYPD noted that neither officer involved in the incident had a history of misconduct, and Holland, in fact, had been cited on numerous occasions for heroism. Autopsy results regarding C. J. Johnson's cause of death were pending, in the hands of the city's medical examiner, police officials said. Press briefings would be conducted regularly, they added, acknowledging the public's right to remain informed. Patience and calm pending the outcome of the probe were once again urged.

But pleas for patience and calm, it quickly became apparent, were falling on deaf ears. By darkness the day after the shooting, more than a thousand demonstrators flooded the street in front of the 73rd Precinct station house, charging systemic racism and police misconduct in the shooting of the black teen. Demands were voiced for the suspensions and arrests of the officers involved and the opening of a criminal investigation by the Kings County District Attorney. Similar calls were issued for a comprehensive review of NYPD policing practices.

Before long, a sense of foreboding had settled like a toxic cloud over Brownsville. Merchants began boarding up shop windows. Wooden barricades were erected in front of the station house. Tactical Patrol Force units, along with Emergency Services reinforcements, were placed on standby. Status reports were relayed to NYPD headquarters, where anxious officials girded for violence.

They didn't have to wait long.

Although raucous and emotionally charged, the demonstration in front of the 73rd Precinct station house remained peaceful for nearly two hours. Then, without apparent provocation, several dozen youths broke free from the body of protestors and raced about randomly, hurling bottles, bricks, and trashcan lids at store windows and passing cars. Police rushed in to intervene. Several of the youths were tossed against a patrol car, handcuffed, and arrested. Angry words were exchanged, curses hurled.

Then, the violence erupted in earnest.

Amidst a stream of curses, threats, and shouts, a pack of young men took to the streets. Armed with baseball bats, metal pipes, crowbars, and tire irons, they careened about aimlessly, toppling trashcans, tripping burglar alarms, kicking in doors, and smashing in store windows. Joined quickly by others, the frenzied mob surged down the street, splintering off in packs. Parking meters were wrested from sidewalks and tossed through store windows. Rioters leapt onto parked cars, smashing in windshields, stomping on hoods and roofs, blocking intersections. Phone booths were toppled, coin boxes torn from their moorings and carried away. A Molotov cocktail was thrown into the open window of a police car, setting the vehicle ablaze.

Then, the rioters began looting. Climbing through broken windows and smashing barricaded doors, hordes of marauding youths toppled store displays, hoisting up armfuls of merchandise before quickly dispersing. Some shopkeepers, struggling to save inventory and cash, used broomsticks and baseball bats to beat back looters. Others simply fled. One by one, stores were raided and plundered, merchandise mutilated or toted away, store after store reduced to rubble.

The NYPD, caught off guard by the escalating violence, scrambled to respond. Borough task forces were mobilized. Emergency alerts were broadcast. Patrol cars, sirens wailing, streamed into Brownsville, along with police reinforcements and Emergency Services trucks toting shotguns, sniper rifles, tear gas projectiles, and lifesaving gear.

Taken aback by the intensity of the violence, police responded haphazardly. In some cases, helmeted, nightstick-wielding officers charged looters, jumping curbs with their patrol cars before leaping from the vehicles to chase rioters, shove them to the ground, cuff, and drag them to mass-arrest centers. In other instances, hastily organized teams of police, donning riot gear, formed human wedges and waded into crowds of rioters. Stragglers were overrun and clubbed with nightsticks, blackjacks, and handguns. Clouds of tear gas were released, followed by a phalanx of gas-masked officers. Officers on horseback sealed off streets. Police helicopters swooped overhead, searchlights sweeping streets. Sharpshooters toting rifles and shotguns were posted on rooftops. Several officers fired warning shots into the air.

Even in the face of the forceful response, the rioters battled back. Hiding on rooftops and behind parked cars, or darting out suddenly from alleyways, they pelted police with rocks, bottles, bricks, mortar blocks, and empty tear-gas canisters. Bands of rioters barricaded streets with debris and abandoned vehicles. Molotov cocktails, lobbed from rooftops, exploded in fiery splashes. Several patrol cars were immobilized, their tires flattened. Others were toppled and torched.

Then the fires started for real.

The first blaze began in an abandoned building. Fueled by gasoline and turpentine, it spread quickly through a common cockloft to a row of dilapidated brownstones. Within minutes, half a city block was engulfed. Squawk boxes came alive in firehouses throughout Brooklyn. One alarm turned into three, then five. Ladder trucks, pumpers, and rescue units, sirens and horns blaring, roared into Brownsville. Ambulances raced to the scene.

The fires advanced relentlessly. Flames licked at the walls of buildings and burst from windows with ferocious popping sounds. Twisting towers of flame rose like giant torches, leapfrogging from one house to the next. Siding melted. Tiles exploded from rooftops. Plumes of thick black smoke belched out onto the street. Ashes were blown about like snowflakes by the fire's howling drafts.

By now, it had escalated into a full borough alarm, a signal of impending catastrophe. Seventy-five pieces of equipment and nearly five hundred firefighters streamed into Brownsville from nearly every firehouse in the city.

The FDNY fought heroically, attacking the firestorm from every angle. Air packs strapped to their backs, firefighters climbed cherry pickers to pluck people from windows and stood atop tower ladders, directing torrents of water onto the fires. Others—toting hoses, ropes, axes, and circular saws—waded into buildings, forcing open doors and cellar grates, chopping through walls, and tearing down ceilings. Hoses snaked across intersections, and around cars and over curbs, burst with jets of water that sizzled and vaporized as they hit the flames. The spray from hoses, illuminated through banks of searchlights, lingered in the air.

The firefighters soon faced other obstacles. False alarms began streaming in, sending FDNY units scurrying off on "dumb runs," where they were pelted from rooftops and windows with a barrage of debris. Police cars raced back and forth to protect the firefighters, who soon turned their hoses on demonstrators. "Hot zones" were established, where firefighters would answer calls only if accompanied by police. Soon, only major sightings were responded to. False alarms were ignored. Trashcan fires and bonfires were permitted to burn. Even structural fires in especially dangerous locations went ignored.

The firefighters did everything they could, but it was hardly enough. All through the night, fires raged. Buildings disappeared under blankets of smoke and flame. Exhausted firefighters, their faces grimy and sweaty, their eyes dull with fatigue, took turns resting alongside their equipment, hacking up phlegm as medical personnel poured water over their heads. Brownsville residents, faces blackened with soot, towels and clothing pressed to their faces, huddled on sidewalks, and watched helplessly as their possessions smoldered in the streets. Many wept. In other quarters of Brownsville, some people openly cheered, chanting "Burn it down! Burn it down!" as the flames soared high, illuminating the nighttime sky.

By the time order was restored, shortly after midnight, it would turn out to be the worst incident of rioting in the modern history of New York. More than two hundred fire and emergency medical dispatches had been reported. Brownsville had suffered fifteen million dollars in property damage. Nearly forty homes had burned to the ground, another fifty would have to be razed, and some three hundred families had been rendered homeless. The city had lost or suffered damage to a dozen police and fire vehicles and had sustained an overtime bill of three million dollars. More than two hundred people had been arrested on charges ranging from aggravated riot, arson, and burglary to disorderly conduct, unlawful assembly, and resisting arrest.

While no one, miraculously, had been killed, injuries were numerous. In all, thirteen firefighters, eighteen police officers, and fifty-eight civilians were sent to hospitals, some with serious burns. A looter, shot by a shopkeeper, was left partially paralyzed. Others suffered concussions, teargas wounds, contusions, and broken limbs. Dozens had been cut by flying shards of glass and debris.

That, of course, was only the damage that could be measured. The true damage wrought by the rioting was far more subtle, but every bit as real. No one could measure, for example, the precise toll the violence had taken on the neighborhood's vitality. No one knew how many businesses and residents had been driven, once and for all, from Brownsville—or how many dreams had been destroyed, or how long the sense of disarray and loss would linger.

None of that was tangible.

What *was* clear, though, was that the shooting of C. J. Johnson had quickly become a tragedy that far outweighed the death of the innocent young boy. More than ever, Brownsville seemed a lost community within the City of New York, damaged and hopeless and dying, its delicate fabric shredded and coming all undone.

Chapter 27

EVEN AS THE FIRESTORM RAGED in Brownsville, police brass was convening at the NYPD's Emergency Operations Center, the city's central monitoring site for crisis management.

Police commanders, it was obvious, were confronting a crisis on several fronts. Foremost was the challenge of mounting an effective tactical response to the civil unrest threatening to consume major swaths of Brownsville. Equal weight lied in mounting a thorough, impartial, transparent, and timely investigation into the C. J. Johnson shooting, and deciding what, if any, action should be taken against Matt Holland and Rachel Cook—all while assisting the Kings County D.A. with a potential criminal probe. Last, but certainly not least, was the thorny issue of how to deal with the fallout from the police shooting: the inevitable, and potentially conflicting, reactions from minority activists, city residents, political leaders, and the thirty-thousand-member Patrolmen's Benevolent Association, the world's most powerful municipal police union.

Just as the shooting had exposed a gaping schism between Brownsville's predominately Black residents and the city's mostly White police force, it was also serving to spotlight sharp divisions about how to prevent the civil unrest from worsening. Indeed, while public officials had spent years studying how protestors behaved during urban riots, opinions differed widely about how police should respond to such crises.

"This city has a major problem on its hands, and we need to make some quick and enlightened decisions," said NYPD Chief of Department Patrick Delaney, presiding over a hastily convened summit at One Police Plaza in downtown Manhattan.

Delaney, the NYPD's highest-ranking uniformed officer—and second in command only to out-of-town Police Commissioner William Dunne—sat at the head of a conference table, adjacent to a bank of hotline telephones providing links to federal and state law enforcement agencies. Directly behind Delaney, a floor-to-ceiling window offered a panoramic view of a large swatch of Brooklyn's industrial heartland, a sprawling tableau of factories, oil refineries, chemical plants, coal yards, and rail links. Visible beyond that were thick plumes of smoke rising from the smoldering fires in Brownsville.

"What's happened in Brownsville is a disaster to the city and a blight on the NYPD," said Delaney. "The situation got completely out of hand. We can't allow that to happen again."

A towering, square-jawed officer whose crisply pressed white shirt was adorned with medals, Delaney surveyed the room. Present were more than a dozen high-ranking commanders, including Chief of Patrol Frederick Barnes, responsible for the NYPD's seven borough commands, Deputy Chief Clinton Ward, commanding officer of the ten-precinct Brooklyn North, and Deputy Inspector Lloyd Dineen, head of the NYPD's Strategic Response Group. Commissioner Dunne, attending a police convention, was unavailable. 73rd Precinct Commander Capt. Joseph Borelli was being piped in by speaker phone.

"What's needed is a tactical response to the rioting that will balance a show of force with a goal of not provoking further violence," Delaney said. "What we can't afford to do is simply emulate failed riot strategies of the past."

His eyes fell upon the commander seated at his right elbow.

"Lloyd, give us the latest thinking on this," he said.

Lloyd Dineen, gaunt and scholarly-looking behind wire-rimmed eyeglasses, had served as a consultant to the Kerner Commission, a Johnson Administration panel which found that police heavy-handedness had played a major role in fueling race riots in the 1960s. In his current post, Dineen was charged with coordinating the NYPD's response to civil disturbances. His new-age theories, however, were a radical departure from traditional police wisdom, and had never truly been tested.

"I think we have to walk a fine line," Dineen said. "The playbook on urban riots isn't straightforward. Our response can't be just a roll of the dice."

"I need specifics," Delaney said. "There's no room for vagaries."

"Well, one thing that's certain is that when police respond to violent protests with escalating force, it doesn't work," Dineen said. "In fact, escalating force can make protests even more violent because it only reinforces the fear and mistrust that minorities have of the police, and antagonizes protestors."

"So, what are you saying?" Delaney asked.

"I'm saying that tactical techniques like wearing riot gear, bringing in mounted police, conducting mass arrests, and deploying tear gas are ineffective in deterring rioting," Dineen replied. "They may clear the streets in the short term, but there's a 'rebound effect.' Demonstrating force is a failed mindset, a primal response that only makes things worse. People riot, the police overreact … and before long, it's all-out war."

"Well, with all due respect, I think that's a crock of shit!" bellowed Chief of Patrol Frederick Barnes. "You're telling me that we're supposed to just sit back and let people commit crimes? Destroy a community? Endanger other citizens, including police officers, as we stand off to the side? Uh-uh! I think we need a massive show of force … and soon!"

Nodding, Delaney yielded the floor to his bullnecked Chief of Patrol.

A dozen years earlier, Barnes had been commander of the 28th Precinct in Harlem, where six nights of rioting had erupted after a Black teen was fatally shot by a White officer. Rioting in Harlem had also been ignited following the assassination of the Rev. Dr. Martin Luther King Jr. in 1968. In each case, at Barnes's direction, the police response had been aggressive—although there'd been a hefty price paid in terms of injury, property damage, and community resentment toward police.

"In my estimation, we have to tackle disorder head on, with a zero-tolerance approach," Barnes said. "Forceful order-maintenance. No show of indecisiveness or weakness. People so much as break a window, we throw their ass in jail. And if we don't have enough firepower, we call in the National Guard!"

Dineen recoiled. "You'd call the National Guard into Brownsville?"

"You're goddamned right!" Barnes seethed. "I think we need to send a message that the NYPD won't abide by lawlessness ... that we're in charge of this city, not a bunch of out-of-control looters looking to exploit a tragedy for their own selfish gain!"

Just then, a voice poured through the conference table's speaker phone.

"I'd like to offer my perspective, if I could, from the front lines," said Capt. Joseph Borelli.

At forty-eight years old, Borelli was one of a new breed of college-educated police commanders gaining prominence within the NYPD. Combining street savvy with modern management skills, he'd replaced a longtime commander whose heavy-handed policies had ruffled feathers among many Blacks in Brownsville. While not every officer at the 73rd Precinct agreed with Borelli's more-conciliatory approach, he was nevertheless a battle-tested, highly respected, veteran cop who had earned widespread approbation during his eight-year tenure as 73rd Precinct commander.

"Please proceed, Joe," Delaney said, granting Borelli permission to speak.

"I think that we've got to tackle the unrest in a way that imposes order but still respects the civil liberties of people, the constitutional right they have to take their voices to the street," Borelli said.

"Civil liberties?" Barnes snapped. "People who commit mayhem have abdicated their civil liberties!"

"Let Joe have his say," Delaney ordered. Barnes backed down.

"I hope we've learned something from the mistakes police have made in past riots," Borelli resumed. "One of them is that while the National Guard may be effective in policing large public events or assisting with natural disasters, dealing with a crisis like we have in Brownsville is a different story. This isn't a rock concert or the Indy 500 we're talking about."

Borelli had the commanders' ears.

"I think bringing in the Guard would send a signal that we've lost control," he said. "Do we really want military vehicles in Brownsville, or a bunch of heavily armed, part-time soldiers trying to police our streets?"

"If they're needed, why the hell not?" Barnes grumbled.

"Well, for one thing, they're not trained for sophisticated crisis management," Borelli said. "They have no riot-control capabilities. Frankly, half those guys would probably shit in their pants if they were anywhere near a close-in, minority ghetto like Brownsville. Bringing in the National Guard will only throw fuel on the fire. I don't think we should consider that option at all."

"I agree," said Lloyd Dineen. "Responding with force would prove not only tactically ineffective, but also potentially catastrophic. In instances of civil disorder, we've seen that escalating force by police only leads to more violence, not less. It tends to create 'feedback loops.'"

"What the fuck is that?" Barnes snarled, derisively.

"It's a situation in which protesters escalate their actions against police, police escalate even further, and both sides become increasingly aggressive," Dineen said. "It's like causing an explosion by putting two chemicals together. We bring more firepower in, and all we'll do is make matters worse. We'll be carrying people out of Brownsville in body bags."

"Just as consequential," said Borelli, "it might create a permanent breach between police and the community—and that would make my job far tougher. We can't afford to win a battle but lose the larger war."

"So, what are you suggesting?" Delaney turned to Dineen.

"I'm saying that we need to handle this situation differently from that in the past," Dineen said. "Our job is to contain the disorder but do it with regard for people's lives and the sanctity of property. There's a lot of innocent, law-abiding people in Brownsville—and a lot of businesses—to consider. If we start breaking heads, what happens then?"

Barnes leaned forward, seeming exasperated.

"There are goddamned criminals running around on the streets of Brownsville, and who knows if the rioting might spread!" he growled. "I say we go in with everything we've got and clamp down on the violence before it worsens. We've got to show people who's running this city. The only way you deal with criminals is in the strongest possible terms."

"Sure, there are criminals on the streets here, and people who are exploiting the situation for personal gain, I'll grant you that," Capt. Borelli piped in. "But there are also a lot of people here who are not the 'enemy.' There's a lot of good people Brownsville, people who depend on the police and are on our side. The entire neighborhood doesn't consist of criminals."

"I side with Joe," said Brooklyn North commander Clinton Ward, a burly, highly decorated cop, and the first Black to achieve the rank of Deputy Chief in the NYPD's history.

All eyes shifted toward Ward. Delaney, with a nod, cleared him to speak.

"A heavy-handed response makes protestors feel like the police are an occupying force," Ward said. "This only amplifies tensions and provokes protesters. The harder we come at these people, the harder they'll come back at us."

"That's utter bullshit!" Barnes snapped. "We need to gain control of this situation. We can't get people get away with lawlessness! We've got to answer back!"

"I say we *do* answer back," Dineen said. "Our answer, however, is not to meet the unrest with force, but rather with finesse—to consciously exercise restraint, and allow brains to prevail over brawn."

Dineen then outlined a de-escalation strategy, counter to conventional tactics, that would prove to be a watershed in the way police would handle civil unrest in New York and elsewhere. The safety of citizens and officers, Dineen said, would be the top priority, along with a strategic containment of destruction. Police would try to minimize property damage, but not always prevent it. Officers would be instructed not to respond to rioters' taunts and provocations. Instead, they'd be ordered to exercise an unprecedented level of self-control, even if it meant ignoring cases of looting. Directives by officers would be communicated in a calm, measured tone. A "negotiated management" approach would also be employed, with Borelli and other senior officers meeting with community activists to empathize with their grievances and establish ground rules governing future demonstrations. Peaceful protests would be permitted.

In adopting Dineen's strategy, the NYPD would also consciously avoid an occupation-army brand of policing. The idea, Dineen said, was to make an impressive show of force so that crowds would disperse without the need for mass arrests. Police response to lawlessness would be proportional, with minor violations such as billposting and littering ignored. Riot-control teams would sweep through trouble spots, arrest quickly when necessary, and keep everyone in motion. No roadblocks or stationary police posts would be set up as potential targets for rioters' fury. Arrest and detention would be carried out in accordance with law, not as a means of punishment for peaceful participation. Once a decision was made to disperse an assembly, the order to disperse would be clearly communicated, with sufficient time allotted to disperse. Tactical Patrol Forces, SWAT personnel, snipers, and police hardware would be less visible. Police helicopters would be grounded. There'd be no intimidation of rioters. No beatings. And under no circumstances were shots to be fired.

"We're probably looking at three to four days before things settle down," Dineen said. "Things may actually get *worse* before they get better."

"How can things get *worse*?" Barnes asked.

"A lot of people," said Dineen, "could get killed."

The commanders signed off on the plan. A hierarchy of supervisory officers—including Dineen, Clinton Ward, and officers from the NYPD's Strategic Response Group—were dispatched to the 73rd Precinct to assist Borelli in managing the crisis first-hand. Declaring a formal state of emergency, a 9:00 PM curfew was imposed on all of Brownsville, an additional eight thousand cops mobilized for special twelve-hour shifts, and the number of officers assigned to the neighborhood quadrupled. The NYPD, it was agreed, would revert to its previous, more aggressive response if Dineen's de-escalation approach failed to curtail the violence.

Delaney reported the agreed-upon strategy to Police Commissioner Dunne, and then to anxious officials gathered at City Hall.

"I hope we're right about the approach we've decided to take," Delaney said, as the commanders left the conference room.

"God help us," said Lloyd Dineen, "if we're wrong."

Chapter 28

By MORNING, a tense calm had settled over Brownsville, the scent of smoke from smoldering fires lingering like an acrid fog over the battered neighborhood.

Virtually deserted now, most streets looked as if they'd been ravaged by a violent tornado. Charred beams of burned-out buildings jutted skyward like pitchforks. Cars were buried under mounds of rubble. Telephone booths rested on their sides. Sidewalks were littered with newspapers, tires, trash, and other debris. With most businesses either shuttered or destroyed, commerce had all but ceased, power to many homes cut for fear of fire. Nonessential traffic into and out of the neighborhood was banned, mail service, sanitation, and public transportation suspended. Corrugated grates and sheets of plywood blocked the entrances to most storefronts.

By midday, bulldozers were moving in to demolish dangerous structures and clear the neighborhood of rubble and debris. Search-and-rescue teams combed through smoldering bricks, water-soaked ashes, and other wreckage to locate victims. Workmen boarded up shattered windows. Tow trucks removed the burned-out shells of police patrol cars. Insurance agents moved through mangled businesses, assessing damage. Underway, too, were efforts at assistance. Operating from a makeshift command center, city officials attempted to find temporary shelter for the displaced. Red Cross and Salvation Army workers provided clothing, food, medication, and other essentials. Medical personnel tended to injured riot victims. Volunteers reached out to elderly residents and shut-ins dependent on social services.

Amid the relief and cleanup efforts, scavengers descended on abandoned buildings, stripping them of plumbing fixtures and copper pipes, and stealing whatever valuables they could peddle. All the while, merchants sifted through the wreckage of their businesses. Some gathered outside vandalized or fire-damaged stores, consoling one another, trying to come to terms with what had occurred. Many were longtime merchants, both White and Black, who had vowed for years to remain in Brownsville even in the face of the neighborhood's encroaching poverty and soaring crime. Now, like Brownsville itself, many seemed intractably broken. Some vowed to carry on. Others declared bitterly that the rioting was the final straw. It was time to shutter their businesses, pack their bags, and leave.

Even as they spoke, a new round of protests was being planned by militant activists, a growing number of whom were poised not simply to condemn alleged systemic racism and brutality, but to declare all-out war on the city's police.

* * *

As darkness descended upon Brownsville, another round of protests began, the most vocal of which took place in front of the 73rd Precinct station house, where a floodtide of angry demonstrators squared off with a column of helmeted officers positioned behind wooden barricades and sandbags.

"Stop the killing! Stop the killing! Stop the killing!" protestors chanted, raising their fists in a sign of solidarity.

Their banners, tee-shirts, and signs voiced similar messaging:

POLICE KILLINGS MUST STOP!

MURDERERS IN BLUE!

WE DEMAND JUSTICE!

"Police in America have declared open war on the Black community!" a dashiki-clad speaker named Ibrahim Shabazz shouted into a bullhorn.

Shabazz, a thirty-year-old activist born Tyrone Prince, had changed his birth name in favor of his current Bantu Muslim appellation, part of a growing trend among militant Blacks. His white tee-shirt was emblazoned with the words *Citizens Against Police Brutality*, the name of an activist group he'd formed as the result of complaints against police. His afro-styled hair was tucked beneath a red beret.

Fiery, eloquent, and streetwise, Shabazz was highly adept at attracting both public and media attention. And now, his ankles supported by a pair of cohorts, he climbed atop the hood of a parked car to address a sea of people that stretched nearly an entire city block.

"We got an end to slavery in America, and an end to Jim Crow," Shabazz shouted into his bullhorn. "We got laws that ended segregation and other social injustices. But with all that so-called progress, we've still got wanton racism and brutality! All that 'progress' and we've still got another Black child dead at the hands of police!"

The crowd cheered, wildly.

"The shooting of C. J. Johnson is just the latest in an endless string of brutal and callous police murders!" Shabazz charged. "Another White cop has shot another innocent victim! Why? Because that person was Black, no other reason. It's business as usual in Brownsville! Nothing has changed! Nothing ever changes! The only way police will stop the killing is if we *make* them stop!"

Then he shook his fist.

"What do we want?" he shouted.

"Justice!" the protestors replied in unison.

"When do we want it?"

"Now!"

"It's time to make a statement!" Shabazz exhorted. "It's time to deliver the message that police violence against Blacks will be answered. There'll be no more forgiveness, no more turning the other cheek, no more saying it was just a 'good policeman doing his job.'"

Again, the crowd let out a rousing cheer.

"We're sick and tired of being terrorized by the people we pay to protect us!" Shabazz shouted. "If we let the police get away with this shooting, they're going to think they can get away with it forever. This case is as important for civil rights as the Boston Tea Party was for the American Revolution! It's no longer just about a shooting. It's an issue of black versus white. We've achieved equality under the law. Now we need to eliminate police brutality. We want violent and racist officers weeded out. We want the city to suspend the cops involved in this shooting. Take their guns, their badges, their freedom! Bring them up on charges that they murdered this innocent Black boy!"

Again, the crowd roared—even louder this time.

"No justice … no peace!" they chanted.

"Stop killer cops!"

"End police brutality!"

All the while, the officers guarding the station house stood stone-faced and unmoving, nightsticks chest high. Under orders to exercise restraint, they made no effort to disperse the demonstrators, some of whom stood eyeball to eyeball with the cops, shaking their fists, cursing, and banging on patrol cars.

"No justice, no peace!" they shouted.

"Stop killer cops!"

"End police brutality!"

Then, as if on cue, violence erupted again. At a nearby auto dealership, a plate-glass window was shattered, and hordes of looters stormed in. Down the street, a pharmacy was ransacked, a hardware store vandalized, a grocery store fleeced. And quickly, the rioting spread.

This time, the looters seemed better organized than on the previous day. Many had donned ski masks and hoods to shield their identities, striking simultaneously at multiple locations so that police couldn't focus a tactical response. Within minutes, the 73rd Precinct also began receiving a stream of telephone threats, warning that a white police officer would be killed to avenge C. J. Johnson's death. The precinct switchboard also began lighting up with calls for phony 10-13s. Diversionary in nature, like the false fire alarms a day earlier, they sent all available police units scrambling to the locations in question. Parts of the neighborhood left unprotected were then targeted for mayhem.

By now, it was apparent that protestors from outside Brownsville had joined in the violence. Youth gang members were among those embracing the C. J. Johnson shooting as a call to action, flocking to Brownsville from every quarter of the city, and spray-painting colorful gang symbols on sidewalks, street signs, and tenement walls. Adding to the chaos, the outsiders—while embraced in some quarters of the neighborhood—were spurned in others. Fights erupted between rioters and peaceful protestors. Residents on rooftops tried to harass looters by pouring buckets of water on them, or by alerting police to their presence. A group of merchants joined PBA representatives in providing shelter to battle-weary officers and delivering food, water, and other supplies to the 73rd Precinct station house.

Adopting the de-escalation tactics proposed by NYPD Deputy Inspector Lloyd Dineen, police offered only selective resistance to the violence, safeguarding innocent lives—and guarding banks, the precinct station house, and other key locations—but making no effort at mass arrests or wading into crowds with nightsticks or vehicles. Military-style equipment and mounted police units remained blocks away. Sharpshooters were ordered to stand down from rooftop posts. Sound trucks circulated throughout the neighborhood, with city officials, local clergymen, and community leaders appealing for peace. And as quickly as the disturbance flared, it fizzled out—a tense, curfew-driven calm settling in for the night.

Chapter 29

AT THE 73RD PRECINCT STATION HOUSE shortly after the outbreak, a group of activists was ushered in for a meeting with precinct commander Joseph Borelli and other police officials, including Brooklyn North Commander Clinton Ward and riot-control expert Lloyd Dineen.

"On behalf of the city and NYPD, I want to express our heartfelt sorrow over the death of C. J. Johnson," said Dineen, straddling Capt. Borelli's desk.

"I'll add my own sentiments to that," said Clinton Ward, a hulking Black man who stood alongside half a dozen other somber, high-ranking officers, all of them White. "Our sympathy and prayers go out to the Johnson family," Ward said.

"Your sympathy is appreciated," Ibrahim Shabazz said, icily, "but frankly your words seem hollow in light of the way your 'storm troopers' carry out their supposed mission."

"Storm troopers?" Ward said, resentfully.

"The word 'cowboys' might be a better description," Shabazz said.

The protest leader glared, steely-eyed, at the police commanders. Seated alongside him, at the foot of Capt. Borelli's desk, was Wilfred Clark, a professor of African-American studies at NYU. The pair was accompanied by a quartet of strapping Black youths in red berets, sunglasses, and white tee-shirts—arms crossed defiantly at their chests.

"I assure you that our sympathy over this unfortunate tragedy is heartfelt," Dineen said.

"Again, that's not what we're here to talk about," Clark replied, curtly. "What we're seeking has little to do with sympathy. What we want is action!"

Instantly, the atmosphere grew testy, accented by the clamor of demonstrators chanting anti-police slogans outside the station house.

"I assure you that action is precisely what you're getting," Dineen said. "I'm sure you're aware of today's press briefing at City Hall."

At that briefing, the second in as many days, NYPD officials had provided an update on the status of the shooting probe—although investigative findings remained scant, no timetable for conclusion of the departmental investigation was offered, and the identities of Holland and Cook were not disclosed. The release of additional details, police officials said, would only undermine the integrity of the probe, compromise due process for the officers, and taint potential jury pools if the case proceeded to criminal trial.

"A thorough and impartial investigation into this shooting is well underway," Dineen reiterated. "Like you, we also want answers. The NYPD—and the Kings County D.A., if necessary—will get to the bottom of what occurred, and action will be taken if the investigation finds policy violations or criminal wrongdoing."

"And exactly what do you expect that your so-called thorough and impartial investigation will yield?" Shabazz asked, wryly.

"As of now, we simply don't know," Dineen replied.

"What's there *not* to know?" Shabazz laughed, sarcastically. "What happened, quite simply, is that two of your officers—based on racial bias, poor training, and fear—wantonly killed an innocent Black boy, confident that the system will protect them … as it always does for cops. They took the easy way out. And what we're expecting is just another police whitewash!"

"How can you make that claim without knowing the facts?" Dineen said.

"Because the 'facts,'" said Shabazz, "will never come to light."

"How can you be sure?"

"Because when it comes to police shootings," Shabazz said, "the facts *never* do!"

Again, the tension in the office ratcheted up, the police commanders squirrely, the young Black bodyguards stolid and resolute.

"Let me predict how this situation will play out," said Wilfred Clark, a gaunt, bespectacled disciple of slain Nation of Islam leader Malcolm X.

"The killing of C. J. Johnson is just the latest in an epidemic of deadly shootings of unarmed citizens by police in this country," Clark said. "While circumstances vary, each case has common threads. The first, of course, is that the officers are invariably White and the victims Black."

"The second," Shabazz interjected, "is that the shootings are always somehow justified. In each case, the Black victim is said to be presenting a threat, brandishing a weapon, or committing a crime. It's always 'objectively reasonable' for officers to open fire, declaring they were in imminent danger. Invariably, investigations turn up nothing definitive, criminal justice systems fail to prosecute, police unions protect officers from accountability, and the cops get off scot-free. No one gets reprimanded. No one gets suspended. No one spends a minute in jail. In truth, the only 'crime' the victims were committing is that they're Black. The color of their skin automatically makes them criminals. Their race makes them armed and dangerous."

"Does that pattern sound familiar?" Clark asked, sarcastically.

"And you think that this so-called pattern automatically means that the officers in this case are callous and racist and criminal, that they killed the boy simply because he was Black, and the officers believe they could get away with it?" Dineen challenged.

"That's exactly what we think!" Shabazz said. "Racial bias? Yes. Systemic cover up? Yes. A glossing over of the facts. It's impossible not to conclude that."

"Our point," Clark resumed, "is that brutal, racist cops almost always get a pass on killing Blacks. These callous acts of racism and police brutality have gone on for far too long. The practice of 'shoot-to-kill-and-let's-sort-out-the-details-later' is no longer acceptable. Instead of escaping justice, officers who automatically resort to deadly force must be held accountable. We want more than phony investigations and lip service. We want justice."

"And what you mean by 'justice'?" Lloyd Dineen asked.

"What it means," said Shabazz, "is accountability! We want to send a message that these kinds of killings, and the racism that provokes them, are no longer acceptable!"

"In other words, we want the C. J. Johnson case promptly, independently, and impartially investigated—not simply swept under the rug," Clark said. "And pending the outcome of that investigation, we want the rogue officers responsible for the shooting suspended, prosecuted, and tried for murder and hate crimes."

"Whoa!" Capt. Borelli said. "Don't you think you're jumping the gun?"

"Not at all."

"Well, we disagree," Borelli said. "These so-called brutal, racist, rogue officers you're referring to? Well, both have exemplary records. No history of misconduct. No civilian complaints. They're among the finest officers we have in the seven-three, and they deserve the benefit of due process—a comprehensive, unbiased probe—same as any citizen. What you're advocating, instead, is nothing less than a kneejerk reaction, a rush to judgment based on history, stereotypes, and an animus toward police."

"You're applying the same false standard to police," said Dineen, "as you say we're applying unilaterally to Blacks. And that's just as wrong. Instead, we need to take a reasoned approach in reacting to what happened."

"What do you mean by 'reasoned'?" Clark snapped.

"What I mean is that we need to objectively examine the evidence and discover the truth about what happened ... not what we think might've happened."

Shabazz brushed off his dashiki, as casually as if he were shooing a gnat.

"This city, I'm afraid, has a short memory," he said. "Incidents like this have taken place before and are seemingly resolved to a point where people forget they ever happened. But the conditions that breed them remain in place. Peace in neighborhoods like Brownsville is fragile. All it takes to ignite a firestorm is a spark. This incident is that spark. It's brought things to the surface, opened old wounds. What you're seeing, gentlemen, shouldn't be a surprise. It's a result of problems that have been simmering for years."

"We're convinced," Clark added, "that the officers involved in this shooting could've found a way to address the situation without the use of deadly force. We also know that the officers answered that call with a predetermined mindset—a racial bias and a 'shoot-first' mentality that pervades police culture. We believe they took the easy way out."

"And how do you know that?" Capt. Borelli asked.

"We know it," said Clark, "because that's the way it always is."

For a taut, fleeting moment, the verbal standoff grew silent. Outside, the anti-police chants were growing louder, more sustained.

"No justice … no peace!" demonstrators shouted in unison.

"Stop killer cops! Stop killer cops! Stop killer cops!"

"What we know for sure," Shabazz resumed, "is that Black people continue to die at an alarming rate at the hands of police. We also know that another Black child—in this case, an innocent eighth-grader—has been slaughtered in an act that was callous, overzealous, brutal, and, almost certainly racist. And no one is being held accountable."

"As I said," Dineen replied, "the incident is the focus of an exhaustive, objective investigation. We'll see where the facts lead us, and that justice gets done. You have my word."

"And what we're saying," said Shabazz, "is that we have no reason to believe you. There's no such thing as 'objective' when it comes to police. Your 'word' means nothing. History has destroyed our trust, shown that the NYPD—like all police departments—is entrenched in self-preservation. The department *can't* police itself or investigate its own!"

With that, the conversation stalled, the two sides at loggerheads.

"So where does all of this leave us?" Clinton Ward broke a protracted silence. "We're pulling our officers back to avoid confrontation and allow peaceful protests to be staged. But the lawlessness that's erupting—the looting, the property destruction, and the threat to people's lives—that's got to stop now!"

The activists studied the Brooklyn North Commander, a decorated, veteran Black officer whose viewpoint was distinctly at odds with theirs.

"The people causing these violent disturbances need to let the city do its job," Ward said. "You may not have faith in the system. But tempers need to cool off or people are going to die."

"Rioting is not the way to resolve the issues you're raising," Capt. Borelli added. "Rest assured your voices have been heard. Now it's time to stand down and help prevent the crisis from escalating. We're on the brink of real trouble here."

"Actually, we're far *past* the brink," Shabazz said. "There's lot of angry people in Brownsville. Things could get a whole lot worse."

"That kind of comment borders on the inflammatory," Ward said, sternly.

"It's only the truth," Shabazz said. "You're calling for calm, but there's a lot of people who feel they have every reason to be agitated. Maybe things *do* have to get out of hand. That's apparently the only way people can get the city's attention."

"By rioting?" Ward asked. "Through senseless acts of blind rage?"

"Do you think what you're seeing with these riots is simply blind rage?" Clark asked.

"I don't know what else to call it," Capt. Borelli said.

"Well," added Ward, facetiously, "we can always call it 'criminality,' 'lawlessness-disguised-as-protest,' and people using an unfortunate tragedy as an excuse for senseless, random violence, an impulse to anarchy. Some might even call it opportunism. I mean, lots of TVs and appliances are being looted, aren't they? Lots of bicycles and groceries and Nike sneakers!"

Clark shook his head, grimly.

"You fail to see what's really happening, don't you?" he said.

"Enlighten us," Ward said, acidly.

"What you're seeing on these streets is not random, senseless violence," said Clark. "Instead, it's an emotional outcry, a spontaneous, last-ditch outpouring of suppressed frustration, anger, and grief—a reaction not just to one event, but a symptom of a much deeper illness. Civil unrest, as Martin Luther King once said, is the 'language of the unheard,' people who are at the very bottom of the country's social scale, people whose souls have resided for years in darkness."

"The people in Brownsville have been brutalized and dehumanized, pushed for decades to the point of desperation," Shabazz added. "You can't imagine their frustration, how they're suffering. Rioting is their only recourse to express the powerlessness, frustration, bitterness, resentment, and desperation that has engulfed so many, the only way they feel they can be heard."

"Heard about *what*?" Ward asked.

"Racial injustice, urban decay, government oppression, lack of opportunity, poverty, unemployment, homelessness, drug addiction, poor schools, police brutality, and other inequities that have gone unpunished in black communities," Shabazz stated.

"So, they resort to rioting?" Ward scoffed.

"You're missing the point," Clark said. "What we're saying is that people destroy neighborhoods like Brownsville because they're intolerable places to live, breeding grounds for resentment and rage. They loot because they can't have things they want. They riot because their patience has run out. They resort to violence because they're frustrated and suffering, and desperate to break free from the things that are destroying them. They strike out at police because police are mistrusted and perceived as an enemy. The actions you're seeing are fueled by bitter, repressed emotions. Some of those people would rather die than be ignored any longer."

"Well, perhaps," said Ward, "their actions are more an issue of people acting out simply because they believe they can get away with it. Maybe their attitude is: 'Here's my chance to get something for myself. I have an excuse. No one is around to stop me.' It's a mob psychology … a festival of lawlessness and greed, an attempt by outside agitators to cause mayhem, tear down society, attack cops, and give criminals a free pass."

"You seem to be suggesting that because people are socially deprived, we ought to overlook their criminality," Capt. Borelli said. "Protestors have responsibilities, as well as needs. Anarchy in the streets is not a legitimate part of any dialogue we can possibly conduct. You talk about people dying rather than being ignored anymore? Well, I'm afraid that some people—including innocent, law-abiding residents—just might die if this violence persists."

"Even if no one dies, these kinds of riots are terribly destructive to the community," Ward observed. "Brownsville residents are being terrorized. Lives are being disrupted. Even after the violence stops, all that happens is that property values decline, insurance premiums rise, retail outlets close, businesses and job opportunities evaporate, people move away. Riots are not how you're going to achieve the goals you're seeking. They're only counter-productive. And we can't let them continue. We need calmer heads to prevail. The violence and lawlessness, quite simply, must stop!"

"There can be no tranquility," Clark said, "as long as the status quo persists. I'll repeat what I hinted at earlier: Brownsville is a powder keg now. If the issues regarding the C. J. Johnson shooting aren't addressed swiftly, as per our demands, I can assure you this neighborhood will go up in flames and there's very little that I, or anyone, can do to stop it. If people don't start listening to the voices on those streets, you'll need the U.S. Army to march in here and liberate Brownsville."

And on that abrupt note, the meeting disbanded—Shabazz, Clark, and the angry young men accompanying them filing out of the station house and back to the streets.

Chapter 30

THE FOLLOWING MORNING, a chilling new wrinkle impacted the burgeoning drama gripping New York: Matt Holland's and Rachel Cook's names and photographs were leaked by an unidentified source to the city's newspapers.

It didn't take long, either, for those former confidentialities to make their way into the hands of anti-police protestors. Indeed, within hours of the published leak, Old-West-style posters were being taped to utility poles and street signs throughout Brownsville. Printed on the posters were photos of Holland and Cook, beneath which a bold-faced caption read simply:

WANTED FOR MURDER: KILLER COPS!

That message, accompanied by charges of a longstanding pattern of racially motivated police shootings, was soon being voiced in demonstrations that were equally vocal—and even more skillfully orchestrated—as those of the past two days. Just as neighborhood youth gangs had embraced the C. J. Johnson shooting as a cause célèbre, a broadening circle of social justice activists was viewing the shooting as a rallying cry, the incident emerging as a lightning rod for a growing breed of activism that would shape public discourse about police shootings for decades in America.

Militant protestors, many with reputations for voicing their anti-police views not merely through reflexive acts of violence but through organized political acts, were flooding into Brownsville now from cities as far away as Chicago. Nationally known and media-savvy, the new wave of dissidents was keenly aware that the C. J. Johnson shooting might enable them to galvanize a broad new constituency whose agenda was defined by demands for racial justice, police accountability, and law enforcement reform. New York, the media capital of America, would be their most visible stage yet.

And so, for the first time ever, Brownsville residents were exposed to the kind of flamboyant, persuasive rhetoric they'd previously only read about or witnessed on television, in movie theaters, or from their pew at church.

"When I was a baby, I hollered when I was hungry, I hollered when I was tired, and I hollered when I was wet!" proclaimed Ibrahim Shabazz, standing atop a flatbed truck across the street from the Unity Funeral Chapel, where the body of C. J. Johnson lied in repose.

"I hollered because I knew that sometimes you've got to holler to get yourself heard!" Shabazz shouted into a bullhorn. "Yes—you've got to holler to get what you want, holler to get results, holler to let the people in power hear your outrage and pain, holler to let 'em know you want action, you want justice, you want change!"

"Tell 'em, brother!" someone shouted. "Tell 'em, loud and clear!"

"I'm not afraid to holler!" Shabazz said, his amplified voice echoing off the facades of nearby buildings. "I'm not afraid to make some noise! Are *you*?"

"Hell, no!" the crowd chanted in response.

"I'm not afraid to take our case to the power corridors of our city. Are *you*?"

"Hell, no!"

"I'm not afraid to push for change. Are *you*?"

"Hell, no!" the crowd roared. "Hell, no! Hell, no! Hell, no!"

As Shabazz riled the crowd, several hundred demonstrators gathered behind police barricades at the entrance to the Unity Funeral Chapel, where they faced off with a row of helmeted officers. Dozens of other cops, under instructions to remain as unobtrusive as possible, rung the perimeter of the demonstration or manned posts on nearby rooftops, eyeing the scene warily.

For nearly thirty minutes, Shabazz and other speakers voiced pleas for justice in the C. J. Johnson shooting, coupled with calls for the dismissal, arrest, and prosecution of Officers Holland and Cook.

"Never again will we allow wanton police shootings to take innocent Black lives!" Shabazz shouted. "Never again will we allow murderers in uniform to patrol our streets! Never again will we tolerate the blue wall of silence that protects criminal cops!"

"Never again!" the crowd shouted in union.

"Never again! Never again! Never again!"

Then several of the *WANTED* posters of Holland and Cook were stripped from a nearby utility pole, shredded, and set ablaze.

"Guilty!" the demonstrators intoned. "Guil-ty! Guil-ty! Guilty!"

The demonstrators waved banners and placards, chanted, and sang. Some carried placards with photos of previous Black victims of alleged police brutality. Insults and obscenities were hurled at the cops. A raw egg, lobbed from somewhere behind the barricade, splattered against a police car. A bottle shattered against the sidewalk, sending glass shards flying. A protestor rushed toward the line of police.

"You pig motherfuckers!" he sneered. "I'll cut your fucking hearts out!"

The protestor grew closer, cursing and taunting the cops. The line of officers edged forward, nightsticks at their chests, faces set like stone.

"C'mon, pig bastards!" the protestor shouted. "I'm Black and I ain't done nothin' wrong! C'mon ... why don't you shoot me, too?"

Someone hurled another egg, and an irate demonstrator squared off with a white-shirted police lieutenant. Demonstrators jeered at cops. Insults, obscenities, and taunts grew more venomous, more belligerent.

Then the violence flared once again.

Visitors to the funeral chapel—many of them in denim jackets emblazoned with gang insignias—had waited outside for hours to pay their respects. Entry, however, was restricted to the Johnson family, public officials, and invited guests. Left to languish on the street, the frustrated youths tried to shove their way past chapel staff members. Denied entry, they bolted down the street, overturning trashcans, smashing windows, and tossing bottles and rocks. Police sirens wailed. Patrol cars careened around street corners. Tactical Patrol Force reinforcements flooded in. Cops on bullhorns ordered the marauding protestors to disperse. In about thirty minutes they did, disappearing into alleyways, cellars, and abandoned buildings while promising to regroup and return.

All the while, police brass and city officials worked feverishly to keep a lid on further trouble. NYPD community relations specialists circulated in sound trucks, urging calm. Statements calling for peace were distributed at churches and other sites. A chain of Black ministers, arms linked in a gesture of peaceful unity, moved along streets, conversing with residents. An interfaith memorial service for C. J. Johnson drew nearly a thousand worshippers who sang hymns and joined hands in silent prayer, the sounds of gospel music and voices of a children's choir spilling through the open doors of the Good Shepherd Baptist Church and mingling with the chants of demonstrators out on the streets.

Chapter 31

CONFINED SINCE THE SHOOTING to NYPD headquarters, Matt Holland and Rachel Cook had far different roles now than the community policing duties they'd been assigned to for the past eight months. Officially, both officers had been removed from street patrol and handed nebulous administrative functions. Their singular task, however, was to assist in the department's probe of the C. J. Johnson shooting.

That investigation, underway in the glare of the public spotlight now, was proceeding apace, widening rapidly in the face of public pressure. Since neither body-worn video nor commercial surveillance cameras were yet in use, crime-scene analysts were forced to reconstruct the shooting incident using traditional forensics, ballistics, and evidence-gathering techniques—all while considering the testimony of Holland and Cook, the dozen or so officers who'd responded as backup, and any number of supposed witnesses.

Although investigative findings had yet to be completed, it had already been determined that the only people in the cellar at the time of the shooting were Holland, Cook, C. J. Johnson, and five other teenagers—all friends of the slain youth. Three had managed to escape seconds before the fatal shot was fired, and had later been taken into custody, questioned, and released without charges. The other two, hiding under the stairway to the courtyard at the time of the shooting, had been apprehended by Cook, and similarly questioned and released. Investigators had also concluded that, based on the way the incident had unfolded, and given the absence of light in the cellar, it was highly unlikely that anyone other than Holland and Cook had witnessed the shooting itself. Nevertheless, nearly a hundred purported witnesses emerged as a product of neighborhood canvassing.

One by one, the supposed witnesses were marched to the 73rd Precinct and interviewed by NYPD detectives, their testimony documented for the most part in scornful silence. Ranging from the highly improbable to the downright impossible, every account taken lacked credibility—often conflicting with, and occasionally contradicting, one another. Witnesses who'd provided preliminary statements at the scene had dramatically different stories to tell now. Several went so far as to demand compensation or special favors in exchange for their testimony. Others suggested that previous accounts could be amended for a price or admitted that they'd provided initial false statements in fear of retribution for telling the truth.

But despite their inconsistencies and incredulity, each of the supposed eyewitness accounts contained a trio of common threads. Invariably, they charged that Matt Holland had shot C. J. Johnson in cold blood. Invariably, they were laced with a venomous anti-police bias. And invariably, they were promptly disregarded by investigators.

Even in the face of the overwhelming animosity toward police, investigators could not uncover anything that either contradicted or discredited the written and verbal accounts of Holland and Cook. Illuminometers, used to measure lighting conditions in the cellar, concluded that visibility, as both officers contended, could indeed have been a factor in the shooting. Blood tests on the officers had proven free of alcohol, drugs, or other substances that might have impaired their judgment. Similarly, blood tests on C. J. Johnson had come back clean. Neither the slain teenager, nor anyone at the scene, had a criminal history. Neither weapons nor drugs had been found.

Other investigative findings similarly reinforced the officers' accounts of the shooting. Ballistics determined that the single gunshot fired by Holland had indeed traveled upward and ricocheted off the cellar ceiling, supporting the officer's claim that the fatal shot, likely unintended, was triggered by a sudden jolt from the victim. The city's medical examiner also concluded that the bullet from Holland's firearm had pierced C. J. Johnson's skull at the junction of the frontal and parietal bones—medical terms for the soft spot found atop a baby's head—and had exited just beneath the boy's left ear. Tests revealed no close-range shooting to the torso, no exit wound, and no powder burns on the victim's clothing. For all intents and purposes, it was as if C. J. Johnson had been shot from above.

Holland's story, like Cook's, was also holding up under the scrutiny of Homicide and Internal Affairs investigators. The eyesight of both cops was tested several times and found to be perfect. Their accounts of the incident were unwavering and consistent. Neither story could have been contrived, investigators reasoned, because the two officers had been immediately separated after the shooting with no contact since that time, thereby eliminating any chance for the officers to compare notes or concoct bogus accounts of the incident prior to their separate interrogations.

Nevertheless, both officers' questioning continued nearly nonstop, in sessions that were at times humiliating, exhausting, and even accusatory. Clearly impacted by the pressure and controversy surrounding the incident, investigators—even those whose loyalty may have been to the officers—often seemed confrontational, their questions focused on such minutiae that both Holland and Cook were sometimes at a loss to answer. Each was repeatedly asked to recount precise details of the shooting and the events leading up to it. Each was questioned about distances, elapsed time, the size and the shape of the cellar, and what it contained; where each officer, and others, were positioned at various times during the incident; how quickly C. J. Johnson fell to the floor and what position his body was in when he fell; what words, if any, were exchanged; and what the officers were thinking and doing at all times. Holland and Cook were also probed on procedural matters: Did the two of them knock on the cellar door before entering? Did they barge in or enter calmly? Were they carrying weapons other than what they'd been issued? Were they certain they'd properly identified themselves?

"You're aware, Detective Sergeant Holland, are you not, that the *NYPD Patrol Guide* provides guidelines for police use of force, display of shield, and other measures to avoid incidents like this?" an internal affairs investigator inquired during Holland's third round of questioning.

"I am," Matt Holland replied.

"As a sixteen-year veteran, you're well versed in those guidelines, I suspect ... are you not?" the investigator probed.

"I am."

"You're also aware, are you not," the investigator said, "that among those guidelines is the stipulation that any use of force must be 'reasonable' under the circumstances, and if the force used is 'unreasonable,' it will be deemed excessive in violation of department policy?"

"I'm aware of that," Holland said.

"Then you must be aware that deadly force is to be used only as a last resort ... to protect your life or the lives of others, correct?"

"Yes, that's correct."

"Would you say then that the use of your firearm was based on a careful assessment of the situation and was consistent with the guidelines set forth by the *NYPD Patrol Guide*?"

Holland winced. "I'd say that, with all due respect to the *NYPD Patrol Guide*, it doesn't address situations like the one I encountered. I didn't have time to make a rational assessment or to consult a manual ... only to react on reflex."

"Well, couldn't you have reacted, perhaps, a little *less* on reflex and exercised more prudence and caution?" the investigator asked. "Couldn't you, for example, have wrestled the victim to the ground?"

"I never even saw the victim until he was lying on the floor, shot," Holland said.

"In retrospect, do you feel that you made a mistake in discharging your service revolver?" the investigator asked.

"A *mistake*?" Holland shook his head. "No, I wish the incident hadn't happened, but I feel the actions that I took were entirely justified under the circumstances. I wish I had more time to assess the situation. I wish that it wasn't pitch-black. I wish the boy hadn't come at me out of nowhere and run into me. As I've testified, the gunshot was unintentional. So was the result. But as far as following police guidelines, I feel I did nothing wrong."

Holland was also questioned repeatedly about his and Cook's state of mind. Were the two officers angry, distressed, frightened, panicked? What types of calls had they responded to prior to the shooting? When had they last eaten? What factors other than the cellar's lighting might have contributed to their perceptions?

"Couldn't you tell it was an unarmed boy?" one investigator inquired.

"No," Holland answered. "I didn't know who or what it was—a person or an object, young or old, Black or White, male or female."

"Couldn't you tell the suspect was not out to harm you?"

"No."

"Did it ever occur to you that perhaps the boy mistook you for someone else … and not a police officer?"

"I've only learned that since."

"And there was no way to tell if the victim was armed?"

"That's correct," Holland replied. "As I've testified, it was totally dark at the instant the boy ran into me. Everything happened extremely fast. There was no way of knowing, in the split second I had, if the boy was armed or not. I only realized after the fact that he wasn't."

The investigator sat expressionless as he pored through his notes.

"One final line of questioning," he said, looking up again. "There are supposed witnesses who have contradicted your story. For example, witnesses have claimed that you shouted something at the boy as he lied on the floor. Is that true?"

"No."

"According to one witness, you looked down at the boy, laughed and said, 'You're dead, you motherfucker! Good for you!' Is that true?"

Matt Holland shook his head, sadly.

"Answer for the record, detective."

"No, it's not true," Holland replied.

"Another witness made a statement that, as the victim lay on the floor, you ground your knee into his chest and attempted to handcuff him, then placed your hand over his mouth, as if to stop him from breathing. Is that true?"

"No."

"At any point, did you shout at people not to approach or to touch the victim after he was shot?" the investigator persisted.

"No."

"Did you use abusive language to anyone at the scene?"

"No."

"Did you use physical force on anyone?"

"No."

"Did you exchange any words with the victim?"

"No."

"Did you touch the boy in any way?"

"Yes, I touched his chest to determine if he was breathing."

"Anything else?"

"I placed my hand over his mouth and nose."

"Was he breathing?"

"Not that I could tell."

"Were you not trying to suffocate him?"

"No." Holland shook his head, sadly. "I was trying to determine if he was still alive. I was trying to save him."

On-and-on the questioning went, with different investigators probing every angle of the incident: actions, intent, motivation, verbal communications, bias.

"Were you able to determine the boy's race at the time of the shooting?" an investigator from the District Attorney's office inquired.

"The issue of race never entered my mind," Holland told him. "I saw, and felt, an object approaching me swiftly in the dark. I never saw what color it was."

"But you *presumed* the boy was Black, did you not?"

"I suppose so, yes."

"Why is that?"

"Because most people in Brownsville are Black."

"And you presumed the boy was committing a crime, didn't you?"

"We were called to the scene regarding a possible crime-in-progress," Holland said. "So yes, I thought that a crime being committed was a possibility."

"Did you use the word, 'nigger' at all?"

Holland recoiled. "Excuse me?"

"Did you call the boy, or anyone in that cellar, a 'nigger'?"

Matt Holland stared at the investigator before shaking his head again.

"I don't think I've ever used that word in my entire life," he said.

"A simple 'yes' or 'no' will suffice, detective."

"No."

"We understand from Officer Cook that you dropped to the floor and took the boy in your arms after he'd been shot," the investigator stated. "Is that correct?"

"I recall that … yes."

"What was the reason?"

"I was trying to see if he'd been wounded. I wanted to help him if I could. I very much wanted to save him."

"Did you make any effort to revive him?"

"Yes."

"What actions did you take?"

"I remember using my hand to try and stop his bleeding. At one point, I administered mouth-to-mouth."

"Did you say anything to the boy?"

"Yes."

"And what was that?"

And with that, Matt Holland paused, looked off to someplace far away, then told the investigator how he'd whispered to C. J. Johnson how much he hoped the wounded teen would live, and how sorry he was for having shot him.

Chapter 32

FULLY UNDER WRAPS since the night of the shooting, Rachel Cook was transported to her final interrogation in an unmarked, chauffeur-driven sedan generally reserved for police higher-ups. For the entire hour-long drive from Queens to NYPD headquarters in Manhattan, Cook, clad in a beige summer dress and matching cotton espadrilles, sat nervously in the rear seat, wondering how her ascendant police career had gone so swiftly and terrifyingly awry, and how subsequent events might unfold.

For the past forty-eight hours, the rookie officer had remained out of sight, enmeshed in a jumble of melancholy, anxiety, confusion, and fear in the apartment she shared with a former college classmate. She'd barely eaten or slept in all that time, much of which she'd spent absorbed with TV coverage of the C. J. Johnson shooting and the resultant riots in Brownsville.

In many ways, the enormity of what had occurred—and what might yet happen—had fully settled in and was crashing down on Cook like a mountain avalanche. Not only her career, but also her entire life had been permanently recast by what had taken place in the span of several horrifying seconds, none of it her doing, none of it her fault.

Over and over, Cook recounted the incident in vivid detail, trapped in a state of disbelief, shock, and grief. She grieved for Matt Holland—a decent and honorable man, an exemplary and heroic cop—stained forever by a shooting he never intended. She grieved for C. J. Johnson—an innocent boy killed in a terrible mishap—and for his family, forced to bear the burden of their son's untimely death. She grieved for Brownsville, the poverty-riddled neighborhood that her own family once called home, and for the City of New

York, forced to cope with a racially tinged crisis threatening to grow further out of control.

Mostly, though, Rachel Cook grieved for herself.

Aside from her deepening withdrawal, uncertainty, and depression, Cook was suffering from a worsening range of physical and psychological symptoms. The maddening tinnitus in both her ears, triggered by the sound of Matt Holland's gunshot, had yet to subside—along with the muscle tremors, chills, and headaches Cook had experienced since the shooting. Her pulse rate had risen to a steady hundred-plus beats per minute. Her blood pressure signaled Stage Two hypertension. Whatever food she'd eaten was impossible to hold down. Sleep had been virtually nil.

Concerned for Cook's welfare, her roommate had contacted a local physician who, given the extenuating circumstances, agreed to make a house call to the women's apartment. A genteel, bespectacled man who'd practiced medicine for four decades, Dr. Hyman Rosenbloom, like most of New York's populace, was keenly aware of the C. J. Johnson shooting. Media coverage, after all, had been virtually nonstop—Cook's identity, like Holland's, an open secret now.

"It's very unfortunate what's happened," the elderly physician lamented. "A terrible tragedy for everyone concerned."

The doctor opened his black Gladstone bag and withdrew a stethoscope, placing its metal disc atop Cook's chest, wincing as he listened to her heartbeat. Hunched and wrinkled, the doctor moved tentatively, wire-rimmed spectacles worn halfway down his nose.

"Have you been eating?" he asked.

"Not much," Cook replied.

"Holding it down?"

"Not really."

"How about sleep?"

"Not much of that either."

The doctor pulled the stethoscope's earpieces from his ears.

"What's been bothering you?" he asked

Cook detailed her range of symptoms.

"Well, all that's understandable," the doctor said. "You've been gravely injured."

"Injured?"

"Uh huh." The doctor slipped a thermometer under Cook's tongue, and then used an otoscope to peek into her ear, and a wooden spatula to examine her throat.

"Symptoms like those you're experiencing are typical in response to trauma," the doctor said. "They're not signs of an illness, but rather a reflection of the body's reaction to extreme stress."

He then informed Cook that her blood pressure and pulse rate were dangerously high, and she was seriously dehydrated and one step away from being admitted to a hospital.

"The rush of adrenaline you experienced at the time of the shooting can temporarily mask the injury you've sustained," he said. "Symptoms like yours may not manifest themselves for days, or even longer, following a traumatic incident."

"How long," asked Cook, "can the symptoms last?"

"There's really no telling."

"Will they worsen?"

"Only if they're ignored."

Putting his instruments away, the doctor closed his bag.

"You're terribly run down, *shaina maidel*," he said, Yiddish for "pretty girl."

He took Cook's hands in his, informed her that she needed to eat and sleep, and made an appointment to see her at his office.

"You must take care of yourself, dear," the doctor said. "You have a very dangerous job, in more ways than you might even realize. And you're under an extreme amount of stress."

* * *

The same could be said as Cook sat alongside PBA attorney Eddie Shearson at One Police Plaza, in the company of the same sloe-eyed IAD investigator who'd interrogated her at the 73rd Precinct immediately after the shooting.

"This will be your final round of questioning," the investigator intoned, shuffling through a ream of paperwork, including the *Use-of-Force* report that both Holland and Cook had filed immediately after the shooting.

"There are several ambiguities," the IAD guy said, "that I'd like to clarify."

"Ambiguities?" Eddie Shearson said.

"Well, more like loose ends," the investigator clarified. "Strictly procedural."

"This officer has already been grilled multiple times about the shooting," Shearson protested, angrily. "Both her and Detective Holland have been put through a meatgrinder. And now, to compound matters, her identity—like that of her partner—has been leaked to the press. What a fucking travesty!"

"The leak is unfortunate," the investigator said, "but there's nothing we can do about it now."

"Maybe not," Shearson said. "But you *can* show Officer Cook the consideration she deserves!"

Chastened, the investigator nodded, turning on his tape recorder and turning to Cook.

"You understand, officer," he said, "that it's a violation of department policy to misstate facts or cover up the truth."

"I do," Cook replied, nervously.

"For example," the investigator said, "you'd never say or do anything to protect yourself or a fellow officer from potential wrongdoing, would you?"

"No, I wouldn't," Cook replied.

"You'd never compare notes with a partner, or with other officers, in an effort to fabricate a story or mislead police officials conducting an investigation?"

"No."

"You'd never speak to anyone about the incident, other than union officials, your attorney, or authorized investigative personnel?"

"No," Cook said. "And I haven't."

"Cut the inferences!" Shearson snarled. "I think Officer Cook has made it clear, on multiple occasions, that she has discussed the shooting incident with no one, including her partner, and that her account of what happened is truthful to the best of her recollection. Now, feel free to address your so-called loose ends."

The IAD guy lowered the temperature, but just slightly.

"The *NYPD Patrol Guide* outlines both the criminal and the civil liability that witnessing officers assume if they fail to intervene, if possible, in the use of excessive force by another officer," the investigator said. "You're aware of that, Officer Cook, are you not?"

"I am," Cook replied.

"And so, I ask: were any steps taken by you to reduce or eliminate the necessity for your partner to use deadly force in the incident under investigation?"

"I—" Cook started, haltingly.

"You *what*?"

"I suppose not," Cook said, seeming shaken.

"And why not?"

"There was no time to intervene or do anything to stop what happened," Cook said. "The entire incident took place in the blink of an eye. The boy was shot before I even knew what was going on."

"I understand," the IAD guy persisted. "But was the subject—the boy who was shot—ever assumed by you to be a physical threat, either to yourself, your partner, or others at the scene?"

"No … I suppose not," Cook replied tentatively.

"And why not?"

"Honestly," she said, "the first glimpse I had of the boy was when he was lying on the floor, immobile, bleeding, not making a sound. And then—"

"Then what?"

"Then when his head was being cradled in my partner's arms."

Cook paused, choking up. Shearson handed her a tissue, and she blew her nose. The ringing in her ears, a buzzing sound that initially had been intermittent, pulsed now in sync with her heart. Her entire body felt tingly, weightless.

"You're aware, of course, that an officer should never assume that just because a subject has apparently been incapacitated, he or she is unable to take aggressive action," the investigator said in a snarky tone.

"It seemed obvious to me," said Cook, "that the boy wasn't a threat."

"What about the others in the cellar?" the investigator asked.

"The several who escaped ran up a staircase and into the courtyard," Cook recounted. "The pair who remained in the cellar were unarmed."

"You apprehended them?"

"Yes, I ordered them to emerge from under the stairway where they were hiding, and held them at gunpoint, before calling for an ambulance and backup."

"Were there firearms or other weapons at the scene?"

"Nothing other than a handsaw, a staple gun, a box of thumbtacks, and a hammer. I didn't consider them to be weapons."

"And you were convinced that the suspects you apprehended were secure?"

"Yes."

"And your partner at the time?"

"He was attempting to render lifesaving aid, pending the arrival of backup officers and emergency medical personnel," Cook replied.

The IAD investigator rubbed an eye with his fingertip.

"One final question," he said. "The *NYPD Patrol Guide* mandates—"

"With all due respect," Cook said, "the *NYPD Patrol Guide* doesn't address what my partner and I encountered in that cellar. Nothing in the world could have ever prepared us for what we stumbled into down there."

Chapter 33

LATER THAT SAME DAY, a sleek Mercedes-Benz sedan pulled to a halt in front of 118 Amboy Street. Emerging from the vehicle, a trio of smartly dressed Black men entered the building and proceeded up a winding stairwell to the second-floor apartment of Charles and Eunice Johnson. Their meeting with the grieving parents had been brokered by the Rev. Josiah Watson, who greeted the visitors in the apartment's vestibule before ushering them into the living room, where Charles and Eunice sat waiting.

Its blinds and curtains drawn, the living room was dimly lit and furnished in a mismatched sort of way that the Johnsons felt awkward about. Their visitors, after all, were distinguished public figures. One of the men, Calvin Hobbs, headed the New York office of the NAACP. Another, named Xavier Cooper, was chief counsel for the American Civil Liberties Union. Accompanying the pair was 41st District councilman Samuel Hopkins, well known throughout Brownsville and the adjacent communities he represented.

Cordial and respectful, each man took turns introducing himself to the Johnsons, who sat on a trundle bed that doubled as a couch, their legs beneath a coffee table set with a vase of silk flowers. A pair of club chairs flanked the couch, facing which was a wall adorned with family photos. A portrait of Dr. Martin Luther King hung between a pair of windows looking out at the street.

Rev. Watson positioned the club chairs in a semicircle facing the Johnsons. He pulled up a leather hassock for himself and the visitors took seats.

"Please permit us to express our deepest condolences over the death of your son," said the balding, mustachioed Hopkins, tugging on the vest of a beige, three-piece suit. "I understand that C. J. was a good young man who was popular and doing quite well, despite his challenges."

"We only pray that he's with God," sniffed Eunice, blowing her nose into a tissue she kept beneath the band of her metal wristwatch.

"Amen to that," Rev. Watson said.

"Amen," the other men echoed.

"It's impossible to fathom your grief," Xavier Cooper said. "There's nothing I can think of that's more heart-wrenching for a parent than losing a child. I pray that C.J. rests in peace and you can find comfort in his memory."

"Thank you," Charles said.

Her eyes bloodshot and barely open, Eunice listed like a foundering ship against her husband's side. Charles slipped an arm around her and pulled her close.

"Please allow me to add my sentiments to what has already been expressed," Calvin Hobbs said, hoarsely.

A stately, dignified presence, Hobbs wheezed whenever he exhaled, and dabbed with a handkerchief at rheumy eyes. A confidante of Dr. King himself, the NAACP official had made headlines when he'd accompanied civil rights activists on their famed voting rights march to Montgomery, Alabama, where the marchers were attacked by sheriff's deputies with police dogs, clubs, and tear gas. Eleven years later, Hobbs still suffered from eye-scarring and shortness of breath.

"I hear," Hobbs said to Charles, "that you're originally from the South."

"Yes, sir," Charles nodded. "Born and raised in Claymont, South Carolina."

"The Piedmont!" Hobbs grinned. "I know that region well. Cotton country."

"Yes." Charles nodded. "Cotton was big in Claymont back then."

"And when did you journey north?" Hobbs dabbed his eye.

"Came to Brooklyn in 1950," Charles said.

"And now," Hobbs said, "I understand you work for the Transit Authority here in New York ... is that right?"

"Yes." Charles nodded. "Been with the T.A. for twenty-six years now."

"Charles and Eunice are also two of our most devoted congregants," Rev. Watson added. "Met and married at the Good Shepherd Baptist Church."

The visitors seemed duly impressed. While appreciative of their apparent approbation, Charles felt guarded and out of place in the company of such distinguished men. He was hardly worthy enough, he thought, to be the object of their attention, surely prompted for no reason other than his son being shot to death by a white police officer. He wondered about the purpose for their visit.

"Well, we won't take much of your time," said Cooper, as if on cue. "But we've come to discuss a matter of the utmost importance."

The ACLU attorney leaned forward in his chair.

"As I'm sure you're aware, Mr. Johnson, there are basic rights under the U.S. Constitution that every citizen enjoys—rights such as free speech, freedom of religion, and protection from racial discrimination," he said. "While these rights are not enforceable against a private citizen who violates them, they *are* enforceable against the government."

"A major part of our organizations' mission," Cooper added, "lies in protecting the rights of citizens in cases ranging from unlawful searches and false arrests to improper conduct and excessive use of force by police officers."

"The point," wheezed Hobbs, "is that if your, or a family member's, civil rights have been violated, you have the legal right to file a wrongful death claim against the individual or institutions responsible—in this case Officer Holland, the NYPD, and the City of New York. In other words, you have the right to seek redress based on the conduct of the officer in question."

"Please continue," said Charles, struggling to determine where all of this was heading.

"Our office is dedicated to ensuring that any citizen whose rights have been violated receives the legal representation, and the justice, they deserve," Cooper said. "That 'justice' comes, in large part, through the aggrieved party's ability to secure damages from a city like New York for the misconduct of its police."

"Damages?" Charles squinted.

"In other words, financial compensation for your family," said Hobbs. "Frankly, in your case, Mr. Johnson ... a rather *large* amount."

Charles stiffened. The notion of potential lawsuits or financial compensation hadn't occurred to him, or to Eunice, until that very moment. Lost in their grief, swept up in Brownsville's protests and rioting, the couple hadn't given the topic of potential litigation even a passing thought. Nor were they even aware that they could.

"It's our intent—with your permission, of course—to file a pair of lawsuits," Cooper said. "Both would be filed on behalf of your family. We've come to seek both your blessing and your support."

"What kind of lawsuits are you talking about?" Charles asked.

"The first would be a civil suit, charging the city and the NYPD with wrongful death in the shooting of C. J.," Cooper explained. "The suit would charge Detective Sergeant Holland with misconduct and negligence in the performance of his duties. We would contend that the officer was brutal and overzealous—and that, through his actions, he violated C. J.'s civil rights."

"And the *second* lawsuit?" Charles asked.

"We'll get to that in a moment," Hobbs said.

Cooper reached into his briefcase and produced a thick sheath of papers, which he plopped on the coffee table before Eunice and Charles.

"This," he explained, "is a draft of the initial lawsuit we hope to file. In it, we'd be alleging what I just described, and we'd be seeking redress for the pain and emotional duress your son's death has caused your family."

Charles leaned forward to examine the document, written in a legal parlance he couldn't pretend to comprehend. Eunice leaned lifelessly against his shoulder.

"We anticipate that any grievance we file will result in a civil trial, although there will likely be an attempt by the city to negotiate an out-of-court settlement," Cooper said.

"Actually, *both* sides will try to settle the case without litigating it." Hobbs dabbed at his eye. "That's how most of these cases are settled."

"I'm not sure I understand," Charles admitted.

"Actually, it's fairly simple," said Cooper. "Cities like New York, you see, provide their police officers with civil-liability protection. The city, in fact, shells out millions of dollars in damages each year to settle cases like this. They'll defend the officer publicly if they feel he acted in the proper discharge of his duty—they have no choice, really. They'd lose credibility among their officers if they created the impression that they don't stand behind their cops."

"So why would they want to settle *out* of court?" Rev. Watkins inquired.

"Two reasons," Cooper replied. "For one, the city already has an army of attorneys buried under a mountain of backlogged cases. They hardly need another lawsuit hanging over them, especially involving a controversial case like this."

"Secondly," Hobbs added, "a prolonged court battle could prove extremely costly. The city would rather get the matter resolved as quickly as possible. It's not so much an admission of wrongdoing as it is a question of trial risk. The city, you see, would prefer to pay an agreeable sum that they could negotiate rather than take their chances in court and perhaps pay even more in the long run."

"Believe me, the city will be prepared to agree to a reasonable settlement in this case," Cooper said. "They'll want this to be resolved quickly."

"What do you mean by 'reasonable'?" Rev. Watson asked.

"Actually, a substantial amount of money," Hobbs replied. "Civil rights complaints emanating from wrongful-death claims involving police actions have resulted in verdicts in the millions of dollars."

Charles and Eunice Johnson nearly fell off their couch.

"We recognize that no amount of money will ever bring C. J. back or compensate you for your pain," Cooper said. "But what we're talking about, should you permit us to proceed, would forever eradicate whatever financial burden you may have, and make a life-changing difference in your lives."

Charles sat quietly, deep in thought. Eunice, teary-eyed, leaned against his shoulder.

"But let me be clear, Mr. Johnson," Cooper said. "This is about *more* than simply money. What it's truly about is holding a city accountable for the actions of its police and helping change the social arc of this country. Unless victims of police shootings file civil actions of the kind we're advocating—and hit the city in its coffers—there'll be little incentive for change. In filing a lawsuit, you'd be sending a powerful message: that these kinds of repeated incidents will no longer be tolerated."

Weeping now, Eunice asked to be excused. She needed a moment to compose herself, she said. A moment to rest.

"Please forgive my wife, but we're going through a very difficult time, as I'm sure you can understand," said Charles, rising to help Eunice to the bedroom. "The past few days have been very hard to handle."

"Of course," Cooper said. "I'm sure it must be quite overwhelming."

"It's impossible to put into words," Charles said. "But ... yes."

* * *

Charles helped Eunice into bed, covering her with a blanket and gently massaging her shoulders as she lied there quivering like a newborn fawn.

"Rest, my dear," Charles said. "I'll return soon as I'm done talking to those men."

"Please don't be long," Eunice implored. "It's especially hard for me when I'm alone."

Charles kissed Eunice gently on her cheek, assuring her he'd return in short order. He then headed back to his meeting, all the while thinking of C. J., and all the ways that he missed his son.

There were so many things that had bound them across C. J.'s fourteen years, Charles thought, so many meaningful moments the two of them had shared. C. J., after all, had been at the very core of who Charles was—the son who'd given his father's life purpose, the son for whom Charles had always been there.

Charles was there through the gut-wrenching visits to the clinics and the hospitals where doctors injected experimental chemicals into C. J., to purge the lead toxin from the boy's body. He was there for the visits to the special-Ed and speech teachers, the occupational therapists and hearing specialists; there at the local school board to lobby for C. J. to be mainstreamed into classes with normal children; there at night to read to C. J. and play with him, to help him set up a fish tank and work on his scrapbook and hang posters of his favorite ballplayers, action figures, and comic-book heroes.

He was there to take C. J. places, too.

C. J. could never accompany his father to Ebbets Field; the Dodgers had already abandoned Brooklyn by the time C. J. was born. But the two of them traveled to Shea Stadium to watch C. J.'s favorite team, the Mets, and sometimes they took the D train to the Bronx to see the Yankees play, or the C train to catch the Knicks at Madison Square Garden. Sports, in many ways, was their *lingua franc*a, a common language that bound father and son.

But the thing that bound them just as tightly was the very thing that pulled so many fathers and sons apart. It was Charles's work.

Indeed, within two years after arriving in New York, Charles passed his civil service exam and graduated from cleaning subway cars at night to a day job with the Transit Authority, earning seven thousand dollars a year as a subway token clerk. And sometimes on his days off, he'd take C. J. and his cousin Marcus to show the boys where he worked.

Charles was assigned to the Montrose Avenue station on the BMT's "L" line, a twenty-five-station route that ran from Canarsie, in southern Brooklyn, under the East River to Eighth Avenue and Fourteenth Street in Manhattan. Sections of the line traversed Brownsville. It was easy for Charles to get to work—just walk a few blocks, hop on the train, and ride it eleven stops to Montrose Avenue.

For the two young boys, however, riding the subways was nothing less than a peerless adventure. C. J., in particular, had an ardent fascination for the New York City subways. And cleverly, Charles indulged it.

At a time when the subways were anathema to most New Yorkers, Charles brought them into his home. He purchased reams of tokens—gold slugs the size of a nickel—so that C. J. and Marcus could run chains through the cutout "Y" to start collections, or to wear as jewelry. He took the boys to the New York Transit Museum, where they explored vintage subway cars and played in working signal towers and saw antique turnstiles and trolleys. Patiently, and in great detail, Charles explained to the boys the vital role that subways played in the life of New Yorkers; explained how subways bound the city's boroughs and suburbs, and enabled people to travel to jobs and restaurants, theaters and schools, museums and sporting events; explained how his job, menial though it might seem, played a critical role in helping the city function.

But he went beyond merely that.

Charles saw the New York City subway system for the towering public works achievement it was, an engineering masterpiece of such magnitude that it should never be dismissed as just another urban mundanity. And he made it come alive for the boys in his care.

He told C. J. and Marcus stories about how the subways were built, explaining how tunnels and elevated structures had to be planned with consideration of streets and sewers, water and gas mains, telephone, and power conduits; how the foundations of buildings had to be reinforced to allow for underground work; how reinforced concrete and steel had to be used for the tunnels, and how manhole covers on the streets had to be placed a precise distance apart so that workers had access to electric cables below. He explained how different lines in the system needed different tunnel clearances; how electric power was transferred through miles of cable, and how different types of current had to be used to operate water pumps, signals, lighting, and ventilation. He pointed out the subway's unique architecture—the ornate period ironwork; the shaded, hook-armed lamps; the arched pillars—and explained how the colorful mosaic bands of glazed porcelain tile on station walls were created by skilled tile smiths as works of art. He explained, too, how each station had a different color pattern, geometric shape, and character denoting the station's initial or numeral—and how the walls of his Montrose Avenue station had the most beautiful mosaic band of all: exquisite cut porcelain with brilliant blue stripes and vivid pastel shades of rose, yellow, blue, maize, and white, all on a background of black, raspberry, and grayed lavender.

In this fashion, Charles Johnson was able to transform the subways from a mundane mode of transportation into a living, breathing classroom. And in this way, he helped C. J. learn.

Charles taught his learning-disabled son how you never tugged on a pull-cord unless there was an emergency, and why you never, ever, touched the third rail. He taught C. J. how the different subway lines—BMT, IRT, and IND—were identified by letter, number, and color codes; taught him how to read subway maps, how to travel to certain sections of the city, and how to identify different types of subway cars by the way they were constructed.

In school, C. J. struggled to learn simple arithmetic. Charles, however, described the subway system in mathematical terms that mesmerized his son. He explained how more than thirty million people a year passed through the city's busiest stations, at Times Square and Grand Central Station. He described the physical scope of the subway system in numerical terms that C. J. learned to recite: more than four hundred stations, thirty thousand turnstiles, seven hundred token booths, eighty-two bridges and tunnels, twenty-six thousand signals, relays, and switches, and enough track that, if laid end to end, could stretch all the way from New York to Chicago.

Beyond practical matters, Charles also saw the subways as an opportunity to teach his son about the wondrous city that lay beyond the narrow, squalid confines of Brownsville. The subways allowed C. J. to experience the New York that his father loved, the New York that had drawn Charles from the country roads and cotton fields and Jim Crow racism of the South.

And Charles experienced it alongside him.

As a Transit Authority worker, Charles could ride the subways for free. So could his son. And, for the better of two years, starting when C. J. was eight, Charles spent nearly every Saturday riding the subways with his son.

The New York that Charles showed C. J. was not the New York of world-renowned landmarks and sightseeing destinations. What Charles showed his son, instead, was the magic and mystery of the city's unseen moving parts, the hidden gears and pulleys that set the city in motion and made it work. The two of them rode the A train from upper Manhattan out to Far Rockaway. They rode the Brighton Line from Coney Island over the East River into Manhattan. They took the F train to the former site of the World's Fair, and the Number 1 train up to the northern tip of Manhattan, and the Number 7 line from Times Square to Queens.

All over the city, they traveled.

Charles took C. J. to the train yards in the Bronx, where new subway cars were delivered on flatbed trucks, and then towed by diesels to prepping locations around the city. He took him to the docks where refurbished cars were loaded onto barges heading out to the vast railroad network beyond the city. He took him to sprawling transit complexes where subway cars and motors were repaired around the clock. He took him to the car yard where he used to work, so his son could see how out-of-service trains were serviced and cleaned.

C. J. was having immense difficulty learning in a traditional classroom. But Charles managed to reach him in his own special way; managed to get his son's attention, stimulate his imagination; and make him understand. Besides, they were *together*. That was the magic of it all. That was the joy.

Charles would watch C. J.'s eyes brighten as the trains they rode roared from the darkness of tunnels into bright sunlight, rising steadily up steep, cast-iron elevated structures to race over the rooftops of homes and across long stretches of open track. He'd laugh as C. J. stood on rattan seats and gazed out half-open windows, so that he could feel the wind against his face. He'd cheer as C. J., arms spread wide, held his balance while the train, sparks flying, swerved and screeched through serpentine curves in pitch-black underground tunnels.

Their treks on the New York City subway had ended by the time C. J. was ten. The boy, by then, was on to other pursuits. But for Charles, those train rides were the happiest, most carefree times he ever spent with anyone in his life. C. J., Charles was certain, felt that way too. Charles could see it in his face; hear it in his delighted squeals, his unrestrained laughter.

It was only later when Charles fully realized why C. J. loved those subway rides so much. It wasn't simply the time he was spending with his father, or the places he got to see, or all the things he was able to learn. In truth, it was far simpler than that. It was because one of the few things C. J. could ever hear without the aid of his hearing device was the roar of the subway trains as they rumbled into each station, and the high-pitched screech of their wheels as they tore at breakneck speed through sharp curves in the tunnels beneath New York.

* * *

When Charles rejoined his visitors, the men were standing in the Johnsons' living room, examining the family photos on the wall.

"Wonderful photos," Councilman Hopkins remarked. "Fond memories."

Charles smiled. "Yes, we had some good times as a family."

"That's obvious," the NAACP's Hobbs observed. "It's equally obvious that you loved C. J. very much."

Charles nodded. "We never had much money, of course, and life was a struggle, what with C. J.'s health challenges. But we have many happy memories. And yes ... I loved my son very much."

"That's why we'd like you to consider the potential lawsuit we've brought to your attention," Hobbs said. "I've sat in too many homes with families that are grieving over a loss of a loved one at the hands of police—families, like yours, who've been left hurting. We're helping to provide justice for them, a small measure of relief."

The men drifted back to their seats.

"Please explain your organizations' role in this, should we proceed," Charles inquired.

"It's simple, really," Hobbs said. "Relying on our organizations' expertise and resources, we'd serve as your family's legal counsel, filing suit and assuring that your interests are represented in court or in negotiations with the city. We'd also help advise you, while serving as your family's spokesmen—its liaison to the media, the public, and City Hall."

Lost in thought, Charles said nothing. Like the possibility of lawsuits, the issues being raised now had never occurred to him until this very moment.

Hobbs pointed to the portrait hanging near the windows, an inexpensive rendering that Charles had framed himself.

"I see you're a fan of Dr. King," the NCAA official rasped.

Charles nodded. "Very much so."

"I knew Dr. King well … a great man." Hobbs dabbed with his handkerchief at watery eyes. "But although we were staunch believers in the same cause, we didn't always see eye to eye."

"How so?" Charles asked.

"Well, Dr. King's dream, in many ways, is the 'American Dream'—a dream that we fight for every day," Hobbs said. "But the civil rights movement has been shaped by *many* ideas, not simply one. Some of us, frustrated by the glacial pace of change, believe that Dr. King's ideology of nonviolent activism is not forceful enough to end racial inequality … that a more militant approach is needed, certainly when it comes to legal action."

"But hasn't there been progress?" Charles asked. "I remember what it was like living in the South. Living here in New York is nothing like that."

"Oh, there's been progress," Hobbs rasped, "through decades of grassroots protests, nonviolent resistance, civil-disobedience campaigns, and militant action. Slavery was abolished. Jim Crow was dismantled. The civil rights movement achieved enormous gains in the '60s, with the breakdown of legal segregation."

"But?"

"But as Dr. King said, 'The plant of freedom has grown only a bud and not yet a flower.'"

"And that means—?"

"It means there's a long way to go."

Hobbs rubbed his leaky eye with a fingertip.

"Major inequities, you see, still exist despite the gains we've made," he said. "Racial injustice, as Dr. King said, is the Black man's burden, a hellhound that gnaws at Blacks in every waking movement of our lives. Even as we celebrate America's Bicentennial, and the ideals our founding fathers espoused, the legacy of slavery continues to reverberate, and Blacks remain virtually invisible in a society that's otherwise so affluent. We should never confuse 'progress' with true equality, Mr. Johnson. Equality, I suspect, will be resisted by many people to the death. But so will inequality."

"In other words," Cooper added, "we must continue our movement."

"You see," Hobbs said, turning to Charles, "the Jim Crow violence you experienced in the South is linked in many ways to a northern police callousness, brutality, and abuse against Blacks. The lethal force of systemic racism that killed C. J. is simply a reflection of racial fissures that have existed in America for hundreds of years. Those fissures have claimed an untold number of Black lives, and they're killing the possibility of democracy for all."

"But the response that we're seeing, the riots," Charles said. "They're so destructive."

"The riots are deplorable, I agree," Hobbs said. "But Dr. King called them 'derivative crimes'—crimes born of even greater crimes: discrimination, poverty, unemployment, racism, and police officers making a mockery of the law."

"The killing of C. J. is simply the latest in a series of killings of unarmed Black people by police in America," Cooper said, "and a growing number of us refuse to accept what's been 'normal' for far too long. We believe that the protests we're seeing, abhorrent as some are, are setting in motion a period of sustained social and political change. We believe that the shooting of C. J. may prove to be a powerful catalyst, a tipping point that's truly consequential. There are critical issues at stake. We believe that this case may well catapult our movement into the national spotlight."

"Our movement, as Mr. Cooper suggested, is marching on a path through neighborhoods like Brownsville," Hobbs rasped. "Police shooting cases, in many respects, are the 'new frontier' of the civil rights movement. You can stand by and watch, or you can do something concrete. You can be part of our movement and help make the city accountable for the actions of its police."

"All we're asking," said Cooper, "is that you give us the opportunity to push city officials in that direction, help you navigate tricky legal waters, and serve as your liaison to the outside world. In other words, allow yourself to focus on the things that are most important—taking care of your family and allowing yourself to grieve. As far as representing and protecting your interests, and getting the justice you deserve, we're asking that you leave that to us."

"Are your services expensive?" Charles asked.

"Not at all," Cooper said. "Everything our organizations would do would be *pro bono*. In other words, because this case is so important, we'd secure no compensation whatsoever in exchange for our services. And any financial redress you might receive from the city would be yours to keep."

"Aside from benefitting personally, there are many worthy things you can do with the money," said Hobbs. "Your church, I'm sure, could find a use for a donation. There's a multitude of causes you can support, as well—including, of course, civil rights organizations like the ACLU."

"Political campaigns, too," Councilman Hopkins winked.

All of them laughed.

"Well, I think I understand what you're asking," said Charles.

"Do we have your permission to proceed?" Hobbs inquired.

"Well, I'd like to think it over for a while, and discuss it with my wife," Charles said.

"Of course," Hobbs said. "And please don't forget … there's the matter of a second lawsuit—an equally important issue—that we'd like to discuss."

"Understood," Charles said. "But that will also have to wait. Right now, you see, Eunice and I have to get ready to bury our son."

Chapter 34

THE FOLLOWING DAY broke peacefully over Brownsville, the funeral service for C. J. Johnson giving rise to a temporary lull in the anti-police demonstrations rocking the neighborhood.

Some two thousand people marched silently over the six-block route from the Johnsons' apartment building to the Good Shepherd Baptist Church, an ornate, wattle-and-daub temple that had served as a neighborhood landmark since the 1920s. Leading the procession was a sleek, white hearse—paid for by a coalition of civil rights organizations—behind which Charles and Eunice Johnson walked arm in arm with C. J.'s cousin Marcus, several church congregants, and the Rev. Josiah Watson. Immediately following was a row of dignitaries, including New York City Mayor Nathan Worth, NYPD Chief of Department Patrick Delaney, and other city officials, followed by a sea of humanity stretching an entire city block. Scattered onlookers left their sidewalk vantage points to touch the slow-moving hearse in a gesture of silent tribute, C. J. Johnson far larger in death than he'd ever been in life, a symbol now as much as he'd ever been just a boy.

Inside the church, mourners filed solemnly past C. J.'s open casket before greeting the Johnsons in their front-row pew and filling row upon row of wooden benches. Dozens of floral arrangements and colorful sympathy wreathes sat on tripods near the altar. Organ music filled the vaulted sanctuary. Gathering hymns and spirituals were sung by the church choir, followed by a succession of prayers, Gospel readings, and psalms.

What mourners heard next was the temperate, measured voice of Charles Johnson, piped through a loudspeaker to the street, where hundreds of mourners had gathered, many waving fans and huddling under umbrellas to shield themselves from the searing heat.

"I want to thank you on behalf of our family for your outpouring of sympathy and support," said Charles, reading from a statement.

"Yes, we're mourning the loss of our beloved son, Clifford, but we want our voice to be one of calm while the investigations into C. J.'s death proceed," Charles said. "Please allow us to mourn our loss with dignity and respect, and don't use our son's death as a reason for violence. C. J. was a good and gentle soul, innocent and peaceful in life. We hope he can be that way in death, too. Please pray for us and know that your prayers will give us the strength we need to lift ourselves from our grief. We will find peace in knowing that our son is with God."

Then Charles, his voice cracking, closed his remarks.

"Lastly," he said, "we say to every parent who has ever lost a child: we know how deeply you hurt. For every other parent, we ask you to love your children as we loved our son. Love them … and let them know it."

Rev. Watson then invited Mayor Worth to join him at the pulpit.

The son of Russian immigrants, Nathan Worth, had risen from indigent roots on Manhattan's Lower East Side to become the first Jewish mayor in New York's history, a political late bloomer who'd cut his teeth in municipal government as the city's comptroller. A diminutive, slender man, the mayor looked overwhelmed by the enormity of the occasion, though deeply moved by the moment at hand. Rev. Watson and the mayor embraced, before bowing their heads in silent prayer. Mayor Worth then strode to the pulpit, lowering the microphone to his height.

"Words cannot adequately express the sorrow our city feels over the loss of this innocent, young boy," the mayor told the gathering. "I stand before you, apologizing on behalf of New York for this tragic death. We can never undo what happened, but I pledge to every one of you that we will learn from this incident and do everything humanly possible to prevent similar tragedies from occurring again."

"I pray to God," Mayor Worth said, "that I never have to come to another child's funeral anywhere in New York."

The mayor and Rev. Watson embraced. The minister then moved to the pulpit, reading first from the Book of Job, then closing his Bible to address the congregation.

"When a person dies," he said, "part of us dies, too. When that person is as young and beloved as Clifford Johnson, it hurts that much more. Today, we mourn for C. J., for the Johnson family, and for others who've been victims of tragedies like this. We don't point fingers. We don't spew bitterness and hatred. We don't commit acts of violence. We only pray that those who are suffering from the talons of life's hardships find peace."

"Amen," the congregation said as one.

"We are haunted as a people," Rev. Watson said, after a brief silence. "We are haunted by our differences, entrapped by our fears, victimized by the hatred and prejudice that lives within us. Even in the face of history, we deny that there's a racial fault line running through the heart of our nation, and that race is an issue that divides us. But we can no longer deny what has forever frayed the fabric of our society and what diminishes us as human beings. Nor can we hide from it."

Rev. Watson studied the congregation, seated amidst beams of sunlight that poured through the chapel's window mosaics.

"The reaction that has surrounded the shooting of C. J. Johnson has, in many ways, shone a spotlight on the uglier side of who we are as a people," he said. "It has lain bare—through violence and blind accusations, hatred and stereotypes perpetrated even before we know the truth about what happened—that we have far to go and much to learn."

"Amen," several in the congregation said.

"We need to put to rest many of our old ways," the minister continued. "We need to look into secret places in our heart and ask ourselves: Why do we hate? Why do we mistrust? Why do we fear? Why do we see our differences before we see our similarities? Why do we see each other as abstractions and not as people? If the answers are raw and ugly, then that's even more reason to understand them. We are divided but need to come together. We are blind to each other but need to see. We are deaf to one another but need to hear. We are wounded but need to heal."

Rev. Watson lowered his voice again, staring at the congregation.

"God uses ordinary people for purposes that only He understands," he continued. "And although C. J. Johnson may have seemed ordinary in life, he has become extraordinary in death. Let the death of this gentle, innocent boy be a new beginning, a wake-up call for us to confront the issues we need to face. Let it help us find a way toward peace, enable us to bridge our differences. Let it become a defining moment for a new and better city. Let it be the start of healing."

Rev. Watson implored the mourners to pray silently.

"I ask for your calm and your prayers," he then said. "I ask that your only outcry be for a world in which we can live in peace, in which we can repair a broken trust, gain an understanding, boycott hatred and fear, protest prejudice and violence, move forward, and honor Clifford Johnson's memory not by coming apart, but by coming together to build a stronger city."

The reverend looked to the sky.

"Lord, we need to heal," he said. "We pray now for peace and reconciliation. We pray for our neighborhood to be reborn, for people working and laughing and building, for children learning and loving and playing. We pray that the dark cloud over us now can soon be lifted. We ask you, Lord, to give us the wisdom to save us from ourselves. May your love and wisdom light our way."

"Amen," the congregation said as one.

Regal in his Army uniform, Marcus Johnson then offered a tribute to his late cousin and the church's children's choir, joined by the entire congregation, sang *Amazing Grace.* Eunice and Charles Johnson then walked to the casket, leaned in, and kissed their son goodbye.

When the service concluded, the Johnson family led mourners out to the street, as classmates of C. J. released balloons that drifted lazily toward the sky. Once again, people reached out to touch the hearse as it pulled from the church, accompanied by an NYPD motorcycle escort.

As it departed, a man in the crowd held aloft a large sign: *LET THE HEALING BEGIN.*

"Amen to that," someone said aloud.

The hearse carrying C. J. Johnson's casket then left for Kennedy Airport, to be loaded onto a plane and flown to the slain youth's final resting place, a family burial plot near Charles's South Carolina birthplace, adjacent to a former cotton field that Charles labored in once as a child, overgrown now with dandelions that made it appear, in the brilliant southern sunshine, like a shimmering field of gold.

Chapter 35

BUT THE PEACEFUL NEW BEGINNING solicited in the wake of C. J. Johnson's death didn't come without further enmity and turbulence. Nor did it come so soon.

The day that followed the slain teen's funeral service was designated as a "Strike Day" in Brownsville, with businesses urged—and in some cases threatened—to close in symbolic protest of an alleged pattern of police misconduct and systemic racism in the community. Offices, banks, and retail outlets were largely shuttered. With schools closed for summer recess, residents remaining indoors, and most traffic banned from the neighborhood, streets were devoid of everything but police cars and emergency equipment. A 9:00 PM curfew remained in effect.

Although large-scale rioting had subsided by now, Brownsville remained a hotbed of unrest. Teams of police officers scoured buildings, apartments, and streets for troublemakers. Agitators continued to infiltrate the neighborhood. Anonymous phone calls to police precincts and media outlets threatened guerilla warfare against the NYPD. In the adjacent community of Bedford-Stuyvesant, a white officer was ambushed and stabbed by two Black men voicing retaliation for the shooting of C. J. Johnson. Similar attacks took place in Harlem and the Bronx.

"There's blood on the hands of anyone who incites violence against the police under the guise of protest," PBA president Red McLaren told the press. "Police officers are not criminals. Police officers *reduce* crime—including those against Blacks. They're on our streets, day and night, putting their lives on the line while trying to protect the public. We owe them a debt of gratitude instead of unwarranted attacks. They're the only things standing between a lawful society and utter chaos."

But declarations like those did little to alter the prevailing tide. Anti-police protests were gaining momentum by the minute. Nor were they confined solely to Brownsville. Mass demonstrations reminiscent of the antiwar rallies of the '60s were now being staged at City Hall, NYPD headquarters, and the offices of the PBA. Political pressure, at the same time, was being ratcheted up. Representatives from a coalition of grassroots social justice groups met with the editorial boards of the city's leading newspapers to present a case for sweeping police reform, their demands including stricter guidelines for police use of force. The same group—pushing for a grand jury probe and potential criminal charges against Matt Holland and Rachel Cook—met with Kings County D.A. Hal Green.

At noon on "Strike Day," more than three thousand demonstrators, ferried to Manhattan in rented school buses, massed at the foot of the Brooklyn Bridge. Forming a human chain, they marched along Broadway toward City Hall, wreaking havoc on downtown traffic. Cars attempting to inch through the sign-carrying throng were battered and rocked. Angry motorists, horns blaring, shouted at demonstrators. Epithets were hurled back and forth. Fistfights broke out between demonstrators and passersby.

In front of City Hall, demonstrators staged a noisy rally, replete with chants, songs, threats, and taunts. Waving multicolored flags and banging on drums, they stood under a giant banner that read, *STOP KILLER COPS!*

Smaller signs and banners carried similar messages.

STOP POLICE BRUTALITY!

BLACK DOES NOT EQUAL CRIMINAL!

JUSTICE FOR C. J. JOHNSON!

Protest marshals, sporting black tee shirts and white armbands, led calls for the suspensions and arrests of Matt Holland and Rachel Cook. Many of the demonstrators wore T-shirts bearing the likeness of the slain teen. Linking arms, they chanted in unison, their voice echoing off the concrete canyons of Broadway:

"What do we want?"

"JUSTICE!"

"When do we want it?"

"NOW!"

A column of helmeted cops, some on horseback, positioned themselves between the protestors and passing vehicles. Others sealed off the iron-gated City Hall. Undercover officers who'd infiltrated the demonstration worked to monitor the crowd and establish calm. Still, the bitterness prevailed.

"Drop dead!" protestors shouted at the officers.

"Fuck you, pigs!"

"Pigs in a blanket … Fry 'em like bacon!"

Clutching nightsticks, the grim-faced officers eyed the demonstrators with a mixture of apprehension, anger, hatred, and fear. One woman walked up to a cop and defiantly shouted: "Shoot me … I'm Black, too!"

Jaw twitching, face clenched like a fist, the officer did nothing.

"You're killing us!" a Black man sneered, standing nose to nose with a White cop. "You're killing our children! You gonna kill me, too?"

The officer, blinking away rivers of sweat, took no action.

A demonstrator then held a young Black child high over his head.

"Here's another innocent Black boy," he shouted to cops. "Why don't you motherfuckers shoot him, too?"

* * *

While demonstrators rallied outside, protest leaders squared off yet again with NYPD brass, this time in City Hall's ornate Governor's Room, where grievances were reiterated and demands repeated for the suspension, arrest, and prosecution of Matt Holland and Rachel Cook.

As before, City officials countered with assurances that both the NYPD's internal probe and a parallel investigation by the Kings County D.A. were proceeding aggressively, and urged restraint by those seeking a kneejerk condemnation of the officers. Police officials, for the first time, also made public Holland's and Cook's separate accounts of the C. J. Johnson shooting, including both officers' claims that the incident had been nothing more than a tragic accident, rather than a racially motivated instance of police abuse. Hours earlier, Charles and Eunice Johnson had been afforded a private briefing regarding the officers' formal statements about the incident.

"We understand the nature of your protests, but we cannot condone an atmosphere that's inflammatory and divisive," said Robert Turetsky, chief of staff for Mayor Nathan Worth. "The rhetoric has gotten out of control. This is a time to mourn a tragic death and to investigate the factors that contributed to it, so that incidents like this don't reoccur and justice is rendered."

Present, aside from Turetsky, was a pair of officials from the Mayor's Office of Operations, which oversaw the city's law enforcement agencies. Present, too, was NYPD Chief of Department Patrick Delaney. Mayor Worth and Police Commissioner Dunne, protest leaders were informed, were involved in separate, closed-door meetings on the same topic.

"This is not a time for politics, speculation, or blind accusation—nor is it a time for rumor, racial mudslinging, and mass hysteria," said Turetsky, a bespectacled veteran of city government. "We must remain open-minded and allow the investigations to proceed without racial overtones or the pressure of public opinion. The last thing we need is a rush to judgment. We must let the system work."

"The problem is that the system that's currently in place *doesn't* work," charged Wilfred Clark, the NYU professor who'd met with police officials in the aftermath of the riots. "It's a system that's one-sided, biased, and flawed. Why should we wait for the outcome of an investigation when the 'outcome' is a foregone conclusion? It'll be the same outcome as past 'investigations' into police officers who kill."

"We don't know that for certain—and to suggest it is irresponsible," Turetsky said. "What's happened in the past is no excuse for jumping to conclusions based on passion and prejudice. We can't punish these officers while we await answers, and we can't cast a shadow over the entire NYPD because of what happened. We just need time to bring the facts to light."

"You don't *have* time!" Clark said. "People want action *now*!"

"We recognize that," Turetsky said. "But this matter requires time. It involves a process that must proceed carefully, objectively, and free of emotion. Racial prejudices and anti-police bias have no place here. We need the truth for the sake of everyone, including the officers. They should be neither blindly vilified nor blindly defended based on false and biased assumptions."

"You're missing the point!" Clark argued. "Our protests aren't about this singular incident—they're about a *pattern*, an irresponsible use of firearms by police that's reached epidemic proportions. Every case like this has striking parallels: a White officer, a Black victim, public outrage, accusations, denials, investigations. The officer says one thing, witnesses something else. And then, always the same result: the Black victim is dead, the police officer walks, and eventually all of it goes away … only to happen again."

"No!" Clark's cohort, Ibrahim Shabazz, slammed his fist on the conference table. "Our protests are about years of incidents like this! They're about out-of-control police officers feeling like they can do as they wish and then hiding behind a 'blue wall of silence,' with no accountability or culpability. Quite frankly, police officers in America feel as though they're above the law."

"And the way things are now, that feeling is justified," Clark added. "When all is said and done, the officers involved in this shooting will be vindicated. You'll see. They'll be back on the street before anyone can bat an eye."

"Frankly, I resent that!" Chief of Department Delaney barked, and all eyes swung to him. "No one in the NYPD gets thrown an automatic lifeline! If officers break the law, they're held accountable, just like anyone. Our investigations into officer-related shootings are rigorous. No one wants officers who wantonly use deadly force out on the street."

"Then how come so many of them are?" Shabazz said. "And how come they always seem to get away with their crimes? Giving officers a gun and a shield doesn't give them a green light to commit crimes and make excuses for their wrongdoing. Nor does it allow them to be treated under a different set of rules than others. Police would be far less likely to kill Black people if they didn't think they could continue to get away with it."

"You make it sound as if police shootings happen every day," said Delaney.

"Don't they?"

"In fact, they don't. Shootings like this may get a lot of publicity but, in reality, they're aberrations."

"That's your opinion," Clark scoffed.

"It's not an opinion; it's a fact!" Delaney said. "Police in America make millions of contacts with civilians each year. Only a handful results in the use of deadly force."

"Maybe so," said Clark, "but when officers *do* shoot, it's usually a Black man on the wrong end of the bullet."

"That's also a fallacy," Delaney retorted. "In truth, most police-shooting victims are actually White."

"With all due respect," Clark said, "you're adding insult to injury by spouting statistics. Numbers won't be accepted as answers. There's no question that police shootings are linked to deep, longstanding racial inequities. Police undervalue Black lives … and you know it!"

"Besides," Shabazz added, "any assertions you make are far less important to us than your assurance that decisive action will be taken against Officers Holland and Cook. To allow them to remain on the job—and even free from jail—is not only infuriating, it may also be criminal."

"As I said," Turetsky replied, "no action will be taken against Officers Holland and Cook until a thorough, impartial investigation establishes the facts. In the meantime, shouting at one another will only further tear this city apart."

The room fell silent but for the muted sound of anti-police demonstrations outside.

"You know," Delaney said, "this shooting is being portrayed as a malicious, brutal murder. You men are creating the deception that our officers shot C. J. Johnson in cold blood because they're callous, brutal, and racist."

"Why should we believe otherwise?" Clark said.

"Because maybe what this incident is," said Delaney, "is a textbook example of the kind of gut-wrenching, life-and-death decisions police officers are sometimes called upon to make. Maybe it's about two officers reacting under intense pressure, relying solely on instinct, reflex, and split-second judgment. It's quite possible—and frankly likely—that this so-called murder was simply an unavoidable accident ... a tragedy, but not the racist act you're alleging."

Delaney sat ramrod straight, his words dripping with contempt. Shabazz and Clark locked eyes with the police commander.

"How many times do we have to hear that shooting incidents like this are just another 'tragic accident'?" Clark said. "And how many of these 'tragic accidents' do we need to have before we recognize that they're not the aberrations you claim they are but are, in fact, part of the pattern we charge? The idea that we can dismiss this as another 'unavoidable accident' or 'isolated incident' is insulting. There have been too many similar incidents disguised in that manner."

"It's strange, isn't it," Shabazz said, "but every time an officer kills an innocent person, *the officer* somehow becomes the victim. The shooting is never the cop's fault. It's always an 'accident ... an innocent, unavoidable mistake.'"

"Most of the time, it is," Delaney said.

"You know what I say to that?" Shabazz said. "I say it's a crock of shit!"

Delaney leaned forward, the tension in the room palpable.

"I can't believe that you're actually trying to solicit sympathy for the cops," Clark said.

"Why not?" Delaney retorted. "They're victims, too."

"Victims? That's laughable!" Shabazz said. "Both officers are alive, aren't they? Both are free. Both are going home tonight to their normal lives. How can you equate whatever hardships they may be facing to the reality that an innocent boy—the *true* victim here—is dead?"

"The officers are alive, that's true," Delaney said, "but, believe me, they're paying a price for what happened. No one ever thinks about that. Police officers put on a uniform and a badge, and they become an 'object,' lose their identity as human beings. Those two officers, I can assure you, are devastated by what has happened. Their careers, and perhaps their freedom, are in jeopardy. Their lives have been turned upside down. They'll have to live with the emotional fallout of this incident for the rest of their lives."

Again, a taut, protracted silence.

"All you're doing now is deflecting attention from the real issue," Clark said. "Our point is that we no longer buy the story you're trying to sell. It's too simplistic to automatically dismiss police shootings as 'unfortunate byproducts' of the work. They're just excuses for killing. Shoot the gun. Claim your life was being threatened. Rest assured that no one will come after you because you're just a 'hard-working cop trying to do his job,' and you can fall into a safety net of protection. Instead of taking the blame, the police blame their mistakes on circumstances. And what happens? The victim gets buried, the cop walks, and the beat goes on. This is bullshit! What happened in that cellar was no accident. It's just another symptom of a greater disease. The real issue is *racism*, pure and simple."

"That, in your words, is what's 'bullshit,'" Delaney bristled. "The officers involved in this shooting were summoned, guns drawn, to what they believed was a crime-in-progress, with suspects still believed to be on the scene in a pitch-black cellar. For all they knew, they were being attacked."

"Attacked?" Clark snickered. "Please! This boy was fourteen years old. Unarmed. Innocent. Handicapped. Does that fit the profile of a criminal?"

"That's a cheap shot … and you know it!" Delaney said.

"Well," said Shabazz, "how can you call what happened an 'attack'?"

Delaney drew a deep breath, struggling to retain control.

"For God's sake, try to understand," he said. "You have two officers responding to a call for an apparent crime-in-progress in a neighborhood with a high crime rate. The officers are emotionally charged. The situation is unfolding rapidly. The lighting is virtually non-existent. Identities are blurred. Intent is undefined. Actions are misinterpreted. Commands are ignored. Now a figure who the officers can barely see comes at one of them rapidly. Decision-making under those circumstances, I can assure you, is a complex calculus. Even the most experienced officers can't distinguish reality from perception."

"What are you trying to say?" Shabazz queried.

"I'm trying to ask you to put yourself in the officer's place," Delaney implored. "In his mind, there was a reasonable belief that his life was in imminent danger. For all he knew, that boy could've been charging at him with a weapon. He had no time to assess the situation. He was in an ambiguous no-man's land, with complex choices that needed to be made in the blink of an eye. Shoot or hold fire? Use force or reason? Arrest or desist? Kill or get killed? There's not a police officer in the world who doesn't dread being in that situation. Who's to say that, under the circumstances, any of us would've acted differently?"

Delaney paused, as if to let his words sink in.

"And yet," he continued, "Detective Sergeant Holland, according to his testimony, still pulled his arm back, willing to give the victim the benefit of the doubt, willing to potentially sacrifice his own life to avoid making a mistake. His action could well have been reflexive or could have occurred on impact. One errant shot. One unfortunate ricochet …"

"Well, perhaps with better training—"

"That's precisely my point!" Delaney interrupted. "The NYPD already has the most progressive use-of-force policies in America. We've screened recruits, implemented anti-bias practices, and trained our officers in cultural awareness, crisis intervention, and de-escalation techniques. The truth is, *no* amount of training can prepare anyone for what those officers encountered in that cellar, nor can it prevent tragedies from happening. We can train our officers in many ways, but we can't train them to be psychics."

"Perhaps not," Shabazz stated, "but you can train them to be correct."

"That's my other point," Delaney said. "We don't require that our officers always be correct. The only thing we require is that they be reasonable. The questions we ask are, 'Did they follow proper procedure? Did their actions conform to regulations? Could they have resolved the situation differently?'"

Delaney paused, drew a deep breath, and then said, "Based on everything I can tell, police brutality had nothing to do with this shooting. Nor did race. I believe this shooting would have happened if the boy were Black, White, purple, or green. Race wasn't a factor at all."

Shabazz recoiled. "Are you saying that the NYPD's investigation has already concluded … that your statement is definitive?"

"No," Delaney said. "There are still loose ends to tie up. But what I am saying is that, in my view, the two officers involved in this incident did everything by the book. They followed their training, adhered to department protocol. According to the officers' testimony, Detective Sergeant Holland didn't mean to shoot the boy. His gunshot was unintentional, a ricochet. On top of that, he made a desperate attempt at lifesaving resuscitation. Doesn't *that* count? Do you think the officer would have rendered that sort of aid if he wanted the boy to die?"

"And you believe the officers' accounts?" Shabazz challenged.

"Based on their records and the plausibility of their testimony," Delaney said, "we have no reason *not* to believe them."

"Well, we beg to differ," Clark said. "Race is always a factor in cases like this. We deny it because it frightens us, and we don't want to admit to it. But denial is just another symptom of the illness. All it does is make the problem more intractable."

"Tell us this," said Shabazz, "how come we never hear about white kids getting killed by white cops, or about Black kids being killed by Black cops? Do you really think that someone would've gotten shot if those officers had been summoned to a similar call in a White neighborhood? Would they have been as fearful? Would they have drawn their guns and burst into that cellar? Would the kids have run?"

No one answered.

"Your silence," Clark observed, "is just another way of saying 'no.' In fact, I'm sure the officers would've handled the whole thing differently. They would've knocked at the door, politely asked for an explanation, received one, and gone on their way. Instead, there was an assumption that whoever was in that cellar was antagonistic. The only 'threat' that C. J. Johnson represented was that he was Black. He was prejudged as a criminal, doomed by his race. It's dangerous to be Black in this country. We already know that. Is it now also dangerous to be young and unarmed and innocent? Is everyone in neighborhoods like Brownsville a criminal to police? In the mindset those cops had—"

"Excuse me," Delaney interjected, "but what mindset do you think those officers should have had, given the circumstances. Sure, they were on guard, suspicious, fearful. They'd have been brain-dead if they weren't. What you fail to see is that our officers may have profound suspicions of the people they police, but those suspicions in many cases are legitimate."

"Are you saying that the outcome of a situation like this is justified?"

"No, I'm saying that it was tragic and regrettable. But it was also reasonable and explainable, given the facts as we know them."

"Those officers 'profiled' that boy . . . plain and simple," Shabazz charged.

"Yeah?" Delaney asked. "And what about the caller who phoned police in the first place—the one who assumed there was a crime-in-progress?"

"What about her?"

"Well, wasn't she profiling those kids, too—as burglars? And what about the preconceived notion, on the part of the kids in the cellar, that they had to be fearful of the police? Isn't that a form of profiling, too? Why does it only cut one way?"

"Because," Clark said, "innocent Black people are losing their lives!"

Delaney fingered a water glass atop the conference table.

"Look," he conceded, "I'll admit that our officers need to stop seeing every minority they encounter as a stereotype ... and I'll admit that racist police shootings occasionally take place. But what about those instances where the shooting is justified? What happens in cases where a shooting can be explained as nothing more than an unfortunate tragedy? Do we walk blindly down a path toward injustice, and destroy an officer's life, simply to account for past wrongs? Do we make a good cop pay an egregious price that's undeserved? Are we to assume guilt based simply on racial bias that may or may not exist? Are the officers guilty simply because it's time for a cop, however innocent, to pay for the sins of the past?"

The room fell silent again.

"Perhaps in our quest to right past wrongs," Delaney said, "the pendulum is swinging too far in the other direction. Perhaps in our rush to win 'justice' for the minority community, we're allowing our emotions and prejudices to stand in the way of the truth, letting our anger and our biases lead us down a path rutted with false conclusions, and doing a grave injustice to a pair of innocent cops."

"Your officers need to stop seeing every Black person they encounter through racist eyes," Shabazz said. "Plain and simple!"

"And the Black community needs to stop seeing every White cop as a racist enemy," Delaney said. "This incident is being used to bash the entire police department and paint everyone in it with the same broad brush. Frankly, you're exhibiting the same kind of blind prejudice toward police that you claim they exhibit to you. Don't the same rules apply to everyone? Or is it taboo to consider the possibility that all of us—White and Black—harbor stereotypes, hatred, and mistrust?"

"Well, if you're telling us that this shooting was within NYPD guidelines, then the department's guidelines need to be rewritten," Clark said.

"And how would you suggest we do that?" Delaney asked. "Should we put into the *NYPD Patrol Guide* that there'll be no more confrontations between White officers and Black civilians in dark cellars or streets? Should we revise our policies to eliminate fear and confusion and references to past cases where officers were killed because they hesitated? In truth, there's no way to avoid these kinds of incidents. Our officers are human, and the nature of their job makes incidents like this a reality. No matter how good we are at what we do, mistakes will be made, tragedies like this will occur. To take action against the officer before the facts are in would simply layer a grave injustice upon the tragedy."

Clark and Shabazz rose from their seats now.

"Well, we're not ready to accept that," Shabazz said. "We're not ready to stand by and watch old wounds continually get reopened. I fear, gentlemen, that our capacity to understand each other has been lost, and the distance between us is too wide to bridge. Quite frankly, I fear that this city is headed toward an abyss."

Chapter 36

As ANTI-POLICE PROTESTS RAGED mere blocks away, Matt and Katie Holland met at Patrolmen's Benevolent Association headquarters with PBA president Red McLaren and the union's legal counsel, Eddie Shearson.

Chain-smoking Marlboros, McLaren was ensconced behind a desk set before a wall filled with photos, citations, and other police memorabilia. Shearson sat in a guest chair alongside the Hollands, who clasped hands as the attorney provided an update on the C. J. Johnson shooting case.

"Let me explain it in the simplest possible terms," Shearson said. "As you know, Matt has been placed on paid administrative leave pending the outcome of the department's internal investigation. It's routine in police-shooting cases. Matt's 'job' for the foreseeable future is to answer questions and cooperate to the fullest extent possible with investigators."

Holland nodded, squeezing his wife's hand.

"How long will they be putting Matt through the ringer?" Katie asked.

"Could be a while," Shearson lamented.

"What does that mean?"

"Weeks ... maybe even months."

"But the same questions, over and over?" Katie blanched. "Confrontational, almost accusatory ... as if Matt is some kind of criminal?"

"I'm afraid so." Shearson pulled on his cigarette. "The process is excruciating and unfair, but that's the way these interrogations are handled."

"They're looking under every rock," Red McLaren explained.

"They're also trying to establish consistency," Shearson said. "The fact is, immediately after a shooting, an officer may be too shaken up to recall events accurately. As time passes, and memories become more distinct, information obtained during initial rounds of questioning may conflict with later statements."

"Stories can also change," said McLaren. "It's happened before."

"Nothing has changed in the accounts Matt has provided," Katie said. "And nothing *will* change, either. The truth is unassailable, regardless of how people wish to twist it."

"And the truth," Shearson said, "is very much in Matt's favor."

"The only question," Red McLaren added, "is will the truth be enough?"

"It'll have to be," Shearson said, "because the truth is all we've got."

Under NYPD guidelines, the attorney explained, an officer was considered justified in discharging his firearm if he or she had reasonable cause to believe that an attacker could cause death or serious bodily injury to the officer or to others.

"This 'green light' applies if the threat is either overt or perceived," Shearson explained. "Reasonable cause to shoot could be based on an officer seeing a suspect make a sudden or threatening movement. In this case, the fact that the cellar was pitch-black at the time of the shooting, the victim made physical contact with Matt, and the fatal shot was a ricochet, renders Matt's actions defensible."

"Even if people charge that it was a callous, racially motivated act?" McLaren asked, facetiously.

"The facts speak for themselves," Shearson said. "Hopefully, those facts will come to light."

In essence, Shearson explained, Matt Holland would be subject to several simultaneous investigations. One was being conducted by a unit of the Internal Affairs Division, a panel of five senior officers whose role would be to determine if the officer violated department guidelines. Once the panel determined whether the shooting was justified, they'd forward the case to the NYPD's in-house prosecutor for a departmental trial, its verdict to be rendered by an administrative law judge. A decision on any disciplinary action, including potential suspension and loss of pension, would rest with Police Commissioner William Dunne.

"We're confident," said McClaren, "that Matt will clear all of those bars."

"But then," Shearson warned, "there's the matter of the D.A."

The Kings County District Attorney, like New York's four other D.A.s, Shearson explained, exercised enormous discretion over which of thousands of potential criminal cases would be prosecuted—and how vigorously—along with which cases could be plea-bargained and which pleas would be accepted.

"In that sense, a D.A.'s personal biases and political allegiance are instrumental in shaping the tone of criminal justice in New York," Shearson said. "It's entirely up to the D.A. to decide whether this matter could wind up in criminal court and, if Matt is charged criminally, what those charges might be."

"Charged criminally?" said Katie, alarmed. "I don't understand."

"Well, regardless of what the NYPD decides based on its investigation, a D.A. could find enough evidence to present the matter to a grand jury for a possible indictment, or he could find insufficient evidence and drop the matter entirely," Shearson explained. "If the evidence for a potential criminal charge does go to a grand jury, the case could be dismissed, or Matt could be indicted and later tried."

"And frankly," Shearson added, "that scares the hell out of me."

Katie Holland blanched. Her husband twisted in his chair.

"But don't D.A.s historically favor cops in shooting cases?" McLaren asked.

"Historically, yes." Shearson lit another cigarette. "But there are extenuating circumstances in this case."

"What do you mean by 'extenuating'?"

"There's an election on tap," Shearson said. "That changes the calculus."

Shearson's concerns were well-founded. The District Attorney for Brooklyn, known formally as Kings County, was a veteran prosecutor named Hal Green, whose tenure had been notable, among other things, for its staunch advocacy of minority communities. While Green was seen as a straight shooter—his reputation solid among prosecutors, judges, and defense attorneys—his current four-year term was soon to expire. Indeed, Green was up for re-election in November, running on the same Democratic ticket as Mayor Worth, in what political pollsters were calling a historically tight race.

"So, what can we expect from Hal Green?" Red McLaren asked.

"Under normal circumstances, I think Matt would get a fair shake," Shearson said. "But to be honest with you, now I just don't know."

"What does that mean?" McLaren inquired.

"It means," said Shearson, "that these are not 'normal' times. The political winds are shifting to the left."

"D.A.s are turning up the heat on cops, huh?" McLaren asked.

"Yeah," Shearson nodded. "Most social justice advocates believe that police have gotten away with too much in the past: systemic racism, brutality, unjustified use of force, you name it. In any number of cases, frankly, their charges are justified … though you'll never hear me say that publicly."

"And people," McLaren said, "are hell-bent on correcting past 'sins,' right?"

"That's the reality," Shearson said. "Police departments are under mounting pressure to weed out 'bad apples.' Reformers are pushing for change. Grand juries are starting to indict. Some prosecutors are looking to press charges—in some cases simply to placate the minority community or to advance their careers."

"In other words, Hal Green may be looking to set an example," Red McLaren said. "He may be out to hang a cop."

Katie Holland, teary-eyed, looked as if she were about to fall from her chair. "And the facts surrounding the shooting?" she sputtered.

"Frankly," Shearson said, "the facts may be irrelevant." The attorney took another poke on his cigarette. "I'm afraid," he said, "that Matt is as much a victim of bad timing as the kid he shot was a victim of bad luck. Truth be told, it's not a 'good time' to be a police officer in an America torn by racial strife."

Shearson's office grew quiet, the air difficult to breathe. Outside on the street, the chants of protestors were audible, angry.

"*ARREST KILLER COPS!*" demonstrators chanted. "*ARREST KILLER COPS! ARREST KILLER COPS!*"

"So where does this leave Hal Green?" McLaren broke a stifling silence.

"Green has a fine line to walk, and he'll be experiencing enormous heat from the Black community—and possibly the city, as well." Shearson exhaled a streamlet of smoke. "He's got to be seen as impartial and fair to all sides. At the same time, he's got to be particularly 'sensitive' and 'responsive' to the Black community because he desperately needs their vote. We've just got to hope for an investigation that's immune to any pressure … hope that City Hall doesn't knuckle under and force the D.A.'s hand."

"In the end," Shearson said, "Green may just decide to do the 'safe' thing."

"What's that?" Red McLaren asked.

"Punt the case to a grand jury and let them decide," Shearson said. "Show favoritism to neither the police nor the Black community."

"In other words," McLaren said, "cover his ass."

The attorney shrugged. "Like I said, you never know when it comes to a D.A. They're nothing more than political animals, after all."

Matt Holland slumped in his chair. Katie whimpered.

"You said earlier that there'd be 'multiple' investigations," Katie asked, turning to Shearson. "What else can we expect?"

"Well," Shearson said, "the U.S. Attorney's office may jump in, too."

"The Justice Department?" McLaren asked. "What's that about?"

"My understanding is that the feds may be conducting their own review of both this shooting and overall NYPD practices," Shearson replied. "They'll be pressured to examine how cops interact with minorities, looking at potential civil rights violations. The Johnson family will also likely file a civil suit seeking damages from the city. It's standard practice now for these kinds of cases."

"Fuck!" Red McLaren mumbled.

"Look, I'm not going to sugarcoat this," Shearson told the Hollands. "I'm afraid this incident has opened up a huge can of worms. What we've got are three or four separate hurdles to clear before Matt can be fully exonerated. And the outcome of each investigation could be different because each requires a different burden of proof. Matt could conceivably clear all the legal proceedings but still be convicted of either civil rights violations, department transgressions, or both."

Shearson doused his cigarette into an ashtray.

"In other words, Matt can face potential double or even triple jeopardy," the attorney said. "If the feds step in, he'd be tried a second time for essentially the same alleged offenses, even if he's never indicted, or even if he's indicted and then acquitted. In many ways, he's being deprived of the civil rights of an ordinary citizen. The fact that he's a police officer takes priority over the fact that he's a citizen. Regrettable, but true."

Katie and Matt Holland studied Shearson, looking for something they could hang their hats on. There was nothing encouraging, however, that the attorney could offer.

"There's one other thing you need to know," Shearson said, turning his gaze to Matt. "It's very likely that you'll be suspended."

"Before anything is even decided?" Matt asked.

"Uh-huh."

"Even after everything Matt has done for the NYPD?" Katie seemed on the verge of tears. "Despite his reputation, his service to the city?"

"I'm sorry, but that doesn't mean much now," Shearson said. "An automatic-suspension policy has been in place ever since the Knapp Commission findings, when the NYPD decided to crack down on cops who drew salaries, sometimes for years, while awaiting trial on corruption charges. The rule also applies to officers under suspicion of violating departmental policies. They do make exceptions, but those are not likely to apply in this case."

"Is that just?" Katie asked.

"Just or not, it's part of the department's anti-corruption machinery," Shearson said. "The department feels it's got to suspend any cop who's under a cloud if they're going to maintain public faith in the system. Regardless of the rule's merits, the reality is that Matt will probably be off the job for an indefinite amount of time. There's nothing we can do about it."

Katie's features seemed to melt like a candle in heat. Shearson offered her a glass of water. Matt raised a hand to his face, as if to shield it from an unexpected blow.

"We're bucking the automatic-suspension policy in our contract talks with the city," McLaren grumbled. "What horseshit! They say they're moving to restore public faith, but in reality, all they're doing is caving in to community pressure and selling cops down the river. What about extending the same due process to police officers that's guaranteed to every other citizen? Innocent until proven guilty, right? But when you're a cop, everything is backward. Even the most outrageous allegation can get you suspended. You're presumed guilty the instant you're charged. The accusation alone stains you for life, even if you're proven innocent. Until then, you live under a cloud of suspicion, uncertainty, and grief."

Katie stood and started to wander the office. Matt rose to embrace her.

"How long will this process take?" he asked. "How long do we have to live under this so-called cloud?"

"Unfortunately, an incident that took seconds to unfold could take years to reach an outcome," Shearson replied.

"*Years*?"

"I'm sorry," the attorney said. "Those are the rules."

"But what do we do until then?" asked Katie, crying now.

"Until then, the two of you have to find a way to carry on," Shearson said. "You've got to muster up whatever strength, love, and faith you have, so that you can somehow get through this. The two of you are walking in a political minefield now. You've got to find a way to keep your lives from falling completely apart."

Chapter 37

WITH ANTI-POLICE SENTIMENT STILL SEETHING a week after the C. J. Johnson shooting, Rachel Cook was summoned to the 73rd Precinct for a meeting with Capt. Joseph Borelli. There, Cook was informed that while the NYPD's internal investigation had yet to formally conclude, preliminary findings revealed that the rookie officer had no culpability whatsoever in the incident—and, in fact, had discharged her duties to the highest possible standards, completely in compliance with department protocols. An announcement would be made imminently, Capt. Borelli said.

"You'll be completely absolved of any departmental violations or criminality in this tragic incident," the precinct commander told Cook, who instantly dissolved in tearful relief.

"Your interrogation is officially over, Rachel," Capt. Borelli said. "You'll be returned tomorrow to uniformed street patrol."

"And my partner?" Cook sniffled.

"I'm afraid that your partner, as the shooter, has a higher bar to clear," Capt. Borelli said. "Unfortunately, that will take more time."

"Well, I'm very relieved about my own situation, sir," Cook said. "Needless to say, the past week has been extremely difficult."

"It certainly has … for everyone," Capt. Borelli said. "But just know, Rachel, that none of what happened is in any way your fault. I assure you that you retain the NYPD's complete confidence. You encountered an extraordinarily difficult set of circumstances and did everything by the book. I and the department are proud of the way you handled yourself and we thank you for the service you've rendered thus far."

"Thank you." Cook exhaled. "That means a lot to me."

Then, just as abruptly, the captain informed Cook that she was being transferred, effective immediately, to another command.

"What?" Cook recoiled. "Where?"

"The 60th Precinct," Capt. Borelli told her. "Coney Island."

Cook felt as if she had been kicked squarely in the gut.

"I want you to know, Rachel, that this decision is in no way a form of condemnation or punishment," Capt. Borelli said. "Rather, it's being made for your own wellbeing."

"My wellbeing?"

"For your physical safety and, frankly, for the sake of neighborhood peace," the captain said. "As you know, we're working hard to restore a sense of normalcy to Brownsville. Passions need to cool. Relations between police and the community need to heal. We can't risk further inflaming tensions ... with your presence."

"But captain, I—" Cook sputtered.

"Based on circumstances, NYPD brass believes it's imperative that you be removed from patrol in Brownsville," Capt. Borelli said. "Sadly, I have to concur."

"But—"

"Rachel, the situation at the 73rd Precinct has become untenable for you," the captain said. "The decision has been made. I'm sorry, but we feel it's impossible for you to work in Brownsville anymore."

And that was that.

Capt. Borelli took great pains to assure Cook that the NYPD still had an immense deal of faith in her, that her performance to date had been exemplary, and that she still had a bright future in the NYPD. That sentiment was difficult to believe, however, given the nature of Cook's new assignment.

To Cook, being reassigned to the 60th Precinct was like falling from the sky into a neck-deep pit of slime. Once a budding superstar, she'd been reduced to performing virtually meaningless tasks in what was arguably the most demoralizing neighborhood in all of Brooklyn—banished to what cops derisively called a "shit-fixer" post on a desolate stretch of the Coney Island boardwalk. Equally problematic, after eight months of stellar performance with a steady partner she adored in Brownsville, she now had to start from scratch in an unfamiliar precinct with a new cast of partners, investigations pending, and a city very much on edge.

* * *

Like Cook's police career, Coney Island was but a faded shadow of its former self—a dreamy, summer playground for New York's working class, and the blueprint for the twentieth-century urban amusement park. And, like the Brownsville of Cook's childhood, the four-mile-long peninsula had once been bathed in what seemed to be brilliant, perpetual sunshine—its sounds those of carefree laughter, carnival music, and the roar of thrill rides; its smell a mix of saltwater and hot dogs, pretzels and popcorn, cotton candy and sweet corn.

For decades, Coney Island had been both a major seaside resort and a prime destination for summer vacationers, its hotels packed with visitors, its beaches teeming with bathers, its world-renowned boardwalk lined with arcades and eateries, vaudeville theaters and funhouse attractions, dance halls and beer gardens. Circus sideshows featured sword swallowers, fire eaters, carnival freaks, and fortune tellers. Crowds swarmed the streets in front of concession stands, pizza parlors, and Nathans Famous. Couples tumbled into each other's arms at Steeplechase Park, Dreamland, and Luna Park. Rides like the Cyclone, Wonder Wheel, and Parachute Jump filled the summer nights with joyous shouts of glee.

But no more.

Like Brownsville, the Coney Island of the past was long gone now, smothered, over time, by radio and TV, rising costs and airline travel, modern theme parks and the flight of New York's middle class to cleaner, less congested area beaches. The Island's glory and spectacle were buried deep in New York's past. All that remained were washed-out signs, faded imagery, and other symbols of urban decline: noiseless, windblown streets; boarded-up former attractions; rubble-strewn plots of dormant land, and a rundown sprawl of rickety, old homes. Drug use was rampant. Deadly shootings and other felony crimes were epidemic. Prostitutes and petty criminals roamed the neighborhood at night.

Patrolling its streets now, it was nearly impossible for Rachel Cook to remember, or even imagine, what Coney Island once had been. Steeplechase, Dreamland, and Luna Park had long since burned to the ground and been paved over with parking lots. Hulking housing projects cast giant shadows over the old amusement area. Most of the former hotels, restaurants, theaters, and community centers were boarded shut. Many of the rides and attractions were gone as well, replaced by seedy gin mills, strip joints, and dilapidated arcades. The huge mushroom-shaped Parachute Jump, brought to Coney Island from the 1939 World's Fair, loomed over the boardwalk like a ghostly metal sculpture, its rusted chains swaying like gallows nooses in the ocean breeze.

Rachel Cook, bundled against the chill, manned her new post on the boardwalk, and took it all in. All that was left of the Coney Island she'd once known, she thought, was the ocean itself. And all that was left of her shattered police career, or so it seemed, was the uniform she was still permitted to wear, the police shield on her chest, and the service revolver that weighed more heavily than ever in her holster.

To make matters worse, Cook's reception at the 60th Precinct had been even more hostile and dispiriting than the neighborhood in which she now worked. The story of the C. J. Johnson shooting and resultant rioting in Brownville had, of course, preceded the rookie officer's arrival, grossly tainting her persona. While no one openly suggested that Cook was at fault for the incident, she was received at the station house as if possessed of bad karma, rejected from the moment she reported for work.

Or maybe it was simply a matter of gender.

Whatever the reason, nearly all the fifty cops assigned to the 60th Precinct subtly—and, in some cases, openly—went out of their way to shun the new arrival. A goodly number seemed resentful over the hubbub that the shooting incident had provoked, implying that the incident had given police a black eye in the city's minority communities and made their job that much harder. But the presence of those sentiments paled in comparison to a far more toxic dilemma that Cook suddenly faced. Worse than her supposed bad karma was the fact that most male cops at Cook's new command harbored a deeply ingrained resistance to having females as patrol partners. Indeed, there was a substantial group of men, backed subtly by the precinct's captain, who made it resoundingly clear that women were unwelcome intruders on their sacred turf. And those men seemed hell-bent on making life miserable for Cook.

On her first day at the 60th Precinct, a dead mouse, along with several pornographic photos, was placed in Cook's locker. Minutes later, the male officer assigned as her partner flatly refused to enter their patrol car. His replacement agreed, under protest, to ride with Cook, but he refused to interact with his female partner throughout their entire eight hours together. For most of the tour, he simply slept, or pretended to sleep, in the patrol car. When awake, he barely moved or said a word, simply peering out the passenger-side window while Cook drove. On calls, he remained in their car, laughing aloud when Cook was razzed over the radio with anonymous kissing sounds, whistles, and catcalls.

"I don't mind telling you flat-out … I'm not happy being on patrol with you," he griped, after several hours of silent stewing.

"Gee, I couldn't really tell," Cook said, facetiously. "But tell me: why do you feel that way?"

"It's simple, really," the male cop said. "I think this 'gender-neutral' stuff the NYPD is shoving down our throats is nothing but horseshit. I don't believe you belong on street patrol."

"But you don't even know me," Cook said.

"I don't have to know you," the cop said icily. "Who you are has nothing to do with the way I feel. I don't believe *any* woman belongs on street patrol."

"Where *do* we belong?"

"At home. In bed. Taking care of children. Ironing clothes. Making meals."

"So, you're saying that women can't be cops," Cook asked, "just because they're women?"

"Sure, women can be cops," he said. "They can handle rape and domestic-violence cases. They can work on special details, intelligence, investigative stuff. Any 'tit' job you can think of ... just not street patrol."

"*Tit* jobs?"

"Yeah. Jobs suited expressly for women."

"Well, I think you're wrong about me," Cook said, "and I know you're wrong about women."

"The fuck I am."

But right or wrong, the male cop's refrain was all too familiar. Female officers at station houses throughout New York were evoking similar reactions. Vulgar cartoons and girlie centerfolds, with penciled-in references to female cops, were being posted on precinct bulletin boards. Used condoms and sex toys were found in females' lockers. Men's language and gestures were often overtly cruder and sexually explicit when women were present. Female officers were bestowed with nicknames based on real or imagined physical characteristics. One woman at the 60th Precinct was called "The Dumper." Another was referred to as "Blow Jo," and a third as "Thunder Thighs." Cook could only imagine what nickname the cops had assigned to her.

For Cook, having Matt Holland as her partner had always been a major plus. Not only had Holland accepted the female rookie, but he'd gone out of his way to endorse Cook, extolling her virtues to others at the 73rd Precinct. Holland's endorsement, based on his stellar reputation, had carried considerable weight. At the seven-three, Cook had been largely free of the ridicule, rejection, and harassment that greeted other female cops.

But that wasn't the case anymore.

Nine months on the job by now, Cook was nearing the end of her probationary period. But Matt Holland was no longer around. There was no one present to shore Cook up when she took a misstep, no one to vouch for her with neighborhood residents or to put in a good word for her with the boys at the station house. She was totally on her own when it came to lobbying for acceptance and getting her male partners to view her as competent and dependable, intelligent and well-trained.

"I understand how you feel about working with women," she told several of the 60th Precinct's male officers. "I agree we should prove ourselves. But at least give me a chance. I'm not trying to play 'superwoman,' or prove a point, or compete with you. I'm just trying to do my job. I'm qualified. I've proven myself. I'll pull my weight. I won't back down if you ever need me. Try to treat me the same way you'd treat a man."

But not many men would.

When it came to the deployment of female patrol officers, the jury was still out. Women were being studied, evaluated, and judged like no cops before or since. Critics were pouncing on their mistakes. Advocates were heralding their triumphs. And stories were flying.

Rumors ran rampant about female cops who'd allegedly froze during confrontations, and others who'd supposedly panicked or acted irrationally in the face of trouble. There were stories about female cops who supposedly locked themselves in patrol cars when circumstances turned harrowing, who summoned backup officers on routine calls, and who remained in patrol cars until their male partners chivalrously opened their door. It didn't matter that there were countervailing stories of women performing competently and even heroically: making arrests, taking risks, making sacrifices. It didn't matter, either, that female officers were bringing an important new dimension to police work, acting as deterrents to violence, providing a calming influence, and assisting with crime victims. Nor did it matter that the evaluations of female officers were generally favorable … or that women were judged as possessing patrol styles and activity levels practically indistinguishable from the men's … or that women were seen to be more articulate, more intelligent, less violence-prone, easier to supervise, more respectful, and possessed of better work habits.

None of that mattered. Women were neither wanted nor welcome on street patrol. Once again, that was that.

* * *

Amid the hubbub and hysteria, Rachel Cook tried to work, bearing witness as female officers tried to cope with the unrelenting scrutiny, ridicule, and rejection. She watched as police commanders consistently demanded a higher level of proficiency for women than they did for men. She watched female officers become crippled with anxiety over potentially committing a mistake and costing a fellow officer his life. She watched as other women, desperately vying for acceptance, exhibited bizarre displays of faux masculinity—spewing crude obscenities, becoming overly aggressive, even refusing to summon backup when truly needed, for fear of being denigrated as inept or weak.

The struggle for acceptance was endless, Cook found—each day a battle to dispel stereotypes, myths, and the status inferiority assigned to women purely on the basis of gender. There was no margin for failure, no room for creating doubt. As a standard-bearer for the women's movement, Cook knew she had to be better than the men she served alongside, or she'd take the movement down. It was taxing and unnerving. It was grossly unfair. But that's the way it was.

Status inferiority, however, wasn't even the worst of what Cook faced now.

When she wasn't dealing with the resistance of male officers, Cook found herself relegated to another new assignment: She was placed on call to conduct strip searches of female prisoners at lockup facilities throughout New York.

Once such a rising star, it was as if Cook was being tossed, through no fault of her own, on the NYPD's scrap heap. Having once seen police work in its brightest possible light, while working with Matt Holland, Cook was being exposed now to the job's seedy underbelly. It appalled and sickened her as much as her work in Brownsville had once made her feel so worthwhile and alive.

Considered a routine part of the arrest process, strip searches were employed by the NYPD to detect contraband and protect officers from attacks with concealed weapons. The practice was also under attack, however, criticized as an invasion of an arrestee's constitutional right to privacy, and an unjustified and traumatic abuse of power. It was being criticized at the same time by female officers, who charged that the NYPD unfairly discriminated against women by requiring them alone to handle the ghastly, dehumanizing task. Unlike male officers, females could not only be denied patrol duties, but could be pulled from their command at a moment's notice, even denied a transfer or a day off, simply because they had to be available for matron duty. And the sharp rise in female crime, coupled with a paucity of available personnel, meant that female officers could spend entire tours doing little more than conducting strip searches.

The strip search was another one of those tasks that officers could learn only on the job. Indeed, at the Police Academy, Cook had received but a single, hour-long lecture on the procedure. "Always disarm yourself," she was instructed. "Take off and check any wigs the prisoners might be wearing. Have them disrobe. Check their clothing carefully. Go through their hair. Make them lift their breasts. Make them squat. Most importantly, be thorough." More than anything, Cook and the other recruits were instructed, never take searches lightly. After all, she was informed, attacks on cops by prisoners were commonplace. Prisoners could conceal virtually anything on themselves, and those things could easily go undetected during routine pat-downs. Knives, hairpins, and razor blades could be hidden in hair and hosiery. Guns and contraband could be strapped to arms and legs. Evidence could be concealed inside vaginas and rectums.

Adding to the challenges was the fact that there was no standardized procedure for the search. Some cops forced prisoners to strip completely, first checking their clothing and only then proceeding with the body search. Others had prisoners undress in stages. Equally varied were the searchers' styles: Some were soft, lenient, even apologetic. Others were disdainful, the threat of violence implicit in their commands.

Cook was soft at the start—an apologist almost.

"Don't worry," she'd tell arrestees. "This is simply a routine procedure. I'll make it as quick and easy on you as possible."

But once her script was recited and the search begun, the entire chemistry changed.

Some of the women Cook searched were frightened. Their bodies would quake. They'd barely be able to speak. They'd tell Cook that they'd never been arrested before. They'd ask what was going to happen next. Sometimes, they'd cry.

"I'm sorry," Cook would say, "but this is something that has to be done."

"Sorry," she'd say, "I know how embarrassing this must be."

"Sorry, I don't want to do this, but it's my job."

"Sorry, I don't make the rules."

"Sorry—"

Then there were the others. Some, Cook could tell, hated her as much as she hated what she was being compelled to do. They'd stare at her with a scornful silence, eyes on fire, mouths twisted into contemptuous smiles, a rabid loathing flowing from them like an electric current. All the while, there'd be a band-saw tension, something cold and fearful about their demeanor. All the while, Cook would feel their anger and hatred swirling around inside them in dark, deep pools. Some of them would be openly resentful and belligerent. They'd laugh at Cook, curse her, mock her. Sometimes, they'd spit on her and call her names.

One time, she was dispatched to Queens at 5:00 AM to search a group of women who'd been arrested the previous night. There'd been a post change in the middle of a tour. Cook had to relieve the officer on guard. All the prisoners had been searched before and had been in their cells for hours. But with the change in guard, procedures mandated that they be searched again.

The women were nickel-and-dime hookers—angry, hard women. There were ten of them, asleep on wooden slats that folded out of the walls of the cells. Cook went from cell to cell, banging on the bars with her nightstick to awaken them.

"Sheeeet, not again!" the first one snarled. "I already been searched. What you gonna search me again for? I got nothin' on me. I ain't even been out of jail."

"Regulations," Cook explained.

"Shit. Just take my fuckin' word for it."

"Sorry, I can't do that."

Inside the cell, Cook felt nauseous, claustrophobic. She had the woman undress from the waist up, feeling through her blouse and brassiere. She had her lift her breasts. She ran her fingers through the woman's hair.

Be a good cop, Cook thought. *Do everything by the book. Do the job right. Do what you have to do. Try not to think.*

Cook tried to close down, shut off her emotions, detach herself in some robotic way from the moment. The woman pulled up her skirt to reveal torn silk stockings and thighs crisscrossed with bulging, blue veins.

"Here ... get a good look, bitch," she snarled at Cook.

Cook went to do the next search. This woman was unbathed, her skin caked with dirt, her hair matted, her clothing tattered, her body odor unbearable. She was menstruating and had worn the same sanitary napkin for days. She pulled it out and stood holding it, blood trickling down her thighs, while Cook did the search.

"Here," she said, offering the napkin to Cook. "Wanna search this, too?"

On to the next cell Cook went.

"What ... again?"

"I'm taking over. I'm relieving the guard here."

"Bitch!"

Again and again, on and on it went, just like that, through all the searches—ten of them, right in a row.

"You get your kicks from this shit?"

No.

"Is this fun for you?"

No, it wasn't fun.

The last woman taunted her.

"Here," she said, "you want a good look?"

Bending over, spreading her cheeks, her rectum wide open, she asked: "How's this ... pig motherfucker? Is this okay? Are you happy?"

No, it wasn't okay.

And no, Rachel Cook wasn't happy.

Chapter 38

RETURNING TO BROWNSVILLE from C. J.'s interment in South Carolina, Charles Johnson found himself a radically changed man.

It wasn't simply that with the death of his beloved son an essential part of Charles had been excised, his insides hollowed out and forever scarred. Charles had been transformed in more nuanced ways, as well. C. J.'s shooting death, along with the racially charged firestorm it had sparked, had rendered the grieving father more contemplative, more spiritual, and far more cognizant of social issues that far transcended the narrow scope of an existence focused until now entirely on family, work, and vacuous distractions.

Even the three-day journey to his ancestral home, where C. J. was laid to rest alongside the firebombed church where Charles once attended school, was a vivid reminder of how profoundly Charles's life had changed in the span of mere days. For one thing, Claymont was barely recognizable anymore—a victim, like many Piedmont mill towns, of a post-World War II wave of civic bankruptcies, abandonment, and financial ruin. America's cotton trade had long since decamped almost entirely from the South, and Claymont's cotton mill had closed its doors for good. The hulking brick building that was once the hub of Claymont's existence lay abandoned and decaying, its crumbled remains a metaphor for the town itself. Mill workers had fled the area. Former banks, shops, and churches sat ramshackle and boarded up. Streets were cluttered with debris, pavements fissured and overgrown with weeds. The clapboard house in which Charles grew up had collapsed in a heap. Even the Ku Klux Klan was nowhere to be found. All that remained of what Charles once knew were the remnants of former cotton and tobacco fields, a handful of dirt farms, and the searing southern heat.

Charles thought long and hard about all of that as he and Eunice returned to their apartment and the gaping chasm created by C. J.'s death. He thought about the horrific, White-supremacist landscape that haunted him as a child, and how desperately he'd wanted his journey north to recast his fate, purge painful memories, and salve his Deep South wounds. He thought about how his hero, Dr. King, had spoken about the "evil" of poverty and how it spread its tentacles into country towns like Claymont and urban neighborhoods like Brownsville, leaving legions of blacks trapped in an endless cycle of indigence, invisible in a society that was otherwise so affluent. He thought about the enormous hurdles overcome by the civil rights activists he'd met; the momentous struggles they'd endured; the substantive gains they'd made with respect to voting rights, housing, employment, and education; the campaigns they were waging even now against police-related improprieties in towns and cities across America.

Charles also thought about where he fit into the overall scheme of things, now that so many issues had become top of mind. Was it possible that a hitherto-trifling man like him—a subway token clerk possessed of no more than a grade-school education—might have a role to play in the civil rights movement, now that his family had been thrust into the limelight by C. J.'s untimely death? Had Charles's otherwise-lowly life assumed a more meaningful arc now that his support was being solicited by organizations like the NAACP and the ACLU? Was there some positive way he could impact the racial storm raging in Brownsville, counter the divisiveness and the hatred, and convey the core values—dignity, decency, integrity, righteousness, truth—that he held most dear? Was there some small way he could help his city recover, heal, find peace?

Charles wasn't sure.

What he *was* convinced about, however—convinced beyond a shadow of a doubt—was that something larger than himself, something spiritual, something divine, was now at work in shaping the trajectory of his life. Charles was convinced, deep in his soul, that the God he'd put his faith in, the God he trusted and revered, had a plan in place for Charles, and that He, that God, would use Charles as an instrument for executing that plan. The tragedy of C. J.'s death, Charles believed, would have some lasting and positive meaning. Painful as it was, it would somehow help people heal and Charles, in his own small way, would be the architect of that healing.

* * *

All those thoughts were front and center when Charles convened for a second time with the civil rights leaders seeking his support for their proposed wrongful-death lawsuit against the city and the NYPD.

The meeting this time took place not at Charles's apartment, as before, but at the office of 41st District Councilman Samuel Hopkins, located in a converted hardware store in the heart of Brownsville.

Hopkins' office, unlike other storefronts, had survived the recent rioting, but only barely. Even now, six days after the conflagration, the acrid scent of smoke permeated the office, whose front window was boarded with plywood, its walls and ceilings damaged from fire and water.

Charles was ushered into a closet-sized meeting room consumed almost entirely by a mahogany conference table and leather swivel chairs. Plastered on the walls were photos of Hopkins posing with assorted luminaries, including Mayor Worth and Police Commissioner Dunne, as well as political posters touting Jimmy Carter for president and several Democratic candidates for state and local office.

Awaiting Charles, aside from Councilman Hopkins, was Xavier Cooper, the ACLU attorney who'd visited the Johnsons' apartment in the aftermath of C. J.'s shooting, along with another Black man, who Hopkins introduced as Carlton Rutledge of the New York Urban League. A former college basketball star, Rutledge was by far the most arresting of the group, athletic in a well-tailored suit, with cocoa-colored skin, close-cropped steel-gray hair, and a penetrating gaze.

"These gentlemen are extremely involved in the effort to change the nature of police-community relations in America," Hopkins told Charles. "Their presence here demonstrates the importance of what has been set in motion by C. J.'s death."

The men took turns expressing their condolences to Charles, before taking seats around the conference table.

"We'd like to bring you up to date on where matters stand, and further outline our goals," Xavier Cooper began, turning to Charles.

Charles nodded politely. "Please do."

"There are many ways people can react to what happened to your son," Cooper said. "One way, of course, is to mount violent protests of the kind we've seen in Brownsville. Another is to wage more thoughtful, peaceful protests about police misconduct, systemic racism, and lack of accountability. Obviously, people have followed both of those paths."

Charles lowered his head.

"You seem disturbed, Mr. Johnson," Cooper observed, astutely.

"I am," Charles said. "My wife and I are law-abiding people and deeply disturbed by the rioting. We believe violence only begets further violence, divides people, and opens new wounds. Lawlessness benefits no one. People in Brownsville will have to live for years with the damage from the riots."

"True." Councilman Hopkins nodded. "There'll certainly be lasting scars."

"We agree, as well," Cooper said. "Rioting certainly draws attention, but there are other, more effective, ways to make one's case. For example, we believe that the most viable means for addressing wrongful police shootings is not by spastic violence, but by applying a powerful form of legal pressure in the appropriate venues. As we've said, it's our aim, with your support, to pursue that course of action."

"I've given much thought to that," Charles said. "Can you further explain?"

"Certainly," Cooper nodded. "As we've noted, we're talking about potential civil litigation—independent of any punitive action the NYPD, the district attorney, or perhaps even the Justice Department may take—as a means for seeking redress for the shooting death of your son."

"Let me be more explicit," Carlton Rutledge said. "The shooting of C. J., and what has transpired in its wake, are far more important than they might initially seem. What happened, Mr. Johnson, is far bigger than simply two police officers, bigger than Brownsville, and bigger than just your family. What it's really about, sir, is power."

Rutledge's intensity made him a compelling presence. At six-foot-seven, his physical stature added an exclamation point to his comments.

"I grew up in a neighborhood like Brownsville, so I understand how power works," Rutledge said. "Most kids I attended school with were Black, but I used to sit in class each day—the so-called *slower* classes, of course—and I'd always ask myself the same question: 'If all the students in school were Black, why was the principal white, and why was the vice principal white, and why were all the teachers white'?"

Councilman Hopkins snickered.

"And then I'd look outside and see the same thing," Rutledge continued. "White businessmen. White public officials. White judges. White police officers."

He glanced around the conference table. "Sounds familiar?"

The men all smiled and nodded.

"So, then I wondered," Rutledge resumed. "If more of us here are Black, why is everyone who has power White? Don't we have a voice? Don't we have any power? And if we don't, why should we expect people with power to make concessions to the powerless?"

Rutledge paused. "Well, the answer is that power *doesn't* make concessions—unless it has no choice."

He stared at Charles. "Our aim," he said, "is to force concessions by exerting our own form of power."

Everyone was silent, riveted by Rutledge's intensity.

"Rest assured, Mr. Johnson," he said, "there are very impactful people supporting our efforts, people who understand the levers of power. Many are deeply troubled over what has happened in Brownsville. Your son's shooting has done more than simply raise awareness of the struggles Blacks face when it comes to the police—it has also fanned a flame. For the first time ever, sir, we're achieving national attention because of this incident. Our voices are finally being heard. We're on the cusp of something historic. This case, Mr. Johnson, could be a major inflection point."

"Carlton's right," Cooper said. "We're dealing with issues that hit at the heart of race relations in America. We're living at a pivotal time now. The civil rights movement has made enormous strides, but we've got to push for greater concessions, greater power. We've already won the *rights* of citizens. Now we're trying to win the right to be *treated* like citizens."

Charles nodded, equally intrigued and impressed. He felt privileged to be in the company of men with such intellect and vision—grateful to be considered, even marginally, as important to their cause. Men like these, Charles had only heard about; it stirred him that they wanted him to stand at their side. Charles was also struck by Rutledge's comments regarding power. In all his life, he'd never felt powerful or impactful in any way, except perhaps in the eyes of his son. But now he thought that C. J.'s death, in an ironic way, may have granted him a power he'd never possessed before. And he wondered if there was some way that he might leverage that power to help people heal, and repair things that were broken.

"This morning," Cooper said, "ACLU representatives met with federal officials to request that the Civil Rights Division of the Justice Department step into the investigation of C. J.'s shooting. We've also asked that the Justice Department create a special unit to probe police practices throughout America."

"Similar requests for federal involvement in police-shooting cases have been made before," Rutledge elaborated. "But the timing of this case may have finally moved the government to take action."

"What will the feds be doing?" Councilman Hopkins asked.

"For one thing, the U.S. Attorney's office will be working closely with the Kings County D.A., while criminal charges are being considered against Detective Sergeant Holland," Cooper said. "Federal officials will monitor both the incident and its related investigations for possible civil rights violations and patterns of police misconduct. This is significant. Typically, federal prosecutors don't enter cases like this until much later, if at all. They prefer to let local jurisdictions handle them. So, it's highly unusual, and very encouraging, that the feds are getting involved now."

"Your son's shooting may have finally sparked action, and moved the government to get involved," Rutledge said.

"But—" Charles sputtered, and then stopped, fearful he'd sound naïve.

"Please, Mr. Johnson," Cooper said. "Say what's on your mind."

"Well, I was just thinking," said Charles. "Shouldn't we wait until the outcome of the NYPD's investigation before we pass judgment about what happened in C. J.'s case?"

Cooper and Rutledge exchanged glances.

"It really doesn't matter what the NYPD investigation finds," Rutledge said.

"Why not?"

"Well, the sad fact is that we can't trust the NYPD to police its own," Rutledge said. "Self-policing is self-defeating. All it results in is a whitewash."

"That's why we want to bring federal authorities in," Cooper said. "To put it bluntly, they don't have the same conflict of interest with police investigations as local authorities. They'll turn up the heat far more than city officials."

"Police in the U.S. kill hundreds of people a year," Rutledge said. "Most of those deaths are labeled 'justifiable homicides'—incidents in which the suspect is killed to prevent death or injury to the officer or another person. The investigations into these shootings aren't, shall we say, quite as 'thorough' as they are for the general population. We know for a fact that many departments ignore evidence, witnesses' testimony, and other information that may raise questions about officers' accounts."

"Efforts to scrutinize police shootings are generally stonewalled, investigated in a shroud of secrecy," Cooper added. "Details are impossible to come by. Cover-ups are common."

"It's the infamous 'Blue Wall of Silence,'" Rutledge added. "Cops take care of their own. Their 'investigations' are nothing but a crock of shit."

"In the meantime," Cooper said, "the families of police-shooting victims typically face months, even years, of legal wrangling to learn what really happened … and they usually find out only when a judge intercedes."

"Something's clearly amiss," Rutledge said. "The fact is … there's far too much deference to cops. They always get the benefit of any doubt. No matter how grievous their actions, they're always claiming to be acting in defense of their own lives. Their argument is always, 'We protect you people, so you have to protect us.' Their lawyers play on the public's emotions. They portray the cop who shot as the poor soul who had a horrific split-second decision to make and was simply doing his job. Then they cast aspersions on the victim—condition people to think, 'So what? You people are *lucky* the victim was killed before he had a chance to mug your wife or rape your daughter.' After a while, who cares if the victim got killed? People figure it was justified. One less 'rotten egg' to worry about."

"What about District Attorneys?" Charles asked. "Can't they be trusted?"

"Usually, it's the same story," Cooper replied. "Most D.A.s are hesitant to second-guess police officers who commit line-of-duty shootings."

"Truth is, they don't feel comfortable investigating police shootings," added Rutledge. "There's a different set of standards for cops than for other killers. Cops are almost never charged with crimes. Judges, juries, the public, prosecutors, the press—they're generally sympathetic, as well. So, D.A.s drag their feet. They're not going to prosecute or indict a cop."

"Prosecutors face a conflict of interest similar to that of police investigators," Cooper said. "They generally have to work closely with cops. If they start pressing for officers' indictments, they know they'll never get cooperation in the future. So, they show leniency. It's a case of one hand washing the other."

"The result," Rutledge said, "is that police officers are literally getting away with murder."

"But can't the NYPD punish its 'rotten apples' even if no one else will?" Charles asked.

"Good question," Cooper replied. "The answer is yes. The NYPD, to its credit, has fired cops who've been charged, and then acquitted, after departmental hearings in which the officers were found guilty of firing their gun without just cause."

"How is that possible?" Charles asked.

"Well, departmental trials are civil, not criminal, proceedings and consequently the burden of proof is not the same as in a criminal case," Cooper explained. "It's far harder to prove guilt in a criminal case."

With that, Rutledge leaned forward in his seat and stared at Charles. "Mr. Johnson," he said, "many people are rallying to our side now: civil libertarians, liberal politicians, even D.A.s and judges. At long last, police are being watched, called out, losing their status in the courtroom. Their credibility has bottomed out. People, for the first time ever, are challenging them."

Rutledge then nodded at Cooper, inviting the attorney to speak.

"Mr. Johnson," Cooper said. "Do you remember that 'second' lawsuit we mentioned at your apartment, the one we never got around to discussing?"

Charles nodded.

"Well, permit me to tell you about it," Cooper said, "because while it may not have as much of a personal impact on you as the proposed civil lawsuit, in many ways it's far more important."

The ACLU attorney then began to outline the organization's plan to file a federal class-action lawsuit, without precedent in the U.S., charging police in New York with engaging in a longstanding pattern of harassment, brutality, and other discriminatory practices against minorities.

"Here, we're not simply asking for federal intervention," Cooper said. "Instead, we're demanding change."

"Our claim," Rutledge said, "will be that for years police have violated the civil rights of minorities. We will assert that C. J.'s shooting falls into a national pattern of police abuse against blacks. We'll be breaking new ground for the civil rights movement with this action. We'll be making history, Mr. Johnson, trying to fundamentally change the way police officers deal with minorities in America."

"Let me state it another way," Cooper said. "See, we believe that the killing of C. J. is not just another police-blotter case. Instead, it's closely tied to civil rights issues like police abuse, and something called 'racial profiling.'"

"I've never heard of that," Charles said.

"Most people haven't—*yet*," Cooper said, "but I can assure you they'll be hearing about it a lot more in the future. The practice has been around for years as a law enforcement technique in minority communities, but it's only now being seen for what it really is—racial bias against Blacks."

"C. J.'s shooting," Rutledge said, "parallels dozens of others: white police officers shooting unarmed, innocent minorities; claims by the officers of self-defense; poor visibility; commands that were ignored; identities that were mistaken; weapons that were assumed; victims acting in a 'threatening manner'; firings that were 'accidental.'"

"Sound familiar?" Cooper asked rhetorically.

Deep in thought, Charles said nothing.

"And in each case," Rutledge continued, "despite sharp protests from the community, the cop walked—either cleared by their department because they supposedly followed shooting guidelines, cleared by a prosecutor who found insufficient evidence to file a charge, or cleared by a jury which found reasonable doubt about the officer's guilt."

"Some cases, especially the shootings like C. J.'s, make headlines," Cooper said. "But just as insidious are the cases that don't. ACLU affiliates field hundreds of civilian complaints about police misconduct each year. The grievances go beyond physical mistreatment. There are verbal slurs and double standards. People get choked and beaten without provocation, addressed with vulgar language, frisked for no apparent reason, questioned without probable cause, harassed, cursed at, demeaned, humiliated. We've heard stories about black doctors, attorneys, teachers, and businessmen being pushed around, hassled, and made to feel like lawbreakers. And why? Because they 'fit the description'? Because they 'look' like a criminal? Because they have their hands in a pocket or a bulge in their jacket?"

"I assure you, a White man stopped under similar circumstances would be treated far differently," Rutledge said.

"Carlton's right," Cooper said. "It's not surprising that the majority of the civil rights violations take place in minority neighborhoods. The fact is, cops react differently if your skin is dark, if you're dressed a certain way, if you live in a certain neighborhood. Everyone's a 'suspect.' Even neutral behavior is viewed suspiciously in places like Brownsville."

"We know that what cops are really doing is establishing authority, exerting power," Rutledge said. "But are their actions really necessary to make the community safer? Hardly. What they are, instead, are forms of harassment and racism, violations of people's civil liberties. What happened to C. J. is not isolated. Your son is not the *only* victim of racial profiling, he's merely the latest. There's something wrong when minorities have a justifiable fear of police officers who are supposed to be protecting them. There's something wrong when cops erode the public trust and create an atmosphere of apprehension and hatred. It simply must stop! To whom does the Constitution apply? Is it applicable only in White communities?"

Charles, quietly, took this all in.

"The civil rights case you mentioned … can you tell me about that?" he finally asked.

"The case will involve numerous entities," Cooper said. "That's why it's called a 'class-action' suit. You'd be among many plaintiffs, including relatives of other police-shooting victims. We would file a complaint on your family's behalf, charging that Detective Sergeant Holland not only acted negligently, carelessly, and with callous disregard for C. J.'s life, but also that he was motivated by racial bias. We're going to make the case that the officer acted as he did because C. J. was Black and that he used his 'color of office' to violate C. J.'s civil rights."

"In other words," Rutledge interjected, "we're going to argue that the circumstances for this shooting were shaped by a preconceived notion that a crime was being committed and that Detective Sergeant Holland and his partner, Officer Cook, felt they were in danger simply because your son and his friends were Black."

"It's a clear case of racial profiling," Cooper said. "It's our contention that the officer would not have had his weapon drawn, and would not have fired his gun, if he had not been in a Black neighborhood—and fearful of people who, in fact, were not criminals and did not represent a threat, except in the officer's mind."

Charles reflected for several seconds on all of this.

"So, what type of support," he finally asked, "are you seeking from me?"

"We simply want you to join us," Cooper replied. "What we're seeking, quite frankly, is a symbol. Your son can be that symbol. All we're looking for is for you to stand with us and tell the world that you're fully on our side."

"By joining us," Rutledge said, "you'll be helping spearhead an important cause. In your son's death lies an opportunity to make a difference. We want police in America to understand that, in a democracy, civil rights violations will not be tolerated. If you stand with us, C. J.'s death will not have been in vain."

Charles hesitated, inspired by Rutledge's sentiments although finding himself equally troubled, reluctant to divulge what he was thinking for fear of sounding contradictory or, worse yet, unenlightened.

"I sense some hesitancy," Cooper observed.

"I suppose so," Charles admitted.

"May I ask why?"

Charles inhaled. "Let me ask a question that may seem odd in light of all that we've discussed: what happens to the officers through all of this?"

"Who gives a fuck?" Rutledge snapped.

Charles flinched, seeming disturbed by the glib response.

"As we've said," Cooper clarified, "we're hoping that Detective Sergeant Holland, and perhaps Officer Cook, will be charged with misconduct, permanently suspended, and perhaps prosecuted criminally. Racist, trigger-happy cops like them must be held accountable for their actions."

Charles looked away.

"Why do you ask?" Rutledge queried. "What would you *like* to see happen?"

"To be honest," Charles said, "I'm not exactly sure."

The others seemed perplexed.

"Don't get me wrong," Charles said. "I can't deny that Detective Sergeant Holland killed C. J., or that there's been far too many police shootings of Blacks in the past. I think the civil rights abuses that you men are trying to address are very real, and I support everything you're trying to achieve. But—"

"But ... *what*?" Cooper queried.

"Well, Eunice and I have talked it over," Charles said, "and while it's easy to condemn Officers Holland and Cook for killing C. J., we have reason to believe there's a strong possibility that the shooting may have been *accidental*, as the officers have claimed."

Cooper and Rutledge stared wordlessly at Charles. Councilman Hopkins twisted in his chair.

"Can I ask what leads you to believe that?" Cooper inquired.

"It just seems—" Charles paused, groping for the right word.

"Plausible?"

"Yes." Charles nodded. "The officers' accounts of what happened seem ... plausible."

Charles continued, growing increasingly emboldened. "The strangest thing," he said, "is that I harbor no real bitterness toward the officers."

"Not even after what they did to your son?" Rutledge seemed incredulous.

"No," Charles said. "In fact, I actually feel sorry for Officers Holland and Cook ... and I'm not sure I want them punished more than they already have been."

"How have they been 'punished'?" Rutledge said. "Nothing's been done to them."

"Oh, I think they've been deeply hurt by everything that's happened," Charles said. "And I think, in some ways, their pain *is* their punishment."

"They're cops," Rutledge said, derisively. "What makes you think they have feelings of remorse? What makes you think they have feelings at all?"

"Oh, I'm certain they have feelings," Charles said. "They're human, after all, aren't they? People ... just like any of us."

"And your own feelings, Mr. Johnson?" Cooper asked.

"Frankly, they're mixed," Charles said. "While I agree that there are 'rotten apples' in the NYPD—cops who are racist and violent—Eunice and I believe that there are also a great many dedicated, hardworking, good cops.

And while public attention is focused, justifiably, on the 'rotten apples,' the good cops far outnumber the bad."

"So that's the reason you're conflicted?" Cooper said.

Charles nodded. "I don't know how I'd feel about being involved in a lawsuit that attacks *all* police in a blanket-kind of way, charging civil rights violations in C.J.'s case even though I know they may be legitimate in others."

Charles looked around the conference table.

"We can't paint all police officers with the same broad brush, can we?" he asked. "Isn't that the very thing we're accusing the police of doing to Blacks … the same *wrong* thing?"

No one said a word.

"I believe your calls for racial justice are warranted," Charles said. "But the same circumstances don't exist for each case, so how can we respond in a uniform way?"

Again, silence.

"And there's even more to it than that," Charles admitted. "To be perfectly candid, there are things I know about the officer who shot my son."

"Things you *know*?" Cooper asked.

"Yes." Charles nodded. "Detective Sergeant Holland, you see, has worked in Brownsville many years. He's well known, and highly respected, in the neighborhood. In fact, I believe he may have had contact with my son—positive contact—on at least one prior occasion."

"What kind of contact?"

"I'm hesitant to say, because I'm still not sure," Charles replied. "Eunice and I are looking into it. But let's just say we aren't ready to jump blindly to conclusions about what the officer has done regarding this incident."

Charles eyeballed the men, inwardly surprised by both his clarity and his growing sense of confidence. Rutledge and Cooper stared blankly at one another, before turning to Charles.

"So where does that leave us with respect to your support for our proposed legal actions?" the ACLU attorney asked.

"Well, I've been thinking," said Charles, surprised by his temerity, yet fully cognizant of what Rutledge had said earlier about the notions of leverage and power—power of a kind Charles found himself suddenly possessed of, for the first time in his life.

"Maybe," he suggested, coyly, "we can make a deal."

Cooper winced. "A deal?"

"Yes … an agreement in exchange for my support," Charles said, "a deal from which everyone here can benefit."

"We're all ears," Rutledge said.

And guided by his instincts, his sense of justice, his innate decency, Charles outlined a set of conditions he'd be seeking in exchange for his family's support regarding both the wrongful-death lawsuit against the city and the federal class-action lawsuit contesting alleged civil rights violations by police.

"Well, that's certainly an out-of-the-box proposal," Cooper reacted. "It's something we'd have to discuss, of course … but I think it's an accommodation we can find a way to agree to."

"Absolutely," Rutledge agreed.

"Good," Charles smiled. "Then I have no problem lending your organizations my family's full support."

Chapter 39

EIGHT DAYS AFTER the C. J. Johnson shooting, Brownsville remained a tinder box, the specter of civil unrest lingering in the air like a volatile fume.

While the NYPD's strategy of purposeful restraint was being credited with blunting further violence, sections of the neighborhood nevertheless resembled an armed camp. Police cars and emergency equipment were stationed at key intersections. The 73rd Precinct station house remained barricaded by concrete barriers and barbed-wire fencing. Corrugated-metal grates protected the windows of most storefronts.

Anxious to restore normalcy to the neighborhood, the city canceled its nighttime curfew and resumed municipal services, including public transportation, mail delivery and trash collection. Sound trucks urged residents to resume daily activities. City officials lobbied state and federal legislators for financial aid to support relocation and rebuilding efforts.

But while the climate in Brownsville had palpably calmed, the issues raised by the C. J. Johnson shooting remained far from resolved. Indeed, protests over the shooting had spread far beyond their scattershot origins, reverberating across the city in a well-organized campaign of sit-ins, marches, and rallies. Thousands of sign-toting demonstrators took part in protests at City Hall and NYPD headquarters. Smaller rallies were staged in minority communities across New York.

The political heat generated by the protests had also dramatically intensified. Protestors' ranks no longer consisted solely of a loose confederation of community activists, youth gang members, and assorted militants. In contrast, demonstrations were being spearheaded now by a steadily broadening coalition of civil rights advocates, religious leaders, student activists, business leaders, and figures from entertainment and sports, many of whom were well-connected to local politicians, media outlets, and corporate interests. The demonstrations had also evolved into a highly choreographed, ritualized form of street theater—entirely new to America's political landscape—the early stirrings of the social justice movement that would be known decades later as "Black Lives Matter." Demonstrators marched, chanted, sang songs, linked arms, and prayed. Others snarled traffic, blocked access to landmarks, and participated in related acts of civil disobedience.

Amid the racially charged mayhem, daily press briefings were also conducted by protest leaders, police brass, and city officials. Social activists continued to level allegations of systemic racism, police brutality, and other deficiencies in law enforcement. Police supporters continued to defend current practices, charging that officers were being unfairly maligned. Reformists advanced proposals for change. Police unions and NYPD brass opposed the proposals, charging that they would tie the hands of police and lead to a spike in crime.

"What we're seeing for the first time in America," Red McLaren charged, "is the evolution of a highly organized 'racial grievance' industry, being whipped into a feeding frenzy, simply to exploit a tragic incident for political purposes."

McLaren, arms linked with the leaders of other police unions, stood behind a wooden horse barricade at the entrance to PBA headquarters.

"What we have on our streets are agitators, fist-shakers, mudslingers, and political opportunists whose acts of civil disobedience are more contrived than heartfelt," the PBA boss said. "The tragic death of a young Black boy has become nothing more than a shameful publicity campaign, political theater elevated to an art form. A coalition of conscience? *Please*! Moral outrage? *Nonsense*! All we're seeing is a shrewd game, a vicious, truth-be-damned form of anti-police bias. This is all about exploiting an unfortunate, isolated incident to establish a political constituency. And all it does is stir the racial pot to a boil."

Predictably, the public took sides in the squabble, which raged, often blindly, along racial, economic, and political lines—White versus Black,

Democrat versus Republican, conservative versus liberal, young versus old. Just as predictably, the media continued to fuel the growing divide, largely for commercial gain. Stories about the C. J. Johnson shooting ran prominently in nearly all the city's daily newspapers. TV- and radio-talk shows buzzed with debate between law-enforcement advocates and civil rights activists. Editorialists and commentators offered sharply differing viewpoints. Sermons both attacking and defending police were delivered at local houses of worship.

Before long, the C. J. Johnson shooting case was dominating nearly all public discourse in America's preeminent city, and much of the country, impacting both the mayoral campaign and the presidential race. Protest leaders placed full-page ads in the city's newspapers, charging that the PBA protected "out-of-control killer cops." The police union countered with ads portraying its officers as dedicated public servants interested solely in the public welfare. *Support a Cop* messages began appearing on buses, billboards, and subway trains. *Officer Needs Assistance* tee shirts were donned by supporters of the police.

Nor was the growing divisiveness defined strictly along racial, politic, or socioeconomic lines. Apparent, too, were rifts within the Black community itself. Black Power advocates called for everything from passive resistance to overt violence. Moderate Blacks were accused of being excessively obedient and servile to Whites. White New Yorkers were similarly divided, with liberals, progressives and the city's intelligentsia standing with anti-police protestors in opposition to conservative, blue-collar residents. Even the ranks of the NYPD itself were divided—with the Guardians, an organization of Black officers, protesting alleged abuse of minorities by white cops, while refuting the prevailing viewpoint of the PBA, the union to which most of the Black officers belonged.

Then the protests turned ugly again—but this time in a far more personal way.

Somehow, a group of militant protestors obtained the Hollands' home address and phone number, and began a stream of obscenity-laced calls, threatening the wellbeing of Matt and Katie Holland, and their children.

Fearing reprisals against the embattled officer, the PBA requested formal police protection for the Hollands—a request that was summarily denied, based on some nebulous legal formality. Taking their denial one step further, NYPD officials requested that Matt Holland sign a waiver releasing the city from liability should anything happen to the officer or his family. Outraged and bitter, Red McLaren advised Holland to shun the request. PBA volunteers, instead, began guarding the officer's house, with Holland shuttled each day by off-duty cops to and from his duties at police headquarters.

All of this, however, did nothing to stop protestors from staging demonstrations outside the Hollands' home. At one of the rallies, a group of Black men carrying a casket with a photo of C. J. Johnson taped to its lid marched solemnly around the cul-de-sac in front of the house. Trailed by several women in mourning garb, the protestors chanted slogans, raised fists, and called for Holland's arrest. Police immediately closed off the street and disbanded the mock funeral, but not before the demonstration was witnessed by Thomas Holland, who ran to his room, crouching in fear beneath his bed.

"Just give me one shot at those fuckin' jungle bunnies!" an off-duty cop said, leering from behind drawn blinds inside the Hollands' home. "Just one shot! I'll solve the racial problem in New York real fast!"

Then he turned to Katie Holland.

"Here," he said, offering her a loaded shotgun. "You better learn how to use this, if you want your family to live."

Chapter 40

At the second City Hall meeting in as many days, a coalition of law-enforcement reformists presented a lengthy list of demands to city officials. This time, Mayor Worth himself presided over the hour-long confab, joined by a team of minority community advisers and Police Commissioner Dunne.

Representing the reformists this time were several Black activists, including New York Urban League president Carlton Rutledge and Calvin Hobbs of the NAACP, both of whom were spearheading out-of-court negotiations in the wrongful-death lawsuit filed on behalf of Charles and Eunice Johnson. Present, as well, was 41st District Councilman Samuel Hopkins, along with a trio of Brownsville's ministers, including the Rev. Josiah Watson. Notable by their exclusion were militant firebrands Ibrahim Shabazz and Wilfred Clark, who immediately charged city officials with marginalizing the pair in an effort to undermine their credibility.

"The city is seeking to drive a wedge between the protestors of the racially motivated police shooting of C. J. Johnson in an attempt to weaken our ranks," Shabazz told reporters.

"Regardless, we will remain steadfast in our demand for justice, accountability, and police reform," Clark added, "even if city officials choose to listen only to 'conciliatory' Black voices—or should I dare call them 'Uncle Toms.'"

But while the latest cohort of meeting attendees was far less militant than Shabazz and Clark, their demands were all too similar. Foremost among them was a renewed call for the suspensions of Matt Holland and Rachel Cook, as well as a speedy resolution to the multiple investigations into the controversial police shooting. Beyond that, their demands focused on stricter oversight of the NYPD, a weeding out of violent cops, and upgraded training in the use of firearms.

"The minority community feels as if it's under siege by its police," Calvin Hobbs declared. "New York, like other cities, needs to recognize that many complaints about its police are legitimate. In many ways, what we have now is a perversion of the traditional view that the police are an ally and protector. Instead, the police have become an enemy to the community."

"Far too many officers," Carlton Rutledge added, "are seen as callous, racist bullies who are on duty solely to harass and intimidate Black communities. Credibility and trust have eroded. There's enormous bitterness and resentment. Police departments have light years to go in gaining trust."

"No one in the NYPD condones racism or police brutality, but we believe the number of brutality cases is being grossly overstated," Police Commissioner Dunne said. "Our officers aren't brutal or racist. They're simply trying to do a difficult job, often under the worst of circumstances. The use of deadly force by our officers should not carry an automatic charge of police abuse or racism. And overly restrictive shooting policies will only hamstring police and put lives in jeopardy."

"Maybe so," Hobbs conceded, "but you need to recognize that repeated deadly-force incidents have polarized police and civilians."

"And what about all the *positive* contacts between police and the public, the instances when police are called upon to help?" Dunne queried.

"There's no question about those," Councilman Hopkins said. "We have many hardworking, excellent police officers in this city—the vast majority, I'd say. To condemn all of them is unfair, a gross disservice."

"Please understand, we're not anti-cop," Rev. Watkins said. "We're only anti-racist cop, anti-brutal cop. But unfortunately, those few 'rotten apples' have created the distinct impression that most police officers are like that. It may be a false stereotype, but it's real."

"There are stereotypes on *both* sides of this issue," Dunne said. "Blacks are often as much to blame as Whites."

"No one is denying that," said Rutledge. "The truth is that even as America celebrates the two-hundredth anniversary of its founding, we find ourselves mired in the same racially charged issues that led to slavery and Jim Crow. The sad reality is that the values and ideals of our country are in sharp contrast with what happens on our streets. We claim to be a nation of equal rights and justice for all, but that rings hollow in the face of what we see. Racial differences still haunt us, still stain who we are as a people."

"The bottom line," said Hobbs, "is that major change is needed, and we need to bring that change about—starting *now*."

"This city has responded in the past to minority complaints about police," Mayor Worth said. "Many reforms have been implemented. We've addressed police misconduct, corruption, and use-of-force. We've improved recruitment efforts, instituted better training, improved police accountability."

"Perhaps so," said Rutledge, "but those reforms have failed to fix a system that's broken ... a deeply entrenched, dysfunctional system that heavily favors police, prevents meaningful scrutiny, and allows officers to commit abuses with impunity."

"It's a system," Hobbs said, "that needs to be fixed."

Hobbs and Rutledge then took turns detailing the reformists' viewpoint that law enforcement traditionally investigates police misconduct in ways that seemed aimed at establishing officers' innocence rather than exposing the truth.

"Mechanisms for oversight have failed to monitor police conduct or hold officers to account," Hobbs said. "Police exercise enormous discretion, and far too much leeway, in carrying out their duties. Essentially, no one monitors their work. Police departments, tasked with investigating and disciplining their own personnel, systematically protect officers from meaningful scrutiny—in part to shield themselves from liability, preserve their power, and validate their own tactics."

"At the same time," Rutledge said, "civilian complaints about police misconduct generally go ignored and prosecutors repeatedly fail to bring charges against officers, because they're not fully independent of police and function with an inherent conflict of interest. The courts are also reluctant to second-guess the decisions of officers. Judges and juries generally sympathize with the cops. Legal standards are disregarded."

"Then there's the unions," Hobbs said. "In the name of due process, police unions negotiate contracts that give officers protection from discipline and accountability, shield those who violate policy or commit crimes, and resist pressure against efforts at oversight and reform."

"The bottom line," said Rutledge, "is that police officers are unlikely to face any disciplinary or legal consequences, even for the most egregious offenses. Only in a handful of cases is anything done. Investigations usually take months to complete, and even longer before any disposition on discipline. Cases rarely result in serious discipline. The system leaves victims of abuse with few options to seek redress. The entire system is rigged. In many ways, it's a cover-up, a farce."

"The only way forward is to change the *culture* of policing," Hobbs said. "Trust must be restored between communities and the officers sworn to serve them. For police officers to be credible, they must be held accountable."

The City Hall meeting, even with the sharp differences in opinion, ended amicably. Several of the reformists' demands, including civilian oversight of the NYPD, were rejected out of hand. Others, such as upgraded firearms training, would be taken under advisement, Mayor Worth pledged. The meeting, he noted, should be viewed as a sign of progress. There was certainly a wide range of police-related issues to be addressed, he said, but at least people were talking about them openly and with a semblance of civility.

"I just hope we're capable of making enough progress to stop what's threatening to tear our city apart," the mayor said. "We need to find a common ground and balance the rights of citizens with the realities of policing. Dialogue, good faith, and mutual respect must prevail. So does an understanding, absent of racial overtones."

"You're right about that," the Rev. Josiah Watson said. "We've got to find a way to work together. We can't afford a race war on the streets of America's greatest city."

Chapter 41

As the drumbeat of protests continued, the dual investigations by the NYPD and Kings County D.A. Hal Green plodded along, with neither a timetable for completion nor an outcome even remotely in sight. Citing the potential to compromise the probes, investigatory officials refused to publicly discuss the C. J. Johnson shooting case, except to say that it was in everyone's best interests to proceed methodically and allow the inquiries to take an unfettered course.

"I assure you that our only objective is to uncover the truth and then respond appropriately to it," D.A. Green told the press. "I recognize the need to put this matter behind us, but high-profile police shootings like this must be handled with the utmost integrity. Our investigations will conclude when we've examined all the evidence, not a moment sooner. We're trying to be responsive to community sentiment, but we can't afford a rush to judgment."

But while the outcome of the investigations remained uncertain, what was eminently clear was that city officials were walking a politically charged tightrope. While facing enormous and growing pressure to respond quickly to protestors' demands, they also had to separate emotion from fact and demonstrate to the city's thirty-thousand-plus police officers, and the public at large, that just as they'd punish an officer who violated police guidelines or the law, they'd support one who performed his job properly.

City Hall officials were clearly between a rock and a hard place. Indeed, political pundits were calling the handling of the C. J. Johnson shooting case a litmus test for Nathan Worth, a defining moment for his four-year-old mayoral administration. Facing re-election in a scant three months, Worth was in the throes of a hotly contested campaign, narrowly leading his GOP opponent in the polls but being squeezed from all sides of the political spectrum. Already under fire for budget cuts imposed while trying to reduce municipal debt, Worth was being pummeled by progressives for being unresponsive to minority demands while simultaneously being censured by conservatives for being too soft on crime.

The political vise had grown far tighter in the wake of the C. J. Johnson shooting. At the risk of alienating itself from New York's police and their multitude of supporters, the Worth administration was being heavily pressured to suspend Matt Holland prior to the outcome of any investigation. Such an act, it was said, would be seen as a gesture of City Hall's willingness to admit to past police sins, while demonstrating its sensitivity to minority concerns. It would be a way to heal old wounds, even if it risked opening new ones, proponents said—a way to cement relations with a constituency that Worth desperately needed in his re-election bid.

With the sound of anti-police demonstrations echoing outside his Gracie Mansion residence, Worth convened a closed-door meeting at which the mayor and his team of advisers, including Police Commissioner Dunne, met to consider their options.

* * *

While the city wrestled with its burgeoning racial crisis, Matt Holland's interrogations continued unabated, expanded now to include not only investigators from the office of Kings County D.A. Hal Green, but also others from the U.S. Attorney for the Eastern District of New York, drawn into the case to probe potential civil rights violations alleged in the class-action lawsuit filed on behalf of police-shooting victims' families, including Charles and Eunice Johnson.

When he wasn't busy answering the nonstop barrage of questions, Holland was busy with mind-numbing, non-patrol duties at the NYPD's Communications Unit, a detail known as a dumping ground for disgraced cops. There, he worked in a cramped basement known as the "snake pit," essentially reduced to little more than a 911 operator. The remainder of his time, or so it seemed, was involved with trying to help his family cope with the events that had turned their lives upside down.

The Hollands' eight-year-old twin girls, Angie and Jenny, remained sequestered at Katie's parents' Jersey beach house, homeschooled by tutors and protected by off-duty cops. Despite his gnawing fears, however, Thomas steadfastly refused to leave his parents' side.

"You're a very brave young man to want to stay with us, but it'd be better if you stayed at your grandparents' house for the time being," Katie told her son.

"I won't leave you and Dad," Thomas declared, adamantly.

At twelve years old, Thomas was the image of his father—towheaded, bright-eyed, and resolute. Ever since the C. J. Johnson shooting, he'd taken to sleeping on an air mattress alongside his parents' bed and, like his mother, had become a virtual prisoner inside their home. Thomas hadn't left the house even once since the anti-police demonstrations began, and he trailed Katie around like a puppy, fearful of the telephone threats and potential protest rallies at the house.

"What's a mob?" Thomas asked his mother one night.

"A mob is a group of people who are out of control and sometimes do things that are wrong, like destroy property and hurt people," Katie explained.

"Are the people who were demonstrating outside our house a 'mob'?"

"No, I wouldn't call them that."

"What about the people who've been rioting?"

"Yes, that's more like a mob."

"Are they coming to get us?"

Katie Holland embraced her son.

"No, Thomas," she assured him. "No one is coming to get us. I promise you. There are many police officers here to protect us, and the people outside the house are just demonstrating to voice an opinion they believe in. Nothing will happen to you—or to any of us."

Thomas nodded, but in a puzzled kind of way.

"But Dad really killed that boy, right?"

"Yes, we've told you that," Katie replied. "But we've also explained that Dad didn't mean to do it … that it was a terrible accident, nothing more."

Thomas blinked but said nothing.

"I think you know your father well enough," Katie said. "You know he'd never harm an innocent boy intentionally or do anything to violate police policy."

"But the newspapers say Dad shot the boy because was Black. That's not true, is it?"

"Thomas, you know better than that. You father would never shoot a person because of their race. You know how respected he is in Brownsville, right?"

"Yes."

"And haven't we always taught you about not being prejudiced or bigoted?"

"Uh-huh."

"So, doesn't that answer your question?"

Thomas nodded and his mother drew him close.

"Thomas, sometimes, you may see or hear or read things that aren't true, or aren't fair, or don't tell the entire story," Katie said. "Sometimes, rumors start, and people distort the facts."

"But why?"

"Because people are out to make a point. Many people in Brownsville dislike the police and don't want them around."

"But even *Dad*? Why Dad? He's always been good to the people there."

"The people who are demonstrating and rioting don't know your father, Thomas." Katie stroked her son's hair. "To them, he's just a symbol. They're striking out against *all* police officers, not just your father."

"But why?"

"Many of them are angry about the way they've been treated by police."

"Are they right?"

"In many cases, sadly, yes. To be honest with you, there are bad police officers, just like there are good ones. The Black people in Brownsville are right when they say that some white officers treat them poorly. But they're not right to say that *all* officers treat them that way. And they're not right to show their anger by rioting or by singling out your father or by judging him as guilty before they know what really happened."

Thomas seemed perplexed.

"Black and White people really hate each other, don't they?" he asked.

"Not all of them. But unfortunately, in many cases—yes. And the hatred runs both ways, I'm sorry to say."

"How does it start?"

"Misunderstanding. Stereotypes. Fear."

"What's a 'stereotype'?"

"It's a general belief that many people have about a particular group of other people, in this case Blacks or Whites. It's an expectation that people have about every person of a particular group—how they look, how they act, how they think."

"But where does it come from?"

"It's passed from one person to another."

"But who starts it?"

"That, nobody knows," Katie said. "What matters most is that it's there, and that it's wrong. It's blind and it's ignorant and hurtful and sad."

Thomas listened intently.

"I know this is difficult to understand," Katie said, "but the main thing I want you to remember for now is that everything's going to be okay again. I'm not going to tell you everything is okay right now, because it's not. You're frightened and confused and sad. I know. All of us are. Your feelings are normal. But everything that's going on is only temporary. So are your feelings. One day, everything will be okay again, and you won't feel all these things anymore."

"When will that be?"

"That, I can't tell you ... but hopefully soon. Right now, you just have to give things time. You need to be strong and brave and try to help Dad and me and the twins get through this ordeal together."

Then she held her son closely to her chest and simply let him cry.

* * *

Later that night, Thomas had similar questions for his father.

"A lot of kids die in Brownsville, don't they?" Thomas asked.

Matt Holland was in bed now—wide awake, as usual. Katie had fallen asleep. Thomas lied on his air mattress, at the foot of his parents' bed.

"Yes, Thomas." His father sighed. "Sadly, kids die in Brownsville all the time."

Matt Holland fought the impulse to cry. He'd been brought up to believe that men never cried, certainly not in front of their children—and that police officers cried even less. He knew none of that was true. But still, he didn't want his twelve-year-old son to see him cry now. He wanted to appear strong and in control, even though he felt uncertain and weak.

"I just want you to know, Thomas, that I didn't mean to kill that boy," he said. "I was just doing my job, same as always. This happened because a lot of things went wrong. I'm sorry for that. The boy I shot was a good boy and didn't deserve to die. But sometimes bad things happen when you're a police officer. You pray to God that they won't—and usually they don't—but sometimes they do anyway."

"Do you feel bad about it?" Thomas asked.

"How do you think I feel?"

"Bad."

"Well, you're right. I feel very bad. Bad for the boy and his family. Bad about what's happening in Brownsville and around New York. Bad for all of us."

Thomas stood, his silhouette dark against the bedroom window. "Were you scared down there?" he asked.

"Where?"

"In that cellar."

"Yes, Thomas, I was scared."

"Did you think you were going to die?"

"It briefly passed through my mind."

"And Officer Cook?"

"Yes, I was afraid that she might die, too."

"What about now?"

"I'm still frightened, Thomas, but in a different way. Down in the cellar, I was frightened that I or Officer Cook might get hurt, or even die. Now, I'm afraid of other things."

"Like what?"

"Like losing my job, or going to jail, or having things in the city get worse than they already are. It's hard to explain. Part of me is even afraid of what might happen between you and me, and between Mom and me, because of this."

"What do you mean?"

"Well, you know how everyone always said I was this big 'hero' because of the things I once did? And you know how you've always looked up to me."

"Yeah."

"Well, part of me is afraid now that everything that's happened may make you stop feeling that way. Know what I mean?"

"I think so."

"See, Thomas, I've never wanted to do anything to ever let you down, but I'm afraid that's happened now. I'm afraid you might stop believing in me because of this. Sometimes, I'm afraid you might even stop loving me."

Slipping into the bed, Thomas squirmed into the narrow space between his mother and his father, placing an arm across his father's chest.

"You don't have to worry about that, Dad," Thomas said. "There's nothing you could ever do that would make me stop loving you."

Chapter 42

MATT HOLLAND'S ASSIGNMENT as a 911 operator didn't last long. Indeed, less than a month into his punitive demotion, six weeks after the C. J. Johnson shooting, the former hero cop was suspended, indefinitely and without pay, in a calculated, politically tainted ruling by New York City Police Commissioner William Dunne.

The rationale for Dunne's decision, arrived at in consultation with Mayor Nathan Worth, seemed contradictory—and in some ways, nonsensical—on its face. While Holland's account of the shooting had been supported by overwhelming evidence, including supposed eyewitnesses recanting their groundless accusations, homicide detectives, at Dunne's direction, had forwarded the evidence they'd gathered to Kings County D.A. Hal Green, as well as to Justice Department officials. In other words, even while the NYPD's internal investigation concluded that Holland had acted in conformity with department guidelines—and that the C. J. Johnson shooting was simply a tragic accident—Matt Holland bore the consequences now of not only an interminable, unpaid suspension, but of potential criminal culpability. As PBA attorney Eddie Shearson had presaged, the officer was facing the likelihood of double and perhaps even triple jeopardy. Since both the D.A. and the Justice Department's probes were still very much alive, the NYPD technically had no choice, Dunne concluded, but to impose its automatic-suspension rule.

And so, what should have been vindication for Matt Holland in the court of public opinion became merely a pyrrhic victory. His suspension, in effect, was an indictment implying guilt.

The PBA was livid.

"This is a dark day for law enforcement in America," Red McLaren told the press. "The summary treatment of Matt Holland is nothing less than a gutless surrender to political pressure, a rush to judgment brought about by a desire to appease the minority community and 'do the right thing.' The city is being blackmailed. Police officers are being betrayed. As a trade-off for 'peace' in Brownsville, a good man is being vilified, betrayed, and prejudged as guilty."

"Matt Holland was once the NYPD's role model, and deservedly so," McLaren said, "but now he has become the department's sacrificial lamb, a symbol of the 'rotten, bigoted, violent cop,' thrown to the wolves in the interest of good public relations, simply to calm the political storms."

McLaren spread a collection of pink arrest records across his desk, symbolizing what the PBA president said was once the most exemplary of law-enforcement careers.

"Everyone's vision has become obscured," McLaren said. "We've lost all perspective and become incapable of viewing incidents like the shooting of C. J. Johnson as entities unto themselves. People are bending over backwards to make a point and correct past abuses. But this has left the realm of civil rights and entered the realm of character assassination. Matt Holland is an innocent man who's being made to bear the weight of every police injustice ever perpetuated in this country. He's a pariah, a whipping boy, a scapegoat. Who he *really* is means nothing. Neither does his record—or, for that matter, the truth."

"Matt Holland is a White cop who has shot a Black child—period—and for that he'll pay for the misdeeds of every cop who, rightly or wrongly, ever shot a black person," McLaren added. "An errant gunshot cost an innocent boy his life. Now, politics will cost a good and honest man his career, perhaps even his life."

The PBA's protestations fell on deaf ears, however. Neither the NYPD nor City Hall was moved. Indeed, anti-police protest leaders not only cheered the news of Holland's suspension, but many claimed that the penalty didn't go far enough. Holland, they said, needed to be criminally charged, as well.

Other people, of course, received news of Holland's suspension far differently. Chief of Department Patrick Delaney and Robert Turetsky, Mayor Worth's chief of staff, each resigned in protest of the decision. In Brownsville, angry police officers tore down the *WANTED* posters of Holland and Rachel Cook and set them ablaze. The American flag outside the entrance to the 73rd Precinct was also lowered, as a symbolic sign of mourning, to half-staff.

Then a large group of rebellious off-duty officers mounted a protest of their own. Repudiating oath and obligation, defying pleas from the PBA, they took their anger to the streets. Police barricades were erected at the entrance to the Brooklyn Bridge, creating a huge, rush-hour traffic jam. Toting American flags, along with banners and signs, the dissident cops then marched on City Hall.

"No justice, no police!" they chanted. "No justice, no police!"

The banners and signs they carried mirrored their sentiments.

POLICE OFFICERS ARE PEOPLE TOO!

MATT HOLLAND = SCAPEGOAT!

IT'S A TRAGEDY, NOT A CRIME!

LET US FORGIVE ACCIDENTS!

LET THE TRUTH PREVAIL

Some cops vented their frustration by letting the air out of automobile tires. Others battered cars, terrorizing stunned motorists. Still others hurled beer cans and shouted obscenities at uniformed officers and commanders who waded through the demonstration, pleading fruitlessly with the dissidents to desist.

In his homily at Saint Patrick's Cathedral that evening, the Archbishop of New York urged an end to the citywide divisiveness. In a skillfully worded message, he called for healing, dialogue, and reconciliation.

"No government authority, no amount of public outcry can compensate for the tragic death of this young boy," Cardinal Francis Regan told a packed cathedral. "Nothing can assuage the sorrow of the Johnson family or the ordeal of the Hollands. All we can do is express our regrets and pray that incidents like this never happen again. But nothing should bring us to denounce the thousands of noble, dedicated, and selfless officers who serve our city each day. The mistakes, sins, treacheries, and even the violence perpetuated by a handful cannot blind us to the nobility, integrity, decency, sacrifice, and service of the vast majority.

"We must push racial hatred aside, eradicate racism in all its forms," the Cardinal added. "If there are injustices, we must correct them rather than deny them, learn from them rather than ignore them. But we must look at these cases one at a time if we're ever to achieve true justice."

He then offered a prayer for the Johnson family, for Matt Holland, and for the City of New York.

The Cardinal's words, however, seemingly had little impact. The racial divide in New York never seemed as cavernous, or as impossible to bridge, as it was at this moment, and the city never seemed so wounded and disjointed. It was as if New York itself might implode from the weight of all its troubles—its crisis seeming, for the moment, beyond even the power of prayer.

Part 3

You may not know it, but at the far end of despair,
there is a white clearing where one is almost happy.

—Jean Anouilh, *Restless Heart,* 1934

Chapter 43

IT FELT, in many ways, like tumbling headlong into a dark and bottomless pit. Down and down Matt Holland and Rachel Cook plummeted, in an agonizing freefall into a lonely and terrifying purgatory where neither officer had imagined they'd ever go.

Unlike the racially charged drama unfolding on New York's public stage, Holland's and Cook's heartrending downfalls took place entirely behind closed doors. Few bore witness; even fewer cared. But no matter: within seconds of the C. J. Johnson shooting, and hastened by subsequent events, Holland and Cook found themselves plunging into separate personal hells—their reputations tarnished, their lives in shambles, their psyches unraveling in harrowing, unimaginable ways.

Abandoned by a city that hailed him once as a hero, buried under a mountain of accusations and doubt, facing months of uncertainty and potential jail time, Matt Holland faltered intractably. Jobless and scorned, wounded in a way that seemingly intensified with each passing day, he closed a door on the world, retreating into a home guarded round the clock by armed, off-duty cops. Silent and withdrawn, haunted by what had happened, Holland threw himself into the construction of the bedroom he'd been building for his twin daughters, working night and day, as if the physical effort alone could somehow mitigate the citywide furor threatening to swallow him whole. Family matters had become mere afterthoughts now. Weekend sojourns to the Jersey shore had ceased. Coaching Thomas in Little League had been put on hold. So, of course, had the annual Labor Day Weekend camping trip with the special-needs children from Brownsville.

In place of those cheerful pastimes was a form of penance served largely in solitary confinement. Rarely did Holland spend time with Katie anymore. Rarely did he spend time with anyone. At night, incapable of sleep, he paced the house aimlessly, chatting with his PBA brethren and peering furtively out of windows in search of would-be assailants. On the few occasions when he managed to nod off, he slept tucked securely inside a sleeping bag on the floor of the bedroom he was building. Shortly after his suspension was announced, he pulled the display case containing his NYPD commendations from the living room wall.

"I don't deserve these honors," he told Katie, retreating into a cesspool of self-loathing and pity. "I took an oath to protect and serve, but I betrayed my badge. I killed an innocent boy, and I'm saddened and ashamed. I'm nothing but a fraud. All I deserve is to be punished."

Reluctant to express his condolences verbally for fear they might be seen as contrived or disingenuous—or, worse, as if he was the one in need of sympathy—Holland wrote a statement that was released to the public through the PBA. It read:

> *My heartfelt condolences go out to the Johnson family. I am deeply sorry for the loss and pain that my actions have caused. If there was any way I could turn back the clock and bring their son back, I would. I have been a police officer for 16 years and have always valued human life. In that cellar, I reacted purely on instinct. I did my best to protect my partner and myself, and to perform my job. What happened was an accident and had nothing to do with race. I do not see color on my job. I don't know what else to say other than that I am sorry for this tragic accident and will continue to cooperate fully in any investigations going forward. I am a parent, too. I cannot imagine what it must be like to lose a child. I will have a pain in my heart forever over this. When I look at my own three children, I will see that boy and remember that a big part of me died along with him down in that cellar.*

Matt Holland, of course, was right about that. Indeed, it felt now as if part of him had died. Each day, he relived the shooting incident in minute detail, second-guessing every action, every thought, every decision. Could he and Cook have avoided the encounter altogether? Should he have kept his firearm holstered? Did the partners, as accused, "profile" C. J. Johnson, prejudging the boy as a criminal simply because he was Black? Was the shooting truly the tragic accident that Holland claimed it was, or just a flimsy excuse for a fuck-up? A cheap alibi? An easy way out?

Holland dwelled almost endlessly on C. J. Johnson, too. He wondered what the boy felt as he lay mortally wounded on the cellar floor. *Was it terror? Hatred? Anger? Confusion? Loneliness? Pain?*

He wondered what C. J. was thinking when he inadvertently ran into Holland in the pitch-darkness. *Did he understand he'd made a fatal error in judgment, mistaking a uniformed police officer for his cousin Marcus? Was he sorry he'd left his hearing aid at home? Did he realize the officer never meant to harm him?*

Matt Holland wondered, endlessly.

At times, he tried to console himself with the thought that C. J. looked oddly peaceful as he lay wounded on the floor, his eyes staring up in seeming wonderment, as if gazing at a constellation of stars. Holland remembered what it was like to try and breathe life into the teen: how he'd pried C. J.'s lips open and pressed them to his own, the boy's spittle salty in the officer's mouth. He remembered how he'd wished, fleetingly, that if C. J. was going to die, he'd die quickly, so as not to suffer. He remembered how he'd wished that he'd never seen C.J.'s face because maybe it would be easier that way. Maybe he wouldn't be as tormented and empty and lost.

Holland also felt culpable for the fact that his own son was struggling now, too. Always an excellent student, Thomas, like his father, had grown quiet and withdrawn in recent weeks. At school, his attention drifted constantly, and he couldn't focus on homework. Often, he complained of physical symptoms—headaches, stomach aches, dizziness, muscle fatigue—that were vague and undetectable. Friendships, afterschool activities, and household chores were off-limits. Like his sisters, he was escorted to and from school by the same off-duty cops who guarded the Hollands' house. After school, the twelve-year-old stayed indoors, clinging tightly to his mother. At night, he kept a light on to help him sleep. He had also started, much to his shame, to wet his bed.

Katie Holland was a pillar of strength for her son, constantly comforting and reassuring Thomas; helping him put his feelings into words; helping with the humiliation of his bedwetting; helping separate myths from realities:

"No, Dad isn't out there killing people all the time."

"No, Dad isn't the racist pig he's being called."

"No, a mob of angry Black people isn't coming to the house to kill them."

"Yes, things will eventually return to a semblance of normalcy."

"I know that you're frightened and bewildered by all of this," Katie told her son. "This has been extremely upsetting because of how it has been portrayed and how it has turned our lives upside down. It's unfair what's happened to you, Thomas … because you did nothing wrong."

Thomas peered at her, his eyes wide and glistening.

"All your feelings are understandable," Katie said, patiently, "even though some of your behavior is not. I'll accept 'good-enough' schoolwork for now, but I expect you to try harder, pay attention in school, do your homework, and do the things you need to do around the house."

"Are you angry at me?" Thomas asked.

"Of course not. But remember how I said how you need to be brave and grown-up now?"

"Yes."

"Well, I need you to remember that. We're in this nightmare together—as a family. We need to pull together for one another, and stay strong, and try to keep on living."

Then she cradled Thomas in her arms as if he were a toddler, and sat with him, stroking his hair until, slowly, he did what his father seemed entirely incapable of—closing his eyes and drifting off to sleep.

* * *

Rachel Cook, like her former partner, resided in another world now, too—a rancid, hostile realm riddled with bitterness, uncertainty, and fear.

As informed by 73rd Precinct Capt. Robert Borelli, Cook had been formally absolved of any culpability in C. J. Johnson's shooting. But banished largely to strip-search duties and shunned by most male cops at her new command in Coney Island, the rookie officer found herself isolated and terrified as never before. It didn't matter that the 60th Precinct was designated as "B" house, with a lower incidence of crime than Cook's former command. Nor did it matter that the rioting in Brownsville had subsided. Resentment and trepidation stalked the streets of minority neighborhoods in the aftermath of the C. J. Johnson shooting. Anti-police sentiment was spiking again in New York, as it had several years earlier, and officers assigned to neighborhoods like Coney Island remained in a state of heightened alert, the target of hostility and potential retribution.

On some tours, Cook could feel the hatred beating down on her like a relentless, chilling rain. Conversations ceased, people turned away, and children halted in their play as Cook approached warily on foot patrol. Other people proffered hostile glares, mouthed curses, and whispered taunts.

Her heart hammering, her stomach walls taut, Cook walked her beat as quickly and robotically as she could, diverting her eyes or forcing a tepid smile. As she passed by, however, people's feelings were unleashed, usually from the shelter of rooftops, alleyways, and windows.

"White lady pig!"

"Fuck you, bitch!"

"Blow me!"

"Go to hell!"

Desperately, Cook tried to steel herself to the torrent of abuse, pretending she didn't hear it, didn't see it, didn't feel it. Desperately, she tried not to take it personally, fearful of becoming a mirror that might reflect her own budding feelings of contempt for the public, a malice and a rage building slowly inside her.

Cook didn't want to harden herself to the very people she'd been sworn to serve; didn't want to dismiss them as enemies or become numb to their challenges and their pain; didn't want to stereotype them or condemn them for being as allegedly racist as the officers they targeted with their scorn. Inwardly, though, Cook knew she couldn't afford to allow herself to remain vulnerable for very much longer to the avalanche of abuse. She was only human, after all. It would only be a matter of time, she feared, before the sentiments she was exposed to would become reciprocal and she'd start hating, too—and hitting people back as hard as they were hitting her.

But the roots of Rachel Cook's burgeoning fear didn't reside solely on the streets of Coney Island. Instead, they resided *inside* her, born as much from what she couldn't see or hear as everything she could. The heady confidence she'd gained under Matt Holland's tutelage had all but evaporated by now. Devoid of that, Cook felt suddenly vulnerable: conspicuous, susceptible to violence, exposed. Highly visible, female, White, stained by the C. J. Johnson shooting, she saw herself as a prime target for retribution against the police. She envisioned groups of angry Black militants plotting behind closed doors to kidnap, disable, or assassinate her. Walking her beat, her imagination played cruel tricks. Loud noises became gunshots. Swooping birds became hurled objects. An unexpected hand on her shoulder became a sign of attack.

As with Matt Holland, the C. J. Johnson shooting rarely left Cook's mind, haunting her every waking moment. She could still see herself and her former partner barging, guns drawn, into the cellar on Amboy Street. She could still feel the darkness swallow the two of them up; still see the muzzle flash from Holland's service revolver, the mortally wounded boy lying on the floor, the anguished, disbelieving look on her partner's face. Reliving the hours of questioning she'd been subjected to, Cook could still see the investigators' sullen faces, the dubious eyes of senior officers, the terrified look on her mother's face as her fear for her daughter's wellbeing poured from her lips.

Cook tried to deflect her thoughts and focus on her police duties, but the vivid flashbacks, accompanied by jarring rushes of adrenaline, were triggered by almost anything—sometimes by nothing at all.

When she wasn't dwelling on the incident itself, Cook thought about Matt Holland, who she'd neither talked to nor seen since the night of the shooting. She tried to imagine what her former partner—the esteemed cop she'd idolized and even loved—was going through now: the torment, the uncertainty, the isolation, the pressure. To Cook, it was unfathomable how Holland's life had been turned inside out in the blink of an eye—his reputation trashed, his career destroyed, his freedom threatened, his record of service tossed aside. Nothing would ever be the same for Holland or his family. Whatever the outcome of the case, whatever the remaining investigations might uncover, he'd carry the weight of the shooting around with him for the rest of his life.

As would she.

Cook wondered if her former partner would be able to live with the torment and the guilt without becoming hopelessly overwrought. She wondered if he'd ever be able to piece his splintered life together, reconcile the conflicts raging within him, rescue his damaged marriage, mend his wounded family. Matt Holland, such an exemplary officer—such a good and caring man—had been stripped of his identity as a human being and a cop. Cook couldn't get over that, either. Holland was little more than a symbol now, the same way C. J. Johnson was a symbol. To protestors, he was The Killer Cop. To the PBA, he was The Great Pariah. To the NYPD, he was the latest Problem Child. To other cops, he was the poor schnook who'd been in the wrong place at the wrong time, and had to watch helplessly now as his entire life turned to shit.

Equally unfathomable to Cook was how this could have happened to Holland in the first place. Of all the cops she'd met, he seemed the *least* susceptible to something like this. He was such a pro, after all—so experienced, so respected, so hardworking and adept, and so *clean*, too. Never took risks. Never looked for trouble. Not a bigot or a loudmouth or a rabble-rouser, like some of the others. Not one of those jerkoffs who'd hassle people for a laugh or sit on calls that weren't emergencies or fall asleep on the job. Holland was such a *good guy*—that was what was so jarring. Always so honest and dependable. Always kept his distance from the dirt bags in the precinct. Never so much as took a free cup of coffee. Just an honest, dedicated, heroic cop who always tried to do his best. Just a dedicated public servant who probably rather have died himself than kill an innocent kid.

Just like her.

Cook tried to put herself in Holland's place. Faced with the same terrible choices, what do you do? No one's there to lend advice or help you decide. Nothing could prepare you. You can't get on the radio and ask the desk sergeant for guidance. You can't consult the *NYPD Patrol Guide*. You can't stop things from happening because you don't want the complication or the consequences.

What do you do?

Cook couldn't answer that—or all the other questions she posed.

Matt Holland didn't have the luxury of the second-guess. He had to be on guard. He didn't know that he and Cook were walking in on a bunch of teenagers preparing for a surprise party. He didn't know what they'd find in that cellar. What if there *had* been a crime-in-progress? What if C. J. Johnson hadn't been an innocent boy who was hearing impaired? What if Holland was truly being attacked? Seeing what he did, hearing what he did, feeling what he did, thinking what he did, who could truly say he was at fault? Who could say they would have acted any different?

Cook couldn't.

She knew that what had happened that night was an unfortunate and horrifying tragedy, an accident of fate, in many ways unavoidable. And it could happen again. Tomorrow. Today. To any cop. To *her*.

The realization of all that was chilling. It was no longer possible for Cook to minimize the dangers or the implications of police work, or pretend she was immune to similar incidents, similar consequences. The C. J. Johnson shooting had exposed that reality in spades. You never knew when even a routine call would turn complicated and chilling, did you? You never knew when the shit would hit the fan. It could no longer be dismissed as simply a vague abstraction or remote possibility. It had hit too close to home.

Now, suddenly, it was obvious to Cook how each day she walked a fine line between life and death. For the first time, she realized that she, too, could really die on the street—or, almost as horrific, kill an innocent person. For the first time, she realized how fragile her life was, how each moment could change things forever. All it took was a slip of the finger, a mistaken judgment, being in the wrong place at the wrong time, and the whole world could come crashing in on her. There was no running away from it, no margin for error, no hiding.

Suddenly, Cook's entire future seemed murky and uncertain. Nothing was predictable anymore. No longer was she shielded or immune; no longer under the wing of a competent, experienced pro like Matt Holland. To the contrary, she was vulnerable, always on the brink of catastrophe, blind to her fate. She wondered if she could cope with the pressure, the questions, the accusations, the threats that were bombarding Matt Holland every waking moment now. She wondered if she could ever do her job again in quite the same way.

But Cook tried to push her questions and her doubts away, just like she tried to push aside her growing alienation, anxiety, and fear. *Put your head down and plow through it*, she told herself. *Suck it up and tough it out.*

It was just another reality about police work that you tried to put out of your mind, Cook told herself. Just another one of the job-related hazards that you made believe wasn't really there.

Chapter 44

FROM THEIR PEW inside the nave of the Good Shepherd Baptist Church, Charles and Eunice Johnson leaned on the kneelers beneath their bench and silently began to pray.

It was a daily ritual now, their sojourns to the tiny church in Brownsville. More than ever, the couple's faith in God had become their prime source of sustenance, the church their singular refuge, its pastor and congregation their pillar of strength. The grieving parents immersed themselves in all those things—their lives, like those of Matt Holland and Rachel Cook, invisible to the public now. Eunice heightened her involvement with the church choir, its various ministries, its bible study group. She and Charles became active in the church's Palmetto Club, comprised of fifty-plus native South Carolinians. The couple also met weekly with the Rev. Josiah Watson, whom they leaned heavily upon for guidance and support.

"We must trust in the Lord," the pastor told them. "God has a plan for all of us, a reason for everything. C. J. lived and died for a purpose. With time, that purpose will become clear, and you'll find the strength to accept God's wisdom, and help serve Him in your beloved son's name."

Charles clung tightly to those words, using them as a beacon to light the way through his darkest, most uncertain moments. Each day, he prayed that Rev. Watson would be proven right: that God really *did* have a plan for him, and soon that plan would be revealed. Anything was possible, of course, Charles thought. So many things, after all, had been set in motion in the wake of C. J.'s death. The federal class-action lawsuit filed by civil rights leaders, with Charles's blessing, was already being hailed as a landmark piece of litigation. The allegations of alleged racial profiling by police were shining a light on an important issue; indeed, talk was that the tragedy of C. J.'s shooting death could result in lasting changes in police-minority relations across America. At the same time, the wrongful-death lawsuit filed on the Johnsons' behalf was forcing city officials to hold police accountable for their actions.

Charles thought, too, about the terms of the tacit agreement he had privately struck with respect to the civil-liability lawsuit and the potential monetary award tied to a subsequent judgment. He was pleased with the way he'd handled himself in the presence of the esteemed Black leaders; pleased that he'd carried himself with dignity and humility; pleased that a lowly token clerk had gotten such consequential men to consent to the out-of-the-box conditions he'd demanded in exchange for his family's support of the class-action lawsuit now before the U.S. Justice Department.

Charles prayed each day that the outcome of the dual legal actions would somehow be favorable to everyone concerned, just like he prayed for the wellbeing of Eunice and the sanctity of C. J.'s soul. He prayed that both lawsuits would reach a speedy resolution, and that some permanent good would result. Most of all, Charles prayed for healing and recovery: for him and for Eunice and the rest of their family; for his shaken, damaged neighborhood; for his bedraggled, racially divided city.

He prayed for Matt Holland and Rachel Cook, too.

Charles knew in his heart that the two officers, like his own family, had been deeply wounded by everything that had occurred. He sensed that the two of them were hurting and lost. And he prayed that the officers, like everyone touched by the tragedy, could somehow find closure; that they too could move past the misfortune that had befallen them and proceed in God's good grace with the remainder of their lives.

* * *

Matt Holland, much like Charles, spent time in church too, struggling to find absolution for everything that had occurred.

Seated behind a leather curtain in the confession booth at Holy Innocents Roman Catholic Church in Staten Island, the disgraced officer spoke in muted tones through a latticed opening, confessing his sins to the shadowy silhouette of the parish priest.

"I've betrayed both my oath and my faith," Holland said, weeping as he offered his penitence. "I'm a police officer who failed to live up to his duty to protect. I'm a father who killed an innocent child. I'm responsible for the turmoil in our city. I've violated God's commandment and the laws I pledged to uphold."

But the disgraced officer couldn't find solace in the pastor's consolation, or in his assurances of forgiveness, or in any of the Hail Mary prayers he was told to recite. Prayers weren't helping now. Neither were the comforting sentiments of family and friends, nor the support of fellow police officers—nor much of anything, really.

It was mid-October already, three-plus months since the C. J. Johnson shooting, and still Matt Holland awaited some form of legal and emotional closure, an escape from the darkness that had smothered him since that fateful July 4th night. Stripped of his badge and his income, his family disjointed, his fate uncertain, the suspended officer twisted in the city's seesawing political winds, his state of mind irrelevant to the dilatory pace of the two remaining investigations. Until those matters were concluded, and his legal issues resolved, all Holland could do was watch and wait. And so, he did—all the while immersed in his own private hell.

Not nearly as sensational in its current phase, the C. J. Johnson shooting case had all but receded from the public eye. Anti-police demonstrations had for the most part quieted. Accounts about the incident no longer warranted expansive news coverage, periodic updates on the case overshadowed by stories of greater immediacy. Jimmy Carter was headed for apparent victory in the race for U.S. president. The Cincinnati Reds had swept the Yankees to win the World Series. A deranged gunman nicknamed "Son of Sam" was terrorizing the city. Those were the stories that dominated media coverage now. Matt Holland's torment, in contrast, was very much his own.

Father Michael Caruso was among the handful of people who looked in on Holland periodically, trying to assuage the officer's private affliction.

A former U.S. Army colonel, Father Caruso had, for thirty years, been chaplain of the NYPD's Holy Name Society, the department's oldest and largest religious organization. Having served in Europe during World War II, the veteran priest had seen both combat soldiers and police officers shattered by the kind of trauma battering Holland. He understood the price of emotional pain, knew what it took to counsel even the bravest of men plagued by issues of the heart.

"I'm so sorry, Father," Holland told him. "I'm not sure I can live with everything that's happened. Every day, I relive the incident. Every day, I look into that boy's eyes and see him die of a bullet from my gun. Every day, I try desperately to save him, and I fail. I'm trying so hard to get the picture of that night out of my head, but I just can't. It's like a nightmare that won't end."

The two of them were alone in the living room of the officer's home. Father Caruso sat in an easy chair, drinking tea. Holland paced about.

"I was raised a Catholic ... brought up on the commandment 'Thou shalt not kill,'" the embattled cop said. "I've always believed in that, always valued human life. I never wanted to kill anyone. But now, I'm guilty of the greatest sin possible. What happened goes against the grain of everything I've ever stood for. I can never see myself the same way again. How can I be a father? A father *gives* life. How can I be a police officer? A police officer *saves* lives."

"Before you can be a father or a police officer," Father Caruso said, "you need to return to being the *man* you once were."

"I'm not sure I know how to do that," Holland said.

Father Caruso calmly sipped his tea.

"You've always been everyone's knight in shining armor, Matt," he counseled. "You've led an exemplary life. You've loved and been faithful to your wife, provided for your family, given to the community. You've been a police officer that this city has been proud of for years. And now, because of this one tragic accident, you think all of that has been wiped away? You think you've been disgraced in the eyes of God?"

"Haven't I?"

"Of course not," Father Caruso said. "The commandment you're referring to, Matt, means, 'Thou shalt not commit murder.' There's a difference between a murder and a killing. It's the difference between something evil and something that, I believe, will ultimately be found to be accidental. God understands that difference. Don't you?"

"What I've done may be legal, Father, but what about my conscience?" Holland asked. "There's a difference, too, between what's legal and what's moral. Whether I was technically 'right' or 'wrong,' the fact is that I killed an innocent child, and now must live with everything I feel inside: the immorality of my actions; the pain I've caused; the uncertainty I've created for my own family and that of the victim."

Even as he spoke, Holland felt himself spiraling downward, to a dark and fearful place where there seemingly was no way out.

Father Caruso stood and placed an arm around Holland's shoulder.

"You're right, Matt," the priest said, softly. "Surely, you'll have to live with the consequences of your actions. But you can't fail to remember that you never acted with evil or malice. You didn't *want* to kill. Allow yourself to take comfort in that, and to accept that what happened was an accident. God forgives accidents. He'll forgive you, too. What you need to do, Matt, is find a way to forgive yourself."

Then the two of them prayed.

He was sorry, Father Caruso said, that he could offer no more than his meager wisdom and prayers. But he also told Holland that he knew of someone who might be able to help in a more substantive way. And he gave the officer the name and phone number of a fellow cop named Landon Devlin.

Chapter 45

ALTHOUGH THE NYPD had formally cleared Matt Holland and Rachel Cook of departmental violations in the C. J. Johnson shooting, the Patrolmen's Benevolent Association, like police unions across America, was far from pleased with the decision to suspend Holland, and soon began applying its own pressure on city officials.

Meeting with Police Commissioner William Dunne and other police brass, PBA leaders pleaded their case for the NYPD to revise its disciplinary guidelines regarding officers accused of wrongdoing.

"The current policy is to automatically suspend an officer pending the outcome of either a departmental or a criminal trial," union president Red McLaren argued. "But clearly, that's unjust."

Police Commissioner Dunne, magisterial behind his desk at One Police Plaza, shuffled a sheath of papers as PBA officials pleaded their case.

"There's a profound lack of due process in play," McLaren argued. "Matt Holland has been unjustly stripped of his constitutional rights. Why isn't a police officer accused of misconduct or under a cloud of suspicion entitled to the same presumption of innocence that any other citizen enjoys when charged with a crime? Why should the officer be judged guilty before he's had his day in court? How could the department justify suspending an officer, then await the outcome of investigations and possible trials that could take years to complete?"

Commissioner Dunne stifled a yawn.

A ruddy-faced, sloe-eyed ex-cop, Dunne had been immensely popular when named four years earlier to head the NYPD. But the commissioner had fallen out of favor with the city's police during the city's fiscal crisis, when he'd ordered the layoffs of thousands of officers, while freezing salaries and promotions. His popularity had declined even more precipitously when he'd threatened terminations and fines against officers who staged protests over the cutbacks.

"We don't see the harm in the automatic-suspension policy," Dunne said, blithely. "Even if an officer is eventually cleared of wrongdoing, what harm is there in suspending him until the investigation is complete?"

"The harm is to the officer," McLaren retorted. "Don't you see that?"

"Frankly, no," Dunne said.

"Just look what's happening in this case," McLaren argued. "People are shouting, 'Let's hang the White cop … he shot a Black boy because he's racist.' Matt Holland is being demonized, tried, convicted, and crucified in the court of public opinion before the facts are even in. His career has been all but destroyed. His family has been torn to shreds. He faces months of legal uncertainty and no income. On top of that, he has to live with this shooting for the rest of his life. But tell me … has anybody thought about him?"

McLaren eyeballed the other senior officers, all of whom seemed unmoved.

"Tell me," McLaren asked, "what becomes of officers while these investigations are being conducted? What if the officers acted appropriately? What if they're innocent? What if a shooting really was just an unavoidable accident?"

No one said a word.

"I'm not saying police officers want to be above the laws we're asked to enforce, and I understand the outrage over brutal and racist cops," McLaren continued. "Cops should be held to account when they do something wrong. But they should also be supported when they do something right, or when the jury's still out. How can our officers function effectively, if they don't have that minimal level of support—if they're treated like criminals when they might not have committed a wrong?"

Again, there was silence.

"We need balance, if we're truly to be just," McLaren said. "Right now, the city is so anxious to demonstrate that it will move against a cop who acts inappropriately that it has failed to consider that Matt Holland might not have been at fault. By automatically suspending him, we've sent a message that he's guilty before the investigations are even complete. We've done him a grave injustice. It's no longer guilty *as* charged. Now, it's guilty *when* charged. Innocent or not, Matt Holland has been stained for life. He's guilty in the eyes of the world."

"You talk about messages," Dunne said, "well, what about the message we need to send to the Johnson family and the minority community? Don't you think we're sending them a destructive message if we allow Detective Sergeant Holland to remain on the job? If he does prove to be guilty, isn't it only exacerbating his crime by allowing him to remain in a job that the public supports with its tax dollars?"

"The rights of cops are obviously less important than the rights of everyone else, I suppose," McLaren said sarcastically. "But what about a cop's rights as a human being? Do they have to be so callously disregarded? Here, we have a man who's being treated like a criminal and no one seems to give a damn. This is a good man we're talking about—a heroic cop with an exemplary record, not some reckless out-of-control cowboy. But he's an afterthought, isn't he? No one thinks about him as a person. No one has any compassion. Doesn't anyone understand what a crushing weight he's under? Did it ever occur to anyone that he, too, may have been traumatized by what's happened? No ... no one has any time for that. People don't want to know it."

McLaren gazed again at the NYPD officials around him.

"Let's figure out a way to practice some common decency in these kinds of cases," he said. "What we need is balance, consideration for both sides. Not just one."

McLaren and the other PBA representatives spent an hour arguing their case, before being thanked for their time and dismissed. Their comments, they were informed, would be taken under advisement.

Chapter 46

RACHEL COOK DESPISED what was going on, felt so sullied, so disheartened, so betrayed. The way in which the C. J. Johnson shooting had ignited a racial firestorm, and the way the case was being adjudicated, was forcing Cook to see police work, and the world itself, in a whole new way. None of what she was seeing now had been discernable during her first eight months on the job. None of it had been addressed at the Police Academy, or in the *NYPD Patrol Guide*, or by Matt Holland during his training in Brownsville. Besides, Cook had been too naïve to see it prior to now anyway: too blindly idealistic, too sheltered, too green.

But there it was, staring her in the face, impossible to ignore: Everything was about politics, wasn't it? Preserving power. Saving face. Pandering to the right constituency. Winning votes. And worst of all, robbing Cook of her innocence, her wherewithal, and her faith.

Cook saw police work through such a different lens now. It was as if C. J. Johnson's shooting and its aftermath had lifted a curtain on what merely months earlier seemed gilded and pristine. But now the blinders were off, and everything Cook saw seemed tarnished and debased.

Having seen city government once as a shining bastion of public service, Cook saw it now as nothing more than a shifty, bankrupt entity that did little but create mirages and smokescreens, always trying to paint itself in a favorable light, always moving solely in its own self-interests. She saw City Hall as being overrun by gutless political hacks—ass-kissers and reprobates, backstabbers, conformists, and wannabes who spent their days stalking the corridors of power, striking bargains, pulling strings, undercutting rivals, and wrangling for a cherished piece of turf. She saw the primary instruments of government—the legislature, the judiciary, the media—in the same soiled light. Law-enforcement reformists were vacuous, politically motivated noisemakers. Anti-police protestors were little more than purblind ingénues and clueless do-gooders. Newspaper columnists and TV commentators were ratings-driven talking heads; the public-at-large, ill-informed, apathetic, and self-absorbed.

Worse of all was how Cook saw the NYPD.

It seemed hard to believe now, but merely months earlier Cook had seen the NYPD as a rock-ribbed pillar of gravitas, integrity, and resolve. No more. Now she saw it as a frail, pathetic reed that shifted with the winds of public opinion, heeding the call when the power brokers beckoned and the special interests called. She saw top brass as nothing more than grace-and-favor appointments, subject to the flick of a mayor's broom; saw the chain of command as a litany of wormy, feckless sycophants anchored to a rigid bureaucracy, adhering to the status quo; saw police commanders who began their career as patrol officers, then got swallowed up by the hierarchy and lost touch with the cop on the street, vying simply to put in their twenty years and walk away with a hefty, lifelong pension.

But it didn't stop there.

Literally everything about the job seemed exasperating, infuriating, even farcical, to Cook now. Judgment was needed, but rarely was taught. Merit was inconsequential, careers built by doling out favors and stroking the right egos. Policies were implemented and then scrapped on a whim. There were rules to obey, but they changed constantly and few of them addressed reality. You were told to be aggressive, but never go overboard; ordered to make arrests, but not too many and not too few and never for the wrong reason. Open-and-shut cases went unresolved, swallowed up by the system. Judges were obstructive, prosecutors hostile, attorneys derisive, juries indifferent, criminals set free on technicalities. When the crime rate spiked, the police were blamed; when it declined, some hapless empty suit took the credit. Worst of all, police officers were empowered to make split-second, life-and-death decisions but then were scrutinized, second-guessed, sanctioned, scorned, and betrayed not only when they were wrong, but sometimes even when they were *right*.

And all of it stung.

Having formerly seen the NYPD as benevolent, an ally, a beacon of light, Cook was wounded by the narrow-minded, fickle bureaucracy it really seemed to be. How could you possibly love an entity like that? How could you remain faithful to it? How could you give yourself to it fully and freely, body and soul?

Cook was no longer sure.

She thought: *So, this is how the game is played? A heroic, veteran cop like Matt Holland—acting in the interests of the city, doing his job by the book, free of malice and prejudice, pure of heart and mind—becomes entangled in an unwonted, unintended tragedy and gets hung out to dry because it's politically expedient? A good man gets sold down the river because issues are sensitive and special interests need stroking and other considerations take on greater importance?*

To Rachel Cook now, that's the way things worked: The merits of a case mattered little. Facts were irrelevant. The truth got lost in the shuffle. Politics and emotions prevailed. All people cared about was scoring points, advancing an agenda. And everyone was the same. It was simply a matter of which side you were on.

To protestors and law-enforcement reformists, the C. J. Johnson shooting was solely about police brutality and racial profiling—period. To police unions, it was all about blindly protecting cops. To the media, it was about creating headlines, attracting eyeballs, and peddling ad space. To city officials, it was a political hot potato that needed to be cooled. To the NYPD, it was an internal dilemma that needed to be resolved regardless of cost. In the final analysis, no one other than his family truly gave a damn about C. J. Johnson. And Matt Holland? He too meant little in the overall scheme of things. He was expendable, disposable, a pawn. His life could be flushed down the toilet, but so what? The political outcome was all that mattered, quieting things down until the next big crisis came along.

Suddenly, Rachel Cook perceived the role she played in an entirely new light. Police officers were fodder, nothing more. They could never win, had no real power. They were just out there jerking themselves off, making believe they could make a difference, putting their lives on the line, working their asses off for a pittance, and putting their fate in the hands of higher-ups they could never to truly believe in or trust.

As if the C. J. shooting and its repercussions weren't unsettling enough, Rachel Cook was disheartened by her revelations, the politics and discord fouling the air like the stench of rotting trash. All the more reason, she thought, to cover her ass, take no chances, and steel herself to the realities of the job. All the more reason to salve her growing wounds by donning a suit of armor and not allowing herself to trust the things she saw, or believe in the things she once held dear, or care as deeply as she had when she took her solemn oath of office, not so long ago.

Chapter 47

In a tiny office adjacent to the Queens County Courthouse, Matt and Katie Holland huddled with PBA President Red McLaren and union attorney Eddie Shearson in a weekly ritual to review the status of the remaining C. J. Johnson shooting investigations.

It was early November now, four months since the shooting had inflamed racial tensions across New York, roiling the lives of the people closest to the incident. Matt Holland remained under suspension, his career in shambles, his life in disarray, no end in sight to the probes still underway by Kings County D.A. Hal Green and Justice Department officials.

As usual, Eddie Shearson pulled no punches in providing an update on the case. As usual, there were questions, conjecture, and grave concerns.

"In my best judgment, there's insufficient evidence for Hal Green to bring this case before a grand jury," Shearson said. "It was a 'clean shoot'—an unfortunate tragedy for sure, but a justifiable, defensible act. It should be an open-and-shut case, in Matt's favor."

"You did everything by the book, Matty," Red McLaren concurred. "For this to go to a grand jury would be based more on politics and emotion than on merit."

"That's exactly what concerns me," Shearson warned.

"What do you mean?" Katie tightened the grip on her husband's hand.

"What I mean," said Shearson, "is that nothing matters more than politics and emotion in police-shooting cases—not right or wrong, not facts, not the truth. And this case is a political hot potato, a lightning rod for pro- and anti-police supporters."

"What are your sources saying, Eddie?" McLaren asked.

"They're saying," said Shearson, "that Hal Green is getting his nuts squeezed by everyone imaginable—the Black community, civil rights leaders, police reformists, City Hall bureaucrats, NYPD higher-ups, the media, the PBA."

Shearson dragged on a cigarette. Matt Holland slumped in his chair. Katie, pale and gaunt, looked as if she was about to get sick.

"This whole matter probably would've been put to bed weeks ago, and in Matt's favor, if it weren't for the political pressures being applied," Shearson said.

"It's all a political calculation and everyone's out to cover their ass," McLaren said. "Let face it … it's not a good time any more to be a cop."

"It's a lot easier to throw a police officer under the bus than it is to defend one," Shearson said, "even when the officer is right."

"So, what's the bottom line here, Eddie?" Red McLaren asked.

"Given today's political climate," Shearson said, "I think Hal Green will play it safe and make a statement that his office is being responsive to the concerns of the Black community."

"Regardless of merit?"

"It's the D.A.'s safest bet," Shearson said. "Hal Green has nothing to lose by punting whatever evidence he's gathered to a grand jury and letting an 'independent panel of citizens' be the ones to decide on potential criminality."

"And what does that mean for us?" Katie asked.

"It means," said Shearson, "that you continue to wait."

"The waiting," Katie said, "is squeezing the life from us."

"I'm sure it is," Shearson said. "I'm afraid, though, that you have no other choice."

* * *

As usual, Eddie Shearson proved as prescient as he was well-informed. One week after the attorney's final meeting with Matt and Katie Holland, the C. J. Johnson shooting case was handed up from the office of Hal Green to a state grand jury.

Like other city officials, the King's County D.A. had bowed to political expedience, and decided to play it safe. While Brooklyn's top prosecutor opted to file no charges on his own, a decision regarding potential criminal culpability for Matt Holland would rest in the hands of a twelve-person panel of New Yorkers convened to hear the case. Among the potential charges the officer faced were those of criminally negligent homicide, second-degree manslaughter, and reckless endangerment. If found guilty of even one of the charges, Holland could spend the better part of his remaining life behind bars.

For law-enforcement reformists, Green's decision was a major step forward in achieving accountability for police shootings. For the PBA and other police advocates, it was a miscarriage of justice, a slap in the face to cops across America. For Matt Holland and his family, it was a dreadful blow, the worst possible news.

"There's no way that Matt Holland should be exposed to potential criminal charges in this case," Red McLaren told the press. "Taking this to a grand jury is a travesty. People have caved in to political pressure, anti-police bias, and scapegoating. It's not surprising, when you consider today's racially charged climate, but this entire case has become a political sideshow."

The PBA demanded that district attorney prosecutors publicly share the evidence that supported the potential charges against Matt Holland. Hal Green refused. Then all hell broke loose once again between New York City and its cops.

"The implications of District Attorney Green's decision are clear," Red McLaren charged. "This is an exercise aimed solely at demonstrating to the minority community that the city won't simply sweep matters like this under the rug … that it will punish its 'rotten apples.' Like everyone else, the D.A. is cowering before the mobs and bending over backward to imply there's been wrongdoing. Why? Because it's politically expedient. This case has become a racial issue, not an issue of right and wrong. The city is more interested in sending a message than it is in uncovering the truth. It's obvious which way City Hall wants this to go. In the meantime, Matt Holland—and every other police officer in America—has been thrown under the bus, as the city slips further toward anarchy."

New York City cops took the PBA's protest one step further, with hundreds of veteran officers taking their pension and resigning, and hundreds of others phoning in sick in opposition to both Holland's suspension and the D.A.'s action.

"What we're seeing," Red McLaren said, "is not a *de facto* strike and not the 'blue flu.' Instead, it's an effort by police officers to protest a grave injustice resulting from cowardice, political pressure, and an effort to assuage mobs seeing vengeance for alleged past incidents."

"Police officers are not being treated fairly in America anymore," McLaren said. "They're being held hostage to political pressure. Morale among cops is at an all-time low, and I'm not sure it can ever be repaired."

None of the rhetoric mattered, however. Matt Holland's fate had moved past the investigatory phase and was now in the hands of a state grand jury, with potential criminal charges very much on the table and up to thirty years in prison the officer's potential fate.

Chapter 48

MATT HOLLAND CRADLED the framing lumber in the palm of his hand, running his fingers along the two-by-four to check it for warping, splits, and other defects. Then, pulling a measuring tape from his work belt, he spaced the eight-foot length of lumber sixteen inches to center from the vertical stud alongside it, before pulling out a hammer and nailing the stud in place.

Holland knew that the traditional framing method he used for building walls was outdated, and that current construction codes permitted him to space the studs as far as twenty-four inches apart; he knew he was building a wall that was stronger than legally mandated. But this was the way he'd been taught to build, and this was the way he preferred it. It was the *right* way, after all. And when his twin daughters—forced to live for the past five weeks with Katie's parents—finally came home, their new bedroom would be built the way it was supposed to be. It would never collapse like the rickety tenement the officer rescued those children from years earlier in Brownsville. It would never fall apart like the rest of his life.

Matt Holland worked round the clock on his daughters' new bedroom now. It felt good to keep busy and divert his attention from the shooting tragedy that had reshaped his life; it felt equally good to build something worthy of his expertise, something with love at its core. If only he could lose himself forever in that kind of endeavor, Holland thought, he wouldn't have to think about how everything he'd built across sixteen years as a cop had been destroyed by a single, errant bullet from his gun. If only he could keep working like this, he wouldn't have to confront the turmoil he'd caused outside his home, or the pain he'd caused within it.

But the pleasure that Holland derived from building was merely a fleeting escape. In truth, the veteran cop seemed a broken man. There was a sadness about him that had settled in his eyes, his voice, the way he saw the world. In many ways, he'd stopped living almost entirely.

Taciturn and withdrawn, the once-engaging husband and father was no longer an active participant in family life. He'd abandoned his regular household chores, leaving Katie to carry the entire weight of their family. His interactions with his children were truncated, trancelike. Often, he was virtually invisible, in many ways a prisoner inside himself. In the evenings, he made token appearances at dinner, picked at his food, then quietly drifted away. He and Katie rarely spoke of anything substantive anymore. They hadn't made love in eighteen weeks.

But that wasn't even the worst of it on Holland's sad and lonely days. Nighttime was far worse.

Holland was suffering now from nyctophobia, an irrational, pathological fear of the dark. For the disgraced officer, it wasn't a childlike phobia about ghosts or monsters, strange noises or sleeping alone. Darkness instead was a reminder of untimely occurrences, a doorway to the terrifying and unknown, a trigger for flashbacks to the cellar on Amboy Street. Nighttime sparked a loss of control, an urge to hide, an overwhelming shame, and panic-like symptoms: chest tightness, trouble breathing, dizziness, and even imminent death.

In the rare instances when Holland slept at all, he slept in troubled spurts by daylight or with a nightlight in his room. In the instances when he'd nod off, he'd waken suddenly to an imagined explosion of gunshots, muzzle flashes, and an illusion of C. J. Johnson lying on the cellar floor, staring at Holland through murky, puzzled eyes.

"I never imagined in a million years that I'd lose you to your job, Matt," Katie said one night, holding a pair of houseplants wilted from the lack of sunlight in their shade-drawn, guarded home. "I've always fought that fear, the reality I saw in so many police marriages," Katie said. "I'd write you notes, give you photos, send you reminders about the need to stay the gentle, loving man you've always been ... for us to stay together as husband and wife."

Katie slumped her shoulders, leaned against doorway, and slowly began to weep. "But I guess I've failed as a wife, haven't I?" she said. "Despite all my efforts, I've lost you, after all."

"What are you saying?" Holland asked.

"Oh, can't you see what has happened, Matt?" Katie shuddered as if catching a sudden chill. "We used to be on the same page as husband and wife, parents to three wonderful children. And now all of it has fallen apart. Our life is an utter wreck. You've become a prisoner in a bedroom you're building for children who can't come home for fear of their lives. Worse than that, Matt ... you've become a prisoner to your emotions."

It was, of course, true. Matt Holland had become closed off to the entire world now, even to Katie. He could neither be reached nor express how his emotions were gnawing at his insides, draining him of everything that was once joyful about his life. It was as if there was a voice inside of him desperate to be heard, but the words were trapped in his larynx, choking his airways, deadening him like the houseplants in Katie's hand.

"I feel like I've lost not only my husband, but also my best friend." Katie leaned against the doorway and cried. "I feel completely shut out of your life, Matt. We don't spend time together anymore. We don't talk, don't dream, don't make love, don't smile."

"*Smile*?" Holland rasped. "Tell me, Katie—what's there to smile about? Don't you understand the enormity of what's happened?"

"I understand it, Matt," Katie said. "I understand every horrible, tragic detail of it. An innocent boy is dead, his family is mourning, a city is in turmoil—and all of that is deeply troubling and sad. I know you're grieving for that boy, just like you're grieving for the parts of yourself that you think you've lost: your reputation, your career, your self-esteem. But there's more than just *one* victim of this nightmare we're trapped in, Matt. Everyone in your family is a victim. Every one of us is hurting and lost. And if we allow it, our marriage will be a victim, too."

Katie Holland fixed her gaze on her husband, swallowing hard. "What I'm really saying, Matt, is that ... I'm afraid of losing you."

Holland inched forward, arms dangling helplessly at his side.

"You're not losing me, Katie," he said. "I'm not going anywhere."

"Maybe not physically, Matt. But mentally, you've retreated somewhere inside yourself, somewhere no one else can go," Katie said. "And in doing that, you've been unfaithful to me."

"*Unfaithful*? How can you possibly say that?"

"You're being unfaithful to our marriage," Katie said. "By bottling your feelings up. By holding me captive to your silence. By pushing me away."

Matt leaned against a doorway to the bedroom he was building.

"What do you want me to do?" he asked, head down. "I'm doing everything I can just to hold myself together."

"I want you to let me in!" Katie stammered. "Talk to me! Let me help you!"

"I've told you the story a hundred times," Matt said. "I'm tired of telling it."

"I'm not interested in the story, Matt—I'm interested in *you*. I can't make what happened go away, and I can't talk you out of your feelings. But don't bury your emotions so deep inside of you that you forget they're there. Don't force me to sit by helplessly and watch you remain lost inside yourself, hurting and confused. Don't destroy our marriage with this wall you've built around yourself!"

Katie moved closer. "Matty, listen to me carefully," she whimpered. "Somewhere along the line, we've got to put this tragedy behind us and stop what has happened from sucking the very life from us."

Holland, drawing back further, said nothing. And with that, Katie suddenly spun around and hurled one plant, and then the other, against a wall—soil and dried leaves and pieces of the ceramic pots flying every which way. Then she fell to her knees, her sobs echoing through the empty, half-finished room.

"Matt, I miss our girls and I want them home!" She cried unabashedly. "I miss the sunshine in our house, and I want it back! I miss what we had as a couple, and I want that back! I want our lives to be what they once were. I want to be together again, safe and loving and normal."

"I can't give you that now, Katie," Matt stammered. "Don't you see? We can't snap our fingers and go back to the way things were just because you want to. That's not possible. Not now … maybe not ever."

"No," she said, "we can't go back. But we can try to move past what we have now, instead of drowning in it, move past feeling miserable and sorry for ourselves. We've become a poster couple for self-pity, Matt, and I'm tired of it! If you don't want to recover from what happened, fine. That's your choice. But I want to. And I will!"

"What in God's name do you want me to do?" Matt said, exasperated. "This is tearing me to pieces, too! Can't you see that? But I don't know what to do, or how to deal with it."

"Your whole life, you've always helped other people," said Katie, still on her knees, "but now *you're* the one who needs the help. Understand? You've got to open yourself up to the possibility of support and guidance, and some form of recovery."

Matt looked down at his sobbing wife, his own eyes welling with everything he wanted to say but couldn't put into words.

"Please let me help you, Matty," Katie said, reaching up to hold him around the knees. "Let me be your partner, your backup. Let's figure out a way, together, to find some way to escape this living hell."

Chapter 49

At the Emanuel Cellar Federal Building in downtown Brooklyn, the dozen grand jurors for the U.S. District Court convened inside their chambers to sift through the evidence gathered by investigators probing the C. J. Johnson shooting.

The jurors' mandate was explicit: Serving as the conscience of the public, the racially mixed panel—a mirror of New York's tangled demographics—was to decide if criminal charges should be brought against Matt Holland. If the grand jury ruled affirmatively, it would return an indictment detailing the charges, and the case would proceed to a criminal trial. If the panel found that the evidence did not warrant an indictment, they'd return a "no bill" and Holland would be instantly cleared. Their decision would be based on a standard that was equally explicit: whether they thought Matt Holland reasonably believed that either he or someone else was in imminent danger when he fired his gun, and/or whether his use of deadly force was reasonable, justifiable, or accidental.

The indictment possibilities were wide-ranging. Under the law, Holland could be charged with second-degree murder, meaning he intended to kill C. J. Johnson, displayed a depraved indifference to the boy's life, and acted so recklessly that he caused the boy's death. More likely, the officer could be hit with the lesser charges of either manslaughter—for exhibiting a reckless disregard for human life—or criminally negligent homicide. The presumptive penalties, should Holland be found guilty, ranged from imprisonment for fifteen to thirty years.

"If their decision is depraved indifference and murder-two, then you know that this is strictly a 'racial' case," Eddie Shearson said, explaining the indictment options to Matt and Katie Holland. "A finding like that means that the grand jury is just out to get a White cop, knee-jerk revenge for killing an innocent Black boy."

"How likely is that?" Katie asked.

"It's hard to tell," Shearson replied. "I'm afraid that in the current political climate, anything's possible."

"You mean that Matt can go to jail for nothing more than a tragic accident?"

Shearson looked away. "I'm afraid so."

Katie, head bowed, began to quake, her husband embracing her consolingly.

"Let's pray that the grand jurors are capable of seeing this case for what it really is," Shearson said. "We've got to have faith that a group of conscientious, objective people can look beyond race, and beyond the hysteria surrounding this case. We've got to have faith that they can see the truth, and not make this a witch-hunt."

"Can they?" Katie sniffled.

"It's a lot to ask," Shearson replied. "But yes ... it is possible."

No one knew, however, what the grand jury was seeing, thinking, or feeling. As was customary, their deliberations were conducted fully behind closed doors, cloaked in a shroud of secrecy.

In theory, the grand jurors were immune to outside influence, insulated from the conflicting pressures inherent in police-shooting cases, their anonymity allowing them to render an impartial decision and then return without fanfare to their private lives. Reality, however, was far different. In truth, it was impossible to fully shield the panel from the controversy and scrutiny enveloping the case, or the issues at stake. Exposed like most New Yorkers to a steady stream of media coverage, the grand jurors were keenly aware of public sentiment on both sides of the case, as well as the potential consequences of their decision. To make matters worse, each day on their way to the courthouse the panel was bused past a gauntlet of anti- and pro-police demonstrators who carried banners, waved signs, and chanted slogans reflecting their sentiments.

"Do the *right* thing!" anti-police protestors chanted as the panelists entered the courthouse.

"Do the *fair* thing!" PBA supporters chanted in counterpoint.

For the time being, however, it was impossible to predict exactly what the grand jury would do. All anyone could do for the time being was wait.

Chapter 50

WHEN CHARLES JOHNSON wasn't immersed in work or at church, he spent a fair amount of time sifting through the pile of correspondence that continued almost daily to arrive at the Johnsons' apartment.

There were expressions of grief and pity from family, friends, co-workers, and church congregants. A group of C. J.'s former classmates had written condolence letters as a school project. Mayor Worth, Police Commissioner Dunne, and even several officers from the 73rd Precinct, all penned sympathy notes. Other correspondence had arrived from strangers across America: people whose lives had been impacted by similar police-shooting tragedies; others who commended Charles for his support of the class-action racial-profiling lawsuit, and still others who'd been moved in some meaningful way by C. J.'s death.

Sadly, not all the correspondence was sympathetic or supportive. Hate letters were targeted at the Johnsons, as well—vile, demeaning, crudely written expressions of racism, bitterness, and ignorance. The bereaved parents, more than once, were scorned as lowlife niggers whose worthless son had been slain for good reason, and whose family was at the root of New York's racial divide. Others denounced Charles for not adding his voice to anti-police protests or issuing a condemnation of allegedly bigoted, trigger-happy White cops. Still others accused Charles and Eunice of being greedy, get-rich-quick opportunists, schemers and bloodsuckers bent on monetizing their son's death through their civil lawsuit against the city.

But the hate mail, distressing as it was, paled in comparison to the outpouring from people who were sympathetic to the Johnsons' grief, and who saw C. J. as more than simply an abstraction, but rather as a real boy who'd lived and dreamed, laughed and loved, and worked hard to overcome the challenges wrought by the lead poisoning that contributed to his demise. Correspondence of that sort was a source of immense comfort to Charles and Eunice, even as they cleaned out C. J.'s room and donated or discarded his clothing and cherished possessions. It was heartening for the bereaved couple to know how many people had been affected by the Johnsons' tragedy, and who commended the family's calls for healing and peace in the face of their unspeakable tragedy.

Charles read those letters and cards, repeatedly. One, in particular, moved him deeply. It read:

> *Dear Mr. and Mrs. Johnson:*
>
> *I am writing to you to say I am very sorry that your son C. J. died. I never met him, but he sounds like he was a nice boy and a very good son. I wish I could have known him. We might have been friends.*
>
> *The other reason I am writing is to say that I hope one day you might forgive my father for shooting C. J. He feels very bad about what happened. One time I heard him tell my mother he feels so bad that he wishes he had died himself instead of your son. Please don't believe all the bad things people are saying about him. My dad is a very good father and a very good policeman. I know he would have never done anything on purpose to hurt your son.*
>
> *If you can't forgive my father, I will understand because I know it must hurt very much to lose a son that you love. But even if you don't forgive my father now, I hope that maybe you can change your mind someday. Then he might be able to forgive himself, too.*
>
> *I wish I could do something to bring C. J. back, but I know that I can't. I am sorry about that too. I will say a prayer for him at night and pray too that your hurt can someday go away.*

The letter was signed, Thomas Michael Holland.

"Will you take a look at this?" Charles said to Eunice when he read the impassioned missive.

"Is that who I think it is?" Eunice asked.

"It is," Charles nodded.

"Oh, my Lord," Eunice said. "That poor, sweet boy."

Charles and Eunice Johnson embraced one another and cried for a long while as they placed Thomas Holland's letter in a bedroom drawer. Then they wondered aloud if there was some way the two of them could respond in a personal and meaningful manner to the twelve-year-old child of the police officer who'd tragically slain their son.

Chapter 51

THE DISCOTHÈQUE WAS JUMPING well past midnight, jammed wall to wall with young, hip revelers. Out on the dance floor, and along the entire length of the disco's hundred-foot-long bar, patrons stood shoulder to shoulder—dancing, talking, and scarfing drinks, as music blared and strobe lights flashed and the nightclub pulsed with motion, chitter-chatter and blatant sexuality. And Rachel Cook sat in a tiny nook at the end of the bar, nursing her third vodka tonic of the night, sullen and distant and alone.

The nightclubs and discos on Manhattan's East Side were a world away from the streets of Brownsville and Coney Island, far from the hubbub of the C. J. Johnson shooting and the racial strife roiling New York. And that's where Cook went these days to find a measure of solace and escape.

They were the only places that she could.

One year into her police job, four months after the shooting incident that transformed her life, Cook embraced the notion of boozy escape as fervently as she'd once embraced the notion of a groundbreaking, bold adventure in the NYPD. Drawn to police work for its promise of fulfillment and excitement, she now sought shelter from its sights and sounds, refuge from its demands, and ways to turn down the volume on her jagged, muddled emotions.

Locked reclusively inside her apartment after most tours, her melancholy a painful, lonely prison, she spent hours escaping into vacuous romance novels, witless magazines, and an endless stream of mindless TV sit-coms. She lit candles, burned incense, gobbled sedatives, smoked pot, and immersed herself in yoga, meditation, Tai chi, and other relaxation techniques. On occasion, she embarked on long, solitary drives to remote locations outside the city, as if she could lose herself on some desolate beach or stretch of country road. Mostly, she journeyed across the city's singles landscape: places where it was too raucous to think and too public to cry; places where she could bleed into an unruffled anonymity; places where she could nurse a few drinks, listen to music, and buttress her waning belief that human contact—however unlikely these days—was still at least a possibility.

But there was no substantive human contact to speak of anymore, not for Cook—no one to talk to, no one to be with, no one to have or to hold. Cook was all alone now, adrift in a sea of heartbreak and confusion, tortured by a dream gone awry, empty and cut off, fragile and forsaken.

While the events tied to C. J. Johnson's shooting had dramatically deepened Cook's sense of isolation, her life had been heading in that direction for months, yet another of police work's damaging byproducts. Former friendships, stifled by rotating tours and odd days off, had wilted. A guy she'd been dating prior to the shooting had run for cover. Contacts with her mother and siblings had all but ceased. Social activities had dried up. So had contact with anyone outside the job.

Indeed, Cook did everything she could now to *avoid* most contact. Other cops, she kept at arm's length. Dour and cynical, most of them only griped about their status and reminded Cook of job-related issues she desperately wanted to forget. Contacts with civilians were even more scrupulously avoided; they only made Cook feel awkward and wary. She was far too judgmental and argumentative to hold even a simple conversation. There was no such thing anymore as a simple give-and-take. Who wanted to listen to peoples' sob stories? Cook heard enough of that on the job. Who had the patience for barroom raps or casual encounters? Those lacked substance or relevance. Who wanted to discuss thorny, real-life issues? Those were too insoluble, too depressing. There was no longer room for debate now either—not for Cook. Issues were one-sided, cut-and-dried. You either saw things through the eyes of a cop or you were full of shit. And most people, to Cook, were full of shit. All they did was make snap judgments about issues they knew nothing about, blinded themselves to realities Cook was forced to confront, or offered glib solutions to problems that seemed, in many ways, unsolvable.

Fuck them! Stupid bastards! What did they know anyway?

Besides, there was nothing much to talk about anymore. Discussions about police work were strictly off-limits. Cook had long since grown weary of telling war stories, or of being seen as a novelty or a role model for schoolkids. She was tired of engaging in testy, unresolved debates, or of having to serve as an apologist for the supposed failures of law enforcement. She certainly wasn't inclined to discuss the C. J. Johnson shooting, even if she was permitted to do so. Besides, no civilian, it seemed, really gave a damn about what police officers experienced or thought about or felt. Cops were pariahs. No one outside the job wanted to get close. No one could possibly understand.

Cook's isolation was reinforced by the realization that she resided in a different world than most people—and, in that world, people outside the job weren't to be trusted; they were suspects and skeptics, adversaries and critics, "scrotes" and "skels" who'd slit your throat in a heartbeat if given the chance. And they were everywhere: the friendly guy reaching in his pocket; the motorist you pulled over for running a red light; the suspect you were strip-searching; the would-be assailant lurking in the shadows. All of them were out there, pretending to be your ally, waiting for you to drop your guard, ready to attack.

"Can I buy you a drink?" a guy at the disco would ask.

"Uh-uh," Cook would reply, standoffish, guarded, hostile.

Outsiders were not to be trusted, not to be believed, not to be granted access.

"Would you like to dance?"

"Sorry, no."

The only way to survive was to build an impenetrable wall around yourself.

"Would you like some company?"

"No."

You had to be untrusting and unapproachable. It wasn't paranoia. It was a trick of the trade, a form of self-preservation.

"Could I have your phone number?"

"Fuck, no."

People were bad medicine. *Better to close yourself off, stay away.*

That was the way it was for Rachel Cook now, on the nights she escaped into Manhattan—it was that way all the time. Vodka tonics were Cook's trustiest companion these days. Vodka tonics made no demands, offered no opinions, posed no threats. Vodka tonics numbed the senses, dulled the anguish, made Cook forget. So did the marijuana and the sleeping pills Cook bummed from her roommate, the sole person she trusted enough to grant access.

So, Cook sat in the nightclubs and the discos of Manhattan's East Side, pent up and silent and alone, and watched from a corner of her eye as people danced and talked and laughed. She spurned advances, eavesdropped on conversations, and chuckled at her own private jokes, the irony of feeling so alone in the midst of so many others.

And she drank.

Even on her inaugural anniversary as a pioneering female cop, her probationary period at an end, truly one of "New York's Finest" now, Cook sat in empty celebration, threw down her vodka tonics, and numbed her pain alone.

But beyond Cook's cavernous emptiness, there was an envy, a sadness, a longing. Everyone around her seemed so free of the emotional baggage Cook carried, so absent of the torment and clutter. She wanted to be like all the others, even if she was trapped inside a melancholy, sorrowful persona. She wanted to talk to someone but didn't know where to start. She wanted to connect with someone but couldn't remember how. She wanted to stop feeling empty and alone but didn't know if she could. She wanted to be touched by another human being but wasn't sure she could open herself up to such a risky possibility.

And so, Rachel Cook, off-duty revolver strapped to her ankle—symbolic now of her isolation and torment—sat in the single joints of Manhattan's East Side, stripped of her illusions, drowning in loneliness, trying to reach for the only form of escape she could find: a slow descent into a boozy, mindless numbness that could dull the edges of her biting, relentless pain.

Then, when she found what she was seeking, she'd slip anonymously into the swirl of midtown traffic to somehow find her way back to her apartment—and, if she was lucky, into a sleep filled with dreams of walks with her parents through the streets of Brownsville, when the three of them were innocent and happy and young.

Chapter 52

RISING FROM BEHIND A CLUTTERED WORK DESK, Landon Devlin greeted Matt and Katie Holland warmly as the couple entered his office, housed in a tiny, converted loft atop PBA headquarters in Manhattan.

Barely in his thirties, Devlin had deep-set, emerald eyes, chin-length brown hair, and a scraggly mustache he habitually stroked with his fingertips. Clad in washed-out jeans and a denim shirt, he looked more like a hippie than the New York City cop that he was.

The mental-health specialist that NYPD chaplain Michael Caruso referred the Hollands to, Landon Devlin had spent a decade at the 41st Precinct in the South Bronx, considered the toughest command in the city. As a rookie, he'd won the Police Combat Cross, the NYPD's second-highest commendation, for saving his partner in a shootout that claimed two lives. But it was another harrowing incident that profoundly altered the arc of Devlin's life.

Responding to a violent domestic dispute, Devlin and a partner found themselves confronting a deranged assailant wielding an eight-inch butcher knife. The officers attempted desperately to calm the man, who'd already stabbed two people, but nothing they tried could defuse the situation. The knife-wielder pleaded with the cops to shoot him because he wanted to die. When the officers refused, he rushed the two of them, stabbing Devlin's partner in the stomach and slashing Devlin across his face. Devlin had no choice but to shoot the assailant dead.

Tortured by the incident, unable to reconcile his conflicting emotions, Devlin completely fell apart. Day and night, he relived the incident repeatedly, alternating between feelings of contrition and despair, guilt and shame. He found himself growing increasingly irritable and plagued with doubt and self-loathing. His personal life spiraled downward. He began to drink. His relationship with a fiancée fell apart. He became alienated, reclusive, absent of self-worth. It took three years before he sought the professional help that he needed to turn his life around.

No longer assigned to street patrol, Devlin was among a cadre of young instructors at the John Jay School of Criminal Justice. Working toward a master's degree in psychology, he'd also organized an NYPD-sanctioned pilot program known as COPS, an acronym for "Coping with Police Stress." Tailored expressly for police officers and family members, the program provided peer support and counseling for officers experiencing job-related trauma.

"First off, you need to recognize that you've suffered a traumatic injury," Devlin told Matt Holland minutes after they met. "You've been deeply wounded by what has occurred."

"Wounded?" said Katie. "Explain that, please."

"The 'wound' Matt has sustained is not to his body, but to his mind—his psyche," Devlin told the couple. "It's not as obvious as a physical wound, but it's just as real, and in some ways even more painful. Mental-health professionals are calling it 'Post Traumatic Stress Disorder'—PTSD, for short. But it's not so much an 'illness' as a reaction to situations that are emotionally overwhelming. Unlike a physical injury, this type of wound is not visible, except through a person's actions, emotions, and thoughts."

"Like shell shock or combat fatigue?" Katie asked.

"That's a good way of describing it," Devlin said, "but it's not confined only to soldiers. We've seen it in police officers, firefighters, emergency workers, medical personnel, and untold numbers of others."

"Please continue," Katie said.

"A line-of-duty shooting is probably the most traumatic event a police officer can experience," Devlin said. "It's almost always followed by a psychological aftermath that can be debilitating—and, if unaddressed, can leave permanent scars."

Devlin trained his eyes on Matt, who seemed attentive.

"The impact of an incident like the one Matt experienced can be especially powerful if the shooting is ambiguous or accidental, or involves a child," Devlin said. "Shooting a child is especially traumatic for police officers because they see themselves as 'protectors.' It's even worse when an incident causes a public uproar. But even in the most clear-cut police-shooting cases, the aftermath can become more traumatic than the shooting itself."

"Why is that?" Katie asked.

"Because once the smoke clears, you have to deal with your emotions. And that's harder than anything—especially for a cop."

Devlin winked at Holland.

"I'm right ... aren't I, Matt?" Devlin asked, drawing a reluctant grin.

"The truth is," Devlin continued, "most police officers have no idea what to do with their emotions, or how to cope with them. They're uncomfortable with 'feelings,' rarely talk about them. Shrinks? *Forget it*! No cop wants to go a psychologist. Most cops think psychologists are naïve do-gooders, too touchy-feely, out of touch with reality. To most cops, therapists can't possibly relate, don't understand, can't really help."

Familiar with the mindset, Holland chuckled.

"Look at that," Devlin quipped. "We're already making progress."

Katie smiled, too—for the first time in months.

"Seriously," Devlin resumed, "aside from being uncomfortable with their emotions, there's a stigma among cops about seeking help. It's part of the police culture. Cops are tough, stoic. Most believe they can handle things on their own, live with their emotions, and push their feelings aside. Sure, some guys may let off a little steam during 'choir practice,' at the local tavern. But that's about it. Few cops ever seek real help."

Devlin stroked his mustache. "Am I right, Matt?"

Again, Holland smiled.

"See, going for help is a sign of weakness to police officers," Devlin continued. "Most are afraid of repercussions, from the department or from fellow cops; afraid of being labeled a 'psycho,' someone who cracked under pressure, who's unstable and unreliable, who's less than a 'real man.' In the police officers' world, 'real men' don't whine, don't complain, don't discuss their feelings, and don't need support."

"What do they do then?" Katie asked.

"Most of the time," Devlin said, "they suffer in silence."

"What do you mean 'suffer'?"

"Everyone reacts differently to trauma like the kind Matt experienced," Devlin explained. "How severe the symptoms are—and how fully and quickly people recover—depends on their personalities, their coping skills, their mental well-being, how troubling the incident was, and the support they're willing to accept. A lot of factors come into play. People react to traumatic events in very different ways, but there are common patterns."

"What are they?" Katie queried.

"Acute physical symptoms, anxiety disorders, and behavioral reactions," Devlin said. "Panic attacks. Insomnia. Flashbacks. Night terrors. Hypertension. Impotence. You name it."

Katie recoiled.

"But that's not even the worst of it," Devlin said. "The psychological wounds resulting from line-of-duty shootings can not only be devastating, but they can also make officers feel as if they're losing emotional control. I'm talking about serious bouts of depression, guilt, disbelief, despair, betrayal, restlessness, anger, frustration, suspiciousness, confusion, apathy, vulnerability, and fear—just to name a few. Some officers obsess over a shooting, abuse alcohol or drugs, make poor decisions, break ties with family, lose interest in life. Often, their symptoms are simply camouflaged emotions that are being stifled, normal human reactions, and not signs of mental illness—but very damaging."

Katie glanced at Matt, Devlin's words all too familiar.

"How long can all of this last?" she asked.

"There's no way of knowing," Devlin said. "A lot depends upon the incident, the public reaction, the type of peer and family support, and the officer's coping skills. In some cases, trauma can trigger cognitive, emotional, and behavioral reactions that can last for months—even years. Normal coping strategies are often inadequate. Everything may seem fine, then, out of the blue, the hurt and the memories tumble out. Emotional or visual triggers can make someone relive the event. Before they know it, they're in a tailspin. Things unravel. People think they're going crazy. They wonder if anything will ever be normal again, if their life has any meaning, if living itself is pointless."

Devlin, aware he was touching a raw nerve, shifted in his chair.

"PTSD can get very ugly," he continued. "Situations like what Matt is going through can shake someone's belief system, disrupt their sense of control, test their most basic assumptions. You start to see the world differently. You can't function. You lose interest in things you love. You feel bottled up inside. Some people resort to drinking, drugs, smoking, gambling, and other addictions. They shut down emotionally and stop communicating. Marriage and friendships crumble. Families can be destroyed. More than a few cops have eaten their guns."

"Oh, my God!" Katie began to tremble.

Rising from his chair, Devlin led the couple to a closed door. "Let me show you something," he said, opening the door slightly. In an adjoining room, a small group of people sat in a circle, talking quietly.

"Our organization throws cops and their families a lifeline, tries to give them something to lean on," Devlin told Matt and Katie. "Our meetings are closed and confidential. No notes are taken. No records are kept. No department brass is around. No one sits in judgment. This is peer support, pure and simple. It's an outlet. We talk about our feelings. There's no fear, no guilt, no shame. You can say anything you want. It's a catharsis. What we offer, ultimately, is a way to help pull each other through."

Devlin ushered the couple back outside, and the trio took seats again.

"Police departments are still in the Stone Age when it comes to things like this," Devlin said. "There's no safety net for cops who suffer trauma: No debriefing, no counseling, no peer support, and no critical-incident stress intervention. In many ways, in fact, the department makes things even *worse* by the way they handle things. They take your gun and your shield, the symbols that make you special. Your actions are challenged. You face reprimands and suspension, not to mention lawsuits, public criticism, and the possibility of going to prison. What the department inflicts, in many ways, is a 'second wound.' You expect it to be sympathetic and supportive, but it's callous and punitive. You feel abandoned and betrayed, even though you've always been loyal. You feel bad enough over what happened; then the department injures you again."

"How can the two of us get past this?" Katie asked.

"There are no magic cures—only, patience, persistence, and hard work," Devlin said. "Recovery is slow. You get better one day at a time."

"But how?"

"In a normal recovery, an officer comes to terms with the emotional impact of a traumatic shooting incident," Devlin said. "They begin to accept what has happened, understand what they've been experiencing, and learn productive ways to handle it. You've got to understand that you've been changed forever, and that your feelings are normal. You've got to recognize what you've lost and try to regain whatever you need to move on. In other words, you've got to let the trauma dissipate, make it part of the past, make it part of who you are. That's what survivors do."

"They stop being victims," Katie said.

"That's right." Devlin nodded. "Trauma survivors overcome, make things normal again. The events that reshaped their lives may have been powerful, but they gain wisdom from what happened. The memory may be lasting, but they stop it from being a daily torment. You'll never completely purge yourself of what happened, but you learn to live with it. It's all part of a healing process."

"This 'healing process,'" Katie asked. "How does it work?"

"First, you need to remember," Devlin observed.

"It's too painful to remember," Matt said. "I'm trying, instead, to forget."

"I understand, but you can't allow yourself to stop remembering," Devlin said. "It's impossible to heal what you can't remember."

"So, you 'remember,'" Katie said. "Then what?"

"Then you break free of the classic 'tough guy' role and recognize that you're human and have feelings," Devlin said. "You need to value your feelings as much as you value your toughness, your bravery, and your street smarts. You need to understand that your psyche is not bulletproof. You need to accept the fact that you have to be helped through this, and that getting help is a sign of strength, not weakness."

"And then?"

"And then, you talk."

"What good does that do?" Matt said. "Talking doesn't change what happened."

"No, but it helps let you out of the prison you're in now," Devlin said. "The one thing that can keep you locked in that prison, and destroy you, is to keep your feelings bottled up. The only thing that can save us from ourselves is to share our feelings with other people."

"Can the two of us recover?" Katie asked.

"What amazes me more than anything about PTSD is the resiliency of the human spirit, the ability of people to recover." Devlin smiled. "Most people, over time, do okay. And you've got more going for you than most cops I run into."

"How's that?" Matt asked.

Devlin looked at the two of them. "You have each other," he said. "You're partners in this. Your love and togetherness can pull you through."

Just then, the door to the meeting room opened and people came filing out.

"Want to be helped?" Devlin asked, offering the Hollands his hand. "Good," he said, accepting their handshakes. "We can start right away."

Then, almost as an afterthought, he asked, "What about your partner, Officer Cook? How is she?"

"I don't know," Matt said. "We haven't been in contact for months."

"Well, she might need a lifeline, too," Devlin suggested. "She didn't pull the trigger, but she may be going through a lot of the same things that you are. She's a rookie, as I recall. In some ways, she may be in an even worse kind of hell."

"That hadn't occurred to us," Katie said.

"Well," said Devlin, "I don't see how it could hurt if I gave her a call."

Chapter 53

By now, the commanding officer of the 60th Precinct was strongly considering placing Rachel Cook on indefinite administrative leave—and Cook was thinking about applying for it. Both those considerations seemed entirely justified.

In many ways, it was as if her job as a police officer was sucking the very life from Cook. In the months since the C. J. Johnson shooting, she had lost twenty pounds, and appeared on the verge of malnutrition. Barely able to eat, sleep, or hold down food, she suffered from debilitating migraines and bouts of diarrhea. Her skin was mottled and blotchy. Clumps of hair were falling out. Weeks earlier, she'd abruptly dropped the graduate classes she'd been taking twice a week. The workload, coupled with the clamor of nearby anti-police protests, was more than Cook could bear.

So, in many ways, was the daily grind of work.

The C. J. Johnson shooting, and its aftermath, had taken a grievous toll on the young officer. Cook's anxiety and dread, reinforced during weeks of patrol in Coney Island, had altered not merely her perceptions but her patrol patterns. So had the steady stream of rejection heaped on female officers by most men. Cook was far less confident now, infinitely less assertive. For weeks, she had made no arrests and issued few citations. When she rode in a patrol car, her door remained locked, her window closed. On foot patrol, she remained constantly in motion, trying to avoid civilian interactions, subtly seeking shelter frequently in buildings and coffee shops. Revolting as they were, strip searches by now had become almost a relief. At least then, Cook could control events. At least then, she was behind closed doors, surrounded by fellow officers, not outdoors in the line of fire.

It was hard to believe that, less than a year earlier, Cook had so loved the *very idea* of being a cop, let alone the job itself. In contrast, her enthusiasm now had ebbed almost entirely. Each day, she scrupulously watched the clock, anxiously waiting for her tour to end so she could rush home, barricade herself inside her apartment, gulp a tranquilizer, and collapse into bed. Sleep was sporadic, storm-tossed, flush with dark, recurrent, nightmares. Cook dreamed of young black boys running toward her, bleeding from their head. She dreamed that her service revolver stalked furtively around her apartment at night, slipping out the door to the sound of gunshots and screams. She dreamed of bearing witness to her own Inspector's Funeral—seeing her mother, windblown and weeping, standing curbside as columns of police officers, wearing prayer shawls and black tape over their shields, marched solemnly behind a coffin draped in a white-and-green NYPD flag.

More than ever, Cook felt betrayed, disillusioned, soiled. But something equally disturbing had happened to her in the months since the C. J. Johnson shooting: Cook found that, in many ways, she could no longer *feel at all*—that she'd grown, for all intents and purposes, emotionless, hard-hearted, numb.

By now, Cook had conducted countless strip searches and, they—like the shooting itself—had taken a grievous toll. Slowly, the officer had crawled into a shell somewhere inside herself, sprouting a body armor that was all but impenetrable. It was the only way, she found, she could do her job. Cook needed a wall around her now, simply to survive. The price of feeling, she'd come to believe, was far too great.

It was a strange new world that Cook resided in now, a world devoid of the color and weight of nearly all emotion; a world in which the door to most of her feelings was bolted shut; a world in which Cook could no longer be shocked or sickened, saddened or humiliated, frightened or hurt.

Cook had managed, through sheer force of will, to shut down almost completely, close her eyes and cover her ears and push the most troubling of her feelings away. Emotions were no longer welcome. Mind over matter was her modus operandi. Detachment was her stock in trade.

Cook functioned smoothly, almost robotically, on the job. Most things, she found, simply rolled off her back. Nothing she saw or heard or felt seemed quite as tragic, or disgraceful, or as much of an outrage as it once had been. Everything was pretty much routine. Even strip searches weren't nearly as revolting anymore. Over and over, Cook conducted the searches now, in all kinds of settings. She wasn't heartsick or repelled. She wasn't nauseated or disgusted or demeaned. She didn't feel sorry for the people she searched. She didn't feel much of anything. The people she searched were *objects*, that was all. Part of the landscape. Absent of any emotion themselves.

But there was something troubling Cook that she couldn't bring herself to reconcile, or close her eyes to, or ignore. It was the feeling that police work had transformed and crippled her in some profound, elemental way—rendered her cold and callous, robotic and hard-edged—and that she'd never return to the person she once was, never be the same. Something was missing from her now, something that had once made her human, happy, alive. And its absence, while helpful in a practical kind of way, was demoralizing and hurtful.

Cook wondered if she could ever truly bring herself to feel *anything* ever again—if the numbness wrought by police work would ever thaw. She wondered if she'd ever be touched or warmed or affected again, if the world around her could ever move her in the same way it once had. She wondered if she could ever love, or be loved by, another human being ever again.

Something valuable had been stolen from Rachel Cook in the months since the C. J. Johnson shooting: her innocence, her enthusiasm, her emotionality—the part of her that had once been hopeful and optimistic and young. She was no longer sure if she could ever rediscover those qualities or make her way in the world without them.

Chapter 54

THE STATE GRAND JURY opened its deliberations by reviewing the written accounts that Matt Holland and Rachel Cook had provided investigators regarding the C. J. Johnson shooting, along with the officers' testimony during their multiple rounds of questioning. The panel then spent several days poring through reams of data from the city's medical examiner, crime-scene analysts, ballistics experts, and ancillary evidence collected by the office of D.A. Hal Green. The jurors were then bused to Brownsville, to inspect the shooting scene itself.

As their gray, New York City Department of Corrections bus wheezed to a stop at the entrance to 118 Amboy Street, the dozen grand jurors were greeted by the sing-song chants of sign-carrying demonstrators poised behind wooden police barricades.

INDICT THE OFFICER! their signs read.

DO THE RIGHT THING!

"We want justice!" the demonstrators shouted in unison.

"We want justice *now*!"

The jurors, faces shielded to conceal their identities, were escorted by court officers into the apartment-building cellar, where they were briefed by D.A. prosecutors and led through an examination of the shooting scene. In the courtyard at the rear of the building they paused to pay their respects at a makeshift shrine erected in honor of C. J. Johnson, the letters *R.I.P.* painted on a wall where several floral wreaths lay wilting near a row of votive candle holders and barren ailanthus trees.

"Remember that boy!" someone shouted from an open window. "Indict the cop! Justice needs to be done!"

Having inspected the shooting scene for more than an hour, the grand jurors were sequestered when they returned to the U.S. District Courthouse. There, they'd conduct deliberations in their closed-door chambers, spending nights and weekends in a nearby hotel for however long it took to render a decision.

But even as the jurors deliberated, powerful new pressures were building behind the scenes. For one thing, rumors were being floated that if Matt Holland were to be criminally charged, Rachel Cook might also be prosecuted as an accessory to the shooting, a none-too-subtle form of coercion aimed at inducing Cook to testify against her former partner. Indeed, using PBA attorney Eddie Shearson as an intermediary, D.A. Hal Green's office contacted Cook with a pledge of immunity from prosecution if she'd serve as a cooperating witness against Holland. Aghast at the hint that she was culpable in the shooting, Cook, on Shearson's advice, refused the D.A.'s offer, standing by the testimony she'd already supplied—and taking her chances that that was enough to ensure her innocence.

At this point, the most important question was whether Matt Holland would waive the immunity he was entitled to and testify in his own defense.

"Absolutely not!" PBA attorney Eddie Shearson said, when the possibility of Holland appearing before the grand jury was broached.

"It would be 'noble' of you, I suppose, but it's piss-poor legal strategy," Shearson advised. "I must advise you—no, I must *warn* you—against testifying. The risk is far greater than any potential reward. You'd have everything to lose and almost nothing to gain."

Holland, however, wasn't convinced.

"I understand what you're saying," the officer told Shearson. "But I have no problem telling the grand jury what happened and why, or in answering any questions they have. What could be the harm in testifying?"

"The harm," Shearson said, "is that you can hang yourself."

"How?"

"It's simple, really. Fact is anything you say to a grand jury could be used against you if the panel decides to indict. One misstep—even an innocent, innocuous statement—could destroy your credibility and cast doubt on your account of the shooting if things go to trial. And because you'll have waived immunity, it could expose you to criminal prosecution ... even years in jail."

"In other words, Matty, by not testifying," Red McLaren added, "you avoid the risk of making statements that could be picked apart later for inconsistencies or contradictions."

"But there are no inconsistencies or contradictions in what I have to say—there's only the truth," Holland said. "By testifying, couldn't I explain why I acted how I did? How can a grand jury determine the most important thing about the incident—my state of mind—without hearing directly from me?"

"They have the written and verbal testimony that you and Officer Cook provided," Shearson replied. "They also have the findings of the NYPD's internal probe. The fact that the NYPD cleared you of policy violations or misconduct speaks volumes. The grand jury has enough evidence to render a decision, hopefully in your favor. They don't need to hear from you."

Still, Holland seemed hesitant, torn. "But if I don't tell my side of the story," he said, "won't that appear like a ploy, as if I'm trying to hide behind some legal technicality and somehow skirt the truth?"

"You'd be walking in a minefield if you testify," Shearson said, "literally taking your life in your hands."

"No more so than I did every day as a cop," Holland said.

"Listen to Eddie's advice, Matty," Red McLaren cautioned. "Fact is you don't have to testify. Like any citizen, police officers under criminal investigation are protected by due process against self-incrimination. Testifying is way too risky. We won't let you bury yourself. Say the wrong thing, however well-meaning, and you can kiss your wife, your family, your whole life goodbye."

Matt Holland sat staring at the police memorabilia on the wall behind Red McLaren's desk.

"What chance do I have that the grand jury will return a no bill?" he asked, after a lengthy pause.

"To be perfectly honest, I'm not sure," Shearson said. "I won't lie to you, Matt. The grand jury is under enormous pressure to return an indictment. We're banking on them staying immune to all of that—remaining objective and following the facts. In the end, though, they're just *people*. Who's going to stand up to the pressure they're facing and say that what happened was simply an accident, a tragic occurrence that doesn't rise to the level of criminality? I really don't know."

Shearson pulled on a cigarette. "But what I *do* know," he said, "is that there's no way in the world you should testify."

"Follow Eddie's counsel," Red McLaren said. "He knows better than anyone how the game is played."

Holland sat for several seconds, mulling his options.

"I appreciate your advice," he finally said, turning to Eddie Shearson. "But whose decision is this?"

"In the end, it's yours, Matty," Shearson conceded.

"Then I want to think it over and discuss it with Katie," Holland said. "I may be taking a huge gamble but if I didn't walk in there and tell the grand jury, face-to-face, what happened ... somehow it just wouldn't feel right."

Chapter 55

RESPONDING TO THE ONGOING CHORUS of anti-police protests, the NYPD announced that effective immediately it was implementing a sweeping overhaul of its firearms regulations, including the creation of a Firearms Discharge Review Board, charged with probing line-of-duty shootings. The actions were hailed by police reformists as a watershed in the modern-day history of law enforcement; they were denounced just as vocally by police supporters as yet another sellout to minority community pressure.

According to the revised gun code, officers were to use the minimum force necessary to stop crimes-in-progress, exhausting every conceivable tactic before resorting to their firearm. Decades-old police practices were banned. Officers could no longer fire warning shots, nor fire at a moving vehicle, fire to summon assistance, or fire in a situation where bystanders could be struck. Deadly physical force was allowable only in cases of self-defense or to defend an innocent civilian. Firearms were never to be used to as a first option, nor resorted to in lieu of sanctioned de-escalation tactics.

"These new guidelines represent an enlightened step forward in the evolution of law enforcement, and in the rights of citizens to be protected in every way possible from inadvertent police shootings," Mayor Worth said.

"This ill-conceived decision will do nothing but confuse and tie the hands of our officers and make the already challenging job of policing even more dangerous and difficult," PBA President Red McLaren countered.

But objections to the new guidelines fell on deaf ears. Not only was an entirely new set of rules now in effect but tied to those guidelines was a directive that every police officer in the city was to take part in a firearms-refresher course aimed at sharpening their judgment when confronted with unexpected split-second decisions in potentially deadly confrontations with civilians. Within a week, the department was pushing officers in assembly-line fashion through a one-day training course consisting of lectures, interactive videos, role-playing exercises, and close-range target practice. Rachel Cook was one of those cops.

Summoned from her patrol duties in Coney Island, Cook was instructed to report to an NYPD shooting range at a former military camp in a remote section of the Bronx. There, Cook and about forty other officers were ushered into a classroom in a cavernous, hangar-like building set amid wide expanses of vacant land and Quonset-shaped barracks. Facing the officers was a movie screen, alongside which Lieutenant Donald Cooper, the NYPD's top firearms instructor, explained the revised gun code to the cops.

"Anyone can learn to hit a bull's-eye," said Cooper. "What's more important to learn is whether or not you should be shooting in the first place. We're here not so much to sharpen your shooting skills as to sharpen your judgment."

Cooper reviewed the new regulations. "What we're saying is that we want you to think before reacting," he said. "The message is, 'If you shoot, you better be sure you have a good reason.'"

He then dimmed the lights, and the movie screen came to life. On it, the assembled cops were shown a series of documentary-style films depicting hypothetical deadly incidents. In one episode, an officer arrived at the scene of an accident that quickly evolved into a confrontation. Before the officer could calm things, one of the combatants pulled a pistol and fired a shot. He then ran into a nearby playground occupied by young children. Attendees were then asked how they would handle such an incident.

Other scenes followed. In one, a cop checking a driver's license was caught off guard and shot by a passenger in the car. In another, an off-duty cop attempting to thwart a holdup was shot by a gunman he failed to notice.

As each scene unfolded, attending cops were marched, one by one, to the front of the classroom and told to fire a pistol loaded with blanks at the precise moment they'd fire if the situation were real. Some fired; others didn't. Some acted appropriately; others violated the new guidelines. Innocent civilians were accidentally shot. Some cops were informed that if the situation were real, they would have been shot themselves.

Cook and the others then moved to a part of the building that the officers had dubbed "The Funhouse." Sections of the structure had been transformed into a mock tenement, with dilapidated, graffiti-covered walls and a labyrinth of hallways. In those hallways, the officers were exposed to mock "shoot/no-shoot" confrontations that were as harrowing and eye-opening as they were ambiguous and unpredictable. Armed assailants jumped out in ambush from behind hidden doors. Hardened criminals dressed like businessmen fired weapons without warning. Harmless people who resembled criminal stereotypes were mistakenly shot.

Cook moved through the simulated incidents—acting decisively, appropriately, even heroically in some instances. In others, though, she made grievous mistakes. In one case, she killed a young boy who ran into her line of fire. In another skit, second-guessing herself several times in the space of an instant, Cook was shot dead. Hypothetically, of course—but dead as could be.

When the role-playing ended, Cooper solicited questions. There was a shuffle of bodies in their chairs.

Finally, it was too much for one cop to hold back. "Let me make sure I've got this straight," he said. "You're telling us that we now have to think twice, or maybe even three times, before shooting?"

"That's right," Cooper replied. "You should be reluctant to use your gun. If you've got to think about shooting someone, don't shoot because that means your life is not in danger and there's probably another way to handle things."

"But what if we don't have time to think at all?" the cop asked. "And what if the person we're facing isn't as reluctant to shoot as we are?"

"We're not removing your powers," Cooper replied. "You still have the right to defend yourselves. Just be sure you make the right decision."

"This is reassuring," one cop said facetiously. "It's like the department is telling us, 'Do your job, but don't go out on a limb. Get yourself in trouble and it's all over for you. Don't fire your gun when you should, and you could wind up dead. Use it, and you can wind up *worse* than dead.'"

Suddenly, that was the prevailing sentiment among cops in New York.

The city was, indeed, communicating a powerful new message to its police. In effect, what it was saying was that the basic, long-standing relationship between the police department and its officers had changed. Unlike in the past, there'd be no such thing as shoot first and ask questions later. And unlike in the past, there'd no longer be the presumption that if a police officer made a mistake, the department would automatically be there to protect him. The age-old police mindset about the use of firearms could no longer be considered *de rigueur*. Clearly, the message now was: "Don't shoot. If you do, you're on your own. If you make a mistake, there'll be no one to cover your ass."

It was no longer simply a matter now of reacting with an unfettered mind to an unexpected crisis. Judgment, experience, training, and instincts were no longer the only criteria in decision-making. Suddenly, it was just as important to weigh whether the police department would support you, whether your actions might spark civil unrest, and whether your career might be jeopardized, your life threatened, and your sanity tested—not by a mistake, or through misconduct, but by simply doing your job. Decisions that were once difficult enough to make now seemed unspeakably complex. The ramifications of a poor decision seemed overwhelming.

Ironically, the new training only exacerbated this mindset. Designed to achieve clarity, the training, at least for the moment, had succeeded only in creating more confusion by exposing police to all the harrowing possibilities and communicating a message that was contradictory to the word on the street.

"Do you think you could do it?" Cook overheard one cop ask, after the training session was complete. "Do you think you'd shoot someone, if it were just you and some guy, out there on the street?"

"No doubt," answered the cop, whose nameplate read Griffin. "If it's kill or be killed, I'm shooting. If it's either me or him, that bastard's going down. I'm not taking the first bullet. They're not carrying me away in a fucking body bag."

Griffin looked about, as if he wanted to share a secret. "You know the only rule that matters?" he asked. "It's the one that says, 'It's better to be tried by twelve than carried by six.' That's the bottom line: No matter how many questions they ask later, no matter how tough it gets, I'd still rather be talking to a jury than lying dead in a box. I may die on the streets of this city ... but I ain't dying stupid."

Griffin seemed so certain. Cook envied that. Because now, after thirteen months on the job, she wasn't sure herself. Suddenly, Cook felt so strangely unprepared. She knew how to shoot, and when to shoot—she just didn't know any more if she *could*. Could she shoot when the stakes were real and not just playacting? Could she shoot at a real person and not just a paper target? Would she shoot, or hesitate, when she had only a split second to think and nothing more to fall back on than her instincts, her reflexes, and her prayers?

Overwhelmed by her sudden uncertainty, all she could do, Cook knew, was steer clear of trouble. Avoid confrontation. Never, ever, put herself in the kind of position she'd been in with Matt Holland down in the cellar on Amboy Street.

And she wasn't alone.

In making its cops reluctant to use their weapons, the NYPD's new firearms guidelines had also inadvertently made many cops reluctant to act at all. Caution was suddenly the byword. A powerful new message passed through the ranks: Don't get involved. Don't stick your neck out. Don't take a chance on making a mistake because no one will be there to bail you out. If the department deserted a good cop like Matt Holland, it'll sure as hell do the same to you.

In the toxic atmosphere that accompanied the C. J. Johnson shooting investigation, officers in New York now viewed the NYPD itself as a powerful new adversary. It was jarring. With seemingly everyone else lined up against them all these years, the department had always been something to cling to and depend on. No more. Now, even the NYPD was betraying them.

Once again, city residents witnessed the distressing sight of off-duty cops staging demonstrations outside police headquarters and City Hall, as the PBA protested the new firearms code.

The protests had no impact, however. The new firearms policy was fully in effect. And even more changes, the NYPD promised, were on the way. The old ways of conducting police business were being ascribed to ancient history. The C. J. Johnson shooting and the subsequent riots in Brownsville had dramatically accelerated the normal pace of change. Rules and procedures were being rewritten on the fly. Everyone would simply have to feel their way along as developments continued to unfold.

Maybe it would prove positive in the end—a much-needed change as law enforcement moved forward. But for now, all that was obvious was that in the wake of the C. J. Johnson shooting the siege mentality among New York's cops had reached an all-time high, fueled by the sentiment that police leadership was gutless and hopelessly out of touch.

"As cops, we fear that everything that's happening will only make us hesitate a fatal extra second when confronted with a weapon, or make us avoid confrontations altogether, for fear that the trouble we'd cause ourselves would be as bad as getting shot," Red McLaren said. "What we're creating is a 'stay out of trouble' mentality. We're forcing our cops to police New York from hiding spots."

McLaren shook his head, sadly. "I've been around this city for a long time, but I've never seen anything like this," he said. "Our police department is collapsing. Morale is an all-time low. Our city is in a state of paralysis."

Chapter 56

INSIDE THE HOME of Matt and Katie Holland, the protective ring of off-duty cops continued to camp out day and night. Although anti-police demonstrations in front of the house had ceased, the PBA was taking no chances. Union members armed with handguns, shotguns, and rifles guarded the Hollands' home around the clock. Others stood vigil in the cul-de-sac outside, barring anyone other than fellow officers, family members, neighbors, and friends from traversing the street.

Inside the house, officers on rotating shifts—catching naps in sleeping bags on the living-room floor—crouched near doorways and windows, running errands, delivering supplies, and performing household chores. At night, they sat playing cards, watching TV, wolfing down sandwiches and beer, and sinking deeper into a cesspool of betrayal, anger, self-pity, and defeat. There were acerbic observations tossed back and forth about NYPD leadership, lamentations about the fate of America's police officers, and hate-filled, racist humor aimed at Brownsville and its residents.

"You know, they ought to build a gate around Brownsville and charge admission to get in—like a fuckin' zoo," Bobby Foster, a cop from the seven-three, said one night.

Everyone laughed, toasting from high-necked bottles of beer.

"Here's a riddle," Foster said. "Why are firefighters under orders not to answer any calls in Brownsville?"

"Dunno. Why?"

"It's the city's latest 'urban renewal' plan. They've tried everything else. Now they're gonna let the fuckin' shithole burn to the ground, so they can rebuild it from scratch."

They laughed and toasted that one, too.

"The NYPD is so inept it could fuck up a one-car funeral," a retired cop named Phil Nettles said. "I don't even recognize it anymore. When I was on the job, the top brass protected the guys who were lower on the food chain, just 'cause we were all cops. Now, though, it's whole a new ballgame. Here we've got a 'good shoot'—justified, defensible, a fuckin' accident— and they're skewering an honest, hard-working cop, just to get the heat off 'em from the Black community?"

Nettles shook his head sadly. "That's fuckin' bullshit!"

"Matt Holland is a hero, for Christ sakes," Bobby Foster groused. "Without cops like him, the whole fuckin' city falls apart. Don't people see that? The goddamned suits from City Hall ought to genuflect before cops like Matty. They ought to build cops like him a fuckin' statue an' kiss their ass for what they do … instead of pissing all over them."

"It's nothing but a goddamn bunch of politics," Nettles grumbled. "All the NYPD does is try and make itself look good, even if it means selling out its own. Those jerkoffs at the top don't give a shit about the cop on the street. They're gonna protect their own asses, that's all. Cops in America have a right to be pissed off! They're getting screwed every which way and backwards. Nothing makes sense anymore. As far as I'm concerned, the whole damn city is in the shitter."

"Fuck the NYPD!" one cop said. "Fuck the city, too!"

The off-duty cops, laughing riotously, quaffed more beer.

And all the while, Katie Holland tried to maintain her usual evening ritual: an hour on the phone with her parents and the Hollands' twin daughters; another hour or so helping Thomas with his homework; and the rest of her waking moments trying to save her houseplants, handle her household chores and pay the bills—all while listening to the sounds of hammers and circular saws as her husband worked feverishly on their daughter's bedroom addition.

Then another hour or more crying herself to sleep.

Sometimes, when she couldn't drift off, Katie sat listening through an open bedroom door to the off-duty cops downstairs, their voices growing more amplified when TV news coverage shifted to the C. J. Johnson shooting.

"Look at those lowlife welfare cases!" Bobby Foster said one night, pointing to a black protester on TV. "*They're* the ones callin' the shots now?"

Foster took a swig from a bottle of Rheingold. "Gimme a fuckin' break!" he groused. "What's goin' on in America? Everything I hear is: 'Protect the niggers … protect the niggers!'"

Another long swig—and even more venom.

"The niggers never do anything wrong, do they?" Foster growled. "It's never *their* fault, is it? Just ours. They tear their neighborhoods apart and live like animals and commit crimes … but *we're* the problem? They curse us, spit on us, attack us, taunt us, but *we're* the racists? We're plopped down in the middle of their fuckin' shit to keep a lid on things, but *we're* the bad guys? It's okay for us to go out there and get ourselves killed, but God forbid we cap some black asshole. And for what? Fifteen grand a year? Gimme a break! You know what? They hate me? I hate 'em back! They don't want us in their neighborhoods? Fine. Let 'em live with no police! Then we'll see how they feel!"

Foster took a swig of beer and pointed at the TV set, where an anti-police demonstrator was being interviewed.

"I tell you," he ranted, "the pendulum has swung so far in the wrong direction, it's fuckin' pathetic. We're being held hostage by the so-called black leadership an' hung out to dry by the city. The city wants us to stand around with our thumbs up our ass, watching these coons riot and loot? Why? Because if we do anything we might make it worse … might hurt their feelings? What bullshit! They're gonna riot and shut down this city? Over my dead fuckin' body, they will!"

"Calm down, Bobby," one of the other cops playfully chided.

"No!" Foster said. "Fuck this! I've had it up to here with having my hands tied an' seeing good cops get arrested for doing their job. I'm sick an' tired of seeing the city kowtow to these fuckin' jungle bunnies! The city should fuckin' pin a medal on us for getting rid of these miserable cocksuckers. Me … I'd have no trouble blowing one of them away. Threaten me? I'll shove my fuckin' gun up your ass! Look at me the wrong way? Run your 'jiveass' bullshit by me? I'll waste you, motherfucker! No hesitation. No qualms. No regret."

"Ooooh, you're a 'bad boy,' Bobby!" another cop scolded, mockingly. "You know what you are? You're a goddamned *racist*!"

They laughed some more and drank.

"You know what—you're right, an' I don't give a shit who knows it," Foster said. "I'm a goddamned racist! I hate those fuckin' niggers an' what they're doin' to this city! Hate 'em! Ship 'em the fuck back to Africa ... that's what I say!"

"C'mon, that's wrong, Bobby," a cop chided. "It's not politically correct!"

"You didn't hear me," Foster raged. "I don't fuckin' care!"

He emptied his beer and moved menacingly toward the TV.

"Shut the fuck up, you bastards!" he barked at the set. "You don't work, you don't have a voice. You commit crimes, you go to fuckin' jail or you get shot. Quit crying an' making excuses. Find a job. Get off welfare. Take a fuckin' bath. Clean up your neighborhood. Learn to speak English an' stop sponging off society. Do all of that ... an' then *maybe* we'll talk!"

He pointed an imaginary gun at the TV set and pulled its imaginary trigger. "In the meantime, can't we please just *cap* these motherfuckers?" he asked. "I'm beggin' you. Please let us off these motherfuckers!"

Foster's voice, and the laughter of the off-duty cops, reverberated through the house. Upstairs, Katie Holland closed her bedroom door and moved to comfort Thomas, awake on an air mattress alongside his parents' bed, asking why the officers downstairs felt the way they did toward Black people, and if a mob from Brownsville was coming to Staten Island that night to burn down their home.

Chapter 57

RACHEL COOK STEWED in her anger, too. It was always present now—a seething, metathesizing malignancy that simmered deep inside her, threatening to poke its way through her skin and pummel nearly everyone who crossed her path.

Cook was angry all the time now. Everything she'd felt over the past few months—sadness, confusion, bitterness, disappointment, betrayal, despair—all of it had morphed to an intense, relentless rage. Cook was angry at things people said and things they didn't say; angry at friends and family, civilians, and fellow cops; angry at actions and gestures and the way people looked and talked, or laughed or frowned. Nothing escaped her wrath—not NYPD brass nor city officials, not politicians nor judges, public defenders nor the press, the public at large nor anti-police protestors. Much of the time Cook didn't even know what she was angry about, or why—just that she was bottled up with a fiery rage that burned inside her day and night like a low-grade fever.

One day, she found herself railing at her television set during a newscast during which a college professor was discussing community-police relations.

"Goddamned ivory-tower, bleeding-heart intellectual, speaking with such blind certainty about issues you know nothing about!" Cook snarled at the screen. "Here I am, putting my ass on the line every day, jeopardizing my life, open to criticism and second-guessing, trying to solve problems that have no solutions, working under the kind of pressure that most people can't even imagine ... and I have to listen to this fucking crock of bullshit?"

Cook stood in her bedroom, shouting at the TV. "What the fuck do you know, asshole?" she railed. "You're going to tell us what cops ought to do? Why? 'Cause you got your answers out of a fucking textbook? Why don't you get your fat ass out of your safe little classroom and let me rub your goddamned nose in the shit that cops have to deal with? Then we'll see if your academic bullshit works. In the meantime, shut your goddamned stupid mouth and drop the fuck dead, you pathetic, pencil-necked putz!"

Then she sat on the floor in front of the TV set and cried.

All she wanted to do was to *show* people—that's what Cook wanted more than anything now. She wanted to march the naysayers and the intellectuals and the activists and the critics into the firestorm in neighborhoods like Brownsville and Coney Island and rub people's faces in them until they saw and felt everything that she did. She wanted people to get screamed at and cursed and spit upon simply for trying to do a thankless, fruitless job; for trying to keep communities from falling apart, halt lawlessness, protect those in need. She wanted people who criticized cops as being brutal, jaded, callous racists to have to clean up after an accident or move through rat-infested, rancid tenements, and be forced to confront the worst of humanity, the vilest forms of violence and depravity. She wanted them to see children abandoned, beaten and dying on the streets; wanted them to sit in court and see how misguided judges and crooked attorneys and inept public defenders and gaping loopholes in the system stifled justice and beat well-meaning police officers down. She wanted people to be exposed to everything she saw, everything she felt, and be betrayed by the same myths and illusions and half-truths she once so fervently believed in.

Let them go there and see it as it really is, Cook thought. *Then they'll know what I know. Then they'll understand what I feel. Then we can talk, and maybe I won't to have to feel so angry and terrified and disillusioned and alone.*

But none of that happened. All Cook was left with was her burgeoning, explosive anger. And what she was angry at, most of all, was herself.

What a laughingstock I am! she thought. *What an ignorant asshole! Number one in my graduating class at the NYPD Police Academy? Please!*

Cook couldn't believe she'd been so naïve, so hopelessly blind. Look at what she'd gone and done. She'd allowed dime-store novels and B movies and television shows to create an idealized perception of police work that she'd bought into hook, line, and sinker. She'd adopted a secret identity—a modern-day heroine who was going to solve crimes and vanquish villains and rescue the helpless and save the city—that was as bogus and bankrupt as the NYPD leadership she now scorned. She'd allowed fables and myths, fairy tales and fantasies, to fashion a glorious, dreamlike world that was so bloated with youth and unbridled idealism it was only destined to disappoint her once reality set in.

What horseshit! What a fucking joke!

She should have known better, but she hadn't. She should have been smarter, but she wasn't. She should have foreseen what was out there, in the real world, but she didn't. All she had done was set herself up for a fall.

"Asshole!" she cursed herself. "I can't believe I've allowed this to happen!"

Cook felt so useless now, so unworthy, so damaged. It was hard to believe that not so long ago she'd felt so confident, capable, and worthwhile. Now she couldn't bear to even look at herself in the mirror. *She was nothing!* Nothing more than an ugly, useless, sorry sack of shit, a lonely shadow in an empty uniform, struggling to find some cogent reason to continue on the job, struggling to keep from drowning.

You've got no one to blame but yourself, Cook thought. But she managed, nevertheless, to pin the blame on others. And she carried her rage around inside her—a walking, talking, ticking time bomb, wanting to flail away at something or someone, purge herself somehow of the billowing anger consuming her.

It was an unsettling thought—walking around with a nightstick and a gun and feeling the way she did. Cook didn't know if she could ever give her anger free rein without hurting someone badly. She didn't know if she could hold in it much longer without hurting *herself* even more.

Chapter 58

SURROUNDED BY A PROTECTIVE CORDON of off-duty cops, Matt Holland slipped inside the Emanuel Cellar Federal Building, his bodyguards skirting the crowd of anti-police demonstrators outside the main entrance, before accessing the U.S. District Courthouse through a loading dock at the rear.

Holland had made the most consequential decision of his life. After consulting with Katie, and praying with NYPD chaplain Michael Caruso, the officer had decided to eschew the advice of PBA officials, opting to waive his constitutional right to remain silent, testify on his own behalf, and put his fate in the hands of the state grand jury. He'd made the decision, he said, because he believed it was the right thing to do and there was no reason, legal or otherwise, to hide from the truth.

Accompanied by PBA attorney Eddie Shearson, Holland—dressed in a gray suit, white shirt, and gray-and-yellow-striped tie—was ushered into the grand jury chamber and sworn in before the panel, all of whom sat riveted in silence as the officer recounted the night of the C. J. Johnson shooting: the ambiguity and apprehension that he and Rachel Cook experienced in the cellar on Amboy Street; why the officers acted as they had; and what they'd thought and felt before, during, and after the incident.

Holland, although nervous under oath, was detailed and composed throughout his solemn testimony, his observations pensive and sincere. Then, guided by a supervisory judge, the jurors took turns asking questions, many of them personal and probing. Holland answered each one patiently, professionally—and, at times, with emotion that was deeply moving.

The officer then read a statement he'd composed the previous night, with assistance from Katie. The statement read:

I appreciate the opportunity to be heard. I have waived my legal right to immunity from testifying because I want you to hear directly from me what happened in this case. It is the only way I believe you can make a fair and objective decision. I'm here only to tell you the truth. The way I've related the incident is exactly how it happened. I know there are many people passing judgment, calling me a callous, brutal racist, an inept police officer, and even worse, a murderer. But what happened that night was a tragic accident, nothing more. I know you may be skeptical, but that is the truth. My gun discharged when Clifford Johnson unexpectedly ran into me, mistaking me for someone else. All I saw when the lights went out, at the last split-second, was a shadow. I didn't know if it was a man or a woman, Black or White, adult or child, enemy or friend. I didn't have the time to assess the circumstances or consider the consequences. I barely had time to react. But while I'll accept your verdict, regardless of outcome, I want you to know that I didn't shoot Clifford Johnson in cold blood. I am neither a murderer nor a racist. I don't see people in terms of their race, religion, or color. I've been a police officer in Brownsville for sixteen years, my record is unblemished, and I help people impartially. And that night, I was just someone who was trying to do his job, best as I could, under very difficult circumstances. I'm sincerely sorry that all of it happened. I wish it could have turned out differently, but the reality of it is something that I suppose I'll have to live with for the rest of my life.

Then Matt Holland, surrounded again by the ring of police bodyguards, exited via the same rear entrance through which he'd entered, departed the courthouse, and was driven home to wait for the grand jury to decide his fate.

Chapter 59

When Rachel Cook unleashed her pent-up rage, it poured from her with an unbridled fury that frightened her more than anything she'd ever come across as a police officer on the streets of New York.

The onset of winter was approaching by now, and Cook's frightful, lonely past few months had become seasons not simply of disillusionment, alienation, and anger, but of interminable eight-hour tours alternately manning a stationary post on the Coney Island boardwalk and conducting strip searches at the Central Booking Inmate Lockup in downtown Brooklyn.

The amusement area was closed for the season now, the beaches empty, the boardwalk raked with frigid gusts blowing off the ocean. It was at the tail end of such a tour when Cook was summoned to conduct a pair of searches.

The female arrestees she was assigned to search—each eighteen years old and Black—were handcuffed to a row of green plastic-and-metal chairs near a table at which they'd been fingerprinted, photographed, and booked. Both teens, with prior police records, had been charged with larceny and theft. They'd also viciously assaulted the two male officers who'd arrested them.

"Motherfuckin' pigs!" they railed, tugging on their handcuffs, and howling in mock pain when Cook arrived at the lockup. "You cocksuckin' cops! Bastard pigs! Let us go!"

When they caught sight of Cook, their protests grew even more specific.

"Awh, shit!" one of them howled. "Look at this! A fuckin' *lady pig*! Hey, White bitch, I know what you're gonna do. You're gonna make us take off our clothes an' search us, right? Shit! I'm tellin' ya now, you ain't gonna fuckin' touch me. I ain't lettin' no fuckin' white lady pig lay her filthy hands on me."

"They brought this pig in to search us?" the other girl asked, incredulously.

"That's right!"

"Well, that lesbian dyke bitch ain't gonna lay her fuckin' hands on me, either."

Cook's felt her insides churning as she approached a male cop standing guard over the pair.

"I'm not sure why," the cop said, wryly, "but something tells me these exemplary young women don't much desire your company."

"I don't desire their company much either," Cook muttered.

The girls yanked harder on their cuffs, lifting the row of chairs from its mooring and slamming it noisily back to the floor.

"Let us the fuck outta here!" one of them howled.

"Seriously," male cop said, "these two bitches have been belligerent from the start. They won't tell us a thing. We can't even get their names. Had to book 'em as 'Jane Does.'"

Cook glanced at the girls. Both glared back mockingly, sticking their tongues out. Removing her utility belt and taking a deep breath, Cook tried to steel herself, her adrenaline already surging. The male cop released one of the girls from the row of chairs, and then cuffed both her hands in front of her.

"Lemme go, motherfucker!" She squirmed. "Fuckin' pigs ... lemme go!" She then lashed out violently, kicking the male cop squarely in his testicles. He dropped to the floor, writhing in pain.

"Bitch!" the cop howled, twisting the girl's arm behind her back as he struggled to his feet. "I'll crush your goddamned head!"

He shoved the writhing girl toward Cook. "I envy you," he said. "I'd like to have two minutes with this bitch, myself."

The cop pointed to a bathroom in which the search was to be conducted.

"Be careful," he cautioned, "you got yourself a wild one here!"

Cook approached the girl.

"You ain't touchin' me, dyke!" she hollered.

"Listen," Cook said, calmly, "you can call me whatever you want, but this search has to be done, regardless. It doesn't matter if you like me or not, but the quicker we can get this over with, the easier you'll make it for yourself."

"Fuck you, bitch!" the girl bellowed.

Cook took her by the arm.

"Get your motherfuckin' hands offa me," she screamed, pulling away and then spitting, hitting Cook squarely in the face with a gob of phlegm.

Something inside of Cook, something wild and unruly, broke free of its reins. Instantly, she grabbed the girl beneath an armpit, pinched hard, and yanked the girl forcefully toward the bathroom. Screaming and resisting, the girl pulled forcefully in the opposite direction.

"Bitch!" she spit again, her spittle dribbling down Cook's blouse. "You white lesbian pig! I told you to get your motherfuckin' hands off me!"

Mustering all of her strength, Cook tugged at the girl, dragging her into the bathroom and slamming the door behind them. Inside the tiny room, the girl spun free, facing Cook with an even more pronounced fury. She was younger and taller than Cook, rangy and athletic, dressed in jeans and an orange button-down blouse.

Struggling to retain her composure, Cook tried to explain what had to be done, all the while feeling a powerful rage ebbing and flowing. She was squarely on the precipice now. There was no place left to be pushed.

"Fuck off, pig!" Jane Doe snarled.

Since the girl was cuffed, she couldn't remove her own blouse. And since Cook wasn't about to uncuff her, it was obvious the officer would have to remove the girl's blouse herself. She wondered how she'd do that without provoking additional trouble. Just suddenly, she didn't care.

This bitch's blouse is coming off! Cook thought. *It's coming off, whether she likes it or not!*

"I'm going to remove your blouse," Cook said.

"The fuck you are!" Jane Doe shrieked. "Stay away from me. You ain't taking off my clothes … you white, motherfuckin' dyke bitch!"

Cook touched the girl's blouse. The girl ducked, then shuddered like a horse shooing a fly.

"Watch it!" Cook warned, as another surge of adrenaline coursed through her body, mingling with revulsion and contempt. Suddenly, Cook was ready to do things to this girl that she'd never done to another person before. She wanted to pound the girl with her fists, kick her, tear her hair out, rip at her face with her teeth and nails.

The girl then spit in Cook's face again—and that was it! Cook felt something inside of her snap, as if a dam had burst under the strain of an enormous groundswell. Cook grabbed the girl by the shoulders, smacking her in the face repeatedly and shaking her as hard as she could.

"Listen, you badass little fucker!" Cook snarled. "I've had all I'm gonna take from you. I told you to cut your attitude and shut your filthy mouth. Now I'm going to shut you up myself! Here are the rules: You do what I say, when I fucking say it! I don't give a fuck what you *want*. I'm not here to listen to your jive-ass bullshit. This search is gonna happen whether you like it or not. Now just stand still … and shut the fuck up!"

"I don't have nothin' on me," the girl protested. "No weapons. No drugs. Nothing stolen. You ain't gotta do a search. Keep your dirty, White fuckin' hands offa me, or I'll come back with my friends an' we'll cut your fuckin' heart out!"

Her powerful kick caught Cook squarely on the shin, sending a bolt of pain up the officer's leg. Jane Doe laughed. Instantly, Cook's pain disappeared, and all she felt was another surge of anger, this time more forceful than before. She grabbed the girl by her blouse and, grunting, screaming, yanked downward with all her strength. Legs buckling, arms flailing, the girl toppled to the floor. Cook leapt astride her, straddling the girl's chest.

"You stupid, fuckin' bitch!" Cook screamed. "See what you've done? You were looking for trouble … and now you've got it!"

Jane Doe screamed incoherently, kicking, bucking, trying to throw Cook off, as the enraged officer smacked the teen across the face. She then yanked hard on the girl's blouse, tearing it at the breast pocket. The girl's head jerked up, and then slammed against the bathroom's tile floor.

"See?" Cook shouted. "Like I said, I'm gonna search you one way or another … even if I have to rip the fucking clothes off your back!"

Jane Doe thrust her body upward, twisting and sending Cook tumbling sideways to the floor. The girl then lashed out again, this time catching Cook with a kick to the groin and knocking the wind from her.

"You son of a bitch!" Cook gasped.

There'd be no more roles to play now, no cool professional detachment, no holding back. Cook felt nothing but this fierce, savage rage traveling from the pit of her stomach to her legs and fists. She leapt atop Jane Doe and began pummeling the girl about the eyes and mouth, her gasps and grunts and curses echoing off the bathroom's tiled walls. She tore at the girl's blouse, feeling the fabric rip and the buttons pop, as the garment flew open. Then she dug her fingernails underneath the girl's brassiere and yanked, the bra's shoulder strap tearing, its metal hooks popping. Jane Doe fought back, elbows flailing, legs kicking, screaming in protest.

"You like this, huh?" Cook snarled, hands pushing against the girl's face. "Is this the way you want to be searched?"

"Bitch!" the girl screamed. "I'll fuckin' kill you!"

Fists clenched, Cook pounded the girl's face repeatedly.

"You'll kill me, huh?" Cook said. "Let's see who'll kill who!"

God, how Cook hated this girl. She hated more deeply, in that one instant, than she'd hated through the entire sum of her life. She never knew she could be moved to feel this depth of primitive, white-hot emotion. But there she was—her fiery, bottled-up rage unleashed fully. Hating Jane Doe and everything about her. Hating her for her clothing and her language, her blind hostility and the color of her skin. Hating her, more than anything, for luring Cook into another dark cellar—not unlike the one on Amboy Street—a place where tragedies could unfold and lives could be destroyed and strangers could emerge from the shadows to torment and cripple you with emotions you couldn't control.

"Here, bitch!" Cook spewed the hatred within her now, striking Jane Doe repeatedly about the face. Once for the officer's failed dreams. Once for her ruined career. Once for all the wounded cops in the city. Once for Matt Holland.

And once simply because she felt like it.

In truth, the search was never even completed. Bleeding from her nose, her blouse tattered and hanging from her wrists, her breasts exposed, Jane Doe lied on the floor of the bathroom, whimpering, and cursing. Fists clenched, heart racing, Cook rose to stand over her, her own blouse undone—feeling triumphant, then suddenly empty, soiled, and ashamed.

"Fuck you, you White pig!" the girl sobbed.

"Go to hell, bitch!" Cook howled, not sure which of them felt more defeated, sullied, and diminished.

Outside the bathroom, the male cop waited, smiling.

"Nice job in there." He winked, and then held up a blackjack. "Next time, use this. Scum like that deserves even more of beating."

Covered with a blanket, Jane Doe was led from the bathroom by the male cop and cuffed to a chair next to the other girl, who leered and gave the officers the finger.

"Honkey pigs!" she shouted.

"Nigger!" the male cop sneered.

Cook just stared at the floor, working as hard to control her anguish as she'd worked the past few months to control her rage.

"The NYPD ought to give you a medal for what you just did," the male cop said. "These aren't *people* we're dealing with. They're nothing more than worthless pieces of shit!"

"You're right." Cook said. "I guess I never realized that until now."

* * *

Back at her apartment, Cook tried to wash her anguish and rage away in the shower. Her knuckles stung, bloody and raw. Her fingernails were splintered, strands of Jane Doe's hair stuck beneath them. Cook stood in the shower, hot water beating down, wondering if she could ever wash away her emptiness and her pain, wondering if she could ever repair what felt like a permanent tear in the fabric of her soul. Then slowly, she sank to her knees and began to weep. And she remained in the shower as her sobs turned uncontrollably to wails and the water grew cold and Cook was gripped by the same kind of bone-numbing chill she had felt when Matt Holland shot C. J. Johnson, the night that both officers' lives began to come undone.

And when she emerged from the shower and caught a glimpse of herself in the bathroom mirror, Cook looked tinier than she ever had before, distorted and deformed, as if the image staring back at her was merely a crudely drawn caricature, someone she struggled to recognize as the brave and sanguine young woman that she once was, not so long ago.

Chapter 60

MATT HOLLAND COMPLETED the electrical hookups, laid wall-to-wall carpeting, and painted the room addition he'd busied himself with for the past twelve weeks. He then declared the room ready for Angie, one of his twin daughters. Each girl, he said, could have a bedroom of her own now.

"Good news!" Katie smiled. "Now we can bring our daughters home."

The thought of that alone was an immense relief to Katie, a glimmer of sunshine amid a ferocious storm. Pulled from their third-grade classes, the girls had been living for weeks at Katie's parents' house, secreted to the Jersey beachfront location since shortly after the C. J. Johnson shooting, when demonstrations outside the Hollands' home had reduced the eight-year-olds to tears. Matt had seen his daughters only sporadically since their banishment—Katie taking the solitary, two-hour drive to visit the girls twice a week before heading home to care for Thomas and the household. With Matt's paycheck lost to his suspension, Katie had also picked up additional hours at the photo studio where she worked, a routine that drained her to a point of exhaustion. The fact that the couple was falling increasingly behind on their financial obligations had only exacerbated their dire circumstances.

"I want our girls home with us, Matt," Katie said. "This is where they live, and where they need to be."

"I'm not sure that's a good idea." Matt hedged. "I'm not sure it's safe."

By now, Matt's face seemed twisted into a perpetually tortured look, his movements tentative and ponderous. His unkempt hair was flecked a dull gray patina, as if he'd aged a decade in mere months.

"What if we—"

"No!" Katie said. "It's *time*!"

"But—"

"I said no!" she repeated, more sharply this time. "At some point, we need to stop being held hostage by what has happened, Matt. We need to move on with our lives and put this nightmare behind us. I want our girls home with us … period! I want to hug them, see their faces, tuck them into bed at night! I want to be a family again! I want to be a mother! I need that … if there's any chance at all for me to remain sane. And the time for it is now!"

It was two weeks before Thanksgiving already, and the tempest surrounding the C. J. Johnson shooting had quieted almost entirely, unfolding exclusively behind closed doors—in the offices of NYPD officials, D.A. prosecutors, civil rights attorneys, City Hall politicians, grand jurors, and others tied to the case. The headlines had all but faded. No substantive anti-police demonstrations had been staged in weeks. Telephone threats to the Hollands' home had ceased as well, with the change to an unlisted number. Thomas also seemed more settled, back to a normal routine at school, sleeping in his own room, his bedwetting having ceased.

"It's time to turn the page, Matt," Katie said. "I'm hopeful that the worst of our personal hell is over—the demonstrations, the riots, the threats. As far as the uncertainty goes—the district attorney, the grand jury, the civil lawsuit, and everything else—that's just something we're going to have to live with until everything is resolved."

"That could take a long time," Matt said. "Maybe months."

"Hopefully, that won't be the case," Katie said. "But if it is, so be it. I'm in this marriage for the long haul, for better or for worse. I'm not going anywhere … unless you chase me away."

"I'd never do that," Matt said. "But we have to face the possibility that I could be indicted, face criminal trial … even go to prison."

"I'm fully aware of all those possibilities," Katie said, "but let's cross each bridge when we come to it. We've lived with fear, uncertainty, and regret for months. We'll learn to live with them for as long as it takes. The important thing now is to be together again, as a family, and try to heal … to regain some semblance of a normal life."

Reluctantly, Matt relented. And the couple agreed that they'd bring their daughters home the following day.

"There's one other thing," Katie said. "I want the officers guarding our home to leave."

Matt stared at her, quizzically. "Why?"

"We need to take possession of our home again, Matt," Katie said. "Having armed, off-duty cops living with us is another thing I want to move past. I don't want to see rifles and guns . . . or be reminded daily of what we've had to live through. I don't want men camped out here in sleeping bags. Besides, their conversations are disturbing, especially the ones regarding race. I don't want our children exposed to bigoted, angry talk. I don't want Thomas and the girls to hear Blacks called 'jungle bunnies' and 'niggers.' I don't want them to hear how Blacks need to be sent back to Africa or be beaten up and shot."

"Those guys don't mean any harm, Katie," Matt said. "They've been protecting us out of loyalty and support for me. It's what police officers do for one another, Katie. It's part of the brotherhood. You know that."

"And the language they're using?" Katie said. "The cursing and the ranting? The disillusionment and the bitterness? The drinking and the racial epithets?"

"They're just venting, Katie. It's just the way cops talk. They're angry, that's all. They feel betrayed by the way the police department and the city stab their officers in the back. Besides, they've treated you with nothing but respect, haven't they? They'd die in a heartbeat, protecting us. They'd do anything for us."

"I appreciate everything they've done," Katie said. "But it's time they went home to their families, too."

"But they're all I've got," Matt said. "Everyone else has abandoned me."

"That's where you're wrong, Matty," Katie said. "You have me, and you have Thomas. And now you'll have your daughters, too. We all have each other. And maybe our love, and the fact that we'll be together again, can help pull us through the nightmare we've been living all these many months."

Chapter 61

SHORTLY AFTER THANKSGIVING, Landon Devlin phoned Rachel Cook, fresh off the officer's latest in a seemingly endless string of midnight-to-eight tours.

For Cook, it had been another unnerving eight hours. Crime rarely took time off in neighborhoods like Coney Island. Nor did heartache, penury, or racial tensions. There'd been several shootings across Cook's harried tour, as well as a burglary, an attempted rape, and several hours of chasing drug peddlers from their boardwalk haunts. As usual, Cook was wary, exhausted—and reluctant to take the call when her roommate offered her the phone.

"Who the fuck is calling *me*?" the officer snapped, standoffish, guarded.

To Cook, the entire world was an enemy now, and she was under siege. There were few people to believe in, fewer to trust. Cook was disillusioned, angry, wearing the same psychic armor as most of the city's cops.

"It's some guy," her roommate said of the caller. "Said he was a cop."

"What does he want … a fucking date?" Cook snapped.

"He says he just wants to talk," Cook's roommate said. "Says he got your phone number from Matt and Katie Holland."

Instantly, Cook softened. As per investigative guidelines, she hadn't had contact with either Matt or Katie for more than four months. For nearly all that time, she'd agonized over the state of the Hollands' lives, same way she agonized over her own, sympathizing about them, grieving for them, missing them desperately.

"Actually, he sounds pretty nice," Cook's roommate said of the caller. "What do you have to lose, Rachel? You can always just hang up."

"I guess so," said Cook, reluctantly taking the call.

Devlin promptly introduced himself and detailed his connection with the Hollands, as well as the services offered to traumatized police officers through his organization, COPS.

"I've heard some very impressive things about you," he told Cook.

"What kinds of things?"

"Tops in your graduating class at the Police Academy. One of a handful of females on street patrol in New York. Stellar performance as a rookie in an 'A' House in central Brooklyn. A future superstar in the eyes of One Police Plaza."

Devlin laughed. "Hell, the accolades don't get much better than that. I hear you're even taking graduate courses, on the NYPD's ticket, at John Jay, where I teach. Going for a master's degree … bigger and better things."

"Grad school's out for now," Cook said curtly.

"How come?"

"I lost interest."

"Well," Devlin asked, "what *are* you interested in these days?"

"Just keeping my head above water," Cook said.

"Why? You feel as if you're drowning?"

"To tell you the truth … yeah."

"That's understandable," Devlin said. "I'm sure you've had a rough go of it these past few months."

"I've been going through my share of shit," Cook said, coyly.

"I suspect the C. J. Johnson shooting has affected you deeply, hasn't it?" Devlin asked.

"That's not something I'm comfortable talking about," Cook demurred.

"I think that you'd be a lot better off if you did," Devlin said.

"And I suppose you're someone I can talk to?" Cook asked, facetiously.

"I believe that I am," Devlin said.

"Someone who'll wave a magic wand and make my problems disappear?"

"It doesn't work that way."

"Yeah?" Cook said. "Well, how *does* it work?"

"It starts with the recognition that you're in enormous, debilitating emotional pain—coupled with a desire to heal and a willingness to address what you're feeling with wisdom and courage," Devlin said.

"I'm listening," Cook said, after several seconds of silence.

"Are you?"

"Well, I haven't told you to fuck off yet, have I?"

The two of them laughed.

Devlin filled Cook in on his background as a cop, the emotional trauma he'd faced after his line-of-duty shooting, and the recent formation of COPS, to assist police officers in coping with the emotional impact of the job.

"I think you'd benefit from what we do," he said. "If you think it's a waste of your time," he added, jokingly, "you can always shoot me in the head."

Cook thought that was funny. She was also intrigued. There was something reassuring in the tone of Devlin's voice, wisdom in his words. The two of them remained on the phone for nearly an hour. At the end of their conversation, much to Cook's surprise, she agreed to meet Devlin at his Manhattan office.

* * *

Landon Devlin cut to the chase shortly upon Cook's visit, several days after their introductory phone call.

"So, things aren't going according to the 'script' you wrote for yourself when you started on the job, are they?" asked Devlin, taking a seat at his desk after greeting Cook at the door.

"That's an understatement," Cook said, wryly.

Off-duty, she was dressed in civvies—bell-bottom jeans, peasant-style blouse, and wedge sandals—her hair falling loose and curly to her shoulders.

"Thought you'd be like Angie Dickinson in *Policewoman* when you joined the NYPD, huh?" Devlin chuckled. "Or maybe like one of 'Charlie's Angels.'"

Cook, embarrassed, lowered her eyes.

"Seriously," Devlin said. "The truth is that *nothing* about police work goes according to anyone's script … and the biggest dreamers fall the hardest."

"Guess so," Cook sighed.

Devlin eyeballed her closely. "You were a dreamer, weren't you, Rachel?"

Cook nodded. "I suppose."

"Had a bushel of misconceptions about what it was like to be a cop, didn't you?"

"Uh-huh."

"You were going to help save the city, right? Break new ground? Leave a mark? Show the world that women could handle police work as well, or even better, than men?"

"All of those things, I suppose," Cook said and shrugged.

"Then you got slapped around pretty hard, didn't you?" Devlin asked. "Woke up to the harsh realities?"

Cook eyed Devlin guardedly, unsure what to think. He was a fellow cop and apparently knew the landscape—that helped. He was also strikingly handsome and seemingly able to see to the depths of Cook's soul. Still, his confident, easygoing demeanor was more than a bit disquieting. Cook wasn't sure if Devlin was too good to be true. She tried to resist the instinct to ward him off. She wanted to trust someone, anyone—needed to, desperately.

"Being a cop has stirred up a hornet's nest of emotions, isn't that right?" Devlin inquired.

Cook nodded wordlessly.

"Disturbed by the politics, the bureaucracy, the gamesmanship?"

"Uh-huh."

"And the way police officers are scorned by much of the public?"

"That, too."

"Feeling misunderstood, under siege, and angry at the world?"

Cook tried to muster a laugh.

"You've also changed, haven't you, Rachel?" Devlin said. "You're a different person now than you once were—though you're not entirely comfortable with who you've become, and you're not sure you like yourself anymore, right?"

Cook nodded. *Who the hell is this guy*? she thought.

"On top of everything," Devlin said, "your politics have changed, you've grown hardened and callous, untrusting and disillusioned, maybe more bigoted than you once were. You're wondering if the price you're paying for being a cop is worth it. You feel confused, conflicted, numb to your emotions, and very much alone."

"All of those things," Cook confessed.

Then Devlin really hit a raw spot. "And I'll bet that you're probably upset to no end over the fact that your partner fatally shot that boy, and you were there to witness it, right? Heartbroken? Shocked? Upset by the racial politics? Frightened and demoralized by how you and your partner have been demonized and your lives torn to shreds."

Cook felt something inside her become unhinged. Unwittingly, her eyes began to well as all of it bobbed to the surface—a floodtide of emotion, everything she tried so desperately to hold at bay, vivid and harrowing as the instant it occurred.

Struggling to contain herself, Cook began to tremble, growing cold and clammy, on the verge of tears. Devlin reached across his desk and offered her a box of tissues.

"It's okay, Rachel," he said. "Acknowledging that those feelings are there, bottled up inside of you, is the first step to keep from drowning—the *only* way."

Blowing her nose, Cook took a deep breath, struggling to compose herself.

"I suspect that there's lots of things you'd probably like to unburden yourself from," Devlin said.

"I wouldn't know where to start," Cook stammered.

"You can start," said Devlin, "by talking about everything that you feel."

"There's no one," Cook said, "for me to talk to."

"You can talk to me," Devlin said, reassuringly. "And it may help to know that you're not as alone as you may think."

"What do you mean?" Cook sniffled.

"Like many others, you've been through a terrible trauma," Devlin explained. "Officers, like you, who've witnessed a civilian shooting, can be deeply troubled, even if they weren't the person who shot. Keeping your feelings bottled up only makes things worse."

"I suppose so," Cook said, softening.

"But I suspect it's more than just a singular event that's troubling you," Devlin said. "More is going on inside of you than just the C. J. Johnson shooting."

"What are you ... a mind reader?" Cook joked, trying to cut the tension.

"No," Devlin said, "just a fellow cop who understands that police work is a pressure cooker. Every day you deal with powerful emotions, things you can't make sense of or control, things you have no answer for and can't hide from. You see the worst in people, problems you can't begin to solve. You deal with all kinds of demoralizing bureaucratic bullshit. You've got complex, multiple roles to play—doctor, lawyer, psychiatrist, marriage counselor, peacemaker, referee ... sometimes even God."

Cook chuckled, feeling unburdened simply by acknowledging what Devlin was saying.

"As if playing all those roles isn't tough enough," Devlin continued, "you get to play them in front of supervisors, politicians, judges, special interests, the media, civilian review boards, you name it. Months or even years of trauma, stress, and suppressed feelings accumulate. Eventually, your emotional machinery breaks down. You start having trouble functioning. You lose your balance, feel like you're drowning. Things that once were understandable suddenly don't make sense."

Devlin paused, and then smiled.

"Imagine a bucket in a rainfall," he said. "If it keeps raining, what happens?"

"The bucket overflows," said Cook.

"Exactly. And that's what's happening to you now, Rachel. It's common among rookie cops. Veterans, too. Truth is there's an army of people who struggle with the demands that police work puts on them. The job wounds a lot of people, breaks a lot of hearts."

"It does ... doesn't it?" Cook said.

Devlin chuckled. "Do you have any idea what the statistics are on alcoholism, emotional exhaustion, heart disease, and divorce among cops? Do you know how many cops suffer from ulcers and backaches and headaches and skin disorders and muscle spasms and chronic fatigue and hypertension related to stress? Do you know how high the rate of police suicide is? And you know what? No one, other than cops, really gives a damn."

Devlin chuckled, drawing a faint smile from Cook.

"It's sad, but true," he said. "Cops have no one to talk to, no means for learning to deal with the job's demands. Most police departments aren't equipped to assist their people, and the public doesn't care. The public has voided cops of all human characteristics. We're cardboard cutouts to them, not human beings with feelings and problems."

Devlin rose from his chair, walked around to where Cook was sitting, and sat on the edge of his desk.

"You know what the biggest miracle about police work is?" he said. "It's that most cops manage to do it. Don't ask me how, but they do. They manage to handle the job and still function as human beings. It's amazing how resilient people can be, how they can weather the worst of storms and still find a way to carry on."

Devlin stared at Cook, his intensity almost hypnotizing. "Maybe you'd like to figure that out, too," he said.

And by the end of their meeting, Cook had decided that was precisely what she wanted to try—and agreed to attend a trial session at COPS.

Chapter 62

WITH HIS HOUSEHOLD DEBT MOUNTING, and the duration of his unpaid suspension indeterminate, Matt Holland took another job while awaiting the grand jury's ruling on his fate. The job was with Ray Maglio, as a construction supervisor at the homebuilding and remodeling company that Katie's father owned.

Well into the pre-holiday construction season now, RM Builders was especially busy with projects, pushing to pour foundations and frame houses prior to the onset of winter. Before long, Matt was working twelve-hour days, interrupted only to attend weekly meetings at COPS—group sessions that were proving highly beneficial. As Landon Devlin had said, there was much to be gained when officers were courageous enough to acknowledge their pent-up emotions and open themselves up to people who cared. Being outdoors at work was also helping Matt cope. It felt satisfying to be on construction sites in the bracing fall weather, to be building things instead of seeing them destroyed.

Better yet, was to finally have his twin daughters home from their lengthy exile, and Thomas once again fully involved in school, friendships, and his favorite pastimes. Even with the grave uncertainties that hovered over their family, the sights and sounds of children filled Matt and Katie with a joy they'd all but forgotten was possible. With all three children seemingly at ease again, and off-duty cops no longer guarding their house, the air of anxiety that had enveloped the household was no longer as palpable. Matt no longer avoided family interaction or eschewed household chores or paced the house endlessly at night. He no longer felt himself suffocated by grief or frightened of the dark. On the rare occasions when he couldn't sleep, he calmed himself by sitting on the landing outside the children's bedrooms and listening to the peaceful sounds of their sleep. He and Katie had even begun making love again, finding pleasure in each other's arms, in laughter and touching and physical release.

Ray Maglio, in recent days, had also approached Matt with an enticing offer to ponder.

"Listen, Matt," his father-in-law said late one afternoon. "Things are busier than ever these days at our company."

"That's great," Matt said and smiled. "Good for business."

Katie's father hesitated, groping for the right words.

"What I'm trying to say," he began, "is I know you've always loved being a police officer, but with everything you've gone through, I'm wondering if you might want to consider coming to work with us."

"I already am," Matt said.

"No, Matty," his father-in-law said. "I'm talking permanently."

Ray Maglio rubbed a finger across his forehead. His hands were gnarly and callused—workmen's hands like those of Holland's father.

"I'm not sure I understand what you're saying," Matt said.

"You've put in your time on the NYPD, Matty," Ray elaborated. "Sixteen years, and a hell of a job. You know how proud we are of you. But maybe you want to think about letting someone else take their turn now?"

"You mean, pack it in as a cop?"

"Only you can decide that," Katie's father said. "I know you're sitting on a solid pension if you make it on the job twenty years. I'm just asking if you'd give some thought to coming to work with me."

"Oh, I don't know."

"Just think about it," Ray Maglio said. "And I hope you notice I said *with* me ... not *for* me. The truth is, Matt, I'm slowing down and the work isn't getting any easier. We're growing by leaps and bounds, and I can't run this company by myself anymore."

He hesitated again, saying, "Thing is, I could use a partner."

"A partner?"

"Yeah." Ray Maglio nodded. "The only thing missing from my business now is someone to share it with and take it over when I call it quits. I want you as a partner, Matty, because that's what you're like to me. More than that, you're like a son."

Matt drew his father-in-law toward him, and the two men embraced.

"You know everything that I'm facing, don't you?" Matt asked. "The suspension, the grand jury, possible criminal charges, the fallout from the shooting."

"None of that matters," Ray Maglio said. "If God forbid you get charged with a crime, the job will be there for you through the outcome of your trial. If worse yet you go to jail, the job will be there when you're released. Either way, you can start tomorrow, for a hell of a lot more money than you were earning as a cop. The other stuff makes no difference. I know what kind of man you are. That's all that counts."

"Well, I'm flattered and honored that you asked," Matt said, promising that he'd discuss the offer with Katie and give it some serious thought.

Chapter 63

AFTER ATTENDING her third meeting at COPS, Rachel Cook was pulled aside by Landon Devlin on her way out the door.

"I'm not sure I want you attending our meetings anymore," Devlin deadpanned, "unless you'll let me take you to dinner."

Cook was caught off guard. Not only was Devlin's invitation wholly unexpected, but also it had been so long since any man whom Cook even remotely trusted or found attractive had asked her for a date, that she stumbled awkwardly in offering a response.

"Hey," Devlin joked, "is having dinner with me so horrifying a prospect?"

"Not at all," Cook said and smiled. "I just haven't gotten many dinner offers lately."

"You probably haven't felt you'd be very good company, have you?"

"No," Cook sighed. "I guess I haven't."

"Well, how about you let someone else be the judge of that?" Devlin asked. "Give yourself a chance, Rachel. You might be pleasantly surprised."

Cook did. And she was.

After her next COPS meeting, she and Devlin escaped to a local seafood restaurant, near the Lower Manhattan waterfront. Seated dockside, they could see the lights of Battery Park reflecting off the inky waters of New York Harbor. Pleasure boats bobbed on their moorings. Cargo ships and ocean liners, their funnels and running lights aglow, moved across the harbor on their way to sea.

"Feeling any better these days?" asked Devlin, candlelight dancing in his eyes.

"I'm calmer," Cook said.

"Why is that?"

"Mostly, I'm listening to what others in COPS are saying," Cook said. "I realize now that I'm not as alone with my feelings as I thought. That helps a lot."

"Actually," said Devlin, "that's half the battle."

"And the other half?"

"The other half is mustering the courage to get your own feelings on the table. Understand them. Confront them. Talk. Deal with them."

"I'm trying," Cook said as she sipped from a glass of wine. "It doesn't feel very good, building a wall around myself and hiding."

"It will only make your torment worse," Devlin said.

"I understand that now."

And as they shared a lobster dinner, Cook began practicing what Devlin had preached for the past three weeks: she began opening herself up in a way that she'd thought was no longer possible. Haltingly, at times tearfully, she related how the C. J. Johnson shooting and its racially charged aftermath had left her once-promising career in ruins, stripping away her innocence, her illusions, her faith. She talked about the meaningful work that she and Matt Holland had done prior to that fateful night; about her demoralizing transfer to Coney Island; about the public scorn she'd endured, her rejection by male cops, and the degradation of conducting strip searches. She confessed to her newfound loss of confidence, her solitude and emptiness, her numbness and self-loathing, her confusion and fear, and admitted how her pent-up frustration and rage had erupted with her beating of the teenaged arrestee Jane Doe.

All of it came pouring out, like torrents of water from a cloudburst. Cook talked about the racism, the stereotypes, the hypocrisy, and the contempt she'd witnessed from so many sides—Black and White, politicians and bureaucrats, anti- and pro-police advocates—and about how soiled and disheartened it made her feel. She talked about her childhood memories of Brownsville and Coney Island, and how those memories were painfully juxtaposed over the desolation and poverty she witnessed as a cop. She talked about how neighborhoods that were once vibrant and secure had become dumping grounds for the indigent and cold-hearted killing grounds for children like C. J. Johnson.

Cook talked, too, about how vastly the past thirteen months had changed her, transforming her into someone she was uncomfortable with, so unlike the woman she once was, the woman she wanted and needed to be.

"I hate what the job has done to me," she said, misty-eyed in the light of the tabletop's candle. "To be honest with you, I'm not even sure who I am anymore."

"Who do you think you are?" Devlin asked.

"I'm this callous, untrusting, angry bitch who has retreated into a shell and convinced herself that the world is a hostile, ugly place," Cook said. "I'm someone who's at war with everyone and everything, including myself. Suspicious. Unapproachable. Cynical. Hardened. Jaded."

"And unhappy?"

"Yes … that, too."

Cook sipped her wine, treading on sensitive, uncomfortable turf—ready to go, at Devlin's tacit invitation, a step further.

"The shooting, the riots, the anti-police demonstrations, the politics, the job itself—all of it has turned me inside out," she confessed. "The person I once was has been colored over by a new personality, a new way of viewing the world. I don't see things the same way I once did. I've built an impenetrable wall around myself and won't let anyone near me. I'm not sure if the person I once was even exists anymore, or if I want to be who the job has changed me into."

"You're a cop now, Rachel," Devlin said. "What's happened to you comes with the turf."

"That's precisely my point," Cook said. "Becoming a cop was the best thing I ever did with my life—before the shooting and all that's happened since. Now … I just don't know."

"What don't you know?"

"I don't know," said Cook, "if I can continue on the job."

"You'd *quit* the NYPD?"

Cook sighed. "I'm not sure that the NYPD can give me what I need."

"Well, maybe you're looking at it for all the wrong things," Devlin said.

"What does that mean?"

"What it means, Rachel, is that police departments are bureaucracies. They're not human. You can't allow yourself to be dependent on them for things they can't possibly provide. You've got to find the things you need from other people. And you've got to find them within yourself."

"I'm not sure," said Cook, "that I can."

Cook looked away, holding her emotions at bay. Devlin reached across the table and gently laid his hand atop hers. It was the first time in months that Cook had been touched by another person expressing something other than revulsion or contempt. Instinctively, she began drawing her hand back, but left it where it was. The gesture made her privately shudder. Devlin smiled.

"Sure, you've changed, Rachel," he said. "Every cop undergoes a metamorphosis. It's inevitable."

"Inevitable?"

"Uh-huh. For most people being a cop is a rude awakening. The novelty wears off quickly. Expectations shattered. Ideals get tested, illusions crumble, your entire mindset changes."

"The job," said Cook, "shocks the hell out of you."

"Sure, it does," Devlin said. "You're shocked that nothing is the way you imagined it, shocked at the way people live, shocked that leadership is often unsupportive, and your training is inadequate, and the public doesn't welcome you with open arms, and the criminal justice system is just another unwieldy, dysfunctional beast that tears the heart out of you."

"Shocked?" Cook chuckled. "That's a good way of describing it."

"Yeah," said Devlin, "but it's also just the beginning. Police work literally devours people, Rachel. It redefines you, gives you a new personality, a whole new psychology. You become seasoned, the 'streetwise cop.' You sound like a cop and think like a cop. Your view of the world is the cop's view. Your personality is the cop's personality."

"Seasoned, huh?" Cook said. "Sounds kind of sad."

"Maybe," Devlin said, "but in many ways it's also necessary. Becoming 'seasoned' is a cop's ticket to survival out on the street. The only problem is that for every survival technique you pick up, there's a casualty—innocence, idealism, sometimes faith and hope. That's just the way it is. It comes with the tin. Sometimes, it bothers people—all the things that they're losing. Sometimes, it bothers people that they can't turn the police personality on and off, when they clock in and out of work each day."

"I feel that way," Cook said. "All the time."

"And you probably feel a lot more," Devlin said. "It's easy to get apathetic, for instance. And why not? You're out there busting your ass, but you feel like your hands are tied. The problems are unsolvable, but you're asked to solve them. You feel that you care but no one else really gives a damn."

"After a while," Cook interjected, "you feel like it's a losing battle, like you're just shoveling shit against the tide."

"Of course," Devlin said and smiled. "But you fight those feelings, too, don't you? You don't want to feel hopeless, don't want to be someone who just punches a clock and goes home. So, you fight not to let it wear you down and scar you. But after a while, you find that in many ways you're simply going through the motions. That's all you can really do. You hate the system for wounding you, making you feel empty and cheated. You hate it for what it does to good, honest, caring people like you. But you can't fight it. It's too powerful. It defeats you. Then you hate yourself for that even more."

Devlin drained his wine, caught a waiter's attention, and ordered another two glasses. Cook's hand remained tucked beneath his on the tabletop.

"It's the same thing when it comes to people," he said. "You start off really caring, really *giving*. But all too often you find that you're unwanted, unappreciated, shunned. You don't want your attitude toward people to change. After all, you're there to help. But you start hating people for hating you. You can't help it. It's only human."

"It hurts the way people see you as some vile stereotype," Cook said.

"Sure, it hurts," Devlin agreed. "And after a while, you say to yourself: 'I know these people are poor. I know they're facing circumstances I can't even imagine—but screw this. I don't deserve the abuse.' Then you say, 'Hey, enough emotional fragility. Enough feeling sorry for myself. Enough getting stung. People see me as a hollow, malevolent, racial stereotype? Fine, I'll see them the same way. People spit at me? Okay, I'll spit back. Fuck it.' You no longer care if it's right or wrong. And you hurt over that, too."

"Then eventually," Cook said, "that hurt goes away, just like the other hurt."

"Precisely," Devlin said. "You start seeing things in a different light. You get used to it, learn to live with it. You realize that things aren't going to change, so *you* better change. You get acclimated, learn what it takes to get by, drop the excess baggage. After a while, nothing is so shocking or disturbing or painful anymore. You retreat behind your armor. It's all a defense mechanism, a way of preventing yourself from being further hurt."

Cook shrugged. "I guess it's the only way to cope."

"Uh-huh," Devlin nodded. "You need a way of masking your disappointment, of demeaning the value of the prize you can't attain. You convince yourself that none of it was ever that important in the first place. It's easier to shrug and say, 'Hey, it's just a way to make a living.' It doesn't hurt as much. Only, inwardly, it hurts in a different kind of way, because now you hate yourself for not caring or for being unable to admit you still really do care."

"It gets pretty complicated, doesn't it?" Cook asked.

"Yeah," said Devlin, "but you've got to find a way to get through it. You can't let the job defeat you or rob the essence of the person you are. You need to find a way to lift yourself out of the muck. You need to find a way to get back up when the job knocks you down."

"How do I do that?"

"You look for balance, Rachel," Devlin smiled. "You find something good and hang onto it for as long as you can. Just like there's darkness, there's light. Find it … and the darkness goes away."

Devlin's smile was warm and sincere. Cook turned her palm over and held his hand, feeling something inside her melt, like a candle in heat.

"Push your pain aside and find the light, Rachel," Devlin said. "Be the person you really are inside, the person you want the world to see."

"I'll try," Cook vowed.

"Good." Devlin winked. "And maybe we can even do dinner again?"

"Sure." Cook smiled, warmly. "Maybe we can even make a habit out of it."

Chapter 64

Back at work for nearly four months now, Charles Johnson had long ago settled into his daily routine as a Transit Authority token clerk, his job offering a measure of escape from the tragedy that had transformed his life. It was a source of both comfort and reflection, Charles found, to once again be spending eight-hour workdays in the underground caverns of New York, far from the limelight and the racially charged hubbub surrounding his son's fatal shooting.

A metaphor for the city's crumbling subway system, the Montrose Avenue station was dimly lit, its walls grimy and scrawled with graffiti, its platforms scented with tunnel dust and the creosote used to preserve the railroad ties.

Charles's token booth was located at the far end of the city-bound platform, adjacent to a trio of wooden turnstiles and a stairwell leading to the street. There wasn't much inside the cramped, wooden booth, aside from a token dispenser, a cash safe, a fire extinguisher, and an emergency switch that could cut power to the third rail. Charles supplied a portable fan for the dog days of summer, and an electric space heater he utilized on wintry days, when the token booth was as frigid as the street above.

Charles's duties, though loftier than his former job cleaning subway cars, were not especially taxing, except for the two-hour window during the weekday commuter rush, when a steady stream of straphangers queued up to purchase their thirty-cent fare to Manhattan and other stops. In contrast, the balance of Charles's workday was tedious enough so that, often as not, he could busy himself by reading the newspapers or listening to music and ballgames on a tiny transistor radio. Near the conclusion of each shift, he'd gather his turnstile keys, metal token pail and portable alarm transmitter, and leave his booth to empty the turnstiles. Then, he'd use a mechanical counter to run the tokens and secure the day's receipts inside the safe until a Transit Authority agent, escorted by a cop, arrived to collect the money and deliver new tokens.

Other than that, Charles's workdays were quiet but for the roar of subway trains entering and exiting the station at twelve-minute intervals. There was a great deal of time for contemplation. And there was certainly much to think about.

Charles thought about all that had transpired over the past four anguished months. He thought about his frantic race to the hospital on the night C. J. was shot, and how he'd held his son inside the police car, stroking the boy's blood-swaddled head while whispering words of comfort and reassurance. He thought about his vigil at the hospital with the Rev. Josiah Watson, and how the two of them had prayed for C. J.'s survival and the courage to endure should the worst happen. He thought about how C. J.'s funeral procession had wound through the streets of Brownsville to the Good Shepherd Baptist Church, where Charles had offered a gesture of reconciliation, healing, and hope, asking that mourners honor C. J. by curbing the racial discord wrought by his death. He thought about how distinguished men from the NAACP, the ACLU, and other organizations had sought his support for lawsuits aimed at holding police accountable for civil-rights violations against Blacks. He thought about how C. J. had been laid to rest near Charles's birthplace in South Carolina.

So much had happened in a scant four months; so much of consequence had changed. Charles thought about how the anti-police riots had ravaged Brownsville, and how troubled he was not only by the ruinous violence but by how he felt vaguely responsible for what had happened, since it was C. J.'s shooting that had sparked the upheaval. He thought about the racial discord wracking New York, and how the animus was usually so shrouded by a patina of calm that people would forget it was forever present, toxic and volatile, just beneath the surface. He thought about the politics tied to the incident:

... how Matt Holland had been made a scapegoat for police sins of the past.

... how Mayor Nathan Worth, boosted by a surge in Black support, had eked out a victory in his re-election bid, naming William Dunne to another term as police commissioner, and carrying Hal Green to another term as Kings County D.A.

... how police reformists battled with reactionaries over recruitment, training, use-of-force policies, anti-bias practices, crisis intervention, oversight issues, and the culture of policing.

Equally disturbing to Charles was the fact that C. J.'s death had in many ways assumed symbolic proportions that completely obscured how the shooting had impacted the lives of the people tied most closely to it. No one, Charles thought, gave more than a passing thought about those people; no one truly cared. Each of the principals in the tragedy had become, in their own way, objectified, their identities lost amidst the rhetoric and hysteria. C. J. Johnson had become the proverbial Innocent Black Boy Slain by Racist White Cops, his death a cause célèbre in America's decades-long race war. Matt Holland and Rachel Cook had become proxies for every poorly trained, racist cop who'd ever fired their gun in the line of duty. Charles had become the self-serving, heartless, get-rich-quick bloodsucker out to profit off his own son's death. Everyone else—anti-police demonstrators, civil rights leaders, NYPD officials, City Hall politicians, the media, the PBA, the city's cops—had similar roles to play. Facts were secondary, truth clouded by emotion, bias, and personal agendas. No one saw beyond the stereotypes, the hubbub, the contentious issues surrounding the shooting.

Charles thought, too, about how his own personal dream—a hope-filled life free of the Jim Crow racism he'd faced in the South—stood in such stark contrast to the city's current circumstance. C.J.'s shooting had exposed such discouraging fault lines, opened such grievous wounds. In some ways, it seemed as if race relations were no better in New York on America's two-hundredth birthday than in Claymont during the 1920s, and the five decades of progress made by the civil rights movement hadn't truly changed a thing.

Would Charles ever witness anything other than the same racial enmity that for centuries had yielded mistrust and conflict in America?

Would the state of race relations ever become less charged with prejudice, stereotypes, and fear?

When legislation, policy, or judicial rulings ever really matter if people's hearts and minds didn't change?

Would people ever see what they had in common as human beings, rather than what divides them?

Charles thought about all those things, and about how his life would never be the same. Mostly, though, he thought about C. J.—conversations they'd had; moments they'd shared; struggles they'd overcome; connections they'd made.

He thought about how he'd taken C. J. and Marcus on their subway trips around the city, and to ballgames at Yankee and Shea Stadiums. He thought about how father and son had watched on their tiny, black-and-white TV when the Knicks made their championship runs in '69 and '73, and how the entire family had celebrated with pizzas and soda when the Mets won their first World Series in '69. He thought about how he'd helped C. J. with reading and math; how they'd shot hoops at Lincoln Terrace Park, and gone swimming at the Betsy Head pool, and cheered Fly Williams and the other streetball greats at the Soul in the Hole basketball courts, in the heart of the projects.

Charles thought, too, about the Labor Day Weekend camping trips that C. J. attended with other special-needs kids—the annual, three-day trips that had been organized by cops from the 73rd Precinct; the trips on which C. J. had learned how to start a campfire and pitch a tent; the trips on which he'd hiked through the upstate foliage and watched flights of hawks circle overhead and saw stars aglow for the first time ever in the nighttime sky; the same trips on which C. J. had met a Brownsville police officer who had paid the boy such special attention.

Charles thought about how he had always wanted to thank that officer for taking such a special interest in C. J., and for treating him so kindly. He thought about how he'd asked around Brownsville in recent weeks, to confirm the identity of the officer. He also thought about how much he wanted to hate that officer now—but how, strangely, he didn't feel hatred at all, mostly just compassion and sorrow. It was profoundly ironic, Charles thought, that the police officer who'd taken C. J. under his wing and made the boy feel so special on those camping trips was the very same officer who'd wound up taking C. J.'s life.

And now, alone in his token booth, Charles came to the quiet realization that it was highly likely that the police officer who'd slain his son had been honest in his account of the incident, and that the shooting had indeed been a tragic accident wrought by an unfortunate confluence of circumstance—and absent of callousness, malice, or regard to race.

Charles Johnson, a Black man, wanted to hate Matt Holland, a White cop, for taking from him that which was most cherished—his beloved, only son—and for wounding Charles so grievously and testing his faith in God. But now he wished there was some way he could reach out to the officer and let him know that, even with his son's death, Charles was able to see beyond emotion and race, beyond bitterness and prejudice, beyond politics and polemics.

He was able to see the truth.

Somehow, Charles wanted to let Matt Holland know that he recognized that the officer and his family—like Charles and his—was wounded and aggrieved; that he knew Matt Holland, at his core, was a good and honorable man, and a dedicated public servant; that Charles held the officer blameless in C. J.'s death and forgave him for everything that had transpired; that he'd thought about Matt Holland a great deal and wished the officer no further harm.

Chapter 65

RACHEL COOK RETURNED to patrol duties in Coney Island, more determined than ever to stumble upon the kind of radiant, transcendent moment that Landon Devlin assured her was out there waiting to be found—a kind word, a grateful gesture, any nugget of buried treasure that Cook could unearth to rekindle her passion for police work and rediscover the officer, and the woman, she desperately wanted to be.

She didn't have to wait long to find it.

A scant three days after her dinner with Devlin, Cook was working a midnight-to-eight tour alongside a male partner named Tony Silvestri. It was a frigid, moonlit night, unusually light for a Saturday in Coney Island, when Cook and Silvestri were summoned to respond to an emergency call for an aided case requiring medical assistance. They pulled their patrol car up to a rundown tenement on a dilapidated, dead-end thoroughfare eerily reminiscent of Brownsville's Amboy Street. Cook shuddered when the pair of officers clambered up the front stoop.

When they entered the building, a young, Hispanic man greeted them in the vestibule. He was frantic, clad in grease-stained, mechanic's work clothes. His name, he said, was Nestor Alvarez.

Conversing in broken Spanish, Nestor quickly led Cook and Silvestri to his ground-floor apartment. There, the officers found the man's wife, Rosa, in the throes of an intense, premature labor. Lying in the couple's bed, covered by a thin, woolen blanket, Rosa was breathing in rapid, shallow bursts. Her amniotic sac had already ruptured, and her cervical contractions regular and strong.

Instantly, Cook rushed to the woman's bedside, reaching for her utility belt, pulling her radio free, and summoning an ambulance. Tony Silvestri stood flummoxed, immobile.

"What's your wife's name?" Cook called to Nestor.

"Rosa," Nestor replied. "Her name is Rosa."

"Rosa!" Cook turned to the young woman. "Try to relax. Breathe in and out, in and out. An ambulance will be here soon."

Nestor, clutching his wife's hand, translated Cook's instructions.

"Respirar!" he said, frantically. "Respirar! Respirar!"

Biting her lip, Rosa clutched her blanket tightly, her abdomen bulging, her fingertips turning white, rivers of sweat running down her face. Stupefied and helpless, Silvestri retreated to a corner, quaking. Nestor, following Cook's command, raced to the kitchen and brought a damp washcloth, placing it on Rosa's forehead and tamping down gently. Rosa cut loose a scream as a powerful contraction tore through her, then moaned and began to breathe shallowly, in and out, in and out.

"Oh, my God, it's coming!" she screamed in Spanish. "The baby's coming now!"

Cook pulled the blanket off of Rosa, her massive belly bulging as if it would burst. Cook knew that they couldn't wait another minute. The infant was crowning, its tiny head, black-haired and bloody.

"This baby's coming *now*!" Cook yelled. "Tell Rosa to push down hard!" she said, turning to Nestor. "Breathe and push! Breathe and push!"

"Respirar y empuja!" Nestor shouted. "Respira y empuja!"

Rosa pushed for all she was worth, grunting and sliding down the bed, contractions gripping her like a vise. Nestor held her hand and cradled her head. Cook then climbed onto the bed and, on her knees, positioned herself between Rosa's legs. Rosa clamped down and pushed, grunting sharply, again and again. Through the darkness between Rosa's thighs, Cook could see more and more of the infant. Nestor shouted encouragement in Spanish, calling out Rosa's name, crying, praying. Tony Silvestri crouched in a corner of the room, wide-eyed, speechless, unmoving.

Cook then reached toward Rosa, feeling—for the first time in her life—the tiny body of a newborn, wet and slippery, soft and smooth. Rosa pushed again, as Cook pulled gently from around the infant's waist, her hands sliding along its body to just under its tiny, fragile shoulders. The infant wailed, faintly and haltingly at first, and then louder and more persistently. Rosa exhaled, then drew in air and pushed again with all her strength. From the innards of her womb, the remainder of the newborn slid out, its purple-red umbilical cord slick with blood and meconium, its form taking shape in Cook's hands, wailing and squirming and alive. Nestor gasped. Silvestri let out a sigh. Rosa sobbed with joy. And Cook—her uniform flecked with droplets of amniotic fluid and sticky, green meconium—held the couple's newborn son, like a tiny football, in the crook of an arm.

"It's a *boy*!" Nestor shouted joyously. "*El nino muchacho*!"

He began to laugh and cry together, all at the same time.

"*A boy! A boy*!"

Nestor then covered Rosa with the blanket and Cook gently placed the newborn on his mother's chest before climbing off the bed and watching as the new parents gently enfolded the infant, speaking to him gleefully, caressing his face and his head and his tiny, pink hands.

"Thank you!" Nestor exclaimed, looking at the portrait of Jesus Christ above the bed, and then at Cook. "Gracias! Gracias!"

He embraced Cook warmly, and then pumped Silvestri's hand.

"Your son looks like you," Silvestri said, and the young father beamed.

Cook and Silvestri remained with Nestor and Rosa Alvarez, laughing, making small talk, and admiring the infant until paramedics arrived, some fifteen minutes later.

"Everything's under control … thanks to this beautiful woman here!" Silvestri told the ambulance attendants, nodding at Cook.

The EMS crew attended to the new mother and her infant. Then, her umbilical cord severed, they placed the Rosa on a rolling stretcher for the ride to the hospital. Cook walked alongside, cradling the infant, calm and bundled now in a blanket. On the street, a crowd watched as Rosa's stretcher was hoisted into the ambulance.

"Vaya con dios!" Rosa Alvarez said, as they placed her inside the rig.

"Vaya con dios!" Cook replied. "And good luck with your new son."

Before he climbed into the ambulance next to his wife, Nestor Alvarez shook Silvestri's hand once again, and then embraced Cook. When he pulled away, he glanced at the nametag on the breast pocket of Cook's reefer.

"Officer Cook?"

"Yes."

"Please … tell me your first name."

"It's Rachel."

"Ah-ha," he grinned, broadly. "*Rachel Cook.*"

And then he climbed into the ambulance, to accompany his wife to the hospital.

"We were lucky today," he said in broken English. "We were lucky you were the one who came."

"I was just doing my job," Cook said.

"And we'll always remember how well you did it!" Nestor said. "We'll always remember your name and the gift you gave us this night! Gracias, senorita! Thank you!"

Nestor's words filled Cook up, and there was nothing she could say. Whatever gift she'd bestowed on the new parents, she thought, had been reciprocated a thousand times over. Cook felt as if she was flying over the rooftops of Coney Island. Having been so pained by the deaths of children over the past thirteen months, she felt profoundly moved over having brought a newborn child into the world and giving his parents such joy. She watched the ambulance pull from the curb and disappear around a street corner on its way to the hospital. And for the first time in what seemed like a lifetime, she heard the sound of applause riffle through the crowd, and people cheering for something she'd done as a cop.

* * *

Night was lifting by the time Cook clocked out, and a powdery snow was descending on Coney Island, blanketing the boardwalk, the beach, and the tired, old amusement park in a gentle, white shroud.

Warmed by the birth of the Alvarez baby, Cook stood on the steps of the 60th Precinct and watched as the morning, murky and gray, slowly brightened. The neighborhood was quiet now, looking whitewashed and pristine, free of the ruinous scars it had sustained through the years. The way it looked just then it wasn't impossible for Cook to believe she might hear the hopeful cry of yet another infant, or the whisper of other new beginnings.

Maybe it was naïve to presume that things could begin anew in neighborhoods like Brownsville and Coney Island but Cook caught a momentary glimpse of how they might begin anew for her. Maybe it just took moments like these to see things with clarity, she thought. Maybe, as Landon Devlin had said, all she needed to do as a cop was to catch some special call—some glorious, magical moment—then cling to it through the darkness and the doubt, and let it lift her to a place that felt special and right.

She wasn't sure she entirely understood how all of that worked—not fully, not yet. But standing by herself in front of the station house, something became clear to Cook. Maybe the story she'd write for herself as a cop wasn't going to be the grand and glorious symphony she'd envisioned—just a quiet, simple melody she could hum to herself whenever she needed to feel good. Maybe she'd just have to accept the police job for what it was, and not punish herself because it wasn't what she'd thought it would be.

Being a police officer, Cook could finally see, would never go according to some innocent, preordained plan, or be as predictable and perfect as a fantasy. It was a lot like life itself in that way, she thought—chaotic and messy and full of rough edges and unexpected spills. If you were smart enough and strong enough, maybe you'd eventually see that all you could ever really do was take what it dished out, try to roll with the punches, and keep coming back until it all somehow worked out. Some days you'd mourn, other days you'd exult. And most of the time, if you were lucky, you'd find some sort of balance that could help you buy some much-needed inner peace. The key was to grab it, as tightly as you could, and hang on for the ride.

Cook left the 60th Precinct station house then, another tour over. It was one of the job's many ironies, she thought. It had taken awhile to get to the place she found herself now, but this was exactly the way Cook had dreamed about ending her days as a cop—tired but charged, her mind lit up and alive, all the pieces fitting, feeling worthwhile and engaged and fully reconciled to all she was going through. She still couldn't predict how it would all work out. Maybe the assignment she'd once dreamed about—to an elite NYPD unit or to federal law enforcement—would come after all. Maybe it wouldn't. For the moment, however, it hardly mattered.

All Cook knew for now was that she was coming back tomorrow—coming back to see if she could find answers and meaning; coming back to find higher ground; coming back to see if there'd be other mornings like this, and other good and grateful people she'd meet along the way. People like Nestor and Rosa Alvarez. People who were happy she was on the job. People who'd always remember her name.

Chapter 66

IT ENDED AS IT BEGAN, shortly after Christmas, with a simple telephone call.

Six torturous months earlier, a 911 call from a Brownsville resident had summoned Matt Holland and Rachel Cook to an apartment-building cellar for a tragic encounter between the two white officers and an innocent Black teen, triggering a racial conflagration that transformed lives, ravaged America's greatest city, and sparked a debate that would last for decades over the relationship between police and minority communities in America.

Now, a second phone call, placed this time by Kings County District Attorney Hal Green, notified City Hall officials that the grand jury convened to consider criminal charges in the contentious police-shooting case had rendered its decision. The verdict, Green said, would be announced at a noon press conference at the U.S. District Courthouse.

Green's phone call triggered an immediate chain reaction. Within minutes, newspaper, TV and radio reporters, and camera crews were being dispatched to the Emanuel Cellar Federal Building, where shouting, sign-carrying demonstrators on both sides of the controversy were already squaring off behind wooden police barricades. NYPD reinforcements were dispatched to downtown Brooklyn, the 73rd Precinct station house, and One Police Plaza in anticipation of protests. Merchants in Brownsville hurriedly boarded up stores, girding for violent new outbreaks. Residents in the community sought shelter.

Within minutes, rumors about the grand jury's impending ruling were also spreading across the city. Civil rights activists, anticipating a no-bill verdict, mobilized for mass protests. Borough commands and local precincts began receiving phone calls from purported PBA officials, claiming Matt

Holland had been indicted, and urging cops from the city's seventy-five precincts to walk off the job in protest. PBA president Red McLaren and attorney Eddie Shearson raced to the courthouse, preparing to conduct a press conference of their own.

All the while, the principals most closely tied to the case conducted separate private vigils. At the home of Matt and Katie Holland, family members and friends anxiously gathered before a TV set scheduled to carry a live broadcast of D.A. Green's press conference. Rachel Cook sat riveted to radio coverage at the office of Landon Devlin. Charles and Eunice Johnson walked to the Good Shepherd Baptist Church, to join the Rev. Josiah Watson in prayer.

"The past six months have been a harrowing ordeal for our city and for America," said Hal Green, speaking into a cluster of TV and radio microphones. "However, I want to assure the principals involved in this case, as well as the public, that the ruling I'm about to reveal was based on a comprehensive analysis of all the evidence, and the ruling was unfettered by racial bias or public opinion."

"The men and women on the grand jury worked diligently and in good faith," Green said. "Whether people agree with their ruling or not, I'm satisfied that our system has worked flawlessly. People have been clamoring for justice to be done. Well, I can assure everyone that is exactly what has happened."

"Hopefully," Green said, "the events surrounding the shooting of C. J. Johnson have taught us important lessons about the underlying racial tensions that exist in our communities, the life-and-death challenges faced by police, and the harrowing moments when both those things intersect. Hopefully, we've learned about the dangers of a rush to judgment and how anger, bitterness, hysteria, and prejudice—Black and White, civilian and police—can color our perspective on issues that require objectivity, deliberation, and truth."

"Lastly, and most importantly," Green said, "I hope that all of us can find a way to put this incident behind us, learn from it, and come together as a city and a country. The status quo must always be challenged. There is no finish line. Progress may slow, but it's made one step a time, one person at a time."

"We won't fix our racial differences with legislation or policy. Reforms will only take us so far. Instead, we must take account of who we are, and get to a point where incidents like this can be viewed through a lens that's clouded neither by ignorance nor stereotypes, where we're not allowing our emotions and biases to lead us down a path rutted with false conclusions, where the only thing that matters is the truth."

"Somehow," Green said, "we must become better people. Somehow, we must change what's inside our hearts."

The houseful of people in Matt and Katie Holland's home erupted in cheers when Green announced the grand jury's verdict. Rachel Cook and Landon Devlin embraced. Charles and Eunice Johnson wept in each other's arms.

It was a no bill.

After nearly two weeks of deliberations, the grand jury had formally concluded that there were no grounds for an indictment against Matt Holland—no charges to level, no need for a trial. The officer, as in the NYPD's internal probe, was completely absolved of any criminal wrongdoing in the C. J. Johnson shooting. The Justice Department, in a simultaneous announcement, also cleared the officer of alleged civil rights violations pertaining to the slain youth. The private hell that Holland had lived in for the past six months was over. The cloud of accusation and doubt that he'd lived under had finally been lifted.

In a related statement, NYPD brass reiterated that the department's internal investigation had found no violation of police guidelines by either Holland or Rachel Cook. There'd be no reprimands, no recrimination, no dismissals from the police force. Completely vindicated, Holland was ordered restored to duty at his former grade of detective sergeant, with full back pay and no loss of pension time. Cook could continue to remain on the job.

In a departure from protocol barring the disclosure of such information—and to avert renewed violence in Brownsville—Hal Green issued a detailed report on the grand jury's verdict. It stated that the basis for the ruling was that Holland had reasonably believed he and Rachel Cook were in harm's way in the moments before the officer had encountered C. J. Johnson, and that he'd not acted with criminal intent, negligence, bias, or recklessness. The shooting, it was ruled, had not been a callous, racist act of police brutality but an unintended and nightmarish accident, not a crime at all, but a tragic product of circumstance.

Anti-police activists vehemently protested the decision as a continuation of an unjust status quo. Police advocates hailed it as a milestone case in protecting officers' rights.

"While it vindicates the two officers, the grand jury decision is no cause for celebration," Red McLaren told the press. "There are no real 'winners' in this case. Let's never forget that an innocent life was lost, a city was thrown into turmoil, and a heroic police officer saw his life nearly destroyed."

McLaren stared directly at the TV cameras.

"There are saints and sinners on both sides of the issue of race," he said. "I think we've witnessed that. Maybe, through this tragedy, we've also witnessed how bigotry and anger and hatred can blind us to the truth, and how it can divide us. And, maybe, as we move past this, we can find a way to gain an understanding of each other and make our city a better place to live."

In many small ways, that's precisely what happened.

Shortly after New Year's Day, the NYPD unveiled a series of additional policy changes. Overhauled was the policy regarding officers charged with a crime or departmental violation. The automatic-suspension rule was discarded, replaced by guidelines stipulating that police officers under a cloud of suspicion would receive modified, but *real*, assignments in lieu of suspensions. They'd be able to retain their job, as well as their reputation, until their cases were adjudicated; the implication that they were guilty until proven innocent would finally be erased.

Ushered in, as well, was a new era of psychological support services for cops. Public funds were set aside to study the science of human interaction in high-stress, deadly-force encounters, as well as the feasibility of body-worn cameras. Mental-health counseling and critical-incident intervention teams were organized assist officers exposed to trauma. Money was earmarked to support Landon Devlin's COPS program.

Civil rights leaders attained a measure of progress, as well. National attention was focused for the first time on the issue of racial profiling by police. A special panel was formed to weed out police officers with histories of racism or violence. Plans were formulated to add minority officers to the police force, and to actively explore the causes of racial tension in minority communities. On a local level, 73rd Precinct commander Capt. Joseph Borelli launched a program aimed at improving police-community relations in Brownsville, including monthly meetings hosted by local businesses, civic associations, and faith-based organizations that enabled residents to interact with police officials.

"We can't solve deep-seated, decades-old problems overnight," Capt. Borelli said, "but at least we can take good-faith steps in the right direction and make gradual progress in finding higher ground."

Charles and Eunice Johnson also achieved a bit of higher ground.

The settlement with the city in the civil lawsuit filed on the couple's behalf was hand-delivered to the couple's apartment by ACLU attorney Xavier Cooper and New York Urban League president Carlton Rutledge. The out-of-court settlement, negotiated by representatives of the two organizations, represented the largest amount ever awarded in an officer-involved shooting case, a landmark victory for civil rights leaders seeking accountability, redress, and reform.

"Thank you for supporting the cause that we're fighting," said Xavier Cooper, embracing Charles as he handed the Johnsons an envelope containing a certified check from the City of New York for $8.8 million.

Staggered by the amount of the settlement, Charles nearly fell into Cooper's arms. Eunice collapsed in tears into the trundle bed that doubled as a couch.

"Thank you," Carlton Rutledge said, shaking Charles's hand. "Because of people like you, our organizations are making progress on important civil rights issues, a continuation of the legacy of your hero, Dr. King. One day, as Dr. King said, we'll make it to the mountaintop."

Charles was nearly speechless.

"Thank you for all you've done on behalf of my family," he said, overjoyed by his sudden affluence though saddened by the price his family had to pay.

"I'm only sorry you had to lose C. J. to help us get our voices heard," Cooper said. "Sadly, civil rights progress often results from tragedies like the one your family sustained."

"I pray that C. J. rests in peace," Rutledge added, "and I hope you'll find a worthwhile use for the money."

It didn't take long for Charles to do just that.

Even after federal and state taxes, he discovered, $8.8 million went a long way for someone of such modest needs. True to character, Charles spread the money around to a wide range of beneficiaries, fulfilling his aim of making a difference and helping his community heal.

A stipend of $250,000 was proffered to the Good Shepherd Baptist Church for the construction of a new rectory. A similar amount was earmarked for several church-affiliated ministries and a handful of charitable endeavors, including seed money to aid in the formation of a support group for lead-poisoning victims and a community jobs program. Substantial donations were also proffered to the local school board to create an annual scholarship in C. J. Johnson's name; to C. J.'s cousin Marcus to open an electronics-repair shop; to the ACLU, the NAACP, and similar organizations; and to the 73rd Precinct to continue with its Labor Day Weekend camp for special-needs children.

There was yet another beneficiary of both the watershed settlement and Charles's extraordinary largesse. Indeed, as per the deal Charles had struck for civil rights leaders to proceed with their wrongful-death lawsuit, a designated portion of whatever financial settlement the Johnsons might receive had been confidentially earmarked for a specific individual.

Shortly before New Year's, a courier delivered a package to the Staten Island home of Matt and Katie Holland. When Katie opened it, she found an envelope taped to a dog-eared photo album of sports figures. Inside the envelope was a handwritten letter. It read:

Please accept as a gift the beloved scrapbook that once belonged to our son. We hope that your son Thomas can care for it in C. J.'s memory. Perhaps one day we can meet and express our gratitude in person for the sensitivity and kindness you showed our son on a 73rd Precinct camping trip. In the meantime, please accept our additional offering as a way of helping lift the terrible cloud that has hung over all of us for the past six months. We feel that it is only appropriate to compensate you in some small way for the ordeal your family has been through. We know now that our son died for a reason. Sometimes we don't understand what God has in mind, but there is always a plan. We must believe in that plan and move on. From Him, we will find our peace and strength. May you find peace and strength, too, in the love of your family, and may you live a long and happy life.

The note was signed: Charles and Eunice Johnson. Attached was a personal check for $100,000.

* * *

"So, what's Matt going to do?" Rachel Cook inquired of Katie Holland, when the officer was finally able to place the telephone call that she'd wanted so desperately to make for the past six months.

"Is he staying on the job," Cook asked, "or looking to do something else?"

"Well, he's been offered an excellent opportunity, a partnership in my father's construction company, building and remodeling houses in Staten Island," Katie replied.

"That sounds really enticing," Cook said. "I'm certain he'd be great at that kind of work. And it's a lot less hairy than working as a cop in Brownsville … if you know what I mean."

"That's for sure," Katie said and laughed. "But to be honest with you, Rachel, I don't think Matt has made up his mind up yet. He's always loved police work; you know that as well as anyone. The job was good to him for a lot of years, too. I'm sure he'd miss it a lot if he walked away."

"Even after everything that's happened?"

"Hard as that is to believe ... I think so, yes."

"Well, one way or the other, he was a hell of a cop," Cook said. "One of the best this city had."

"And he loved working with you," said Katie.

"Yeah," Cook chuckled, wryly. "The two of us sure cleaned up Brownsville, didn't we?"

"You gave it your best shot," Katie said. "Your hearts were always in the right place. In the end, that's all you can ever give to anything."

"I guess so."

"What about you?" Katie asked. "What are you going to do now?"

"Taking it a day at a time for the foreseeable future," Cook replied. "The department has handed me an exciting new gig."

That, too, was very true. Days earlier, Cook had been reassigned from patrol-and-strip-search duties in Coney Island and fast-tracked to a plain-clothes role in the NYPD's Bureau for Strategic Initiatives, a newly established think tank aimed at developing departmental policies and programs. Despite all that had happened, police officials still obviously believed in Cook's innate talents, still believed she had a bright future, and still believed she had much to offer the city.

"I think I'll hang with this new assignment for now," Cook said, "and see where it takes me."

"Matt will be pleased to hear that," Katie said. "He always believed you had so much to give."

"Yeah," Cook laughed. "I'm sure he'd be pretty pissed off at me if I gave up on the NYPD or the city—or most of all, myself."

"I'm sure he'll want to tell you that," Katie said.

Matt couldn't take her call just then, but he'd get back to her soon enough, Katie assured Cook. He certainly was anxious to talk. For the time being, though, he was outside in the family's backyard, playing with Thomas and his twin girls in the winter's first big snow.

Officers Down *is a work of fiction. While it is based on a composite of similar, real-life incidents that took place in New York and other cities, including a police shooting in the Brownsville section of Brooklyn, its characters are fictional, and any resemblance to real people, living or deceased, is unintended.*